When Push Comes to Shove:
A Clown's Demise

Copyright © 2019 by Donald J. Mackie

Interior design by Michael Ebert

Cover Illustration by Ryan Pedersen

Edited by Linda Franklin

This is a work of fiction. The events described here are imaginary. The settings and characters are fictitious or used in a fictitious manner and do not represent specific places or living or dead people. Any resemblance is entirely coincidental.

All rights reserved. No part of this book may be reproduced or transmitted in any form or by any means whatsoever, including photocopying, recording or by any information storage and retrieval system, without written permission from the publisher and/or author. The views and opinions expressed in this book are those of the author(s) and do not necessarily reflect those of the publisher, and the publisher hereby disclaims any responsibility for them. Neither is the publisher responsible for the content or accuracy of the information provided in this document. Contact Inkwater Press at inkwater.com. 503.968.6777

Publisher: Inkwater Press | www.inkwaterpress.com

Paperback
ISBN-13 978-1-62901-577-4 | ISBN-10 1-62901-577-6

Kindle
ISBN-13 978-1-62901-578-1 | ISBN-10 1-62901-578-4

3 5 7 9 10 8 6 4 2

When Push Comes to Shove

A Clown's Demise

a novel by

Donald J. Mackie

INKWATER PRESS

Dedication

THIS NOVEL IS DEDICATED TO ALL PEOPLE WHO believe the few last vestiges of "natural ecosystems" found on our planet are worth more than all the tea in China, all the gold in Fort Knox, and all the oil in the Arctic National Wildlife Refuge.

Author's Note

W̲ʜᴇɴ Pᴜsʜ Cᴏᴍᴇs ᴛᴏ Sʜᴏᴠᴇ ɪs ᴀ ꜰɪᴄᴛɪᴏɴᴀʟ piece. (Occasionally, you may have to remind yourself of this.) Certain liberties were taken with reality in order to develop and nourish the story. For instance, the Big Eddy Rise geologic formation does not exist. Those of us who trek alongside the beautiful Metolius River know this. The West Wing and White House floor plans were tweaked, somewhat, to facilitate the novel's plot. Also, the big, old, rambling, yellow farmhouse located at 11th and Adams no longer exists. Recent generations of Oregon State students see at this location a tastefully constructed two-story apartment complex. There were other minor transgressions along the way, and hopefully, you can appreciate how they aided and enriched the novel's direction and message. That said, welcome to *When Push Comes to Shove: A Clown's Demise.*

Part One

The President Strikes First

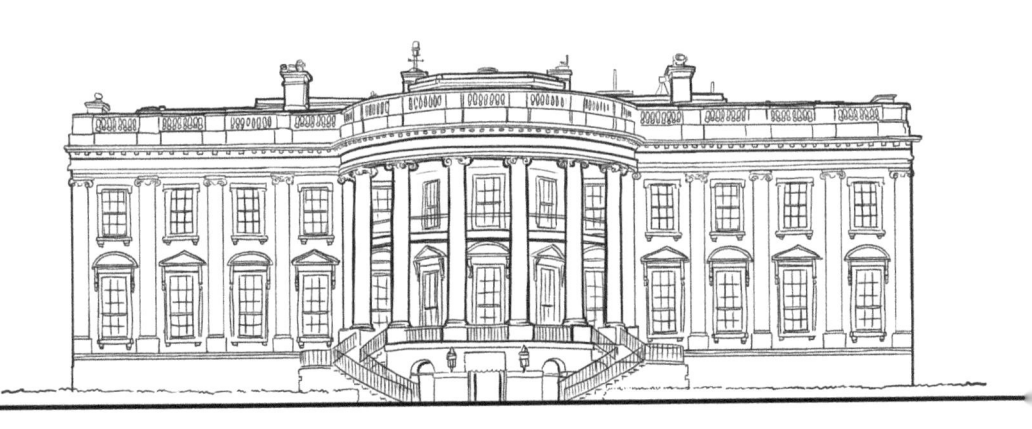

Chapter 1

President McDonald exited his living room on the residence floor of the White House, leaving four flatscreen TVs still tuned to the latest news. His destination was the West Wing, and his presidential workplace, the Oval Office. He avoided the First Family's Elevator by turning right and heading for the second level's Grand Staircase landing. Most presidents had used the elevator because of its discreet location, but President McDonald didn't like its diminutive size, preferring the larger lift dimensions of glitzy hotels and resorts. This elevator felt claustrophobic to him, and more like a domestic lift than a presidential one.

The president liked the White House Grand Staircase, believing it stately and fit for a king. Its white marble steps, covered by a plush red carpet, were regal and the overhead chandelier was worthy of a ballroom. The handrail was polished mahogany, supported by balusters highlighted by a touch of gilding. McDonald would have liked more of the golden sheen, but the subtle use of the metal's brilliance was, in his opinion, very classy.

There was one drawback to the Grand Stairway. McDonald was addicted to his smartphone, and even while walking, would peruse the phone for information of interest. The stairs presented a navigation problem for the president. Not only did he feel compelled to hold the handrail while negotiating the steps, the incline also demanded more attention to movement. He couldn't view his phone and navigate the stairs at the same time. This was a slight annoyance to the president. Even small displeasures could be big problems to McDonald.

While descending to the ground floor, the president was thinking about one Pacific Northwest blue state, Oregon, and a little personal revenge he intended to inflict upon her. He was going to throw dirt into Oregon's political face and call the endeavor an Economic Stimulus Plan.

The president didn't like blue states in general, and the liberal West Coast states, he liked even less. Oregon, with its female governor, was his least favorite. Targeting this domain amused the president and would soon give him a political boost, which his administration desperately needed.

President McDonald knew most Oregonians considered their old forests "gem-like" and didn't want them touched. Most of the old growth in the state resided on federal land that McDonald now held the reins to. He intended to reboot the state's slumbering timber industry by attacking the remaining old growth forests and logging them. By doing this, his "jobs mandate" would generate some tangible, positive numbers. The Commander in Chief had some old cronies who thought this idea held financial promise for their businesses and wanted the president to give it a try. Contemplating the pain the tofu-eating, liberal Oregonians would feel, and the profits his corporate peers would soon realize, pleased McDonald to no end.

The sitting president was a frumpy, sixtyish-looking man with classic male pattern baldness. His shiny dome was surrounded by a partial ring of light gray hair that stiffly descended toward his collar. The slight paunch protruding past his belt betrayed his lack of exercise and fondness for ample servings. The years had dulled his blue eyes to light gray, and gravity had created sagging jowls. A small double chin rounded the once slightly squared jaw of his youth. McDonald looked more like a poorly chosen vice president than the Commander in Chief. His physique didn't bother him, though. Over the years, personal wealth had abolished any negative thoughts about his appearance, and a large ego created in his mind an appreciation for his looks, which he perceived as uniquely sexy.

Traversing the ground floor hallway, McDonald acknowledged the "Good Morning, Mr. President" greetings with a nod. He barely noticed his Secret Service entourage, which was set in motion by his movement. The procession passed by two busts of Lincoln, one etched from black Italian marble and the other chiseled from white. Also, portraits of Washington, LBJ, and JFK gazed upon the staff as it proceeded by. McDonald had not and would not notice any of these art works. Instead, his focus was on media headlines depicted on his phone. CNN had just noted his public approval rating was reaching levels similar to Richard Nixon's. This announcement sent McDonald's pulse racing and completely stopped his forward motion. The whole presidential procession awkwardly came to a halt, causing the Secret Service agents to check their surroundings, noting nothing to be amiss, they looked at the president and waited for his forward motion to resume.

He muttered to no one in particular, "This damn media propaganda needs to stop."

The agents gave each other a knowing glance. Often, these presidential movements halted because of similar circumstances, and the agents were becoming used to their herky-jerky motions.

As the president neared the ground floor kitchen, Vice President Robinson exited the pantry doorway, a sandwich clutched in one hand and a memo held in the other. Formerly a senator from Georgia, Robinson had accepted the GOP's offer to be the next VP of the United States. He was a fit and handsome fortyish African American with a calm demeanor. The vice president was looking at his memo and he didn't notice President McDonald. This lack of attention created a near collision. An uncomfortable moment ensued with an exclamation of apology by the VP and an accepting nod from the president. Both men went their separate ways.

McDonald's procession reached the West Colonnade and the Rose Garden, which provided the exterior hallway's southern backdrop. Its namesake was in late bloom due to an unusually cool and dry summer. Oranges, reds, and numerous values of white adorned the green leafy plants as McDonald strode past. Gazing at his smartphone, he didn't notice the mosaic of color that almost touched him. Again, the procession came to a halt as McDonald read a national news report highlighting retaliatory tariffs being imposed on American exports, and their possible contribution to an alarming rise in the country's trade deficit. This information evoked a lengthy tirade of cursing from the president, followed by a quickened pace, requiring the agents to almost trot next to McDonald in order to keep up. They burst into the West Wing, passed by the Cabinet Room, the president's secretary's office, and finally slowed so that McDonald could enter the Oval Office. His escorts quickly checked his office and his secretary's before ushering the president into his workplace.

The president's official work space was empty, but that would soon change. He had a 10:00 a.m. appointment with Ray Billings, the Secretary of Agriculture. After checking his watch, and noting it was 10:15, McDonald called out to his personal secretary, a well-dressed, nicely shaped, dark-haired and dark eyed mature woman named Janet, to confirm Secretary Billings' whereabouts.

She came to the adjoining doorway. "He's stuck in traffic and won't be here for another ten minutes, sir."

The president mused to himself, *if Billings would only exit his damn limo and walk to the West Wing, he'd get here sooner.* McDonald nodded to Janet and turned to his smartphone. Being so dismissed, Janet returned to her desk and other tasks. After a moment of Twitter browsing, McDonald leaned back in his leather chair, laced his fingers behind his head, and gazed up at his room's lone chandelier. A seldom seen smile spread across his face. He'd enjoy these few minutes by himself, and think about the wrecking ball he'd soon swing toward Oregon, that hippy-dippy, liberal, tree-hugging, West Coast blue state. Billings would arrive soon enough, but for now, the sitting president of the United States would simply enjoy thinking about all those West Coast liberals crying a river over the little Economic Revitalization Plan he'd hatched up just for them.

CHAPTER 2

VICE PRESIDENT ROBINSON'S NEAR COLLISION with the presidential procession diverted his attention from the memo he'd just received. Now that he could focus on it again, he realized he, instead of President McDonald, was to greet the visiting Prime Minister of India in the Diplomatic Reception Room. McDonald was originally slated for this event, but upon hearing of this, pushed it off onto Robinson's plate. It was becoming obvious to the VP and many other White House personnel that McDonald was much more interested in his personal agenda than matters of state. Consequently, Vice President Robinson was performing more and more presidential tasks. Robinson hoped that on this occasion no diplomatic slight would be felt by the Prime Minister, but acknowledged to himself this would be impossible. He was anxious about the awkward meeting that would soon occur. The Vice President was to give the VIP an impromptu tour of the White House, lunch with him in the Green Room, and then discuss trade downstairs in the Map Room. His meeting was set for 11:00 a.m., giving him precious little time for preparation. He needed back-up from the State Department; in particular, someone familiar with trade and business agreements between the two countries would be necessary. Robinson did an about-face and headed for his office in the West Wing. As he passed by the Rose Garden, he stopped to watch a small swirl of tree swallows work a crane fly hatch above the lawn. Lifted by this quick communion with nature, the VP continued on to his office. He checked his watch, hoping an appropriate State Department employee was available.

CHAPTER 3

THE SECRETARY OF AGRICULTURE'S LINCOLN CAME to a stop at the North Entrance to the West Wing. Secretary Billings exited his vehicle, and while waiting for the Marine to open the double doors, checked his watch. He noted how long his transit had taken. Billings was a short, stocky oilman from Texas who loved wearing navy blue suits, highlighted with American flag lapel pins. Gaining entrance to the lobby, Billings quickened his pace. A left turn, down the long hallway, followed by a right turn, brought him to the Oval Office. A Secret Service agent opened the president's hall doors and ushered Billings into the Oval Office. He surveyed the president's work space, noticing little had changed since his boss's predecessor had sat behind the desk. McDonald cared little about furnishings. He was used to hotel suites, spacious condos, and rented mansions, all of which came furnished. Consequently, President McDonald gave little thought to room amenities. He always changed his décor by physically moving to a new address.

Billings' gaze took in the Rose Garden view, provided by expansive windows; returning his attention to the room's interior, he noted McDonald's rich, oak desk, with its glossy finish and the two couches that faced each other in front of the room's fireplace. The sofas were separated just enough so that the Presidential Seal, centered in the room's large, circular carpet, could be completely seen. His eyes finally came to rest on the portrait of Lincoln, whose steady gaze seemed to transfix the whole room.

McDonald saw Billings and exclaimed, "It's about time."

"Traffic slowed me up."

"You could have walked here faster."

Billings mentally rolled his eyes at this comment, and responded, "That's true, Mr. President. The congestion caught me by surprise. It's usually just a five-minute commute. Sorry about my late arrival. Your memo didn't mention any subject for our meeting, just the time. So what can I do for you, today, sir?"

"Those goddamned West Coast states have been constantly slowing down our agenda with bullshit lawsuits and the like. I'd like to give those assholes something personal to fixate on. My secretary was visiting her sister in Portland last week and said she loved walking in the old growth forests up in the mountains, outside of the city. How come those big, goddamned trees are still standing out there?"

Secretary Billings didn't know the answer to this question. His expertise was petroleum and natural gas. He knew a lot about the national and international oil business, but very little about the timber industry.

"I can't give you a good answer for your question, sir, but somebody in my department will have the information you need."

"Well, hell, it isn't going to be anything new. I'll bet you money that tree huggers, regulations, and stupid shit like birds and reptiles have stopped all the lumber commerce."

"That could be, Mr. President. I'll get on it."

As McDonald and Billings talked, both men gravitated to the room's opposing couches and sat down facing each other. McDonald was hungry, and without consulting Billings, hollered to Janet for sandwiches. He ordered ham and cheese on white bread and a carafe of medium roasted coffee to be delivered ASAP. Janet passed on his request to the kitchen and then informed McDonald his order would arrive in a few minutes.

While waiting for Janet's response, McDonald continued relaying his loosely concocted logging plan to Billings.

"We're going to overwhelm those West Coast tree huggers with a full frontal attack on their precious old growth forests. I want numerous logging efforts started pronto. That will take their attention away from my business."

"Mr. President, this could take some time to develop. I'll get my people working on it and get back to you in a week or two with what I've found out."

"The hell you will! I want trees falling in a week, not some damn internal dialogue Agriculture Department staffers have generated."

"Your request doesn't seem possible, Mr. President. Let me..."

"Listen, Billings. If we fart around..."

The president's sentence was interrupted by a knock on the Oval Office hallway door. A Secret Service agent peeked in and noted food service had arrived. President McDonald nodded and a college-aged intern entered carrying a tray filled with sandwiches, cups, and a coffee carafe. McDonald had asked to have these young interns deliver food to him instead of the Secret Service corps. The president liked to ogle the young people. On this occasion, he noted the plainness of this coed and was displeased. She quickly and somewhat nervously set the tray down on the central coffee table and quietly left the Oval Office. The Secret Service agent then shut the door behind her.

McDonald filled his coffee cup, grabbed a sandwich, and motioned for Billings to do the same. After a few bites, McDonald gathered his thoughts and continued.

"Like I was saying, if we fart around, we'll just have a mountain of lawsuits to wade through, and until we can squash whatever regulations are used against us, we'll just be spinning our goddamned wheels with nothing to show for it."

"You know, Mr. President, this could be an impossible task you're asking for."

"God damn it, Billings, I'm the president, you're the Secretary of Agriculture and we should be able to pull anything off. I want trees hitting the ground in a week. So get on it. Do anything you need to, use any resource necessary, and don't worry about stepping on toes."

Secretary Billings could sense his meeting was being terminated. McDonald was already checking his smartphone and looking away from him.

"All right, Mr. President, I'll get on this immediately and results will be forthcoming. Who do you want me to communicate with about these efforts?"

"I'll get Graham up to speed, so either one of us will work."

Graham was President McDonald's chief of staff, with a corner office just down the hall from the Oval Office. McDonald would have Graham pay him a visit later in the morning, and get him on board.

The Secretary of Agriculture exited the president's office. While he retraced his steps, he contacted his driver via cellphone, and when he left the West Wing, his car was already waiting. As he nestled back into the leather seat of his limo, he called his personal secretary and asked her to contact Oregon's lone Republican congressman, Sam Spencer. Billings inherently knew to avoid normal channels. Oregon's elected official would be a good place to start. The secretary knew from D.C. social functions this particular congressman had represented the eastern half of the state for a long time and was an Oregon native. He'd be able to walk Billings through this seemingly impossible task. *Those trees hadn't avoided the axe by sheer luck.*

Secretary Billings was sure this political sleight of hand was going to require savvy and muscle to pull off in addition to just plain old personal swagger. In the international oil community, he was known as a tough-minded mover and shaker. Nobody wished for a head-to-head confrontation with him, and he knew it. This confidence accompanied him into the public sector, and Billings felt as though he could accomplish most any task placed before him. *One week* kept echoing in the secretary's head. *Was this possible?* Billings didn't think so, but if anyone could do it, he could.

The secretary exited his limo, this time emerging in front of his Washington D.C. address. The Jamie L. Whitten Building loomed above him. As he climbed the entrance steps, Billings paused for a moment, lost in thought. He reflected on his meeting with President McDonald. Upon continuing his ascent, he still had one unanswered question: *How in the hell had this asshole become President of the United States?*

CHAPTER 4

McDonald had been the most unlikely of presidential candidates, and with his surprising victory, he became the most unlikely of presidents. To say his presidential bid was a long shot was an incredible understatement, and numerous political insiders dined on crow the evening of his election victory.

He had literally no political experience before running for the highest office in the land. He was known to the general public by tabloid coverage because of his high profile, one-percenter lifestyle, and was always good for an outlandish, almost comical outburst directed at the political system or a particular politician. The tabloids often followed running argumentative battles between McDonald and other prominent Americans. If it wasn't a politician McDonald picked a fight with, it was often a Hollywood celebrity. These fights were usually trivial and mostly boring, except to McDonald, whose personal identity and self-worth seemed to rely on one-upping whomever he dueled with.

President McDonald's noteworthiness was rooted in personal wealth. He was the only son of extremely wealthy, hard-working, conservative parents, who expected him to eventually take over the family's business empire. Like most children from very wealthy families, McDonald did not work as hard as his parents. He more or less fit into their system and didn't rock the boat. This was fine by him. He tired of and became easily bored with corporate tasks. Vacationing on the company's credit was much more enjoyable to McDonald than helping create the assets behind the credit.

The president's parents had warily watched their son's maturation. It was apparent to the elder McDonalds that their boy, from an early age, had a short attention span, was easily angered, and lacked fortitude and drive. Consequently, they allowed him ample free time and slowly pushed him in the direction of their business world and his inevitable corporate responsibilities.

They owned and ran two huge conglomerates. One dealt with real estate, both sales and construction, and the other corporation dealt with banking, mostly focusing on loans, in particular, mortgage transactions. Both entities had Wall Street addresses and extremely high national and international profiles. McDonald's father ran the banking endeavors and Mrs. McDonald headed the real estate/construction corporation.

The two businesses provided a beautiful, symbiotic relationship for each other. The banking side could provide large, unrestricted, and occasionally unrecorded loans that easily passed to the real estate side. This arrangement allowed the real estate corporation to have access to large sums of capital, and this leverage gave the McDonalds an advantage over competitors who, at times, struggled to find loans. The financial relationship enjoyed by the McDonalds worked well for them and allowed their businesses to flourish.

Young McDonald's life calling was never in doubt. He would eventually head one if not both companies. The elder McDonalds encouraged their son to participate in their corporate world in a casual, superficial manner. He had two corporate suites, located in both Wall Street business towers. His corporate title was Vice President of Budgetary Analysis. Several times a year, McDonald was called upon to remedy a departmental problem. He soon acquired, within inner circles, the nickname "Slice and Dice McDonald" because of his tendency to eliminate staff, reduce budgets, and reprioritize department goals as a means of jolting the faltering department's bottom line back into the black. The trauma induced by McDonald's actions upon those who lost jobs and careers was never noticed by him. His self-serving, self-absorbed ego didn't allow for empathy in regards to others, and he became the perfect hatchet man. Righting the ship was all young McDonald cared about.

CHAPTER 5

THE ELDER MCDONALDS PASSED AWAY WITHIN months of each other, and their only son dutifully took control of the corporate reins. As the years progressed, he engaged less and less in managerial functions. He became a hands-off owner who mostly just sat on company boards, and, much as he had done when he was younger, occasionally dealt with problematic departments. "Slice and dice" and "reprioritize" were still his mantras, and he continued to enjoy wielding the axe.

His annual jet-setting cycle of being in the Bahamas for yachting seasons, in the Alps for winter skiing, and anywhere weather permitted for a round of golf pared itself down as he aged. Now, he mostly played golf. He crafted a links routine that allowed for jumping between hemispheres in order to find sunny conditions and quality golfing excursions. Buenos Aires was one of his favorite southern locales for golf, and he often frequented his own resort outside of the sprawling city for extended golf vacations. Usually, he was joined there by several of his lifelong business associates, and they never tired of "eighteen-hole" days followed by long, "nineteenth-hole" cocktail hours. His golfing entourage consisted mostly of wealthy CEOs who made their fortunes by natural resource extractions: oil, coal, uranium, and timber were just a few of the commodities fattening their wallets. The combined wealth held by these individuals far exceeded the entire third world's accumulated assets; these gentlemen were fully aware of this circumstance, and the power their fortunes afforded them. It was at one of their nineteenth-hole social hours that McDonald openly talked about a presidential run. To his satisfaction, all of his peers applauded the idea and offered only encouraging remarks about the potential gains of such an endeavor. In particular, everyone noted if McDonald gained the White House, he could eliminate federal regulations that lately had decreased the profits previously enjoyed by their corporations.

With a gala, enthusiastic toast, McDonald's presidential run materialized. The success of his campaign would eventually astonish Washington D.C. power players and create a situation the likes of which had never before been seen in the nation's capital.

CHAPTER 6

A LARGE-BUDGET, HASTILY THROWN TOGETHER campaign with McDonald at the helm entered the primaries with a thud. His primary run was clumsy, brash, filled with political and social gaffes, and clown-like when compared to his competitors.

McDonald's campaign team saw his lack of political savvy as a positive, and one of their campaign platform pieces became the uncorrupted Washington D.C. outsider fighting against the corrupted insiders. Adding weight to this stance was the real personal dislike for politics and politicians that McDonald had exhibited his entire life. The campaign bumped along and began adding rhetoric that championed downsizing Washington's power, budget, and regulations, which the candidate portrayed as the real culprit behind America's languid GNP, her trade deficit imbalance, and her underemployed working class. The campaign mantra became "Weak Federal Government Equals Strong American Business." He also took a hawkish stance on terrorism and promised to be the toughest president the United States ever wielded in the war on such acts of aggression.

As the dust from primary campaigning settled, one candidate remained standing. McDonald saw numerous candidates, all Washington insiders, fall by the wayside as the political season trailed on. GOP officials became alarmed by his victories and did not know what to expect from him.

McDonald's voting base emerged and began adding real significance to his presidential run. He was gaining support from the unemployed, underemployed, underpaid, and uneducated segments of American society. He also became the far right's favorite and was accepted as the "true leader" by the militant, extremist groups who lived in America's cultural shadows.

When the GOP convention convened to crown its new presidential candidate, most Americans, including many Republicans, and the entire world watched in shock. McDonald was going to get the nod for the GOP presidential run.

Republican insiders and strategists went into survival mode. The general consensus was their candidate had no chance against the Democrats' seasoned and respected adversary. The GOP think tanks searched for any leverage that would allow this presidential race to be at least competitive. The leverage, their advantage, became the vice presidential choice—a young, energetic, charismatic African American senator from Georgia. With this man on the ticket, the Republican Party felt they had a chance.

McDonald's presidential campaign was much the same as his primary race: a herky-jerky, mistake-filled roller coaster ride that somehow didn't "86" its candidate's chances. The polls always showed a tight race, no matter what blunder McDonald recently made. His platform message seemed to resonate with a large portion of the American population. "Weak government equals strong business" was what many disillusioned Americans wanted to hear. The "slice and dice" mentality crafted early on in his business career meshed nicely with his political campaign trail rhetoric of downsizing the federal government and shifting budget resources to departments favoring big business and the military. McDonald promised if he gained the White House, the federal budget would be sliced, the federal deficit would become a thing of the past, the Gross National Product would flourish, the national trade imbalance would favor U.S. products once again, and terrorists would have no safe havens once McDonald set his sights on them. These themes were euphoric calls embraced by voters. His campaign headed into November looking like a contender and not a loser.

After all the votes were counted and recounted in several cases, the seemingly impossible happened. McDonald won the presidency. In just a few months, he would be the new President of the United States. This completely blindsided the Washington elite, including the Republican bosses, who at this moment were frantic because no one actually thought McDonald would win. Consequently, no post-election plans had been designed. In particular, McDonald's cabinet members had not been selected by the GOP brain trust. This process alone could take months.

Washington D.C.'s frenetic reaction to McDonald's win was totally lost on him. He truly was a Washington outsider who believed in his campaign's platform and promises. He didn't need advice from D.C. insiders or Republican strategists. He was going to arm his White House with old friends and people he felt could produce the federal government he had promised. He cared for no one's advice and would govern as he saw fit. In McDonald's mind, and his staff's opinion, Americans had spoken and the new Commander in Chief was ready to deliver on the goods.

CHAPTER 7

Henry Graham walked through President

McDonald's secretary's office. He said hello to the president's secretary, Janet, and then entered the Oval Office through her doorway. McDonald sat on a couch viewing his smartphone and talking to himself.

"Hello, Mr. President. What can I do for you?"

Henry Graham was McDonald's chief of staff. Having known the president for decades, Graham had been a high level executive who helped call the shots at McDonald's banking/mortgage corporation. Graham looked like a Hollywood character actor tapped for the seedy, tough guy parts. He was of average height and build for a fiftyish out-of-shape man. His gray, baggy suits appeared as if he'd slept in them the night before. His hair was straight, thick, and greasy. It often seemed to have been recently roughed up by its owner. Graham preferred a three- or four-day-old stubble covering his face, and along with his hair, age had turned his beard a salt and pepper color.

President McDonald looked up at Graham. "Did you pull an all-nighter last evening, or just drink till you passed out?" Without waiting for a response, the president continued, "Where the hell have you been? I asked Janet to get you here an hour ago."

Graham walked over and sat in the couch that faced the president. "I've been with your press secretary trying to throw water on the latest jobs report. It's not good, Mr. President. We're up to 7% unemployed. When you took office..."

"I know what it was when I took office, Graham. So what did you guys come up with?"

"We're working the 'bad data' angle. We'll get it polished up and ready for a West Wing press show by tomorrow."

"Good, good. Shit, we know it's all Democratic propaganda. Those bastards never quit. Anyway, the unemployment situation is why I called you in here."

"How so, Mr. President?"

"I'm getting old growth trees cut down in Oregon. Can't wait to hear those crybabies over there piss and moan about their big trees falling down."

"I'm not following you, sir?"

"Just what I said. Are you listening? I'm getting logging of old growth trees moving again in Oregon. Billings is setting everything up, and we should have logs entering sawmills in a few days. He'll give us a call, soon, and fill us in on the details."

"That sounds like jobs to me, Mr. President, and a great photo op in the making. This is the best possible rebuttal for a poor unemployment report. We'll get pictures of the whole process and end with some sawmill photos of you talking to workers. This should completely negate the jobs report."

"My thoughts exactly, Graham. So let's get a West Coast trip planned with friendly stops, like Boeing, and then we'll culminate in our hippy-dippy state of Oregon for our photo op. Don't get me an engagement with their governor; I don't want to be seen with her. She's a sorry ass excuse for a woman and an even shittier governor. God, I hate the West Coast."

"Okay, sir. After Billings gets back to us, we'll give the logging efforts a few days of operation, and then we'll pay Oregon a presidential visit."

"You're damn right we will. Well, this will do it for now, Graham. Hey, on the way out, ask Janet where my sandwiches are."

Graham stood up to leave, but before turning away from McDonald, he decided to remind the president about an important upcoming date.

"Janet will be getting an agenda about the full cabinet meeting in her emails pretty soon. This is the gathering you requested regarding government downsizing. Please familiarize yourself with the meeting schedule, and have an introductory greeting scripted to start the session off with. Reporters will be present so we want a polished, smooth-flowing meeting. You've got plenty of time to prepare because the actual assembly isn't until the last part of next week. That said, don't put things off to the last minute. Like I said, things need to be polished."

"Shit, Graham. You sound like an old woman nagging away about our little 'three ring circus.' Don't sweat it. This is going to be fun. I can't wait to run our cabinet secretaries through the wringer and see what they're made of. Don't worry about me. I'll wow the crowd."

"Good, good, Mr. President. I'll drop by in a few days and proofread your intro for you."

"God damn it. Enough about the stupid cabinet meeting. Like I said, 'I'll wow 'em.'"

McDonald looked away from his chief of staff and began scrolling through his smartphone. This action told Graham their meeting was over, so he departed.

As Graham left the Oval Office via Janet's adjoining room, a knock on the hall doorway announced someone's entrance. A young intern entered carrying a tray loaded with ham and cheese sandwiches. McDonald gestured to his coffee table and eyed the young lady. As she set the tray down, his eyes moved to her cleavage. When she straightened up, the intern smiled and asked the president if there was anything else he needed. McDonald answered with a no, and then dismissed her. She turned and left the Oval Office with her serving tray. The president thought to himself, *this latest batch of interns isn't making it, especially flat-chested ones like this last server.* He called out to Janet and asked her to contact the White House chief usher. A few minutes later, Janet called back saying the chief usher was on line one of his desk phone. McDonald walked over to his desk, sandwich in hand, and lifted the receiver. He commenced talking to the man who literally ran the White House. Nothing transpired in this building that the chief usher was not aware of because he planned or helped plan almost everything that had anything to do with White House events, personnel, and upkeep.

"Hey, Peterson, I need a new batch of interns serving me. This present group is pretty damn boring."

Peterson physically looked up to the ceiling at this comment and request. They'd had this same dialogue several times in the last few months. Peterson quietly waited for the president to continue.

"I want some attractive, well-proportioned college kids serving me my food. Hell, this bunch is just plain homely. Let's get some young 'eye candy' walking around in this old antique mall."

"Certainly, Mr. President. I'll interview some prospective interns right away. You'll have some new kids in just a few days."

"Good, good, Peterson. Remember, 'good looking' is the goal, here. Savvy?"

"Certainly, Mr. President. I'll do my best. Anything else, sir?"

"No, Peterson, that's all."

The White House chief usher for thirty years, Don Peterson hung up his phone and viewed his tiny, cramped quarters with a sigh. *Has it really come to this after so many years of government service? Am I really just enslaving young girls for the president of the United States?* He reached for his rolodex directory and its list of nearby colleges and universities and gave George Washington University the first call. They were pretty good about getting kids on board with the Intern Program. *How am I going to ask discreetly for only "well-endowed" coeds? God, this is a new twist to my job description: Don Peterson, White House chief usher and pimp.*

CHAPTER 8

IT WAS MIDAFTERNOON AND RAY BILLINGS' LIMO was once again returning to the Whitten Building. Billings had just left a meeting with "Big AG" representatives. They'd wanted to lesson regulations in regards to the meat packing industry. The secretary was not so inclined and left the gathering with no changes to present policy. His thoughts now drifted back to his early morning conversation with the president which directed him to get old growth clear cuts started in Oregon. His original thoughts resurfaced. He couldn't go through normal departmental channels in his pursuit. Department tree huggers didn't need to be tipped off to his plans. This would have to be an end run catching everybody by surprise and tipping no one off until it was too late. His ride slowly moved onward, allowing the secretary more time to think. Yes, the Oregon congressman, Sam Spencer, would be his man. If anyone outside of his agency had the answers, it would be Spencer.

    Billings' Lincoln pulled up to the Whitten Building's front entrance. The secretary left his ride and strode into the building. He two-stepped the stairs and quickly gained the first floor's huge lobby. Heading for his elevator, the secretary acknowledged staff greetings with a nod or slight hand wave. He rode the lift up to his office floor, exited, and walked through the outer rooms of his suite and into his work space. The secretary sat down behind his ornate, hand-carved cherrywood desk. Its paneled sides portrayed various agricultural scenes in a continuous, hand-carved mural, wrapping completely around the desk. The panels showed wheat fields being harvested by ox-drawn thrashers, apple orchards being picked, and timber being felled. Billings rang up Congressman Sam Spencer's office, which was located in the Rayburn House Office Building, a grand, majestic building completed in the sixties. This was the favorite office space for House members, and only the senior congressmen called this structure their home.

Sam Spencer was reading the *Washington Post* near his exterior window while reclining in his cushioned desk chair. Sam situated his desk close to his Independence Avenue window so a couple leg thrusts got him to his favorite spot next to the window. Also, if he leaned backwards, the Congressman could grasp his desk phone without effort and still remain near the window. He had propped his feet up onto the bottom sill and was using the natural, early afternoon light to read by. Occasionally, Spencer left his article to view the Capitol Building. He never tired of this vista. Sam was perusing a business article that explained China's devaluation of their dollar and its effect on American exports. The reporter's belief was China was purposefully devaluing their currency in retaliation for large American tariffs imposed by McDonald on Chinese goods. By doing this, American products became too expensive for the Chinese and they were losing favor. Already General Motors had noted a large decrease in Asian sales and had recently laid off employees to buoy its bottom line. Spencer was musing over this potential political black eye when his desk phone rang. He reached over and brought the receiver to his ear.

"Hello, Laura, what's up?"

"Secretary Billings is on the line, Sam. Are you available?"

"Sure. Any idea as to what he's after?"

"Nope. Do you want me to find out?"

"No. I'll just take the call."

Representative Spencer rarely talked with Secretary Billings, and had no idea what prompted this call. He pushed the phone's blinking button.

"Hello, Secretary Billings. What can I do for you?"

Billings decided to get right to the point with the Oregon representative.

"Spencer. I need to get some old growth trees cut, on the ground, and shipped off to sawmills from your Congressional District by this time next week."

Upon hearing this, Sam Spencer almost laughed, but controlled himself. This was an incredibly naïve request. The representative knew from Capitol Hill gossip that Billings was an oilman and held little knowledge pertinent to his department. This request blatantly proved, at least, his complete ignorance of Oregon's timber industry.

"Mr. Secretary, this request is impossible. There are numerous steps to the logging process; some are prompted by federal regulations, and they make your request impossible to grant. For instance, the bidding procedure by which 'shows' are awarded to individual companies can take weeks or months to complete. Also, site evaluations must occur to ensure protected species aren't harmed, and site boundaries need to be established. Add to this, the cruises that must occur."

"What must occur?"

"A cruise, sir. This establishes how many board feet exist in the sale, and from this number, we can determine how much to charge the logging company. All this can take many months, Mr. Secretary, and then whoever is awarded the show can wait for market prices to be advantageous before cutting. This whole process can take years."

Sam Spencer didn't know where this conversation was going, but he was sure he didn't want anything more to do with it.

"You know, Mr. Secretary, I'm not your best source of information. You should confer with your departmental staff, and in particular your Forest Service personnel. They work with these scenarios on a daily basis. I'm just shooting from the hip, here."

"Spencer, I'm talking to you because I don't want departmental advice. I know cutting old growth trees is nearly impossible in your state because of federal regulations and a bunch of tree huggers. So we're going to avoid this mess by side-stepping my department. This request comes from the Oval Office, Spencer, and needs to be completed yesterday."

This was beginning to sound like a political nightmare to the representative, and the usage of "we" in regards to this illegal scheme was making Spencer nervous. He needed to get Billings moving on and away from him quickly.

"What I'm going to suggest, Secretary Billings, needs to be 'off the record.' I don't want these comments to bite me in the ass come reelection time. Can we agree to this?"

"Certainly, certainly, Spencer, and be assured my memory is long, and any favors you do for me, I'll reciprocate with in-kind, down the road."

Sam Spencer rolled his head backwards and looked up at the ceiling of his office in dismay at what he'd just heard. Then he continued on with his conversation.

"Thanks, Mr. Secretary. Very considerate of you. The only way to get these trees harvested within your timeline would be to completely ignore normal Forest Service channels and personally contact a district manager with your request. Somehow, maybe by using your departmental title or personal leverage, you need to persuade this forester to do your bidding."

Secretary Billings was beginning to comprehend the impossibility of his initial plan. The large-scale logging of Northwest old growth could be the president's pipe dream.

"Okay, okay, Spencer. What do you think is possible, and where do you think I should start?"

"Well, Mr. Secretary, I'd definitely shoot for a small target here. How about one logging show?"

"Okay, keep going, Spencer."

"I'd target the Deschutes National Forest. It's in the middle of Oregon, and in particular, I'd target the Sisters District Office. Lots of old growth pine in this area. I think this is your best bet, Mr. Secretary."

"I like your logic, Spencer. Your plan seems doable and much more likely to succeed than what the president wanted."

"Thank you, sir. Is there anything else I can do for you?"

"Yes, yes, there is, Congressman. I'd like a list of big GOP donors from your district who own logging companies. Can you provide my information by this afternoon?"

"Yes, Mr. Secretary. Consider it done. Anything else?"

"No, Spencer. That should do it for now."

"Well, good day to you then, Mr. Secretary."

"Good day, Spencer."

After hanging up with Spencer, Billings moved from his desk to the deeply cushioned, overstuffed leather couch that faced his office's electric fireplace. He sat down, letting the soft couch support his frame. *Spencer made sense. The smaller the battle, the less noise to be heard. Let's just get one cutting done, use it for a photo op, and champion the president's latest job creation effort. Play up the whole "big trees going to market," which means lots of jobs for the Pacific Northwest. The president doesn't need to know how scaled back this effort has become. Hell, he'll probably be off on some other tangent tomorrow, completely forgetting about this scheme.* The secretary relaxed even further into his old sofa and mentally roughed out his next moves directed, it seemed, at the Deschutes National Forest and a small domain, the Sisters Ranger District, found within its boundaries.

Sam Spencer hung up his phone after his conversation with the secretary, and returned to gazing out his window. He was shocked by the outlandish discussion he'd just had. On this beautiful, late summer day, the greens of the lawn were vivid, the sky was a solid hue of azure, and the Capitol Building, framed by all this, was more striking than normal. It seemed to shimmer in the sunlit afternoon. *Was Secretary Billings really going to cut down the last big trees in Oregon?* Representative Spencer wasn't sure how he felt about this.

CHAPTER 9

SECRETARY BILLINGS WAS READING A LIST OF names formulated by Congressman Spencer's office. Each name represented a logging family that had donated large sums of money over the years to the GOP. While scanning this info, he was devising his next move. He'd go directly to the Deschutes National Forest as Spencer suggested. The secretary's muscle could probably produce results at this level. He mentally ticked off the strong-arm tactics he planned to use to leave no wiggle room for the Deschutes Forest Director. *Director, Director,* Billings checked his notes, *Director Steve Johnson.* Johnson was a twenty-five-year professional forester. Billings checked his notes some more. This time he was looking for the Sisters District Manager's name. *There it is, Tarri McGrath.* She was a fifteen-year career forester and his notes mentioned she was the first female district manager in Oregon. He reached for the landline resting atop the end table next to his couch. Hopefully this wouldn't take too long, and wouldn't require the "tough guy" tactics he'd prepared.

Director Johnson had just returned from his lunch and was sitting down at his desk. He had dined on a patio adjacent to the Deschutes River. The river was running low now, leaving many riffles flowing between exposed boulders that ended in languid pools. There had been a large, midday, caddis hatch eruption. While Johnson ate his Caesar salad, he watched the fly catchers and swallows swoop in and grab the rising, clumsy insects. This natural phenomenon was a wonderful lunchtime distraction for Steve, who totally appreciated its complex, random interactions. Director Johnson was still reminiscing about his ringside seat when his phone rang. It was his assistant on the line.

"Yes, Rob, what do you need?"

"Are you sitting down, Steve?"

Johnson became nervous. This question was never a good thing.

"I am, Rob. Lay it on me. What's not right in the universe?"

"Billings, our Secretary of Agriculture, is on the other line and wishes to speak with you." Director Johnson sat upright in his chair. No, not another round with this guy. The last time Johnson and the Forest Service had encountered Billings was in response to the secretary's demand to reduce the Forest Service overall budget. Billings' decree cut staff by 25% and hacked from the total budget another 30%. Considering that 50% of their overall funding was earmarked for firefighting, which couldn't be touched, the cuts were to come out of the other 50% of the district's annual budget. Meeting the secretary's parameters devastated and crippled the United States Forest Service. The months following Billings' decree were humiliating for Johnson. People were given pink slips based on seniority. Johnson saw his young energetic, dedicated workforce eliminated. He now had middle-aged, middle-management desk jockeys in the field wearing hard hats and wielding chainsaws. Most projects in his forest were cancelled or put on hold. He was currently monitoring two salvage logging jobs and several restoration programs. These programs cut out unwanted underbrush, small unhealthy trees, and seedling clusters from the old growth pine forests found within his jurisdiction. Continuing this agenda allowed Johnson some satisfaction and relief from the guilt he felt regarding the massive layoffs. Steve also had been directed by higher-ups to close half of his district's campgrounds. This occurred just prior to summer, and was not well received by the public.

Steve Johnson took a deep breath and wondered why this call was directed at him and not the Regional Office in Portland. He placed the receiver to his ear.

"Hello, Secretary Billings. What can the Deschutes National Forest do for you?"

"Hello, Johnson. Well, you can do a lot for me, Director, so I'll get right to the point. This comes directly from the White House. You need to get a logging operation going, and by going I mean old growth Ponderosas laying on the ground, ready to haul off to the sawmill, in a few days."

Director Johnson didn't know what to think of this totally absurd request, but realized the seriousness of the situation due to whom he was speaking with. He immediately decided to reply to this request with his own directness.

"This isn't possible, Mr. Secretary. There are too many regulations standing in the way of your request."

"Johnson, you're forgetting who you're talking to. I am the regulations."

After the verbal punch, Billings pulled out his big guns and continued, "I see here, Johnson, you're a twenty-five-year Forest Service civil servant whose pay grade is at our highest managerial level. You could be retiring comfortably in a few years with a nice pension and pleasant memories, or Johnson, and listen carefully now, you could be retiring with a much reduced pay grade from some crappy job in some backwash location I place you in. Do you get my drift?"

Steve Johnson was feeling nauseated but didn't lose focus on the gravity of the threat or situation he was confronted with. He was good at thinking on his feet and responded quickly to the secretary.

"We have to set boundaries and cruise the show, Mr. Secretary, and this..."

"Charge the logging outfit a dollar a tree, Johnson, and get the platting done by tomorrow."

Johnson recoiled at this statement, but continued on. "The bidding process will require..."

"You're to give the job to Sisters Logging Company. And Johnson, I want the show in old growth Ponderosa pines from your Sisters District. I believe Tarri McGrath is your district boss over there."

"Yes she is, sir."

"Do we see 'eye to eye' on this, Johnson, or do I need to find another director for the Deschutes National Forest?"

Steve Johnson lowered his eyes to his desk top and the family portrait resting there. His wife of twenty years and his two teenage sons sat smiling looking at him. He knew what his answer must be.

"Yes, we're seeing 'eye to eye' here, Mr. Secretary."

"Good, call my Whitten Building office with some satisfactory news in a few days. I'll be talking to the president, soon, and he'll be waiting for your response. Oh, and if McGrath doesn't want to accommodate us, have her give me a call. I'll straighten her out, or send her packing. You can quote me if need be."

"I'm sure she'll follow my directive, Mr. Secretary. She's a team player. You can expect a call from me in a few days' time."

"Great, Johnson. I'm glad you could help the president out."

"Certainly, sir. Is there anything else?"

"No, Johnson. Good day."

"Good day to you, Secretary Billings."

After talking with Johnson, and relaxing in his office for a bit, Billings mused about his conversation with the director. Pushing around a public servant left a different taste in his mouth compared to battling it out with an unconscionable business competitor. The secretary felt somewhat like a bully after his interaction with Johnson. This feeling was unsettling. Threatening good, decent people didn't seem appropriate to Ray Billings at the moment. He needed to rein himself in and find other methods for securing the president's wishes.

Doubting himself was an alien concept, causing him some angst, so Billings turned to a comfort response, and ordered some food from the cafeteria. The kitchen's food was just what the doctor ordered, and after finishing his entrée, he felt more like himself. The secretary began thinking about his forthcoming call to the president. Some needed assurances began to define themselves. Something could always go wrong with plans, so a contingency was needed, a firewall to ensure your success. Billings would have President McDonald create an Executive Order temporarily halting all logging regulations currently in place for the National Forest System and placing them in a review category. This bit of gamesmanship should thwart any efforts to stop the logging process.

Secretary Billings wondered if McDonald could focus long enough to get the decree inked. He wasn't sure. All he wished for was that he'd be off the hook once he told McDonald about his conversations with Spencer and Johnson, and then, hopefully, wouldn't be bothered with this petty little scheme again. Billings thought if the president came back to him with more instructions concerning the logging operation, he would proffer an underling to handle the new details, thus allowing the secretary to distance himself from McDonald's vengeful retaliation.

CHAPTER 10

Steve Johnson cradled his receiver into its base, and only then did he notice his upper torso was stiffly frozen and locked into an upright position. He consciously forced his back to relax and slowly settled into his desk chair. He sat for a moment thinking about the ugly, threatening interaction he'd just participated in, and began to formalize the vague notion that had materialized partway through his conversation with Billings. It became clear to Johnson what he should do. He was not the important piece in the puzzle, nor was Tarri McGrath, whom he'd soon call. No, those big, grand, old growth yellowbellies were the lead cast members. These remaining old trees had been consciously protected by his National Forest for over seventy years, and their continued survival was the important concern, not his job. Johnson knew he'd made the right decision to hold onto his position for whatever length of time he was allowed. This meant some administration puppet wouldn't be calling the shots in the Deschutes National Forest. Director Johnson picked up his phone and called Tarri McGrath at the Sisters Ranger District's headquarters.

Tarri McGrath was an energetic, athletic-looking woman who recently turned thirty-eight. She wore her brunette hair in a short ponytail and enjoyed feeling it bounce in rhythm with her stride. Tarri was not only the first female to run a Deschutes National Forest District, she was also the youngest manager.

When Steve Johnson reached Tarri by phone, she had just returned from the field and was checking her computer for email messages. When her phone rang, Tarri lifted the receiver and greeted her caller.

"Sisters Ranger District. Tarri McGrath speaking."

"Hello, Tarri, this is Steve Johnson."

"Steve, how are you? Are you enjoying this fine summer day? I'm sitting here reading mostly boring emails. They make me want to play hooky, take my float tube up to Three Creek Lake, and try for some of those recently planted brood trout. The afternoon mayfly hatch should be popping off right about now."

"Yes, yes, Tarri. I wish I was there right now. Oh how I wish..." Director Johnson's voice trailed off. For a few seconds their conversation sat in silent awkwardness. Tarri wondered what was wrong.

"What's up, Steve? You don't sound like yourself."

"I'm not, Tarri. I'm in shock and feeling really nervous right now."

Tarri began feeling anxious. She'd never heard this weird, frustrated, remorseful tone in Director Johnson's voice before.

"Tell me what's wrong, Steve. I'm getting a little uneasy over here."

"Okay, Tarri, I really don't know where to start. Bear with me. I just finished a phone call with the Secretary of Agriculture and he threatened to ruin my career if I didn't play ball with him, and yours, too, if you don't do as I say."

"What do you mean?"

"It's a scary, convoluted mess, Tarri, but first let me say, I think I know how to derail this crazy scheme Billings pushed onto me."

"What scheme, Steve?"

"Before I go any further, I need you to trust me now. Really, trust me. I think I'm doing the right thing."

"Of course I trust you. Now what in the world are you talking about?"

"Okay, okay, here's the brunt of it. I've been instructed to create a logging operation in your district that gets old growth Ponderosa trees immediately cut down."

Tarri McGrath paused for a moment, sat back in her chair, and digested the unsophistication of this request.

"Steve, this is impossible."

"Yes, yes, I know, but that's what I've been told to do. Now listen, I think I can '86' this whole ridiculous scheme and protect our jobs."

"Okay, I'm listening."

"Here are the parameters Billings demanded. You need to award the site to Sisters Logging. They get the rights for one dollar a tree, no strings attached, and no regs blocking their way."

"This is unheard of."

"Yeah, I know. Billings said this idea came directly from the president."

"So, we're to break numerous laws just to appease some lunatic who sits in the Oval Office?"

"My plan has us appearing to do so, Tarri. I promise I'll protect your backside. If push comes to shove, I'll swear I forced you to abide by my orders by threatening to fire you."

"Steve, I don't think you'll be able to save my job. I'll go down with you if anybody comes after us, and I'm sure they will if we continue with this plan."

Steve Johnson thought about Tarri's words, and surmised she might be more realistic than he was.

"You could be right, but I don't think so. I actually don't think this clear-cut will ever happen, and here's why: I was told to ignore all federal logging regulations, but I wasn't told to shut down our website, and this, I think, could be our saving grace."

"Where are you going with this?"

"Well, you're going to pick a site, let's say 50–100 acres within your district, and notify me of its location. You're then going to award the site to Sisters Logging Company, and tell them to have at it. I'm going to post on our "logging activity" website all the site information it normally includes. You know how environmentalists monitor our site like hawks. There'll be phone calls, demonstrations in front of our offices, and lawsuits hitting the Ninth Circuit Court of Appeals in San Francisco before the day's end. This cut won't happen if we use our website effectively, and Tarri, anyone can import information into this site. It's not our responsibility to update the page. So, what I'm saying is, if Billings wants to drop the hammer on us, we can argue it was some unknown employee who screwed up his plan by just doing his job."

Tarri listened to Director Johnson's plan and wanted to believe him. She hoped he was right, and environmental groups would block this atrocity from happening. She didn't feel Steve's plan would save her job or his for that matter, but saving the trees was possible. She'd do what Johnson asked and hope for the best. If she worked things right on her end, no one but herself and maybe one more forester would be in danger of losing their jobs. She already knew who to ask for help, and Tarri felt he could actually wriggle out of this mess unscathed.

"Okay, Steve; I'm with you. What exactly do you want me to do?"

"Well, plat the site first. Do it tomorrow. Get the logger on board the next day, and tell him he can start cutting on Friday. Call me as soon as the logger has agreed to terms, and then I'll update our website. Before the chainsaws leave their crummy, we should have all kinds of anti-logging activity in our backyard and lawsuits hitting the courts."

"God, Steve, I hope you're right. I can't believe you've been yanked around like this and this whole mess has fallen into my lap. It really, really...it makes me want to cry thinking maybe, on my watch, my district will start cutting down the few remaining yellowbellies we've so preciously protected."

"I don't think it's going to happen, Tarri. I really don't think it will."

"Okay. Let me get going here. I've got to get the site mapped and awarded."

"Thanks so much. 'Thanks' seems like a pretty trite remark considering what I've asked of you, Tarri, but really, it's all I can think to say. Please contact me right after you've awarded the logging site."

"I will, Director, good-bye."

"Good-bye, Tarri."

As Tarri hung up her phone, her gaze gravitated to a large map on her wall showing the Sisters Forest District. She knew it by heart, and was aware of every old growth stand's location. She had already decided not to ask for any help in locating this logging site. The fewer people involved, the fewer employees hurt by the potential fallout. She walked over to the map and placed a finger on the Metolius River's famous Big Eddy hole. Above the slow water lay a stand of big trees not easily seen from the lower road. The upper road that passed through the Ponderosas was used mostly by locals and some knowledgeable fishermen but was not frequented by tourists. If this stand was logged, Tarri knew most Metolius River visitors would never know it. They'd drive to their campgrounds or visit the fish hatchery and never see the "stumps of mystery" left behind by large-scale clear-cutting. Tarri gazed out her window at the nearby Ponderosa trees, and shook her head in disgust. After thinking a bit, she returned her attention to the immediate task. The platting needed to be completed quickly.

As John Hanson walked past the reception desk in the Sisters District Office, Shelley, the greeter who resided there, mentioned that Tarri wanted to meet with him in her office. Sixty-five years of age, John was one week away from formal retirement. His ducks were all in a row, and his retirement papers were dated and signed. His sixty-five-year-old stride had a new, youthful bounce to it, and with a smile and a nod he headed for his boss's office. John politely knocked and then entered Ms. McGrath's work space. She was standing next to her district map, and motioned for him to join her. When he stood next to her, she regarded him and with a sigh patted his right shoulder.

"John, I've got a terrible job for you. I know you're retiring in a few days and that's why I picked you for this task." Without pausing, Tarri continued on. "Can you get a new timber harvest boundary platted, by yourself, in one day's time? Tomorrow, to be precise?"

"Sure, Tarri. I can do it. One truck is set up with all the equipment I need. I'll have to do more leg work than normal of course, but it's doable."

"Thanks, John. I'd like you to get the boundaries set by tomorrow, and the next day, I'd like you to meet with Sisters Logging at the site, and grant them the show for a dollar a tree."

John couldn't believe what he was hearing, but knew why he was the one hearing it. When the shit hit the fan, he'd be long gone, retired, and safe from the potential danger.

"Okay boss, I can do that."

"Thanks, John. No questions now, okay? Someday, after this mess has resolved itself, I'll fill you in, but for now, the less you know, the better."

"All right, Tarri. I'll take care of these jobs for you. When do you want to hear from me next?"

"Right after you award the cut to Sisters Logging."

"Okay, boss. Consider it done."

As John left the office, he turned back and contemplated Tarri. "Hey, Tarri, I'm sorry you're having to do this. I know it's not your idea."

Tarri McGrath turned away from John Hanson. The tears began to stream down her cheeks. As John left her office, she walked over to her desk, sat down, and uncontrollably sobbed. After a few minutes her convulsions stopped and she began to regain control. She untied the paisley scarf from around her neck and dried her eyes and cheeks with it. While she wiped away tears, she thought, *somebody better be reading our website two days from now and put a stop to this madness.*

CHAPTER 11

THE NEW CHEVY SILVERADO FOREST SERVICE RIG turned west onto U.S. Highway 20 and headed toward the Metolius River. John Hanson was steering toward his last official duty as a U.S. Government Forest Service employee. He was "hanging up his keys" in a few days on his forty-year career, and if you didn't count today's task, when he looked back on his tenure, he had absolutely no regrets. Today's job would mar his perfect record, and John hoped to complete it as quickly and painlessly as possible.

His stint with the Forest Service had been more than rewarding. It allowed him to work outside in the Central Oregon environment that he loved. The 300-plus days of dry, sun-drenched weather he enjoyed each year were perfect for his outdoor labors. John knew he was a lucky man for choosing Sisters as his home, and the Deschutes Forest as his office space. For the last ten years, his district had allowed him to share with the public his knowledge of local geology and indigenous peoples. Several large U.S. campgrounds around Bend had small amphitheaters, and John was the resident ranger who gave informational presentations to the campers. He continued with his Sisters Ranger District responsibilities and added to them his evening "Campfire Lecture" Summer Program. Hanson was passionate about his discourses, and over the years developed a comprehensive delivery, which noted general and regional geology, then shifted to local, unique physical features, and ended by tying one of these exclusive sites to the lives of the Native Peoples who had lived in Central Oregon.

It was somewhat poignant, John thought, that he was currently heading right to the exact spot where he verbally ended his "campfire" presentations. This site was a physical phenomenon of the weirdest level, and he was going to add a little more uniqueness to the local history. *Unbelievable*, thought John, *who came up with this screwball idea? It's like giving the candy store keys to a bunch of middle schoolers.*

Hanson continued west on Highway 20, driving past beautiful stands of Ponderosa pine. He was thinking about his new agreement with Tarri McGrath concerning his "Campfire Lecture" series. She was going to allow him to continue with his summer presentations after official retirement. John was pleased with this arrangement and was anticipating the next camping season.

To help lighten up the trip to the Big Eddy logging site, John revisited his campground delivery in a mentally abridged manner. When he started his lecture he noted that the overall geology and physical features found in Central Oregon were due mainly to plate tectonics. The Cascade Range approximated the subduction zone where the North Pacific Plate met and submerged beneath the North American Continental Plate. Just west of Sisters was where the Columbia Plateau lava flows that occurred about 15 million years ago were eventually covered and disrupted by the volcanic activities of the Cascade Range, which was situated above the subduction cleft. Most intriguingly, some geologists felt the Columbia Plateau flows emanated from the Yellowstone "Hot Spot," a huge molten lava chamber residing below the famous Wyoming National Park.

The Columbia Plateau lava flows oozed across Oregon for millions of years, and in some locations were thousands of feet deep. The lava near Sisters probably originated from fissures near La Grande, Oregon. Wherever rivers dissected Central and Eastern Oregon, these thick flows were cut through by the hydrologic action. You could consequently see any number of these layers exposed to the weather. They created sheer walls with small ledges delineating where one flow was covered by another.

West of Sisters, the La Grande seepage was disrupted by the much younger Cascade Range volcanic development. Mt. Jefferson, one of the Cascades' largest volcanoes, was only about 600,000 years old. Relative to the Columbia Plateau lava flows, Mt. Jefferson was just an infant. All the volcanoes in the Cascades covered the older, molten flows with their own, youthful lavas. John wrapped up this part of the presentation with a simple statement: "The geology of Central Oregon was the result of newer, more youthful volcanic forces colliding with and overriding the older plutonic continental activities." After this comment, John would laugh and add, "Just another example of youth eventually taking over the playing field from us oldsters." This usually elicited a few laughs from the elder audience members.

John's truck drove by Black Butte Ranch, and this local resort community landmark signaled his turn to Camp Sherman was quickly approaching. He'd just passed Black Butte, the volcano for which the ranch was named. This volcano and the Big Eddy site were the two cornerstones of the second part of John's campfire presentation. In this section, he pointed out nearby geologic oddities. He noted

Black Butte appeared to be a completely forested, cinder block volcano, but in reality, it was a complex stratovolcano that due to its shortness did not glaciate like the taller nearby volcanoes. Mt. Hood, located a little north and west of Black Butte, had glaciers cut into its sides, and still had remnant ones clinging to it. Its profile seemed much older, with numerous, jagged ridgelines ascending to its peak. Hood's once circular crater was blown out, and now you saw a partial bowl from the mountain's southern side. This volcano was actually the baby of the two. Mt. Hood was only about 500,000 years old, whereas Black Butte, the little, short, forested hill, was over 1.5 million years old. John always raised his eyebrows with this exclamation and uttered the old adage, "Looks can be deceiving."

John turned off Highway 20 just past Black Butte Ranch and was now heading due north to Camp Sherman. Both sides of the road were still forested by Ponderosas. His thoughts continued with his presentation, and at this point of his delivery, he always became excited discussing how the Big Eddy site was unique because of its geologic quirkiness. Here, the Grande Ronde lava flows were knifed by a small fault, which due to deep internal pressures created a fault block lift on the west side of the Metolius River. This rise exposed two different flows, the younger separated from the lower, older flow by the telltale ledge. The Metolius River chose the fault line as its channel, and this section of river ran straight for about a half mile. Another unique feature, an intrusive rhyolite formation, was exposed by weathering just to the east of the fault line. This orangish rock proved to be harder than the neighboring basalt, and forced the river to curve around its edge. This bend in the river had created the Big Eddy. John then added a third oddity to the regional puzzle that helped define the overall picture of this site. A fissure connecting to a local, deep hot spot cut through multiple layers of the Grand Ronde flows, and as the last flows covered the area, the fissure allowed escaping gases to create a cavernous pocket somewhere in the top lava flows. This process lifted the entire western fault block even more, and produced a gently sloped, flat-topped hill.

Several thousand years ago, the cavern's roof partially collapsed, creating a small crater-like depression at the knoll's summit. The views of this formation were quite different from the two roads that paralleled the river. From the western road, you saw a gently sloping rise, covered with large evenly spaced Ponderosas, terminating in a flat-topped plateau. Down below on the eastern river road, you viewed two sheer, volcanic walls about seventy-five feet in height. These walls were slightly inclined from the south and the north and met at the small mesa-like crown. John noted in his lecture that the crown was a natural fortress and could be protected easily because of its citadel-like structure. Over the years, erosion created a small, wall-like basaltic lip that rimmed the summit's bowl.

Hanson's Forest Service vehicle came to a three-way stop just past the Camp Sherman volunteer fire department's buildings. Turning right would take John to Camp Sherman. Straight ahead would lead him past several riverside summer homes and eventually to the Big Eddy logging site. John slowly drove through the intersection and continued on. He let his thoughts return to his campground discussion, and the grand finale. By this time in his address, John had been talking for about thirty minutes, and usually he lost about a third of the listeners in the process. So like any good speaker, he saved the best for last. He tied together the Big Eddy formation with the "First Peoples" who lived in the region. Hanson shared with his audience two well known, local, Indian legends. When and exactly who created the myths were a mystery to the old forester, although he assumed they were produced by the Warm Springs or Northern Paiutes since they both hunted and gathered in the general vicinity of the Metolius River. Something about the Big Eddy Rise caused it to be used as a spiritual site. Native "rites of passage" as well as other celebrations occurred there. The earliest Euro-Anglo settlers witnessed and wrote about lengthy periods of drumming and chanting emanating from the hill. A sweat lodge resided on site and was observed being used often. Eventually, due to hostilities between whites and local Indians, the spiritual grounds were abandoned. Several indigenous legends remained after the "First Peoples'" departure. John culled from this group two myths he felt were unique to the Big Eddy Rise and still resonated mystical and foreboding tones. First, he would tell of the site's reputation for having a portal to the afterworld. One could go to the rise and be joined by visitors from the underworld. The second legend dealt with the Spiritual Grounds' curse, which was directed at white people. It stated that any Anglo with an evil heart who ventured onto the Big Eddy formation would die a painful and violent death. This last legend usually brought a hush to the audience, and John loved to abruptly end his lecture at this point.

As John finished mentally summarizing his campground presentation, the road turned from the river, and now moved inland just a bit. He passed by one of the last stands of unmanaged forest. It was on the District's to-do list, and when funds resurfaced, it would be cleaned up like the surrounding areas. In another half mile, the road turned back toward the river. John followed the lane for a quarter mile, then pulled off onto an ATV road that ran into the old Ponderosa forest. Turning off the engine, he opened his door and stepped out into the quiet, warm, early September day. Several scrub jays flew off, away from his rig, and a flock of yellow-rumped warblers flitted about in the branches of the closest trees. A doe and her fawn slowly walked away from him, heading for the river, browsing as they departed. Occasionally, the doe would look back at John with her big ears rotated his way. Hanson surveyed the big, old yellowbellies with their orange bark, which appeared scale-like because of the dark-veined irregular furrows that deepened and widened with age. As far as John was concerned, no other conifer could match these Ponderosas for beauty. His eyes focused on the nearest tree and slowly gazed upwards. About thirty feet from the ground, the first big branch protruded from its host. Above it, numerous limbs followed, randomly projecting from the trunk. They progressively grew shorter as they neared the top of the tree. This was a stand of old giants. The average height of yellowbellies was over two hundred feet and at their base, the trees were about five feet in diameter. The green bundles of needles on the branches contrasted beautifully with the orange-colored, dark-veined bark. The needle clusters bunched up at the ends of the branches, leaving long sections of bare limbs. John never tired of viewing these trees.

The forest floor was somewhat barren of vegetation. There were manzanita bushes interspersed among the tree trunks and some wild bunchgrasses also prevailed, but in general, due to the lack of precipitation in this area, not much could compete with the stately trees. The empty space between plants was littered with pinecones and needles. The cones provided great food for chipmunks. You could rarely view the forest floor without seeing several of these natural entertainers scurrying about. John shook his head as he thought about today's job. He would soon hand a contract to Dennis Stafford, the owner/operator of Sisters Logging, allowing him to completely destroy this pristine, beautiful setting. *Unbelievable!*

Off in the distance the sound of a diesel rig caught John's attention and he observed the direction he'd just come from. The truck's progress became louder and the Forest Service employee recognized Dennis' big, heavy-duty crummy coming his way. Hanson looked onto his dashboard at the envelope containing Dennis' contract with the Forest Service signed by both Tarri McGrath and Steve Johnson. Suddenly, John Hanson felt all the weight and guilt of this betrayal press down on his shoulders. It was a staggering load. He'd hoped this moment wouldn't cause him any angst. He was wrong. It hurt. It hurt badly. Stafford's rig pulled up behind John's and the motor shut off. John waved and walked to Dennis. He thought, *the sooner this transaction is over, the better.* With each step, his official and last duty as a Forest Service employee became more and more a reality.

CHAPTER 12

Dennis Stafford stopped his crummy behind the U.S. Forest Service rig. He saw John Hanson walking back his way. Dennis viewed the forest of old trees surrounding him and wondered why they'd stopped here. *This couldn't be the logging site*, he thought to himself. He then noticed a new boundary tag affixed to a nearby tree and wondered even more about this locale. Peering farther into the forest, he saw the spray paint used to denote a "cone tree" marking the trunk of one of the old giants.

Was this his logging show? Dennis hopped out of his truck and walked to meet John. They'd known each other for over twenty years. Ever since Dennis had started running his father's logging company, he had worked with John regarding the company's logging efforts in the Deschutes Forest. Dennis liked John. He was a down-to-earth local who was easy to talk to, and he appreciated a good logging outfit. The two men met and shook hands.

"Hello, John. Hey, I hear you're close to retirement. Is that so?"

"I'm leaving the keys on the desk day after tomorrow."

"Congratulations. Are you staying in the area or moving on?"

"I don't have any long range plans as of yet, but I'll probably stay round. Tarri says I can still do the campsite presentations, and really, I can't think of a better place to live."

"Well, John, for what it's worth, I've always appreciated your professionalism. You're a respectful and considerate person, and those traits have not been lost on me. Not enough people care about another person's well-being like you do."

The two men looked off into the forest for a moment, and then John said, : "How's your mother doing?"

Dennis' mother had just lost her husband six months ago. He had died, suddenly, from cardiac arrest while constructing a log home up in the Wallowa Mountains near Joseph, Oregon. Norma Stafford, his wife, was crushed by his death, but recently had started to regain her composure, and now was doing better.

"She's okay. Dad's death was a blow to all of us. You never expect it to happen, and when it does, it's such a shock. Mom's just now acting more like her old self. Thankfully, my younger brother and his family live right on the ranch, and are with her every day. I think the grandkids are good medicine for her."

"Well, I'm truly sorry for your loss. Be sure and give your mom my condolences when you talk with her next."

"I will, John, and thanks for inquiring about her." The two men once again looked off into the forest. They both noted the doe and fawn returning to the stand, browsing as they walked along.

"She and the youngster just went down to the river for a drink. Looks like they're back for more grub."

"It certainly does. Well, John, we're standing here surrounded by these big trees, and you told me about a logging gift the district had for me. Is this really the logging site I'm looking at, and if it is, I don't believe you."

John headed back to his truck, grabbed the envelope off his dash, and, returning to Dennis, handed it to him. "Open it up."

Dennis Stafford contemplated John Hanson with a quizzical expression. He pulled some reading glasses out of his shirt pocket and positioned them onto his nose. He opened the envelope and retrieved the official logging contract. The contract was only one page long; this was extremely odd. Even odder were the terms of the legal document. It took Dennis less than a minute to read the contract. He tilted his head to one side, raised his eyebrows, and spoke to John. "One dollar a tree, and no regulations to abide by?"

"That's right. I don't know what's going on here, but as you probably noted, it's signed by Tarri, and by Steve Johnson. It's legit."

Dennis looked away from John and viewed the fawn and doe browsing on grasses. He then regarded the old Ponderosas. He hadn't cut a tree like this in twenty years. He returned his attention to John Hanson. "I'm stunned."

"So am I, but like I said, this is legit. You know, Dennis, I'd get logging right away. This is pretty weird, and who knows what will happen next."

Dennis nodded his head in agreement. "Yeah, I'm not going to look this gift horse in the mouth. I've got a few phone calls to make, and if I get the right answers, I can start felling trees day after tomorrow."

"Well, Dennis, hope things go well for you. Oh yeah, you don't have to abide by this request, but I've got several cone trees marked out there, and if you'd leave them standing, I'd greatly appreciate it."

Dennis Stafford looked at the old forester standing in front of him and thought about his father. What great men this generation produced! They were kind, considerate, respectful, and filled with a moral obligation toward responsible behavior.

"Certainly. I'll make sure they're not damaged, and John, thanks for all the good years you put into your job. I really appreciate what you've done."

"Thanks, Dennis. Good luck with the show." The men shook hands.

John Hanson turned away from Dennis Stafford and walked back to his Forest Service truck. Before getting inside, he examined the stately forest. Nearby, the doe and fawn still browsed. Several chipmunks skittered about and a few scrub jays returned and were checking the trees for grubs. John saw the shadow of a large bird ripple across the forest floor and gazed upwards, catching a glimpse of a golden eagle. It turned back, flying a tight circle overhead. The two locked eyes and watched each other, and then, with several powerful wing beats, the bird disappeared behind the closest tree tops. *That's strange,* John thought. *This is not really golden eagle habitat.* John took one more glance at the surrounding forest, then opened his truck's door and sat behind the wheel. He pulled a U-turn, and driving between and around manzanita bushes, he gained the west Metolius River Road and headed back to Highway 20. In his rearview mirror, he saw Dennis Stafford's truck pull onto the road behind him. John hoped this cut wouldn't happen, but at the moment he could not think of anything to stop it..

Chapter 13

THE CRUMMY TURNED EAST ONTO HIGHWAY 20 and headed back toward Sisters. Dennis thumbed through his contacts until his mom's number appeared. He swiped the phone screen and waited for his mom to answer.

"Hello, Dennis, how are you?"

"Hi, Mom. I'm fine, how you doing?"

"All right. It a beautiful day out here."

Dennis knew what his mother would be doing. Right now, she'd be sewing on the quilt she intended to give Dennis and Janice, his wife, for the birth of their third daughter. Her sewing table sat in front of her log cabin's huge picture window, which looked down upon a tranquil, mountain valley scene. The valley was now covered with tall grasses. Grazing the valley floor would be about one hundred Black Angus cows, roughly half of the Staffords' herd. The other half would be up in the National Forest, grazing on the wild bunchgrasses found beneath the fir and pine trees.

"How's the quilt coming along, mom?"

"Oh, I don't know. I hope you and Janice will like it."

"You know we will. Hey, have you seen much of Younger and the family?"

Mrs. Stafford laughed and said, "A little too much. The grandkids are great, but your brother and his wife are a bit too concerned about my well-being. They're always bringing food up here, checking on my meds, and just plain getting in the way."

It was Dennis's turn to laugh. "Well good for them. It shouldn't be any other way."

"Easy for you to say, young man. You don't have to shoo them out the front door every night so you can have a moment to yourself."

"Sorry, but everyone thinks it's the best thing for you right now."

Mrs. Stafford laughed again and continued. "Actually, I agree. The grandkids are really great and so are your brother and his wife."

Dennis' mind shifted gears and he thought about the logging show and the big trees he'd soon have in his possession.

"You won't believe this, but I've got the logging rights to about a hundred acres of old growth pine near Camp Sherman."

After a pause his mother responded, "How did that happen?"

"I'm not really sure, but it's for real, and my memory tells me you've got the only mill capable of handling these big trees. How long would it take to get Seneca up and running again?"

The Staffords' Seneca Mill hadn't run for twenty years. The family shut it down when the supply of old growth pine ended, but instead of scrapping it out, they'd chosen to winterize and mothball the mill. The hope was at some time down the road, more big trees would be made available.

"I'm not sure. Everything would need greasing, motors fired up, electrical circuits checked. We'd need a supply of wood for our power plant. If there were no problems, maybe it would take a couple weeks to get it operational. We'd have to get mill workers. That's probably not a problem, though, but getting a lead sawyer might be. Ed Philips died a few years back, and I really don't know of another big wood sawyer around these parts."

"We could find one. There's one out there someplace, maybe in Northern California or Southern Oregon."

"So what's your plan?"

"Well, I'll start cutting trees and haul them over to Seneca. Hey, is there a loader on site?"

"I believe there is."

"We'll need one. Anyway, I'll stockpile the logs in Seneca. While we're cutting and hauling them, I'll be searching for buyers. There'll be lots of people salivating over the dimensions of these sticks. We'll get top dollar for this lumber."

"I'm sure you're right."

"Anyway, Mom. That's the deal."

"Sounds like we could make some money. Are there any more old growth tracts coming up for bid? The cost of jump-starting the old mill will cut into our profit margin by quite a bit. It would be nice if some more big logs were headed our way."

"I agree. I haven't heard of any other shows. I'll give Tarri McGrath a call, and ask her if more cuts will be coming. You're right about our profit margin. A few more sites would certainly help us out."

Mrs. Stafford chuckled to herself. "Our little town of Seneca won't know what to do with a bunch of millworkers and log truck drivers hanging around, again. I'm not even sure if there's a café operating anymore."

"There is. I was just through there about a month ago. They'll be happy to oblige the workers and their needs. Hey, changing the subject, the girls and I were thinking about visiting you in a couple weeks. Could you stand another son and his family harassing you for a few days?"

Mrs. Stafford laughed again. "I'll give it a try, Dennis. Be on your best behavior, though, or I'll send the lot of you packing."

"Okay. We'll be good. Love you."

"Love you too. Good-bye."

"Good-bye, Mom."

Dennis set his phone down next to him on the bench seat. His mom sounded like her old self for a moment there, which was good. It would be nice to get up into the Ochocos, away from all the Sisters and Bend congestion. Maybe he could help his brother cut out the first batch of yearlings from the herd and get them ready for auction.

Dennis started to mentally tick off his tasks regarding running the logging show. Some of the fellas who worked for him had never cut down an old growth tree. *Boy, they'll be surprised at the sound and feel of one of those big trees hitting the ground.* He reached for his phone and once again accessed the contact list. Time to start putting together his crew. Like John Hanson suggested, the sooner the better.

CHAPTER 14

RUSSEL NELSON STOOD OUTSIDE HIS COLLEGE advisor's office waiting for her to arrive. Russel had just arrived in Washington D.C. the day before and moved into his dorm. He had a small, two-room space in Mitchell Hall, which was part of the Foggy Bottom campus of George Washington University. His roommate hadn't checked in yet, so Russel enjoyed the cramped quarters all to himself. After dinner, he joined a few other early arrival students in the game room and they'd shot pool and played some Xbox together. Before turning in, he tried to reach his friend Bridger, but got his voicemail, so Russel made a mental note to call his friend at about noon the next day.

The redheaded, freckle-faced freshman now waited for the first meeting with his college adviser. He moved down the hall and was looking out the window when a voice called out to him. "Are you Russel Nelson?"

Russel turned around and saw an older, gray-haired lady wearing denim jeans, sandals, and a lightweight, button-up blouse, smiling at him.

"That would be me, Professor Riley."

"Sorry I'm late, Russel. These warm sunny days tend to make me a little lethargic."

"No worries, Professor. I'm still feeling a little jetlag and moving somewhat slowly myself."

Professor Susan Riley unlocked her door and they both entered her small office. Bookshelves lined the walls and Russel noted lots of world history volumes plus many political science books. Near Susan's exterior window sat a large globe, resting on its four-legged stand.

As he moved closer for a better view, Russel perceived its aged appearance. "Wow, this is beautiful, Professor."

Russel reached out and gently turned the globe. Southeast Asia presented itself to him, and he observed Myanmar was denoted as Burma, which told him a little about the globe's age.

"Thank you. I found it in an antique store in upstate New York. Here, Russel."

Susan motioned to a chair sitting across the desk from hers. "Have a seat and let's get to know each other a little bit. I read some of your file, and I'm really impressed, young man. Not many students get a full ride to this university. You should be very proud of your accomplishments up to this date."

Russel sat down and faced his counselor. Behind her, hanging on the wall, was a reprint of Arnold Friberg's painting depicting George Washington kneeling in prayer next to his horse at Valley Forge. This cold, snowy, forested scene was one of Russel's favorite paintings.

"You know, Professor Riley, I'm just a very fortunate person who's getting to follow their dream at an early age."

Susan looked at Russel and knew this young student would do well at George Washington University. She could tell he already possessed a level of maturity most incoming freshmen didn't have. Just as she was about to continue, her desk phone rang and, excusing herself, she answered it. It was her dean, who needed help in finding some new students for the White House Intern Program. Susan replied she'd keep an eye out for any possible candidates and then said her goodbyes. Looking back at Russel, she mentioned, "Would you be interested in a White House internship?"

Professor Riley wasn't aware of the new job category President McDonald created, and she thought Russel would be filling one of the usual positions the White House offered the undergraduates. She had never heard of the "personal presidential service" job category Russel would be ushered into, and if she had, most likely Susan wouldn't have suggested the job to him.

Russel thought for a moment. "Probably. What's it entail and how long a stint would it be?"

"Well, the internship runs for four months, usually, and there are various types of jobs. You could be a White House guide for large tours or special guests. More often, the job entails communication of data, so computer skills are essential. You could end up in any of the nineteen or so White House departments. Your job description is pretty limitless. It really depends on your interest and personal skills."

"Sounds interesting. Yeah, I think I'd like to try it."

"Well, our counseling session will be cut short then. My dean, whom I just spoke with, said applicants are to apply immediately. Let's do your class schedule next Monday. Same time, okay?"

"Sure."

Professor Riley wheeled her chair over to her computer and printed off a letter of introduction for Russel. She filled in her name and Russel's in the appropriate spaces, then scooted back to her desk and handed Russel the letter.

"Don't over-dress, Russel. Just put a tie on, but other than that, be casual. Go to the Pennsylvania Avenue, North Gate, entrance, and show the guards this letter. They're used to interns coming and going and will take care of you immediately."

Russel accepted his letter of introduction from her.

"Good luck, Russel, and welcome to Washington D.C. You're jumping right into the capital life. This will be a great experience for you."

"Thanks, Professor Riley. I'll see you next week about my schedule."

Russel stood up, excused himself, and left his advisor's office. As he departed James Monroe Hall, he headed directly for his dorm, which was only a block away. He'd change into a light, short-sleeved shirt, some light-weight slacks, and a tie before heading over to Pennsylvania Avenue. Russel wasn't worried about time because the North Gate was only five blocks from his dorm room. His mind began to fill with images of all the possible tasks he'd be asked to do. Of all the jobs Russel conjured up, none was remotely similar to the one the White House chief usher, Don Peterson, was going to enlist him for. As Russel hurried up the stairs toward his dorm room to change clothes, he thought Washington D.C. was beginning to get really interesting.

Chapter 15

Russel headed north on 19th Street from Mitchell Hall. The warm, humid, sunny day had him sweating within a hundred yards of his starting point. Fortunately, he only had a few blocks to walk before he reached the North Gate on Pennsylvania Avenue, and thankfully, a few shade trees provided him protection from the sun's rays. As he turned onto G Street, the White House grounds came into view. Reaching 17th, he crossed the thoroughfare and headed around the corner to the North Gate. Everything began to look serious now. Numerous guards were stationed inside and outside of the grounds, and behind a tall, black, wrought-iron fence sat a large gate house. A road from Pennsylvania Avenue ran past the gate house, and, curving through the North Lawn, led to the North Portico. The road then circled back through the lawn and exited the grounds at the far end of the block.

Russel showed his letter of introduction to the nearest D.C. police officer and he directed him to a gated walkway directly in front of the security house. As he stopped in front of the closed gate, a speakered voice asked him about his appointment and Russel lifted his letter up for the interior guard to see. Simultaneously, he mentioned his 1:00 p.m. with the White House chief usher. A metallic click announced the unlocking of the gate. Another guard approached Russel and read his letter of introduction. He handed it back and led Russel over to the gate house, where the sentry left him, entered the small building, and returned with a plastic visitors pass attached to a lanyard.

"You'll need to wear this while you are on the grounds, young man."

As the security guard handed Russel his visitors pass, he looked up at the White House driveway. "Here comes your ride."

An electric cart was rapidly slowing to a stop by the security house. The guard smiled and waved at the vehicle's driver.

"Your chauffeur will give you a lift up to the White House and introduce you to the chief usher. Good luck with your interview."

"Thanks. Hey, how will I leave the grounds?"

"Preston will give you a lift to the exit gate at the other end of the block." The guard smiled again, and added, "Or he may just bring you back here. Kind of depends on his mood."

Preston pulled a sharp U-turn and, coming to a stop, waited for his rider to join him. Russel sat next to the young chauffeur, and the cart lunged off.

"Pleased to meet you, homie. I'm Preston."

He extended his knuckles at Russel and they fist bumped. Preston was a pleasant looking, young African American man with a short Afro haircut. He wore a white button-up jacket, black pants, and black leather lace-up shoes.

"I'm Russel. Thanks for the lift."

Making small talk, Russel added, "Is it always this humid? I'm sweating bullets."

"It most certainly is, my man." Preston laughed. "Welcome to Washington D.C. I hear you're to see the chief usher about an internship."

"That would be right."

"Well, good luck, homie. They've been dropping like flies all summer. You're the second round of meat I've wheeled up to this house since the beginning of summer. You would be the fourth person today, and my notes have me bringing six more of you college kids in for a shake-down."

Preston's dialogue and what he wasn't saying were intriguing Russel. "What's up? How come there's such a turnover?"

"You're part of a new intern position. You'll be serving the president his munchies. It's a job the new boss created."

"Serving him his munchies?"

"That's right, brother. I've even helped train some of you boys. Like I said, most people don't last long. The man must be hard to take care of."

The cart came to an abrupt stop underneath the North Portico roof, and both Preston and Russel stepped out and into the huge roof's shade.

"Come on, brother. I'll show you to the chief usher. His office is just inside the main doors. Preston opened a small side door for Russel and waved him through. He then joined him inside. Just to their right was a substantial wooden door, which was closed. Preston inspected his charge. "Straighten your tie, my man. Are you ready?" Russel nodded an affirmative and his guide knocked twice on the chief usher's door.

Chapter 16

Don Peterson was scrutinizing Russel Nelson's college application, which Susan Riley had emailed him. The application's borders were filled with a few pertinent notes, added by the professor, and the chief usher was now reading them. Peterson didn't need any more work, and was irritated with himself for taking on the responsibility of hiring these special interns. *A full ride*, thought Peterson. *That's pretty unusual.* As he read more of the border notes, a knock resounded from his door.

"Come in."

The door opened, and in walked a redheaded young man wearing a red tie, short-sleeved shirt, and casual slacks. He was accompanied by Preston, whom the chief usher knew and liked.

"Here's your next appointment, sir. I believe this young man deserves special consideration, Mr. Peterson."

Peterson smiled at Preston. He could always count on this young man's humor to help lighten the day's load.

"Thank you, Preston. Your advice is always considered when I make important decisions."

Preston looked at Russel and said, "I'll be waiting for you in the cart. When you're finished, I'll drive you back to the Avenue."

With that said, Preston turned and slowly closed the door behind him. Russel had been observing the chief usher's office while Preston and Peterson conversed. Floor to ceiling bookshelves lined most of the interior walls, making the room feel small. On their shelves, volumes of books were perched, separated by dozens of framed photos. Most pictures showed Peterson posing with various political figures. Russel noted Bill Clinton, both senior and junior Bushes, President Obama, and many others. A beautiful blue and purple Persian rug covered the floor and the chief usher's four-legged writing desk sat close to the room's only window. A couple chairs sat across the desk from the chief usher. He motioned for Russel to sit in one of them.

"I read you just arrived in D.C., and yes, during the summer months, it's always this humid."

Russel laughed at the chief usher's quip. "I'm sure I'll acclimate, sir. I'm from the north Oregon coast, and honestly, I'll take the humidity and sunny weather over the damp, chilly, constant coastal rains I'm used to."

"I'll reference this conversation in a couple months and see how you feel about things when the warmth and humidity give way to cold and endless snowy days."

Russel laughed again. "Four true seasons will be a climatic shock for me, sir, but I'm looking forward to it."

Don Peterson had already made up his mind about Russel Nelson.

"Russel, I'm prepared to offer you an introductory intern position, one you can rotate out of in a couple months if you'd prefer to try another avenue. There are many jobs to choose from, but for now your opening is for the 'presidential service' job. You'll be basically a waiter for the president. You'll help the kitchen staff until the president requests something, and then your waiter duties will take precedence. After a round of 'presidential server,' if you'd like, we'll shift you over into another position."

Russel smiled. "Not quite as glamorous as I'd hoped for, sir, but I accept your offer. Hopefully my efforts will allow me to change course and branch out elsewhere."

"Guaranteed, Russel. This job is only temporary."

Russel glanced out of the chief usher's window onto the North Lawn and farther yet, to the fenced border of the White House grounds.

"I'm sure I'll do a good job for you, Mr. Peterson, and along the way develop a great respect for this beautiful house."

"Most people who work here do just that, Russel. There's a noble feeling to this building."

The White House chief usher regarded his computer screen and accessed the staff's work schedule.

"Can you be here tomorrow at noon? Preston's on then, and I'd like him to be your mentor. He does a great job. Also, you'll get some presidential service calls in the middle of the day, and Preston can show you the proper way to fulfill those duties."

"I most certainly can, sir. What should I wear?"

"We'll have what you need here. There's a closet full of clean uniforms of all sizes ready to go. Do you have any black, laced shoes?"

"No, I'm afraid I don't."

"No worries. There'll be some waiting for you. What size shoe do you wear?"

"10 and ½ D."

"All right, young man. Good luck with your new position. If you have any needs or problems, feel free to contact me."

Don Peterson stood, extending his hand, and Russel grasped it in a firm handshake.

"Thanks, Mr. Peterson."

"It sounded like Preston was going to wait for you in the Portico area. Glad to have you aboard, Russel."

The White House chief usher turned away from Russel and began viewing emails. Russel noticed before he did so, Peterson jotted down his shoe size on a sticky note. He left the chief usher's office and walked to the outside door. *What just happened? Was he really going to serve the president munchies like Preston said? How weird. Well, the next few months should be interesting.* He pushed open the door and emerged once again into the humid D.C. afternoon.

Part Two

The STRONG Alliance Pushes Back

CHAPTER 17

It was a cloud-free, late summer day in Corvallis, Oregon, and OSU senior Tom Weber was sitting in his dorm room perusing the Oregon National Forest's website on his laptop. He sat near his window enjoying the breeze pulled through the room by a fan. His hall doorway was open, allowing for maximum ventilation and an ear to his floor's social activity. When he scanned the Deschutes National Forest's website, Tom did a double take at the "logging activity" section. A logging contract was just posted. The Environmental Science major noted in disbelief that logging was to commence in three days. He examined the description again. *Somebody must have screwed up big time.* Logging sites were always posted well before the tree harvest was to begin, and reading more about the show caused him even more concern because this tract was old growth Ponderosa, near Camp Sherman, Oregon. Tom shouted into the hallway for his friend, Dread, a senior Forestry major whose room was two doors down the hall from his.

"Dread, Dread! You need to see what I'm looking at, now! Right now! Come over here!"

Dread, named for his Rasta style hair, was a tall, lanky student with a scruffy beard and dark eyes. He liked the comfort and style of third world, loose-fitting clothing, and dressed himself accordingly. He'd been lying on his bed next to his dozing girlfriend, reading a periodical, when Tom hollered at him. The urgency in his friend's voice quickly roused him from his prone position, and he now peered into Tom's room from the hallway.

"What's up, Tommy Boy?"

"There's a logging show near Camp Sherman in old growth Ponderosa, which is going to begin in three days."

"No way, man. Somebody made a mistake."

"Dread, the U.S. Forest Service does not mess up on these website pages. This is totally 'spot on.' Look, right here."

Tom pointed at his computer screen. Dread walked over and viewed the "logging activity" category. He read the description of the show and its location.

"Holy shit! I know this spot. Those assholes. I can't believe this."

Dread quickly left his friend's room, ran to his, and grabbed a cowbell and drumstick off his desk. He began beating them together in the hallway.

Dread and Tom plus a few other students had formed a de facto "Earth First" organization on the Oregon State campus. They'd gravitated to the second floor of Callahan Hall, and pretty much had the run of the place since their floor's Resident Assistant was one of the group. They officially called their organization the STRONG Alliance.

Dread noted a few bodies entering the hallway, looking in his direction. Too few, really. His girlfriend, Sasha, roused from her nap due to the racket, stood next to him, stretching and mentally trying to wake up. She was a pretty African American girl from Eugene, Oregon. Her hair was braided into long cornrows that hung to just below her shoulders. She was short with broad shoulders and a nicely proportioned body. Her mixed European and African ancestry had produced a light brown skin tone and black hair. Dark brown eyes sat atop a straight nose and beautiful lips that spread easily into a smile. Sasha, like Dread, enjoyed loose-fitting peasant clothing. She regarded Dread with a questioning expression on her face.

"What's all the noise about, babe?"

"Sasha, you won't believe it!"

Five students joined Dread, Tom, and Sasha in the cramped, narrow dorm room. Dread shared with them what Tom discovered on the Deschutes' website. He suggested to his friends they mobilize immediately and begin a tree hanging/sit-in at the logging show sooner than later. Everybody there was savvy enough about logging regs, and knew lawsuits would be forthcoming. All they had to do was stall the loggers' efforts for a short time. The STRONG Alliance had a number of occupation scenarios already worked out, and they unanimously chose their most aggressive strategy. They all looked forward to deploying this scheme because they felt it would be effective and relatively trouble free. Everyone present knew their roles in undertaking this tactic, but the young college students felt more bodies were needed to successfully forestall the loggers. Sasha was sent off to the Education Building to make fliers to announce a STRONG Alliance meeting in the MU Quad for noon the next day. The group always met beneath the tall cedar trees, adjacent to the Home Economics Building. After Sasha left, Tom departed for the hardware store with a predetermined list, and several Alliance members headed off to the STRONG leader's old school bus to kick tires, check engine fluid levels, and crank over the vehicle's ancient engine. Two more students headed for the grocery store to purchase basic provisions for the occupation.

Dread noted all those present were climbers. This was incredibly fortunate. The success of their strategy required people who could scale big trees. Hopefully, they could get other students to join their effort because good ground support was essential for a tree hanging/sit-in.

The young Forestry major began packing his gear into a large, military-style duffel bag. He smiled to himself as he thought about the "curve ball" local law officers would encounter when they tried to bust their logging site occupation. Dread loved knowing he'd get a firsthand view of the arresting officers' reactions when they saw the surprises awaiting them.

CHAPTER 18

Janet glanced up from her desk as Secretary Billings walked into her office. She liked this conservative oilman from Texas. Billings was much older than Janet, and was a little short for her tastes, but he kept himself relatively fit and had a positive, self-confident attitude. Her attraction was probably caused by some kind of Freudian complex, but it didn't bother her. She'd liked men for weirder reasons. Janet knew he had a rough side, and heard stories about his "tough guy" persona in the oil business, but Billings had always been pleasant and considerate of her. She thought some men were like that: cordial, normal people mostly, but real fighters when they had to be. With a smile, raised eyebrows, and a slight tilt to her head, Janet greeted Secretary Billings.

"Good morning, secretary. What brings you to this neck of the woods?"

"I'm not sure, beautiful. Your boss summoned me. What's going on in the center ring today?"

Janet peered into the Oval Office through her opened doorway, noting the large crowd mingling around the president's desk. She could see the chief of staff, Henry Graham, talking with several White House secretaries whom Janet knew from social events. All of them seemed overdressed for a typical workday. A large German-speaking group of middle-aged men was clustered close to the president's desk. Standing near them was a young intern who conducted White House tours. He seemed a little nervous, and occasionally spoke German with what appeared to be a special tour group he was saddled with. Janet couldn't see the president, and assumed he was sitting at his desk, monitoring his smartphone.

"You know, Ray, I've been left out of the loop on this one. Must have been Graham's idea. By the looks of things, my money is on a photo op, and you're probably the guest of honor."

Billings immediately thought of his suggestion for an Executive Order that suspended logging regulations, and audibly groaned.

Janet smiled and laughed softly. "Oopsy. Did something just bite you in the behind, secretary?"

"Yes. What's that old adage? 'Be careful of what you ask for!' I'm probably going to need a drink or several drinks after this little charade."

Billings contemplated Janet, who was still smiling at him, and impulsively asked her out on a date. "Would you like to help me consume some of those drinks after work today? We could go over to Murphy's and compare notes about our boss, maybe even begin collaborating on a book entitled *Bat Shit Secrets of the Oval Office*."

They both laughed and regarded each other with knowing expressions on their faces. Janet thought, *what took you so long, Mr. Secretary?*

"Invitation accepted, but let's not spend too much time talking about McDonald. I hope we can move on to more interesting topics, quickly, and let this office stuff hang on the line until tomorrow."

Billings smiled. "Good suggestion. I'll meet you at Murphy's at 5:00."

"Great, secretary. Do you want me to announce your arrival, now?"

"No, no. I'll just slip quietly in, and maybe no one will notice."

Billings turned and stepped through the Oval Office doorway. He thought about how nice flirting with Janet was, and for that matter, how nice it had always been. *Her close position to the president must have intimidated me.* Normally, Billings would have asked a woman like her out months ago. She was a single, attractive lady who was smart and charming. He thought to himself, *better late than never.* As he entered the Oval Office, the small cluster of people hiding the presidential desk from view separated somewhat, allowing Billings to view McDonald surfing his smartphone.

As if on cue, McDonald turned his head and caught view of Billings. "What took you so long, Billings? We're all sitting here on our thumbs waiting for your arrival."

Billings checked his watch and noted his conversation with Janet had taken five minutes, causing his tardiness.

"Sorry, Mr. President, but traffic was a little slow due to a demonstration on Pennsylvania Avenue."

The secretary hoped McDonald would ask about the march, but he didn't bite.

"Well, find some alternative routes. We've got a lot to get accomplished here. So timeliness is important."

Graham saved Billings from further berating by clapping his hands together. "Okay, okay, everyone. Let's gather round the president."

Looking at the intern, Graham told him to position his charges around the Oval Office desk in a crescent shape. The young man, speaking in English and German, gestured to his tour group and got them situated around the president.

Graham watched this clumsy task unfold and thought how much easier his job would be if only people wanted to be a part of this administration's accomplishments. It was getting damn hard to put together these photo shoots because nobody wanted to be associated with McDonald's political moves. This gathering completely exemplified the problem. He had asked numerous politicians and Washington higher-ups to participate in the Executive Order signing ritual, and to a person, all had previous engagements that couldn't be broken. Consequently, Graham had gotten several West Wing secretaries to dress up and pose with the president. He also had tracked down a large group of German high-tech businessmen who were taking a break from their D.C. meetings by touring the White House, and baited them into the photo shoot by promising a presidential signed picture of their gathering in the Oval Office. They accepted his invitation and were now shuffling into place with the help of the young intern. On cue, the secretaries positioned themselves evenly throughout the crowd and gazed forward. Graham motioned for Billings to stand to the president's left and he positioned himself on the president's right.

"All right, everyone smile for the cameras."

White House photographers began taking pictures as McDonald signed the Executive Order. The cameras flashed and a video crew worked the scene. The president, with a grand flourish, signed his proclamation and then lifted and turned the official-looking document toward the cameras. He smiled broadly and gave a thumbs-up salute. The chief of staff quickly called an end to the photo session.

"All right, all right, everybody. Nicely done. Thank you, everyone. Young man, could you get me a head count and the hotel where your group is staying? We'll get them their pictures by tomorrow morning. Thanks, ladies. You looked great, and certainly prettied-up this photo session."

Graham began ushering everyone, including the camera crews, out into the West Wing hallway. "Thanks again, everyone."

Then he shut the doors, leaving McDonald, Billings, and himself alone in the Oval Office. "Well, this should stop any attempts to undermine your logging operations, Mr. President."

"You bet your sweet ass, Graham. I love doing this Executive Order maneuver. When the bellyaching starts, all they can do is whine, whine, whine. Almost brings a tear to my eye. How are things going with our tree cutting, Billings?"

"It's all on schedule, Mr. President. Everything's falling into place and progressing nicely. You should have your trees cut down by tomorrow or the next day."

The president and Graham gravitated to the couches and sat down facing each other. Billings, who was still standing, glanced at his watch and raised his eyebrows. "Got to go, gentlemen. I've got a lunch date with the Secretary of the Interior at noon. We're comparing notes on our budget cuts."

"Good job, Billings. Let's get this federal government cut down to size. Give Graham a call when those trees are cut."

"Certainly, Mr. President. Good day."

In his departure, Billings paused at Janet's desk and glanced back at the Oval Office. Seeing no one, he looked back at the secretary and rolled his eyes. He then mouthed, "What an asshole."

Janet smiled up at him and nodded her head in agreement. She reached out and grabbed his hand, gave it a slight squeeze, and mouthed, "See you at five."

Billings squeezed back. Then, letting go of her hand, he turned and entered the hallway.

Using his phone, he called his chauffeur, and as the Marine Guard opened the entrance door for the secretary, his limo came to a stop at the West Wing's formal entrance. He reclined back into the limo's bench seat and exhaled. Maybe now he'd be through with this logging nonsense.

"Mr. Secretary."

"Yes, Jimmy."

"The drive back to your office is going to be a little convoluted."

"What's wrong?"

"The impeachment rally got a little larger than expected and a little rowdy. The marchers are all around the White House and spilling out into the surrounding streets. We'll have to follow the D.C. police directions, and slowly track our way back to the Whitten Building."

"How big did the march get?"

"I've heard upwards of three hundred thousand, Mr. Secretary."

"Okay, Jimmy. Do the best you can."

As the limo slowly headed back to the Whitten Building, Billings thought about McDonald's favorability ratings and how low they were. They had never been high; even after his inauguration they were historically low. But what the president did following his swearing-in caused them to plummet even further, and they hadn't recovered from his stupid blunder. After the January presidential changing of the guard, McDonald shocked America and the world by declaring war on illegal immigrants living within the United States borders. Numerous Executive Orders were hastily signed and crudely put into operation. At first, Latino immigrants were the target of these proclamations but later, other ethnic groups came under fire. Eventually almost any immigrant, legal or illegal, was in danger of deportation.

McDonald's rationale for these moves was simple. Immigrants were taking jobs away from American-born citizens, and his campaign had been all about righting America's economy and creating jobs. He could not ignore American jobs being usurped and filled by immigrants. When McDonald championed this new immigration policy, and backed it up with Executive Orders, the American voting populace and Americans in general felt blindsided by this sucker punch. It was blatantly obvious to most citizens the president had withheld his "war on immigrants" in order not to lose votes. This sleight-of-hand was perceived by many to be a racist, politically motivated ploy, and it totally derailed his emerging presidency. His approval rating drastically dropped and cries for impeachment were constantly thrown in his direction. At this point, less than one year into his term, many Americans, and most of the world, were watching his presidency stumble along, and they hoped his administration would come crashing down, the sooner the better.

Billings' limo crept along the D.C. streets in a roundabout manner, heading mostly toward his office building. Groups of demonstrators passed by calling out "Down with the Clown," and moving their signs in rhythm with their chant. The Secretary of Agriculture viewed D.C. through his tinted limo windows and saw Americans of all types pass by his vehicle. They were unified in numerous ways, but today they focused totally on a sitting president who was incapable of leading their country in a moral, ethical manner and was humiliating them on a daily basis, due to "guilt by association." He thought about his own U.S. Government role. *Am I proud of my efforts? When I bullied Johnson into fulfilling McDonald's orders, was that good for America, or just good for President McDonald's ego? Was it even necessary to begin with? Why didn't I get the Executive Order signed first, then in a civilized manner request Johnson to fulfill the president's bidding?* Billings acknowledged to himself he really wasn't much good as Secretary of Agriculture. Actually, he wasn't sure if he wanted the position. He thought of Texas and the oil fields, which helped define him as a person. He thought of his cattle ranch west of San Antonio, up in the hill country, and the beauty of the savanna-like grasslands with islands of oak trees defining their borders. No, he wasn't much good at Washington politics.

Billings found himself softly repeating what he'd just heard. "Down with the Clown. Down with the Clown."

"What was that, sir?"

"Nothing, Jimmy. Just get me home, please."

"Certainly, Mr. Secretary. We're almost there."

CHAPTER 19

Bob Thompson, known by his friends as Woody, pulled his 4x4 truck onto Highway 101 and headed south. His destination was Corvallis, Oregon. Hiding behind his rig was a small U-Haul trailer, mimicking the Titan's every move. This day marked the culmination of eighteen years of parenting, and as of today, Bob and his wife Karen were empty nesters. Empty nesters for the second time. The young man following Woody in a dark blue VW Jetta TDI was Bob's grandson. He'd been raised by the Thompsons after their daughter, Julie, gave him up to her parents so she could chase her dream of "rock-n-roll" fame. She was the lead singer for an indie band that floated up and down the West Coast playing small venues. Woody and Karen hadn't seen their daughter in years. Their last visit with her was a sad mixture of love, grief, and closure. During the visit, it became apparent Julie's musical career was a charade and drugs and sex were the last vestiges of her indie lifestyle. She hugged her son, Bridger, and blew her parents a kiss as she walked out their door, forever. Woody didn't know if his daughter was alive or dead, and had mostly stopped worrying about her well-being and whereabouts many years ago. The loss of their daughter was tragic for them, but the years of raising, loving, and parenting Bridger eased those bleak feelings created so long ago.

The previous night, Karen and Woody had eaten dinner by themselves. Bridger and his best friend Hang had left the house in the late afternoon to party with schoolmates and say their good-byes. The Thompsons opened a bottle of pinot noir and enjoyed a glass before dining in front of their flatscreen. Watching the local news, they noted the weather conditions for the next day called for clear skies and warm temperatures. A perfect moving day, and one allowing for an early start. Another report on the evening news caught their attention, too. The newscaster noted a 4.5 Richter scale quake occurred offshore in the Cascadia Subduction Zone. Woody and Karen always took note of offshore tremors due to the possibility of a tsunami. Quakes of 4.5 were not large enough to create problems, but any movement along the offshore faults was noteworthy, and reminded Woody of his desire to sell their home and resettle on higher ground.

After a quiet evening, Woody and Karen retired early, allowing Woody to rise with the sun feeling rested and ready to go. Woody rousted Bridger and Hang out of their beds at 5:00 a.m. The two college freshmen grumbled good-naturedly, but dutifully got up, dressed, and enjoyed bowls of cold cereal topped with fresh peaches. They were out the door by six o'clock.

Before Woody started his pick-up, a peculiar sensation roused his attention. The truck seemed to be rocking back and forth slightly. It took him a moment to realize another minor earthquake had just occurred. Returning to the house, he told Karen about the quake, and turned on the emergency radio. The tremor was slight and not likely to create a tsunami, but just in case, he asked her to listen for any bulletins. After that, he rejoined the kids out front, and they headed off for Oregon State University with Bob Thompson in the lead.

The sun was just rising as Woody drove through the small hamlet of Wheeler, Oregon. The hanging baskets above the storefronts still showed off their colors. His departure was too early to stop at his favorite coffee shop, The Roost, for a fresh baked scone and a mocha. South of Wheeler, the road became windy and mimicked the Nehalem River's course, causing Woody to slow up as he drove through the consecutive "S" curves. He rounded one lazy corner and reflexively gripped the wheel tightly. Directly in front of him was a slump in the asphalt. The six-inch drop could not be avoided. Woody went airborne, leaping over the initially unseen drop, and then bounced over the following cut in the road. The light U-Haul trailer vaulted upwards and then returned to the road only to bounce again, but with less force. With the hitch holding tight, the trailer remained behind the truck. A straight stretch followed the road slump, allowing Woody to search in his side mirror for Bridger. The Jetta came around the corner much faster than he had. He watched his grandson's car leap into the middle of the slump, only to be tossed upwards again by the following asphalt lip. Sparks exploded from beneath the Jetta upon its second landing, and miraculously, the small car continued on its southerly route.

Woody's truck rounded Fisherman's Corner, and he lost sight of Bridger. He pulled over in the large wayside overlooking the Nehalem River Estuary and waited for his heart to settle down before moving. Slowly, he stepped out of his truck. Woody automatically looked across the road up to the top of an old slide, hoping to see resident bald eagles adorning the barkless snag that resided at the hill's crest. The great birds were not there. *Too bad.* His nerves could have used a calming visual. Just then, the TDI rolled to a stop behind the U-Haul. Windows smoothly descended, and bluish smoke wafted out of the Jetta. The plume was caught by the sea breeze accompanying the tidal change, and it quickly dissipated into nothingness. Woody's anxiety was somewhat lessened as he walked back to the Jetta, although it was replaced with a little irritation due to the apparent pot smoking in the Jetta. Bob Thompson leaned over next to the Volkswagen's window to gain a better view of his two young charges.

"You boys notice anything unusual back there?"

A moment of silence played out between grandad and grandson, and then two smiling faces grinned at each other.

"Damn, Gramps! We caught big time air! Did you see it? Hang shit himself, and I'm totally messed up."

All three travelers burst into laughter. Hang lowered his head and turned sideways so he could get eye level with Woody.

"Mr. Thompson, could you unlock the trailer? I need to get some new underwear."

"I could, Hang, but you might just consider going commando. Hell, all the freshman students are doing it, now. You'll fit right in with the trendsetters."

More smiles followed this round of bantering. Just then, Woody's parental instincts kicked in and he fixed a serious expression upon the young men.

"I'm a little disappointed in you two. How much pot have you been smoking?"

Bridger and Hang gazed at each other for a moment, then both returned sheepish expressions to Woody. Bridger spoke up.

"Just one hit of 'home grown,' Gramps. It's not very potent. I'm good to drive."

"If your grandmother was here, she'd be pretty amused and annoyed with your statement, but I'm going to take it at face value. However, I'd like you two arriving at our destination in one piece so going forward, I'm going to dictate some traveling rules. Obviously no more pot, and from here to your apartment in Corvallis, you're no more than six car lengths behind me. When my brake lights come on, yours do, too. Same for your turn signals, and anything else I'm forgetting to mention, you're to do also. Understand?"

"All right, Dad. No more pot smoking and our complete attention will be on driving and the road."

During serious moments between grandad and grandson, Woody became Dad and Bridger became Son. He appreciated this subtle sign of respect his grandson bestowed upon him, and thought it endearing and appropriate.

"Sounds good, Son."

Woody patted his grandson on his arm, and while walking back to his truck, inwardly smiled. *It's amazing any of us make it to adulthood.* As he walked past the trailer, he thought about the jumbled puzzle of furniture they'd find upon opening the trailer's doors. Just then, a familiar cry drifted down to Woody. He gazed upward to see two adult bald eagles riding the updraft directly above him. Both birds looked down, their white head and tail feathers contrasted beautifully by dark brown bodies, and they called out once more. The piercing, monotone screech trailed off into the wind. Woody Thompson thought to himself, *a good sign for a good day.*

He looked back to his young grandson and Hang and hollered, "Let's roll!"

CHAPTER 20

Bridger was watching the back of the U-Haul trailer as it bucked along in front of him. He recovered from the unnerving aerial stunt and was trying to remember what he'd left at home. His best friend, Hang, who was so named because of his affinity for free climbing, rappelling down vertical surfaces, and numerous overnighters spent slung in hammocks hundreds of feet above Mother Earth, was doing his best to distract Bridger. Hang was pounding finger impressions into the Volksy's dashboard while rhythmically drumming to Dire Straits' "Down to the Waterline." Bridger gave in to the moment, and began singing along with the chorus lines.

Bridger, Hang, and another amigo, Russel Nelson, were classmates and best friends from elementary school through 12th grade. The trio progressed along grade by grade, teacher by teacher, and building by building. At the end of their schooling, they were flushed out of the system with good GPAs and high school diplomas. They were teammates during football and basketball seasons, and best of friends all year. Their classmates referred to them as the "Three Amigos" in reference to a corny movie seen on late night cable. Their fraternal bond often showed best during after-school functions. Recreational drug consumption, psychology, and human anatomy were mostly the focus of these gatherings, and often the social events were accompanied by simple gamesmanship, comprised mainly of beer pong and corn hole tournaments. Russel mostly got the ladies, Hang usually won the games, and Bridger always had a great time, occasionally succeeding with girls and games. At one time or another, each friend safely deposited the other two into their beds, late at night, while their respective parents slept peacefully.

Russel was a brainiac, pure and simple. The redheaded, freckled young man was a lean, mean machine, wired with a computer for a brain. He'd graduated valedictorian of his class, and was more than intelligent; Russel was insightful, inquisitive, and driven to lead. Class president, football and basketball team captain, and Future Business Leaders of America president, as Russel put it, were only résumé steppingstones. His initial life's goal was the U.S. Foreign Service, and his acceptance into George Washington University with a free ride seemed to suggest this possibility had merit. One characteristic Russel possessed seemed alien to his basic skillset. He could totally freak out and become incredibly nervous during stressful situations. It was as if an emotional switch was cued, completely rewiring his confidence level. Not many people witnessed these meltdowns because they occurred few and far between.

Hang was loose, confident, and competitive. Varsity quarterback and shooting guard came naturally to him. This demeanor was honed by one who challenged himself, daily. After staring down at his possible demise hundreds of times from cliffs and high tree perches, not much fazed him. He had no idea what he wanted to do in the future other than attend college, and this lack of overall direction didn't bother him in the least.

Hang grew up in the foster system. His biological parents were young and careless, and the State of Oregon removed him from their home at an early age. His foster parents were well-meaning, hardworking people who provided him with a roof over his head and regular meals. They tried their hardest to be home for their kids, but monetary constraints required they have multiple jobs. The children were left alone and unsupervised quite a bit. When Hang entered the fourth grade, he and Bridger became fast friends. From that point on, he gravitated to the Thompsons' household and spent most of his time with Bridger and his family. He cared a great deal for his foster parents, but even more for Mr. and Mrs. Thompson.

Bridger Thompson was a people person, a product of his grandparents' upbringing. He enjoyed and respected most everyone. He liked being productive, working side by side with others, and helping a team reach a goal. Thanks again to his grandparents, Bridger had a playful sense of humor developed over the years by watching Woody and Karen jest back and forth. Life was pretty fun for Bridger, and he enjoyed the ebb and flow of growing up in a loving household with friends like Hang and Russel close at hand..

When it came time to pick a college, Bridger and Hang, without thinking, chose Oregon State in Corvallis. The two boys practically grew up there. Woody and Karen were both OSU alums, and often took them to campus events. The boys had traversed the university grounds so often that both of them knew the campus by memory, and had frequented so many college buildings that the school felt like home. It was only natural the two friends chose Oregon State over other local colleges to be their new school. They thought the campus was cool, and of course, the female coeds looked pretty inviting, too. The boys found an ancient, canary yellow, two-story, Midwestern farmhouse style rental close to campus with several apartments carved out of the old building, and managed to obtain an exemption to the rule dictating freshmen live on campus. The old farmhouse was today's destination.

As they listened to music, Bridger and Hang watched their trailer bounce along ahead of them. They wondered what their days would be like, living the life of college freshmen. The boys would soon find out, and their exciting near-mishap south of Wheeler, Oregon, would quickly be forgotten.

CHAPTER 21

THE SMALL CARAVAN CONTINUED SOUTH ALONG Highway 101. The Titan and U-Haul were leading the way, and the small Jetta dutifully followed sixty feet behind. Occasionally, the TDI drifted off of center, but never very far, and it always returned to the safer, middle of the lane, path.

Woody checked his rearview mirror and noted his grandson's location with a pleased smile. Bridger was young, but he wasn't dumb, and he could be trusted to be sensible when need be.

Woody entered Rockaway Beach, a small, middle-class resort town, and tried not to look east. There was only one thing Bob Thompson hated with an emotional, irrational passion, and this nemesis rested directly to his left. Giving in to his weaker self, he surveyed the hills behind Rockaway. The hundred-plus-acre clear-cut he viewed was an abomination. The forest wall surrounding the large wound was the dark color of tree trunks and needle-laden branches. The clear-cut itself was absent of any original vegetation. Small broken logs, branches, and root balls stuck up into the morning light, and a few large piles of slash still stood, waiting for the right weather conditions before being torched.

Woody mentally cringed at the sight. He thought about unsustainable logging techniques, the historical sell-off of public lands by greed-heads from the past, and Rockaway's present drinking water plight. This huge clear-cut behind town had completely denuded their watershed's protective forest, which had helped filter the town's municipal drinking supply. Now, not only did Rockaway inhabitants deal with silt-laden water, but they had to stop drinking their water completely several times a year, due to herbicide spraying. Since the newly planted tree seedlings were vulnerable to faster growing vegetation choking them out, the entire hillside was sprayed with chemicals that targeted broad-leafed plants, killing off unwanted deciduous vegetation, but also killing most other living organisms such as grubs, insects, and birds. In large enough doses, it could harm all the animals up the food chain, including humans. Rockaway tried litigation to resolve this problem, with no success, and now was challenging Oregon's legislature to help them defend their drinking water from the private landowners' chemical practices. Many residences in this small coastal town stopped using their tap water altogether and now used only bottled water.

Woody was disgusted by the logging practices used by private landowners. This scenario was being played out all over Oregon because nobody could stop the large, international consortiums that now owned so much of the state's coastal forested land. These corporations had extremely deep pockets and could outlast most opponents in the court system. To further hinder opposition of these businesses, the State of Oregon showed little inclination to protect its citizens from the unsustainable, chemically laden logging practices being utilized within her borders.

Bob Thompson was glad when he left Rockaway. Seeing the vegetation scar east of town always raised his blood pressure. Clear-cuts in general pissed him off considerably, and he avoided them whenever possible. Woody knew from memory the entire route from here to Corvallis. The caravan would travel through the dairy lands of central Tillamook County, turn east at Hebo, and go through a classic temperate rainforest with moss-laden tree trunks and branches hosting upper canopy parasitic ecosystems filled with lichens, ferns, and even huckleberry plants. Then, before reaching the Willamette Valley, they'd drive through rolling hills covered with small stands of fir and oak trees surrounded by fields of wheat, bunchgrasses, Christmas tree lots, and small vineyards. Eventually, they'd turn south onto 99W and head to Corvallis. This last stretch knifed right through the Willamette Valley's heartland. More vineyards, wheat and bunchgrass fields, an occasional ryegrass field, and a few filbert orchards would line the road's path.

Woody knew only one more seriously depressing view remained: the eastern view from the Tillamook lowlands. This portion of the coastal range appeared as if it had mange. The clear-cuts sawed from these ridges resembled an unplanned, random attack on the standing forests. The overly large cuts in various stages of regrowth seemed to merge with each other, and were barely held apart by small isthmuses of older trees. Woody decided to avoid this view, and he reached into the CD bag sitting next to him in the passenger seat. He loaded up his player with six of his favorite albums from the sixties and seventies and told himself not to look east. He was going to listen to good music, relax, and do some serious daydreaming.

CHAPTER 22

THE TITAN'S CD PLAYER HAD JUST FINISHED PLAYing Springsteen's *Born in the USA* album when Woody, Bridger, and Hang entered the outskirts of Corvallis. Now, it was a simple matter of taking 4th Street right through the downtown area and turning west on Adams. It dead-ended into the college's eastern boundary, where Wilson and McNary Halls formed a large dormitory complex with an eating and commons area. Woody felt the kids chose a great location. They had the freedom of off-campus living coupled with close proximity to the large university atmosphere provided by the Wilson/McNary complex.

Bob Thompson pulled his rig over and parked near the intersection of Adams and 11th Street. The Jetta pulled up right behind the U-Haul. The threesome all observed the old yellow farmhouse across the street. As they viewed the second floor, a dormer that protruded outwards caught the boys' attention.

"I bet the dormer is one of our bedrooms, Hang."

"Yeah, it sure could be."

Their landlord, Mr. Donovan, managed to create four units in the old house. There was a two-bedroom, one-bath apartment downstairs with doorways on both Adams and 11th Street. An add-on became a three-bedroom, one-bath unit with individual kitchen, dining, and living room. Upstairs the old home offered a one-bedroom apartment and the two-bedroom, one-bath unit Bridger and Hang had rented.

Woody stepped out of the Titan and observed Wilson Hall, where he had lived for two years so many decades earlier. Bridger and Hang joined him. They both knew about this mega student living complex because of their many visits to the campus.

"Are you hungry, Gramps?"

"No, how about you guys?"

Hang scanned his new home and answered, "I'm good, Mr. Thompson. Let's move into our new digs."

Bridger surveyed the old, renovated farmhouse. "Yeah, I second the motion. We can eat after the furniture is upstairs."

Woody walked around to the back of the U-Haul and cautiously opened the rear doors. Miraculously, nothing jumped out to greet him. After examining their new home a bit longer, the college freshmen joined Bridger's grandfather and all three gazed into what now appeared to be a large, three-dimensional furniture jigsaw puzzle.

Woody commented, "Well, after our little trip, all of our furniture and gear packed together nicely, didn't it?"

"Egyptians would have been proud of us, Gramps. You can't get a sheet of papyrus between any of those pieces of furniture," quipped Bridger.

His grandfather responded, "Let's be careful now. Easy does it with everything. If we're diligent, we might not end up with too many extra, unidentifiable parts."

Hang joined in. "You got it, Mr. Thompson. I'm going to start by dislodging this armchair."

"Careful, young man, it could be the keystone that's holding everything in place."

"I hear ya. Here goes."

Hang pulled out the old heirloom, overstuffed chair, without a following deluge of furniture. "Hey, success!"

There was a loud round of applause and shouts of encouragement coming from behind the group. All three turned to see a crowd of smiling young people watching their progress. A young, frizzy haired, redheaded girl wearing high-waisted shorts and a crop top introduced the bystanders. "I believe we're your neighbors. Are you moving into the upstairs apartment?"

Bridger responded with an affirmative.

"Well, we're here to help you move in, unless you have objections to untrained, clumsy, student types handling your possessions."

Hang smiled and laughed. "You're the only type of help we'll accept. Let's start putting some more character scratches on this old furniture."

The moving crew consisted of four girls and three boys. The ladies seemed like healthy, friendly, Eastern Oregon farm girls and two of the guys resembled football linebackers, with broad shoulders and impressive biceps. Both had frohawks, ready smiles, and engaging personalities. They immediately grabbed the huge armchair and hauled it upstairs. The last neighbor was a tall, African American, big-boned, slightly overweight young man with an Afro haircut. He had buds in both ears that connected to his shirt pocket via a white audio wire.

"Hello, newbies. I'm Tunes. You've now made our little collective complete. We all wondered when you'd arrive."

Bridger regarded Tunes and smiled. "Never thought I'd be the last one to the party."

He glanced over at Hang, and his friend lifted his hands in a gesture of wonderment. "We might have met our match, Bridger. These guys must be pros."

At this point, the girls pushed the bullshitting boys aside and grabbed pieces of furniture. They headed up the stairs to the empty apartment with their loads. Tunes grabbed an end table and standing lamp, and also moved off to the old house.

Bob Thompson watched the unloading process begin. "Well, boys, this won't take much time. I believe my job is strictly managerial. Considering all the available labor, I'm going upstairs to check out your new home."

Woody walked across the street, climbed the steps, and stopped on the porch. Three doors greeted him. On the left was the entrance to the girls' apartment, straight ahead was the door to the second floor stairwell, and to his right was the entrance to the ballplayers' apartment. The stairwell door was propped open and the moving brigade was passing back and forth like a string of ants hauling the colony to a new location. The boys' new apartment was a simple design with an efficient use of space. They had chosen wisely. All the walls were painted a creamy yellow and the carpeting was a light green color. As Woody took in the apartment's ambiance, the living room became fuller and fuller with furniture and sundries. He had to circle the mound of essentials in order to depart. As he left the apartment, the young redhead came up the stairs with the first article packed into the trailer. Seeing this, Bob Thompson knew his responsibilities were almost finished here. He slowly climbed down the steps and out into the sunny late summer day. The temperature was near 85 degrees, and he noticed how warm he was in his coastal attire of long denim jeans and hooded sweatshirt. A few cumulus clouds drifted overhead. One would undoubtedly block the sun for a moment before sailing off and allowing the warm rays to once again find their target or in this case, targets. A whole batch of young college students, Bridger and Hang's new neighbors and friends, stood on the porch and front lawn. They conversed easily with each other. Intuitively, everyone present knew about the significance of the moment, and waited respectfully for the "rite of passage." Woody walked over to his grandson and hugged him.

Bridger responded in kind. "I love you, Gramps."

"I love you, too."

Bob Thompson then turned to Hang and embraced him. "You two take care of each other."

"Certainly, Mr. Thompson, and I'll make sure your grandson eats his vegetables and flosses twice a day. Anything else you want me to watch out for?"

"Yes. Make sure his contact list has Karen's and my number in it, and he calls us once a week."

"It's a promise, Mr. Thompson."

Woody viewed the young men and women standing around his grandson, and thought about how lucky his boy was. This was a quality group of people that soon would share his grandson's college life with him.

He spoke to Bridger and Hang's new neighbors. "I can tell I'm leaving my son in very good hands here. Thanks for all your help."

With that said, he quickly turned and headed for his truck. Waving over his shoulder, he pulled the Titan's door open and nestled into his driver's seat. Woody didn't mind crying, which he was doing now; he just didn't like company while he did it. His job was done here in so many ways. All these feelings rested heavily upon him, and it would take the long drive home with many CDs before he would lighten up and feel happy once again about this transition. Just then, a rogue cumulus cloud drifted away from under the sun, and the unleashed sunlight lit up the surroundings into beautiful, vibrant shades of green, blue, red, and yellow.

Bob Thompson started the Titan up, released the brake, and headed back home.

CHAPTER 23

Rachael strode up the stairs, two steps at a time, and reached the second floor landing with a flourish of movement. She had switched tops, choosing a less modest, cooler, bikini top to get her through the hottest part of the day. Her red, frizzy hair hung down just below her shoulders. She was barefoot, and her arrival on the second floor went unheard by Bridger and Hang. They were engaged in placing cooking utensils into drawers at the moment, and Rachael, seeing their door was open, walked into the apartment.

"Knock, knock, is everybody decent?"

She quickly gained the common space and found the two boys gazing her way holding various culinary items in their hands.

Hang responded, "No we're not. Come on in!"

This made Rachael laugh. She took a glimpse at the young men and mentally took a deep breath. If she'd been looking, these two would definitely be keepers. Bridger was about 5'11" or 6 feet. He had broad shoulders, narrow hips, and body proportions any portrait artist would love to put together on canvas. His hair was light brown, full bodied, and probably hung to just below his shoulders. Right now it was in a man bun. Bridger was grinning at Rachael and she noted, under the right circumstances, this young man's beguiling smile could disarm her in a heartbeat. Hang stood next to Bridger and offered a much different package. He was tall, slender, long-armed, and long-legged. He seemed like a basketball player. His dark eyes were piercing and his short, dark hair was layered, somewhat wavy, and comfortably covering most of his ears. Hang looked over at his roommate and popped him in the side with his elbow. He'd noticed Bridger's eyes fixated on Rachael's boobs, and hoped to break his trance before she noticed.

"Hey, roomie, introduce us to our new neighbor."

Bridger took his eyes off of Rachael's breasts and refocused. He realized what Hang said was truly in order. No introductions had occurred during this morning's move.

"Hello, I'm Bridger Thompson and this handsome young man is Hang Thorn." Bridger regarded his best friend quizzically and smiled, then continued, "What is your real first name, Hang?"

Hang cocked his head to one side, observed the ceiling with a thoughtful expression, and contemplated for a second.

With a shrug and a shake of his head, he said, "I really don't know. I'd have to check my birth certificate."

Rachael ventured, "How about checking your driver's license?"

Hang thought some more. "No, I'm pretty sure it says Hang on it."

Rachael could not keep from laughing. These two were way fun. "Nice to meet you, boys. I'm Rachael and I'm pretty sure it says Rachael on all my I.D. Hey, I came up here to invite you to our 'get to know you' party we're having tonight. All of your neighbors will be there. You can meet the entire 11th Street collective in one quick, frightening social event. Bring your own beverages and etcetera. I'm cooking burgers for everyone. Bring your 'A' game, too. There'll be beer pong and corn hole tournaments for your delight and sportsmanship."

"What time does this lovely event get under way?"

"How about seven? If you want to come down earlier and just hang out, it's totally fine."

"I can't speak for my roomie, but I'll be making an entrance sooner than later. I just need to find homes for more of this stuff. Then I'll pretty myself up and come join you."

"Great, and you, roomie?"

"Ditto everything Bridger said, but I prefer the more natural look, so what you see is what you'll get."

Rachael smiled and turned toward the door. As she left the apartment, she remarked over her shoulder, "I like what I see, so whatever you do is just fine by me."

Rachael walked out onto the landing and thought if she was looking, she needn't go any farther than this upstairs apartment just a few steps from her own room.

CHAPTER 24

At about 6:30, Bridger started down the stairwell and was greeted by a familiar musical sound. It was CCR's "Proud Mary" gently rolling out of the girl's open doorway. His grandparents had grown up in the sixties when rock and roll was born, and he had listened to all the great bands of that era. Creedence Clearwater Revival was one of his favorites, and he still followed their front man's musical accomplishments. Bridger marveled at the acoustics of the old stairwell, and as he turned into the apartment, he saw why the song sounded so rich. On a low coffee table next to the apartment's living room window sat a stereophonic turntable attached to a tuner amplifier; it in turn was connected to two large, floor Bose speakers. On either side of the turntable sat two, antique wooden apple crates filled with vinyl record jackets. Rachael, who was sitting in front of the music system, stood up and came over to him. She had put a T-shirt on, but hadn't changed her shorts or her friendly smile. Grabbing Bridger's hand, she gently pulled him into the living room.

"Welcome to our little soiree. I see you brought refreshments."

Bridger viewed the three beers he held in his right hand and felt a little embarrassed by his meager contribution to the night's affair.

"My apologies. The cupboards are a little bare right now. I promise next time to be a better guest and bring some munchies to share."

"No need to worry. The burgers are getting overcooked as we speak, so food's not an issue here. Culinary quality may be of concern, but a little beer, a little pot, and some competitive corn hole will make us forget about the cuisine."

Bridger really enjoyed Rachael's humor. It made him think of his grandparents and the fun they had conversing with each other. He really felt comfortable talking with his new neighbor, and holding her hand felt pretty natural, too.

"Hey, whose vinyl collection is this? It's totally sick and I'm totally jealous."

"You're looking at the owner of this ancient, outdated music system, and I guard it with my life."

CCR was now cranking out *Green River* through the speakers. Rachael gave Bridger's hand a squeeze and pulled him over to the stereo. She knelt down onto both knees and coaxed him down next to her.

"Take a look at the albums. Most are vintage recordings from the fifties, sixties, and seventies. Vinyl was king then. They are all analog recordings."

"This is so cool. Digital really sucks. It took all the life out of the music we listen to."

"I know. You won't find any digital here."

Bridger began perusing Rachael's album collection, and they both contemplated jacket covers together, discussing the music and bands she had collected.

Hang walked into the apartment with little fanfare. He noted Bridger and Rachael on the floor examining albums. Straight ahead was the kitchen with a small breakfast nook. To his right was a large couch that supported Tunes and one of Rachael's roommates, who both held beers and were sharing a bowl. He walked over to them and waited for Tunes' long exhale to abate before greeting them.

"Hello, Tunes. Who's your friend?"

"Hey, neighbor. Glad you made it. This is Shelley. Shelley, meet Hang, our new upstairs renter."

"Nice to meet you, Upstairs."

She offered him the pipe, but he politely waved it off.

"I like your place, Shelley. Hey, where should I put these beers?"

Shelley eyed Hang and was impressed with his appearance and casual demeanor. *How lucky did I get?* "Here, let me show you."

She stood up. Hang noticed she was tall, slender, and only a couple inches shorter than himself. They walked into the kitchen, and Shelley opened the refrig. She took Hang's beer, set one on the counter, and placed two inside on the first shelf behind the milk.

"I hid the others behind the moo juice. This trick might keep the raiding Normans from finding them, but if not, there's plenty of PBR in the cooler, outside, on the porch. You're welcome to them. They're the house supply, and it's totally communal property."

"Sounds perfect. I can't lose."

Hang walked over to the breakfast nook and looked outside. It was still light and there was a reverse sunset coloring the mid-valley skies. He noticed a door to his right.

"Is this the pantry?"

"It probably was. It's my bedroom now. I imagine it was one of those big old walk-in farmhouse pantries like my grandparents had."

Shelley opened the door so Hang could see her space. She leaned back against the doorjamb, placed her hand, palm outward, onto her forehead, closed her eyes, and struck a dramatic pose.

"Please don't judge me by my unkempt, dowdy, living conditions. I'm really a much lazier, shallower person than this scene portrays."

Hang laughed heartily at this bit of acting and poked his head into Shelley's bedroom. Her bed was a mound of pillows and blankets. Her closet was purely an ornamental space because the floor, dresser, and chair were covered with her clothing in various stages of disarray.

"Looks pretty normal to me, Shelley. I'm not sure what your concern is here. After seeing this, I totally think you're a despicable, lazy, shallow individual. You shouldn't worry about putting on airs. This is really pretty straightforward."

The two neighbors smiled at each other. Shelley was pleased Hang enjoyed her playfulness. She decided to continue with her hostess responsibilities.

"Follow me. Everyone else is outside in the backyard. I'll properly introduce you to your neighbors, and then kick your butt in a game of corn hole."

Hang grabbed his beer as they departed the kitchen. They took a left and walked down a short hall with bedroom doors on either side, and stepped out onto the covered back porch. It was just large enough for a ping pong table and players, leaving little room for spectators. A lively game was under way, and due to the loudness of laughter and taunting being passed back and forth between teams, it had probably been in progress for quite some time. Shelley waited for the ball to hit its mark, and the required cup of beer to be consumed, before loudly clapping her hands together.

"Hey everyone. Listen up. Time for formal introductions. This is Hang. You've all handled his personal belongings."

This statement brought a round of catcalls and degrading comments from the players. Shelley ignored this outburst and continued on. "But you haven't formally met the man. Hang, on the far side of the table is Lawrence, possibly the best linebacker on the OSU team. Next to Lawrence is Sara, my roommate. Right here," she placed her hand on the shoulder of Lawrence's roommate, who was standing next to her, "is Ridley, the other best linebacker on our team. Last, but not least is Laura, my sweet country girl roommate, who appears to be winning or possibly losing, you decide for yourself, this marathon game of beer pong."

Sara teetered just a bit as she reached out her hand to Hang. He grasped her hand in a friendly shake, then raised his beer to everyone.

"Here's a toast to you all. Thanks for your help today and for your ready acceptance of my humble personage."

Lawrence considered Hang with a serious expression on his face. "What gave you the impression of acceptance?"

Everyone laughed and began shoving and pushing each other in appreciation of their jovial spirit. Lawrence regained some composure and raised his glass. "Here's to acceptance."

All glasses were raised in a salute with lots of "hear-hear" called out to seal the agreement.

Shelley glanced at Hang and, reaching over to the wall, switched on the floodlight, exposing the corn hole boxes ready for use.

"Game on, Hang. That is if you're man enough."

"I'm totally man enough. Bring it on."

They soon had a rousing game of corn hole in progress, and the pong crowd continued with their match. Music wafted out into the backyard. The green grass became cool and moist to the barefoot players' touch, and the crickets began calling back and forth to each other. Somewhere nearby, a number of frogs croaked out their whereabouts and the night sky began to fill with the flittering movements of moths. An occasional bat would fly over the yard, picking off an unlucky evening insect, and then disappear into the night's darkness. Eventually, after they battled through several games of corn hole, Hang turned off the floodlight and both he and Shelley quietly sat on the porch steps. They watched the night's airshow, and listened to the evening's chorus of creature songs.

After their rest, they challenged all present to a single-elimination tournament of bounce beer pong. Tunes, Rachael, and Bridger ventured out and joined the competition. The rules were basically the same, but in this version, to be legal, the ping pong ball had to bounce once in your court and once in your opponent's court before it entered a cup.

The ice chest, originally full of beer, slowly transformed into slush, chilling only itself. Hang and Shelley sent all opponents to the sidelines, and eventually dispatched their last challenging couple, Lawrence and Sara. Everyone was a happy loser due to an abundance of PBR and one-toke homegrown. The chill of the September evening finally sent the party into the living room, where the young people reclined on the floor or sat on the couch, talking and laughing with each other. Rachael strung together empty beer can tabs onto shoelaces that she'd borrowed from Shelley's sneakers and presented these trophy necklaces to Hang and Shelley. The awards were humbly accepted by the champions as the vanquished offered their applause and numerous insults, mostly referring to cheating and fraudulent tactics used by the winning team.

It was well past midnight when the party began to break up. Hang said his goodnights to all and gave Shelley a warm hug before departing. Eventually, only Bridger and Rachael remained in the living room, listening to the Steve Miller Band's *Fly like an Eagle* album. They hadn't drunk very much, so they were still coherent and talkative. They sat side by side on the floor, shoulders touching, with their backs against the couch.

Bridger looked at Rachael and she responded in kind. "Well, it's pumpkin time for me," he said.

"Yeah, it's pretty late. I'll walk you home."

Bridger grinned at this remark. He stood up and helped Rachael to her feet. They stood facing each other. Bridger felt a little nervous standing so close to his new, beautiful neighbor without a distracting audience nearby. He turned, facing the door, and walked outside onto the front porch. Rachael followed him.

The front stoop's light was off, and the two young college students noticed the stairwell was dark, too. Bridger tried both switches, but nothing changed. "That's kind of spooky."

"Yeah, it is. Well, I said I'd walk you home and I'm a girl of my word, so take my hand, young man, and lift those feet up. No tripping allowed."

Rachael grabbed Bridger's hand and both, step-by-step, groped their way to the second floor landing. They stopped in the dark, still holding hands. A thought flitted through Rachael's mind. *I'm not looking, but...*A sensual tingling warmed her groin, and she squeezed her new neighbor's hand. "I'd better see you safely to your room."

Bridger pressed her hand in return, and thought, *this isn't really happening. A beautiful, interesting girl who I've just met wants to sleep with me.* As they stepped into his apartment, Rachael continued, "This darkness is like some kind of omen. I'm really worried for your safety."

Bridger ignored his apartment's hall light and reached for his bedroom's door handle, but Rachael was already opening the door. Together, they stepped into the darkness and stood close to each other. Bridger reached down and turned on his bed stand light. The 40-watt bulb left the room's corners in guarded darkness, but his spindle-headed bed was softly lit by the lamp's glow. The two young people regarded each other and smiled. Rachael pulled her T-shirt up and over her head, allowing it to fall to the floor. She helped Bridger take his off. He looked at her round, firm breasts, which now showed nipples through her bikini fabric. They gently helped each other remove their clothes and embraced, kissing for a moment. Bridger reached down and parted his bedding. They slipped between the sheets, and lying close to one another, shared each other's warmth and nakedness. They kissed again. Bridger leaned backwards and turned off the lamp. The two young lovers regained their embrace and continued exploring their intimacy.

CHAPTER 25

It was another cloudless, late summer day in Corvallis. At 10:00 a.m., Bridger and Hang had already opened all their apartment windows and their front door in order to facilitate a cooling breeze. Bridger, while browsing his Facebook pages, was eating a breakfast of yogurt and fruit at the dining table. Hang was off in his bedroom, repositioning his few items of furniture into another configuration. The dinette was placed next to the apartment's window that faced campus and now had a slight breeze flowing over it. Periodically, Bridger would gaze over at the university and the old, brick, multi-floored dormitories that partially filled his view. He hadn't yet availed himself of the food services offered by the McNary/Wilson complex, but knew he soon would. He was particularly fond of the Mexican food venue found there, and was thinking about having a cheese and chicken enchilada for dinner.

"Knock, knock, is anybody home?"

Bridger's heart missed a beat and a smile spread across his face. Rachael had quietly slipped away during the early morning hours, abandoning Bridger to awaken by himself with only lingering memories of their first night together. *But, oh what a night it had been.*

"I said, is anybody home?" Rachael rounded the corner and saw Bridger, spoon stopped in midair, and gave him a gaze filled with affection. "Hello, beautiful. What are you having for breakfast?"

"Yogurt and fruit. Do you want some?"

"Nope. I just finished off one of those overcooked hamburger patties left over from last night. I covered it with two eggs over medium. It wasn't too bad."

Hang came to his bedroom doorway, and looked across the living room at their guest. "Last night's party was great. You and all our neighbors will make me forget about home, quickly."

"Yeah. I thought the same thing. And after I met you two young men, I couldn't even remember where my home was."

The three friends laughed together. *She is something special*, Bridger thought.

"Hey do you boys want a midmorning tour of campus, culminating with a STRONG Alliance meeting at the MU Quad?"

Bridger replied as he rinsed his bowl and spoon off under the sink's faucet, "If you're leading, I'm following."

"Sounds good to me, too, but what's the STRONG Alliance?" Hang asked.

"I'm not really sure. I suspect they're an Earth First group located here on campus. There's a flyer stapled to our power pole out front, and it mentions stopping a clear-cut near the Metolius River."

"Whoa! A clear-cut near the Metolius? That's crazy! The whole forest there is manicured to perfection. I've fished the Metolius with Gramps since I was five, surrounded and shaded by those magnificent conifers. The whole idea is total bullshit!"

Rachael raised her eyebrows in surprise at Bridger's emotional outburst. "I think I've found the right guy to escort me to the STRONG meeting."

"You bet you have, darling. Let me change clothes, and I'll be ready in five minutes."

Rachael looked over at Hang.

"Ditto, Rachael. I've fished right next to Bridger and his gramps. I can't imagine anyone wanting to cut down those trees."

"Great. Tunes is coming with us, too. So let's meet downstairs in about fifteen minutes."

Rachael turned and walked into the hallway. As she did, she glanced back over her shoulder at Bridger, winked, and blew him a kiss. In a soft voice she said, "I haven't forgotten about last night, young man."

Bridger felt tingles wash over his body. Rachael left the apartment, and knocked on Tunes' door as she passed. "Fifteen minutes, Tunes. We'll be downstairs."

Bridger found some cargo shorts, a tank top, slaps, and some sunscreen. As he rubbed in the sunscreen, his roommate joined him in the living room.

"I can't believe this crap. Cutting down those trees is beyond atrocious."

"I know. I wonder where that idea came from. Certainly not from any of us who frequent the area."

As the boys descended the stairwell, rhythmic drum beats ushered them to the front porch. Tunes was playing his small, shoulder-strapped, djembe drum and producing some hip-moving beats Rachael was taking advantage of as she danced on the front lawn.

"Let's go, gentlemen. Tunes, be the Pied Piper and lead the way to the quad, please."

With a nod, Tunes headed across 11th Street and the procession walked over to Jefferson Avenue. They turned west on Jefferson and headed to the heart of the campus, the Memorial Union. The drum beats bounced off McNary Hall's brick exterior, and drifted over the large, grassy park adjacent to the dorm. Eventually, the rhythm was absorbed by the fringe of trees lining Monroe Avenue. Rachael and Bridger were both wearing cargo shorts and tank tops. Hang felt compelled to tease them about their retro attire, but both ignored his harassment. They were now twirling each other as they walked west on Jefferson, and rhythmically head and shoulder bobbed to the percussion beats. Few people were walking along Jefferson's sidewalks, and in general, the campus was nearly empty. It was, technically, still summer break, and most dormitories were closed.

Jefferson Avenue appeared stately, lined as it was by hundred-year-old deciduous trees. The tree canopies formed a ceiling above the street, and in the late morning sunlight the backlit green leaves seemed to come alive with chandelier-like brilliance. Song birds flitted through the branches, probing the moss and lichens for hidden grubs and insects. An occasional hairy woodpecker hopped on and around the tree trunks and branches, also searching for food.

This beauty was not lost on the small procession. At one point, all four stopped and just stared into the mosaic above them.

"It's so full of life up there," Rachael murmured.

As they peered into the branches, a soft drumming reached them from between the Memorial Union and the newly constructed Student Experience Center.

"Hey, Tunes. I think we've found your comrades. Can you hear drumming?"

Tunes smiled and nodded. He raised his arms dramatically, and rotating his hands in opposite directions, majorette like, he brought them rapidly down to his African drum. The beat he produced joined seamlessly with the new percussion rhythm that found them. The friends walked to the drumming's source. They passed between the huge MU building and the Student Experience Center, coming to a stop next to the stately bronze statue of a pioneer woman adjacent to the Ag Building. From there, the entourage had a complete view of the Memorial Union's massive lawn, easily the size of three football fields resting side by side. Sidewalks radiated outward from a central point, dissecting the massive green space into wedges of lawn. A few students were lying on blankets, sunbathing. Several groups were tossing Frisbees back and forth. Others browsed on their devices, while some simply reclined or sat while engaging in conversation. The drumming emanated from a small grove of trees next to a multi-storied brick building. Two-hundred-foot-tall cedars with their graceful, flat-needled branches, gently sloping toward the ground, shaded the performers, and a small group of people gathered under the giants.

"I predict our STRONG meeting is under those trees."

"You're a winner, Hang. The flyer mentioned a cedar grove. Onward, gentlemen. There lies our destination."

Rachael led them across the quad. Tunes began to drum louder as they neared the percussion group. One of the Alliance drummers heard their approach and alerted the gathering. Shouts of encouragement greeted the newcomers as they arrived under the cedars. The drummers stopped their music, and a dreadlocked student wearing hemp drawstring pants, sandals, and a peasant wedding shirt greeted them.

"Hello, fellow students. Welcome to the Oregon State STRONG Alliance meeting. I'm Dread, and everyone you see here belongs to the Alliance. I assume you saw our flyer, and know we're planning a tree sit-in and are in need of extra people to help us stop a scheduled raping of our forest."

The bearded Forestry major observed the small group that joined them. He noticed the djembe drum held by Tunes, the cargo shorts, and the positive manner portrayed by this entourage. This group seemed like a perfect fit for the Alliance.

He impulsively asked, "Do any of you know how to scale trees and set up hammocks in canopies?"

Hang laughed and raised his hand like a grade schooler. "Been doing it since I was about ten."

Dread viewed him with a mixture of surprise and awe on his face. "I'm glad you're here, amigo."

While Hang and the Alliance leader conversed, several more students joined the gathering. Dread noticed this and continued addressing those present. "We're always looking for more Alliance members, and hopefully some or all of you will consider joining us."

Hang raised his hand, again in grade school fashion, prompting a smile from the Alliance leader.

"Yes, young man?" he cheerfully asked. "What is your question?"

"We just arrived on campus, and don't know much about you guys except your drumming sounds really good." His comment elicited laughter from the gathering. "What does STRONG stand for? I mean, it's an acronym, right?" Hang queried.

The young girl sitting next to Dread stood up, leaving her drum on the ground. As she stood, she grasped her boyfriend's hand, and remained holding it while she spoke. "STRONG stands for Save the Remaining Old Natural Growth. That's what we do. We won't allow any more raping of Oregon's remaining old ecosystems!"

Those in attendance spontaneously clapped and cheered at these words, and then fell silent. Dread looked at his girlfriend and squeezed her hand. He then took the lead and continued.

"There's a logging show due to begin cutting two days from now. This is an unprecedented 'end run' attack upon the few remaining old trees in Oregon. We need to move fast. By fast, I mean leaving campus, today, at around five p.m. We'll be setting up our defensive positions within the clear-cut site by late this evening. All the STRONG members present can pull this off, but we need more people to assist the tree sitters and help maintain our campsite."

Those gathered began to shuffle feet and look questioningly at each other. The Alliance was asking for an immediate commitment and then timely action from those who would volunteer their support.

Sensing the uneasiness, Dread forged on. "I know this is a difficult request on my part, but we need to be in place before the loggers arrive and begin felling trees."

The young militant knew the next statement from him could potentially derail any chance of gaining additional help.

"I must be totally frank and honest with all of you. We'll probably get arrested because of our actions. At some point, local authorities will tire of us and haul us off to the Deschutes County Jail. I can say from experience we won't be held for long. We'll eventually be let out on our own recognizance. I've been arrested three times, and this scenario played out each time. In every case, I received misdemeanor charges, which were dropped. Being arrested is an inconvenience for sure, but our tactics will slow up the loggers, and lawsuits will eventually kill this attack on our trees. I predict we'll tree sit for no more than a week or two, and be back on campus shortly thereafter. For those of you who have just joined us, and have never attempted to stop the destruction of our forests, I'll simply say this: what you'll do in the next two weeks may be the most important, memorable experience of your college career, and for some, it may be the most significant experience of your entire life."

The young people standing and sitting next to the bearded, peasant-dressed speaker were quiet and contemplative for a moment. Rachael turned to her companions and with raised eyebrows and a mirthful smile asked, "Does anyone want to go camping?"

Her voice was loud enough for all to hear, and her humorous banter prompted a surge of nervous laughter and clapping.

Bridger regarded Rachael. "I hate clear-cuts, and even more, I hate clear-cuts next to my fishing hole. I'd love to go camping."

Hang looked at both Rachael and Bridger. "I'm in, boss. Nobody's cutting down those trees on my watch."

They all observed Tunes, who simply nodded an affirmative and began tapping his drum, producing a mellow, body-moving rhythm. Bridger pulled Rachael to him and they embraced. Shifting apart, he gazed into her eyes and said, "You're fantastic. Can I be your Camp Dog?"

"Only if you follow directions and obey my every command."

"If I had a tail, it would be wagging right now."

A unique sound descended upon the small group assembled beneath the oldest grove of trees on the Oregon State campus. It was a chuckling, raspy sound coming from the top branches of one of the old cedars. Bridger peered up and saw two big ravens cocking their heads back and forth and talking to the small group below. The midday sun brightened their bodies, making the blueish-black iridescence of their feathers shine like faceted, dark gemstones. With a squawk, the two birds clumsily lifted off their perch and flew in an easterly direction. They called out several more times before vanishing behind the Agricultural Building.

"Whoa! What a great sign, my good fellows. Let's follow those noble birds to our destiny," Bridger directed.

Hang observed his best friend and laughed. "That sounded pretty ominous, bro. Can we lighten things up just a bit, here?"

Rachael joined in. "Yeah, remember darling, we're just going on a camping trip."

CHAPTER
26

THE ALLIANCE MEETING QUICKLY DISPERSED after Dread mentioned the need for decisive, immediate action. It was 1:00 p.m., and if they were to get rolling by five, everyone present had to move fast.

The 11th Street entourage represented the only recruits for the STRONG Alliance tree sit-in, and Dread was appreciative of their new members. The four friends all agreed helping the Alliance would be a good thing. Classes didn't begin for almost another month, and they felt certain they'd be back in Corvallis in time for fall registration.

On the way back to their apartment, they discussed what was needed for the sit-in. Dread suggested they consider it a backpacking trip and bring small stoves, tents, lightweight sleeping bags, thermorests, headlamps, cooking utensils, and the like. Sasha, Dread's girlfriend, said the Alliance would provide all the basic food they'd need. Any other edibles they desired, beyond the basics, they should purchase for themselves. While the 11th Streeters reversed and retraced their steps, they realized all the gear required was sitting back in their apartments. They had two tents, a couple stoves, and all the other sundries the camping trip necessitated.

Rachael quietly asked Bridger if he'd be her tent mate, and he conditionally accepted her invitation. His terms were simple; if it got cold at night, they'd have to sleep together, naked, in order to fend off potentially deadly symptoms of hypothermia. Rachael thanked Bridger for his thoughtfulness, and agreed to his terms.

As they neared McNary Hall, Bridger invited all to a quick lunch of cheese enchiladas. There was some indecision until Bridger mentioned lunch was on him, and then a unanimous acceptance of his offer was murmured by everyone.

The friends entered the food service area separating McNary and Wilson Halls, and made their way to the Mexican food café. Bridger ordered the enchiladas for everyone, and also got their drink requests. Rachael looked at Bridger as he approached the table carrying everyone's beverage. "You're the perfect host. Can we do this again, soon?"

"Certainly, but first we have a little camping trip to go on. When we return, I'll be glad to spoil you all again."

Bridger gave them each their specified beverage and sat down.

Hang raised his lemonade and presented it to the others. "Here's a toast to saving trees, camping, and being spoiled."

All the others saluted their drinks in Hang's direction. The enchiladas were cheesy and good. The friends quickly devoured them, cleared their space, and headed for the building's east entrance. Their apartment was across the street and about fifty yards away.

Bridger said to no one in particular, "Home Sweet Home."

The group stopped on the Adams Street porch and stood by Rachael's door. She considered each person and said what everyone was thinking. "Are we still sure this is a good idea?"

Tunes spoke first. "Yep, I think so."

Hang and Bridger offered their affirmatives, leaving Rachael the last word.

"Well, I think it's unanimous then. It's a go. I'm going to start packing. It shouldn't take too long." She viewed her phone. "It's 2:00 p.m. I can be ready by 3:00 or 3:30."

Tunes echoed Rachael's timeline, and Hang and Bridger knew they could easily make the 3:00 p.m. deadline.

"Okay, let's get this done, boys."

The friends parted company, each lost in thought, planning for their extended stay in the forest.

Bridger and Hang entered their apartment and headed for their separate bedrooms. After about fifteen minutes, Hang stuck his head into Bridger's room.

"Hey, I'm ready to go. I've got my Insulite and sleeping bag bungeed together. My daypack has clothes, backpacking stove, and fuel in it, and my climbing gear is in a separate bag. The only thing I don't have is a cook set and utensils. Do you have one?"

"Yeah, I do. Do you have a headlamp or flashlight?" Bridger asked.

"I've got both, actually."

"Good, by the looks of things, we'll need plenty of artificial light for tonight's activities. You know, it's hard enough to set up camp in the dark. I can't imagine the Alliance climbing up trees and swinging around like monkeys without any daylight."

"Yeah. It's pretty mind bending. I don't think I'll join in with the hammock hanging. I've got experience with rigging everything, but not in the dark. That sounds a little scary to me," Hang admitted.

"Good call. I'd like you to arrive at your first OSU classes on your own two feet, not aided by crutches or a wheelchair."

"Hey, while everybody's getting ready, let me take the Jetta and make a store run. I'll get a list of everyone's special munchies, buy them, and on the way back, stop and top off the tank."

"Sounds good. Get me some dried fruit, midnight Milky Ways, Gatorade, and a few cans of Pringles; any flavor will do. I'll settle up with you when you get back."

"You got it, boss. Hey, do you need me to pick up any protection for you from the pharmacy?"

Bridger saluted his roommate with his middle finger, causing his friend to smile and respond, "Just asking."

"Don't you have something to do?"

"Right, right. I was just leaving on a store run. Adios."

"Yeah, good. Tootles."

Hang grabbed some dark glasses and a wide-brimmed hat, and headed out the door. Bridger heard him knocking on Tunes' and Rachael's doors, and eventually heard the old diesel engine of his Jetta come to life. The engine noise grew quieter as the car headed into downtown.

CHAPTER 27

Dread pulled his ancient 1950 Chevy, short chassis, school bus into the Burger King parking lot. It was 4:00 and he noted, happily, that Bridger's blue Jetta was already there. He grabbed the door handle, and thrusting it outward, opened the door, allowing about half a dozen Alliance members to bounce down the steps and head for the fast food restaurant. The 11th Street group got up from the sidewalk lawn they were sitting on and walked to the bus. As they approached, Hang eyed the beautiful, antique rig. It was an off yellow with wonderful rounded lines. Dread kept the paint job pretty traditional. There was one black horizontal stripe underneath the windows that ran the entire length of the small bus, which only had four rows of seats. The rounded back end of the bus had a gate-like door with two windows, one at floor level. The chassis itself was rounded over at the top, and the front windshield was steeply inclined into the long, rounded, somewhat pointed, hood covering the big, V8 engine. Two bulbous fenders covered the front tires and rolled over and into the engine housing.

Hang climbed the steps into the bus and greeted Dread, who was still in the driver's seat, and Sasha, who was sitting across the aisle in the forward bench seat.

"Hello, Alliance members. Is this your set of wheels, Dread?"

"Most certainly. It belonged to my grandfather. He rebuilt it years ago. When I left for college, he gave it to me as a high school graduation present. Can you believe he gave me this beautiful old bus? I've run it for four years now, and all I've had to do is change the oil and put gas into it."

The other 11th Streeters joined Hang in the aisle. Tunes with his ever-present earbuds was smiling and bobbing his head to his music. Bridger eyed the interior with appreciation. The old seats had been revinyled and seemed factory new. The back door was mostly hidden behind a mound of backpacks, sleeping bags, coolers, big plastic totes, and some large duffel bags. The back two seats appeared to be covered with cardboard boxes filled with food and gallon water jugs. Bridger turned around and observed Sasha and Dread. They had changed from their peasant attire of the meeting, and now both wore cargo shorts, T-shirts, and climbing boots.

"Looks like you two are going on a major trek. You've got a lot of gear."

Dread responded, "It takes a lot of equipment and food to keep this ragtag band of tree huggers happy. Civil disobedience requires vigilance and sacrifice, but some creature comforts are always welcome." On a more serious note Dread continued, "When we get to the site, things are going to get crazy. All of us will start setting up tree perches. This will be tricky in the dark, but we can do it. Hang, I haven't seen you climb, so I'm going to ask you to help the Camp Dogs. It's going to be dark, I don't know your skill level, and well, I don't want anyone to get hurt."

"Totally understandable. I was actually going to defer tonight's climbing to you pros anyway."

"Good, good, no offense intended."

"None taken."

The Alliance leader viewed the group and smiled. "How do you like the term Camp Dogs, 11th Streeters?"

Rachael laughed and responded, "I've been called worse, and I believe Bridger already volunteered for the job."

"I like it. Camp Dogs sounds perfect," Bridger echoed.

"Thanks for the humble acceptance of your role. You're now officially the 11th Street Camp Dogs. While this peaceful moment continues, let me be more specific about the first few hours of our occupation setup. The Alliance will be getting the hammocks hung and a few other things accomplished. While we are rigging everything, you Dogs will set up the terra firma site. There's a small crater located on a central hill inside the logging show. You'll set up our land camp in it. I've got an old elk tent that needs to be pitched. Any of you set one up before? It's an external pole number."

Hang raised his hand. This action once more brought a smile to Dread's face. "Bridger and I have set up external pole tents lots of times."

Rachael added, "So have I. I think we got it covered."

Dread continued, "Excellent. After the tent is up, rig your own personal stuff and then gather as much firewood as you can. Grab the Ponderosa pinecones and needles, too. They burn great."

Dread focused on Sasha and asked, "Anything else?"

She thought for a moment. "Yeah. It will take us quite a while to sling the hammocks, and if we're not done, and you've finished with what Dread talked about, cook up some rice for all of us. I've got some chicken thighs to add to the rice, too. You know there's twelve of us, so cook up a bunch."

Bridger responded, "This all sounds like Camp Dog territory to me. We'll make you proud."

With a rush of activity, the Alliance members left Burger King with drinks and burger bags in hand.

Dread smiled and said, "Well, here comes chaos."

Sasha joined in. "Duck and cover, everyone."

There was a small traffic jam at the old bus's door as the 11th Street crowd exited and the Alliance members boarded. Everyone exchanged greetings, and before Dread closed the double doors, he told Bridger to leave I-5 at Albany and to take Highway 226 to Lyons. Then at Lyons he should turn east on Highway 22. This route would spare the ancient bus the tougher hills of Highway 20's course through the Cascades. They'd all rendezvous at the wayside below Big Cliff Dam and take a break. Bridger acknowledged he knew the way, and after saying goodbye, he turned and walked back to the Jetta. The 1950 Chevy bus came to life with a cough and a puff of blue smoke exhausting from its tailpipe. Then, with the old V8 purring, it turned east onto Van Buren Street and headed across the Willamette River.

CHAPTER
28

THE TWO VEHICLES TRAVELED THROUGH THE heart of the Willamette Valley, which was nestled between the Cascades on the east and the Coast Range on the west. Harvested wheat fields with only stubble remaining lined both sides of the interstate. This pattern was disrupted, occasionally, by cut bunchgrass fields that now supported flocks of sheep or herds of cattle grazing on them, contributing to the valley's pastoral appearance this time of year.

The caravan left the freeway and headed northeast to Lyons. When the vehicles reached the small hamlet, they turned east and began climbing, slowly, toward the distant pass. The road began to mimic the Santiam River's course. In a moment, they'd pass through Mill City and Gates. Both sat right on the river. After these settlements, they'd drive through Detroit and Idanha. As the vehicles continued, the road's corridor became lined on both sides by tall conifers.

Dread led the way up the Cascade slopes. He shifted gears as needed to keep the old bus's speed relatively constant. He began thinking about historical logging practices in this area. Besides being a Forestry major with "Tourism and Outdoor Leadership" as his course of studies, Dread was a logging history buff, and pretty much knew the entire story of Oregon's timber industry. This knowledge was one of the reasons he was so passionate about saving the last old trees. The big stands of Doug fir, hemlock, and cedar, which lined Highway 22, were really only an illusion of old growth grandeur. Regional foresters did not allow loggers to cut tracts of forests next to major roadways. This tactic produced for travelers the appearance of never-ending, unbroken ancient forests, when, in reality, once you moved inland from the roads, you encountered a hodge-podge assortment of clear-cuts in various stages of regrowth. From the air, this scene resembled a three-dimensional checkerboard of forest land undulating with the up and down inclines of the Cascade Range's ridges and valleys. Only about ten percent of the

Cascades was still covered in old growth. All the remaining acreage was covered by second and sometimes third growth trees that paled in size to their ancient brethren. Most of the remaining ancient trees in Oregon either lined these main Cascade arteries or surrounded the numerous jewel-like, high-altitude lakes nestled in the many bowls found between the mountain ridges.

Most of the small towns Dread and Bridger would soon drive through had been, at one time, mill towns. For the most part, now, they were minor tourist stops, or simply shadows of their original selves.

After the Korean War, logging in this area flourished due to the building boom the United States entered into. The big, ancient conifers of Oregon, especially Doug fir and hemlock, provided perfect wood for the construction industry. Large national lumber companies moved into the area to join the several locally owned corporations. They all began logging at unprecedented levels. The companies all professed sustainable logging practices, and mill towns like Gates, Mill City, and Idanha thrived, producing livelihoods for millworkers, log truck drivers, and loggers. After decades of overcutting, some Oregonians and environmental groups began to realize sustainable logging practices were not occurring. The term "sustainable" was just a propaganda tool being used by large corporations. At some point, the state and federal government realized they'd been duped, too. The industry's cutting schedule was decimating Oregon's forests.

The straw that broke the industry's back was their practice of cutting old growth trees and then sending the unmilled logs overseas for sizable profits. Asia had a huge appetite for the Northwest's old giants. They had denuded their own forests centuries earlier and were willing to pay a premium price for raw logs. Consequently, the "best of the best" logs were sent out of various West Coast ports, heading to the Asian buyers. Once the public became aware of this tactic, their opinion of West Coast logging changed drastically. With negative public and political sentiment targeting the existing overcutting and unsustainable logging practices, regulations soon developed to protect the last old growth trees. One such regulation was the Endangered Species Act. It often provided the muscle behind state and federal efforts that stopped the cutting of these old forests. Timber industry propaganda turned out dialogue blaming environmentalists for the industry's slowdown. The lumber corporations never admitted to their unsustainable logging practices.

The big national and international companies one by one left the Northwest and headed home to timber tracts they'd cleared decades earlier. The small lumber towns like Idanha saw their mills shut down and all the associated jobs dry up. Looking past the collapse of so many small local economies, one of the greatest tragedies caused by the timber industry's overcutting and associated propaganda was the ensuing mistrust between rural Oregon, where most logging jobs existed, and its counterpart, urban Oregon. Urbania became synonymous with environmentalists and government meddling. This dislike and wariness between regions never abated, and still persisted today.

Dread could not think about twentieth-century logging practices without getting angry. He had written his first college term paper about these techniques. It had been a cathartic effort, and in his mind was his best writing to date. His passion about this subject had produced an excellent paper. Unfortunately, an "old school" forestry professor graded his research paper and gave him a C minus with a red, penned footnote mentioning Dread's obvious bias and poorly chosen sources. Dread suggested to his professor, when they met to discuss his paper, that the professor's bias and poorly chosen sources could have influenced his perception of the paper. In the end, both he and the professor agreed to disagree, and the next day, Dread, erring on the side of caution, dropped the class.

CHAPTER 29

As Dread mused about logging and his term paper, the old bus, followed by its satellite car, came to the Big Cliff Dam pullout. Downshifting, he slowed the vehicle, and turned into the large gravel wayside adjacent to the Santiam River. Both vehicles stopped within a few feet of the guardrail, allowing everyone to gaze down into the deep, greenish water flowing past. It appeared awfully cool and inviting.

All the young people exited their vehicles, ready to climb down the river bank for a quick swim, but were instantly met by a cool river breeze coming down the canyon. It was September, and the air temperature had dropped with the afternoon sun, leaving the college students with a beautiful late sunny afternoon but chilly ambient air temperature. The group opted for some munchies and washed them down with cold beers or energy drinks.

After about a fifteen-minute break, Dread called out, "Okay people, we're losing daylight, so let's get rolling. There's still an hour and a half to the logging site."

Everyone hungrily finished off sandwiches, beers, munchies, and energy drinks, and got in one quick toke before getting back into their rigs. The yellow bus again coughed back to life, and Dread slowly ran through the gears. By the time they reached the larger Detroit Dam, the old bus was cruising at 55 mph.

He glanced over at Sasha and asked. "Did you get the bundles of flares painted and taped together?"

She nodded an affirmative and then thoughtfully regarded him. "You know, you should have told the 11th Street group about this."

Dread thought for a moment and then responded, "You're right. I just got too emotional at our meeting, and really, I was afraid it would scare them off."

"Yeah, it could easily have done that."

"I'm not sure what to do about it, now."

"Well, I think you know. When we get to the site, you need to tell them about our plan. This is such a different reality from our other sit-ins."

"Okay, I will. Crap. I hope I didn't screw things up."

"If you say something to them before we set up, you won't have. If they choose to leave, I think we can still get this done."

"Yeah, you're right. I'll talk to them when we unload the gear."

Dread gave Sasha a thoughtful glance, then hollered back, "Hey, Tom, did you get the blasting cord?"

"Affirmative, Captain."

Dread drove through Idanha, the last of the logging ghost towns on their route before they reached the Camp Sherman turn-off. There was an hour of travel left before they unloaded their gear and set up their tree stands and defenses.

CHAPTER 30

The travelers reached the Cascades' summit near Hoodoo, a small ski resort perched atop a nearby peak, and began descending. They passed Suttle Lake and moved into the lee side of the Cascade Range. The rain shadow, produced here by the mountain ridges and the Northern Hemisphere's westerlies, created the perfect environment for Ponderosa pines. The tall trees began to line both sides of the road. A few more miles brought them to their turn-off. The yellow school bus left Highway 20 and headed for Camp Sherman.

At the three-way stop near Camp Sherman, Bridger thought about the funky store to their right. As a small boy, he'd love visiting the classic old grocery, stuffed to the gills with everything a person could want. It even had a fly fishing shop tucked into the back corner. Bridger usually left the store with a new fly pattern clutched in one hand and an ice cream bar in the other.

The vehicles pulled straight ahead and continued on. At a scruffy looking patch of forest, the Chevy came to a stop, and one Alliance member jumped out, waved at the Jetta, and then headed into the closest clump of juvenile trees. They were soon lost from sight due to the tree stands' denseness. The bus moved on. They lost the river for a bit, then turned back toward it. At a sharp left turn corner, the bus's brake lights came on and it pulled to a stop. Its back door swung open and an Alliance member jumped out. Another member started handing gear out the door. Several other students came around from the bus's front and started stacking bags next to the road's edge. Bridger brought the Jetta to a stop. The Camp Dogs got out and walked over to the bus, where Dread and Sasha met them.

Dread addressed the 11th Streeters, "There'll be two piles formed in a minute. You'll be able to discern the Camp Dog pile as it will have the elk tent in it." Dread turned and motioned to the plateau-like top of the hill. "Carry all the gear up to the hill's summit and into the cone."

The huge trees perched on the hill, and all around them, were magnificent in the dusky evening light. The green of the Ponderosa's canopy took on a somber, subdued hue in this light as did the orange bark of the trees. The dark veins, which defined the tree bark, became even blacker and more pronounced, creating a strong, puzzle-like appearance on the giant conifer trunks. Rachael and Tunes had never seen this forest before. They were silent and awed by its beauty. Bridger and Hang actually had been inside the hilltop's crater.

Dread continued, "Bridger, drive your rig down to the turnout by the lower bridge and park. It's about another quarter mile down the road. The bus will follow, shortly, and park there, too. After you park, hump back here and help the others move gear and set up camp."

Hang regarded the Alliance members and asked, "Who'd we lose back there in the forest?"

Dread smiled and said, "Oh yeah. That was Arrow. He's our lookout right now, and has a walkie-talkie in his possession." The young Forestry major reached into one of his pockets and pulled out its mate. "We're connected on channel 11. He's going to alert us if anyone approaches, and hopefully, I won't hear from him. When our bus is parked, Runner will remain with it. He's got another handset and he'll alert us about visitors from his end." Dread was using the Alliance members' aliases, which some of the militants preferred when they engaged in activist movement.

Bridger observed the 11th Streeters. "Are we good, Camp Dogs?"

"You bet," Rachael responded, and the Dogs unloaded their car, allowing Bridger to chauffeur it to the pull-off.

The 11th Streeters began hauling the equipment up to the crater. There were coolers, the elk tent, numerous large totes and duffel bags, propane tanks, a four-legged, two-burner metal cooking range, and their own gear to transport.

As they moved the equipment, Hang watched the Alliance members reach into their packs. They were pulling out climbing gear, headlamps, and big, eighteen-volt-battery flashlights. Hang saw old school climbing gear appear like the spiked boots and lanyards loggers would use. He also noticed piles of apparatus arborist climbers would use. It appeared the Alliance used single rope technique (SRT) climbing methods too, so those piles of equipment were probably filled with waist harnesses, carabiners, hitchhiking devices, foot ascenders, and hand ascenders. As Hang observed the climbers' preparations, the light was slowly fading, and his view was becoming less acute. Soon headlamps and flashlights would be needed.

Several Alliance members were putting on helmets and headlamps, donning their climbing packs, and switching into boots with climbing spikes on their inboard heels. The remaining Alliance members were peering up into nearby trees, and in the dim, remaining daylight, they shined their flashlight beams into them. Dread was with the group peering up into the conifers. After gearing up, Sasha and two other climbers waited for their trees to be located. The flashlight group moved to within ten yards of the road and appeared to be finalizing their choices.

Dread called out to the climbers, "We've got three possibilities for you."

He then took a spray can of fluorescent paint, and moving from tree to tree, painted an X on each trunk. The climbers made their way to these conifers, and the rechargeable battery group split up, allowing each tree scaler his or her personal flashlight attendant.

This part of Dread's plan had caused the STRONG Alliance much soul searching. They needed to hang the pseudo dynamite low on the tree trunks so the bundles could be easily seen. With limited light and time, the quickest technique to use was the spiked boots and lanyard system. The Alliance knew this could be an avenue for disease because with each step, puncture wounds were put into the old trees. The old giants they put flare bundles onto were at risk of potential insect and bacterial assault. As a group, the Alliance agreed with much remorse that potentially killing these conifers was a necessary evil allowing them to save the remaining forest from chainsaws.

Bridger rejoined the 11th Street group and started to help set up camp. Rachael found two Coleman-style camp lanterns and fired them up. She'd also noted two large boulders resting on the crater's floor and set the lamps atop them. The light partially illuminated the bowl. It was strewn with both small and large rocks, and dry, dusty, forest soil was exposed in between the stones. Wearing their headlamps, the group cleared stones from a twelve by twelve section of ground, and quickly erected the elk tent.

After raising the tent, all the Camp Dogs went to the bowl's basaltic lava rim and watched the Alliance members. There was just enough light to see their activities. Sasha and two others were climbing up three trees. Hang watched their rhythmical ascent. Step, step, pause, step, step, pause. This pattern continued upwards on the lower trunks of the chosen trees. With each step the climbers dug into the tree a spike, and when they paused, they leaned slightly forward, taking their weight off the climbing lanyard. With a quick wrist and arm movement, they flung the lanyard upward to a higher level. Then leaning backwards against the lanyard, which now aided their stability, they stepped up again, continuing the pattern. With this rhythmic movement, all three climbers reached a thirty-foot level and stopped. Leaning back, they rested. Eventually, they all reversed their backpacks so the packs lay on their chests and began retrieving items from them.

When the Alliance members descended, Hang could make out what appeared to be climbing ropes hanging to the ground from each tree. He wondered why the group hadn't just belayed down these ropes. For some reason, they descended using their spikes and lanyards again.

The daylight was almost completely gone now, and the Camp Dogs decided to divide into two groups; one would gather firewood and the other would cook the rice and chicken up for the group's late night meal. Bridger and Rachael volunteered to be the camp chefs, and Hang and Tunes went for the wood. Before the young couple set up the stove and started cooking, they found a site for their tent outside of the small crater. It was a section of flat ground overlooking the Metolius River Valley, where the sounds of the rushing water reached up to them.

"Kind of a romantic spot," Bridger announced to Rachael as they pitched their small tent.

"Yes, it is, lover boy. You be sure and pace yourself tonight. I'd like a little energy left in you when we retire to our little nest."

Bridger stood up and contemplated Rachael, who stood on the other side of the tent. "I won't overdo it. I'll be a man of steel when we retire."

Rachael laughed and softly groaned.

With their new understanding in mind, they both returned to the crater and hooked the propane tank to the stove. They positioned the stove next to the large rocks that supported the lanterns. Before starting dinner, they moved over to the camp's basaltic rim and surveyed the forest's floor. There, they saw Hang and Tunes' headlamp beams bounce along through the trees. Occasionally, their lights would stop, angle down, and then, after a moment, continue bobbing around some more. After watching the wood gatherers, the camp cooks located the Alliance members and observed their endeavors. They noticed the group had moved farther up the hill, and were now about thirty yards from the encampment. The light was very poor, and what Bridger observed was curious to him. He saw a "glow in the dark" ball rocket up toward a tree's lower branches and fall quickly back to earth. This maneuver happened several times. After one flight, the ball stopped near a branch, and dangled above the ground, rocking back and forth. Then, the ball slowly descended to the ground. At the base of the Ponderosa, he could see several Alliance members shining lights on the ground as a climber prepared to ascend into the tree. The climber, it appeared to be Sasha, began to rhythmically move up a rope. Like an inchworm ascending on a stick, she rose up, paused, rose up again, paused, and in this manner, reached a lower branch. After watching the unusual show below, Bridger and Rachael's attention went back to their immediate task, and they started to gather together the essentials for dinner: water, rice, cooking pots and pans, and chicken all began to accumulate next to the cooking station. Occasionally, the wood gatherers would return to camp with a bundle of wood. Their fuel pile was growing in size. Rachael had found some large, thick-milled, garbage sacks that the boys grabbed and were now filling with pinecones out on the forest floor.

Hang also was watching the Alliance group's process, and noted that when Sasha descended, her headlamp beam slowly, and in a constant, steady motion, returned to the forest's floor. This prompted him to think she used a single rope and some form of hitchhiker to lower herself down. He also assumed she'd hung her hammock between some stout limbs in the tree's lower canopy. While he watched Sasha detach herself, the lights illuminating her confirmed his assumption of a one-rope system. Hang had used foot ascenders, hitchhikers, and hand ascenders before, so he felt confident he could assist the Alliance in climbing matters if asked to.

Rachael and Bridger put the water pot on top of one burner. It was filled with rice, and they were slow-cooking the chicken thighs in a cast iron frying pan on the other burner. As food was cooking, they walked over to the bowl's rocky edge and held hands while watching the activity below. The Alliance moved over to a second tree and duplicated their previous maneuver. Headlamp and flashlight beams lit up the climber and their work area. Occasionally, a beam would dart off to another area, brightening the tree trunks and branches as it moved. The Alliance's voices could be heard but not understood at this distance; however, a constant line of dialogue was always being uttered.

Bridger and Rachael spotted Hang's and Tunes' lights, and their beams were once again bobbing through the forest. It was a magical, surreal scene playing out below them. The light's dancing movements were almost mesmerizing. Bridger's gaze left the hillside and looked above through an opening in the forest's crown. He saw a few bats darting here and there, grabbing bugs as they flew past. He stared past the night flyers, up to the stars. The Milky Way was shining in its Central Oregon brilliance, and standing on top of the hill, it felt like you could reach out and pluck one of the stars from the black vastness surrounding it. Bridger gazed at Rachael and pulled her close to him. She hugged him in response and they kissed.

"Hey! Get a motel room, you two!"

They turned back into the inner crater to see their friends grinning at them.

"No seriously, I'm getting a hard-on watching the two of you."

The young lovers couldn't help themselves, and both started laughing at Hang's gross comment.

"Hang, you're just jealous. Hey, if you want some quiet time by yourself, I believe the elk tent is presently vacant."

Hang began laughing now. "I think its use won't be necessary, but if you two continue with your sexual exhibitionism, I just may have to avail myself of the tent's privacy."

Rachael grinned and then noticed steam rolling out of the rice's pot. She went over, and seeing the water boiling, placed a lid on the pot and turned down the burner. This prompted Bridger to take note of the chicken progress. As he did so, he checked out Hang's and Tunes' efforts. Along with a huge pile of branches, the fuel gatherers had collected several sacks of cones and one sack of dry pine needles. They'd also found a flat spot some distance from the elk tent, cleared it of burnable material, created a circle of rocks for a fire ring, and were laying the evening's fire. Pine needles, topped off with cones, were mounded together. With one match, Hang had a hot, bright campfire going with flames licking into the night air. Shadows were sent dancing about the campsite as the campfire light illuminated the entire crater. It was about forty feet across, with the tent off center and hugging the river side of the encampment. The campfire was situated near the middle of the bowl. Everybody's gear was stacked near the tent, and the cooking area was about ten feet from the fire. Coolers were placed near the kitchen, and sat up against the two large boulders Rachael rested the lanterns on. On top of these rocks, behind the Coleman lanterns, the food boxes were placed. All in all, the campsite had a tidy, well-designed appearance.

Rachael took in the ambiance of the base camp. It was worthy of a Norman Rockwell painting. The aroma of simmering chicken enticed her curiosity, and she critiqued Bridger's efforts. While doing this, she remembered her curry hadn't been added to the rice. She quickly left the mess area, located her pack, and retrieved the spice. Returning to the gas stove, she called out, "Hey, I've got our Indian cuisine right here in my hands, gentlemen."

Hang observed Rachael. She stood next to the rice pot, and held up the plastic Ziploc bag up for all to see. The firelight lit up her front torso and her red hair appeared more auburn in the dancing light.

"What do you have, Rachael?"

"Some curry spice from the Corvallis Coop."

"Oh yeah, now we're talking," quipped Bridger.

Tunes considered Rachael and gave her the thumbs-up sign.

She checked the progress of the rice pot. "Rice is done."

The young coed removed the rice from the stove and set it on a small flat-topped rock resting near the burners. She added the curry. Bridger deboned the cooked chicken and sliced it into smaller pieces. "Do you want to add the chicken now?"

"Sure, let's let everything sit together for a bit and absorb all the flavors."

Hang examined the camp site. "I think our work is done here. I wonder how the Alliance is doing."

As the Camp Dogs walked to the rim, Bridger told Hang about the "glow in the dark" ball.

"Pretty tricky."

"What's tricky?"

"Well, the Alliance members made their throw ball visible in the dark. They thought of everything."

Hang continued by telling his friend how the Alliance got the climbing rope into place. "They probably used a 'big shot' to get a line over their branch of choice. The line was then used to pull a climbing rope up and over the branch and back down to the ground. After securing the climbing rope to the branch above, Sasha probably used a foot ascender and hand ascender to move up to her perch."

The four friends continued peering down the hill at the flashlight beams that were now focused on the third and last hammock tree. Someone was just now descending. You could see his headlamp beam move slowly to the ground.

Tom detached himself from his climbing rope. He observed his fellow Alliance members. "I'm glad we're done."

Sasha responded to his remark. "Yeah, rigging up was pretty dicey. *Saying* we could do it in the dark was much easier than *doing* it in the dark." She noted the aroma of curry wafting down to the group as she spoke. "No way."

Sasha looked up at the summit. There, backlit by the Coleman stoves and campfire light, stood the Camp Dogs who, noticing headlamps pointed their way, shouted their approval and clapped for the tree climbers. Some reciprocal shouts came back up the hill to the Camp Dogs, and the entire group shared a moment of accomplishment together.

"That would be curry I'm smelling." Sasha watched her friends. "We've got the best Camp Dogs ever."

The group slowly picked their way up to the crater. They eventually reached the summit and entered their base camp.

Dread surveyed the camp set-up. "Holy shit," he exclaimed. "This is beautiful."

Hang loaded the fire up with more cones as the Alliance climbed the hill. Now, the fire's light was bright with four-foot flames jumping skyward. The entire STRONG group started jumping up and down, whooping their approval. They grabbed and hugged the 11th Street members, and in some cases, individuals were lifted off their feet in bear hugs and twirled around and around. The joyous happiness was infectious and slowly played itself out. With laughter and smiles still registering, Dread got everyone's attention by dragging a cooler into the midst of the group. With an appreciative gaze, Dread looked at everyone for a moment, then he reached down, opened the lid, and pulled two six-packs of ale out of the cooler.

"Who wants a beer?"

The simultaneous surge of bodies to his outstretched hands answered his rhetorical question, and within seconds, Dread held two empty six-pack rings in his hand. He examined the vacant rings and in a dramatic voice said, "All right, who took more than one beer?"

A laugh came from behind Dread. Everyone looked past the Alliance leader to see Sasha, one hand raised above her head, holding the missing beers.

"I cannot tell a lie, Sir Knight. I took the extra beers." The fire's flickering light brightened, then darkened Sasha's playful smile. "But, Sir Knight, it is not what it seems. I saved these two beers for our brave and loyal sentinels who are not here to wrest from these lushes what is rightfully theirs. Please, do not judge me wrongfully."

The Alliance leader regarded his girlfriend tenderly. "Fair Princess, your noble deed is recorded in all of our hearts."

He pulled the two beers from Sasha's grasp. She playfully held on tightly to the cans, and tugged back on them a few times before surrendering them. Dread returned the beers to the cooler.

"Fair maidens and knights, I believe our attendants have prepared a feast for us. Let us dine now, under the stars, and then rejoice in our camaraderie. Tomorrow we do battle, so let us feast and revel tonight."

In the firelight, everyone whooped and hollered their approval of Sasha's and Dread's thespian antics. The Dogs rounded up plates, serving spoons, and forks for all and began filling the dishes with their curried chicken rice concoction. The climbers took off their gear, and, after finding safe spots for their equipment, grabbed forks and plates. One by one everyone sat down next to the fire and consumed their food and drink. Dread stood up and visited the cooler once again. He returned with two more six-pack carriers, this time minus two beers, and handed out another round of drink. Paper plates were tossed into the fire, and forks licked clean and placed into pants pockets.

Hang put some substantial wood onto the blaze, lessening the fire's brilliance but maintaining its bonfire appearance. The Alliance members located their drums and were now producing a rich percussion sound with numerous beats blending together. Tunes joined the drumming, and sat smiling, buds in ears, helping to create the soul-tapping rhythm.

Sasha found Dread standing next to the crater's rim, watching and listening to the Metolius River pass beneath them. "You haven't talked to the 11th Streeters yet."

"No. I meant to, but things got going again, and I just let it go."

Sasha stood close to her boyfriend and faced him. She placed both hands on his shoulders and turned him so he faced her. The Big Eddy waters quietly and slowly rotated below them. The slight rockfall above the water hole sent gurgling, rushing sounds up to the couple.

"You can't put it off anymore, Dread. Now's the time."

He looked into Sasha's eyes and realized how lucky he was.

"You're right. I feel like such an asshole. Let's go do this."

The two turned and, seeing Bridger and Rachael sitting together, walked to them. On the way over, they passed Hang, and asked him to join the small group. Looking over to the drummers, they decided not to interrupt Tunes. He could be informed later. When the five young people gathered together, Dread asked them to move over to the crater's west wall, where they all stopped. The young Forestry major bent down and picked up three insulated "two-wire" cords that he'd secured there by placing a heavy rock on them. He held them up for the 11th Street group to see. Sasha left the group and now returned holding an old-school blasting box, with its plunger-style handle in the firing position. The Camp Dogs observed the wire and box presented for their inspection.

Hang spoke up first. "Well that explains my observed, unused climbing ropes. It appears they were really wires dangling down from the trees. What's up, Dread? All this stuff looks like explosive gear to me."

"It is and it isn't."

Hang continued. "Well let's narrow this down, then. Which is it?"

The solemn expressions greeting Dread from his audience told him he'd seriously screwed up. "I should have told you about this much earlier."

Sasha took hold of Dread's hand and held tight.

"I just got so involved in what was happening, I totally messed up, and didn't tell you guys. These wires are connected to flares, and they are bundled together and painted to look like dynamite. The bundles are on three different trees located close to the road. It's a bluff on my part, meant to hold the cops at bay so they won't arrest us. When they arrive, I'll show them the blasting box and tell them if they try arresting us, I'll blow up the trees."

Bridger spoke next. "This is pretty damn serious. This demonstration has now entered the realm of 'eco-terrorism.' You've pushed everything to another, much more dangerous level."

Dread inspected the ground in embarrassment and Sasha spoke next. "We are so, so terribly sorry for our behavior. You all are such wonderful people. We just really screwed up, and lost focus regarding your safety and well-being."

She was tearing up, and her voice began to tremble. "But you can leave now and avoid all of this. No one will ever know you were here."

The three friends turned their heads and viewed each other. Rachael looked back at the Alliance leaders. "We need time to think about this, but you're right, we aren't past the point of no return. We still can leave before anything happens."

The firelight backlit the Camp Dogs, and softly reflected off Dread and Sasha's faces. The warm glow highlighted the soft tones of their complexions and brightened their dark hair. The tears running down Sasha's face glistened in the flames' irregular rhythm. Rachael reached out and touched Sasha's arm in a reassuring manner. "We'll work through this. We're safe now, and will make a decision quickly."

With that, the three friends turned and headed over to Tunes. Rachael glanced back and saw Dread and Sasha embracing. Sasha was crying, her head buried into her boyfriend's chest. His arms enveloped her, and they stood motionless, letting their grief find its course.

Rachael thought to herself, *even the best of people can screw up*. As they approached Tunes, she had already forgiven the young couple who stood behind her at the camp's edge.

The Camp Dogs assembled at Bridger and Rachael's tent. They all sat down next to the basaltic cliff, listening to the river's rock palisade talk to them. Rachael told Tunes about their conversation with the Alliance leader.

Hang spoke next. "Well, our camping trip has gotten a little serious."

"Yeah it has, hasn't it?" replied Bridger.

Tunes spoke next. "Well, let's overlook the dynamite thing. Why'd we come here?" His friends looked and listened. "We came to stop these trees from being harvested, right?"

Everyone nodded their agreement.

"The fake dynamite will certainly aid our goal, but it will also put us in a more precarious position. I think if our goal is to save the trees, then our personal safety takes backseat to the forest's well-being."

Rachael was sitting next to Tunes. She leaned over, tilting her head onto his shoulder, and side hugged him. He lowered his head to hers and they shared each other's respect for a moment.

Bridger responded. "I'm just not sure I want to be jailed on terrorist charges. Dread's previous experiences never incorporated explosives before, and this plan will probably evoke a much more severe response from the authorities. I don't think we're going to get a 'get-out-of-jail-free' card."

More silence prevailed among the friends. They all gazed at and listened to the river below.

Hang broke the silence. "I agree with Tunes, but like you, Bridger, I'm concerned with the legal consequences. I'm sure the Alliance will try and downplay our involvement, but when push comes to shove, lawyers will determine who's guilty of what, and we could get really burned."

Again more contemplative silence followed.

Rachael spoke next. "My gut instinct says run while you can, and then my head says to stay."

Bridger added, "I feel the same way, too."

Hang solidified the discussion. "Me three, Rachael."

Tunes nodded his agreement to Rachael's statement and the four friends fell silent again. A great horned owl called out from a distance, and one closer to them returned the greeting.

Rachael spoke again. "Let's sleep on it. First person awake tomorrow rousts us all up. We'll make our decision then."

The foursome agreed to this suggestion and returned to the camp.

While the Camp Dogs conferred, the lookouts were switched out. Now, the two previous guards sat by the fire drinking their beers and eating. They saluted their 11th Street friends with raised forks and smiles. Dread and Sasha were absent and Rachael thought they'd probably crashed inside the elk tent. Several Alliance members threw Insulite pads down near the crater's perimeter and were already asleep. The fire had been continually fed and still threw off warmth and light in all directions. After finding their sleeping gear, Hang and Tunes wandered off searching for comfortable resting spots. Rachael walked over to the kitchen, and noted the rice pot and cast iron pan were clean. She joined Bridger, smiled, and grasped his hand, quietly saying, "This has been a long day, hasn't it?"

"Yes it has. Can you remember this morning?"

"Barely."

"We started the day with the Alliance meeting. It seems like a year ago."

The two young people walked over to their tent. A crescent moon finally rose high enough to brighten the forest slightly. The September night with its clear sky grew chilly. Rachael contemplated Bridger as they stood outside their tent. "When do I have to start worrying about hypothermia?"

He smiled. "Well, it's getting pretty cold. We might be able to solo tonight and survive, but I see no reason to risk it."

Rachael reached her arms around Bridger's waist, and placed her cheek on his chest. She hugged him. "That's what I love about you. You're so decisive."

She squeezed him again, then cradled her head back, and they kissed.

Letting go of their embrace, Bridger turned and unzipped the tent. "After you, my lady."

Rachael bent down and crawled in. "Wait one moment, let me make a nest before you climb in."

She laid out the Insulites and unzipped the bags, placing one on top of the other. Next, she removed her clothes and climbed between the sleeping bags. The youthful, soft lines of her body caused Bridger's heart to miss a beat.

"Okay, young man, your princess awaits."

As Bridger bent down and pushed back the tent flap, a great horned owl called out. It was answered by another. Bridger, standing up, joined in on the late night conversation. He hooted his greeting to their neighbors, and both birds called back to the newcomer. Across the river, a pine branch bounced upwards as a big owl lifted off and flew up to Big Eddy. It landed closer to the slow water and called out again. "Hooo-Hoo-Hoo-Hoo-Hooo." Bridger responded in kind once more before he entered the tent and zipped the door shut. The thin, crescent moon with the aid of Central Oregon's brilliant night sky slightly lit up the tent's interior. In the dim light, the young college student took off his clothes and joined Rachael under the top bag. Their body warmth created a cozy thermal nest and they hugged each other. Bridger gently rolled Rachael onto her back and then slowly lowered himself down on top of her.

"Oh my, you are a man of steel, Sir Knight."

"Yes, my lady. I paced myself tonight, and reserved my strength just for this moment."

Rachael moaned softly, and pulled Bridger tightly to her.

Down below the small backpacking tent, next to the Metolius River, large padded, four-toed feet left tracks in the soft, moist dirt next to the river. A long tail swished back and forth behind the big cat as it walked along. It stopped at Big Eddy and, lowering itself next to the river, lapped up water. Satisfied, the mountain lion raised itself into a sitting position, and two, yellow eyes raised up for a moment, viewing the orange tent perched high above on the basaltic rim. Turning gracefully, the cat proceeded down the river. Her shoulders rhythmically rose and fell with each step. She stopped once more and raised her head again so she could view the small tent. A low, rumbling growl emerged from the cat's throat. Her warning was silently absorbed by the river's many voices. Then, soundlessly, she turned forward, and walking around the lower bend of the eddy was lost from sight.

CHAPTER 31

THE ONLY ELECTRIC CAR OWNED BY A CAMP Sherman resident quietly stopped at the three-way. Turning right, it headed north on the west river road. Behind the wheel sat the Camp Sherman store owner, Jack Smith. Jack was trying to wake up as he drove by drinking a double shot, sixteen ounce mocha he just made moments before on his new coffee machine. Jack was thinking about the razzing he'd received from the local clientele about his espresso maker. Most of it was good natured, but a few people were truly insulted by the addition of the coffee bar in his store. They told him his parents would never have done that, and truthfully, Jack knew they were right. At the moment though, he was pretty satisfied with his new machine because the double shot was waking him up, which was just what the doctor ordered.

In the back seat was a broken-down St. Croix fly rod with Jack's old Cortland reel on it. This reel was loaded with a sinking tippet, and Jack was headed to the lower river for some nymph fishing. The only sound made by his car as he passed by a scruffy section of forest was the crunch of gravel, and this noise was not enough to roust the sleeping sentinel who rested a few feet away in a dense clump of juvenile trees adjacent to the road.

Jack's vehicle took a sharp right corner and headed directly for the Big Eddy Rise. A column of lazy smoke drifted upwards from the summit. Noticing this, the store owner stopped his car, stepped out of his rig for a better view, and acknowledged to the right of the summit, someone relieving himself. For a moment, their gazes interlocked. Jack watched as the man zipped up his pants and scurried back into the Rise's cone.

As Jack looked away from the summit, he noticed numerous oddities in the trees standing before him. Some conifers had small cables looping from them that ended at the top of Big Eddy Rise. Other Ponderosas, farther up the hill, had ropes hanging down to the ground from their lower branches. Jack walked up to the corner and stood on the road's edge. His new vantage point allowed him a better, more accurate visual. The trees with looping cables also had bundles secured partway up their trunks. The cables leaving these packages took several wraps around nearby branches and then stretched back up the hill. The other trees appeared to have some kind of platform up in their canopies, next to where the ropes were attached.

This all appeared pretty odd to Jack. He had never seen anything quite like this before. Smoke drifting up from the hill's top, suggesting a recent fire, was his major concern. There was a complete fire ban in the Deschutes National Forest because of the tinder dry, late summer conditions. You couldn't even have fires in designated fire pits. Jack also thought camping was relegated only to campgrounds, now. The store owner viewed his watch. It was 6:15 in the morning. He knew a phone call to the sheriff was in order, which required him to return to Camp Sherman. He'd use the store's landline to alert the sheriff, and would also call his friend Brian Larson, and inform him about the oddities he was now witnessing. Brian was the anchor for Channel 19's evening newscast. This was Bend's local TV station. Brian lived in Sisters and might be interested in seeing what he was regarding.

Jack walked back to his vehicle, slipped into the driver's seat, and pushed the ignition button. Nothing happened. He was used to this now. He'd owned the electric car for several months, but was just now becoming familiar with its nuances. The only noticeable change in the vehicle after starting it was the interior gauges all coming to life. Jack was still a little surprised when he pressed on the accelerator and the car began moving. He turned the vehicle around and headed back to the store. His downriver fishing trip would have to wait. Maybe he'd just roll some nymphs along the river bottom near his store. *What the hell did I actually see?* He'd know soon enough, but for now Jack could only speculate. Even in the silence of his electric car, the store owner was unaware of a loud alarm being created on top of Big Eddy as a cowbell was being beat enthusiastically by a tall, lanky, dreadlocked young man. Jack's discovery was the first glimpse of a well-planned act of civil disobedience that would eventually have serious local and national repercussions.

CHAPTER 32

THE LOUD CLANGING OF DREAD'S COWBELL AWOKE Rachael and Bridger from their slumber. The dim light of early morning allowed enough visibility to rise quickly and dress. They hastily threw on shorts, T-shirts, and, after feeling the cool morning air, hooded sweatshirts. They clambered over the crater's basaltic wall and stood near the eastern edge of the compound. Everybody in the bowl was in motion. Tree sitters were putting harnesses on and checking their climbing gear. Dread was affixing the blasting wires to the blasting box, and vocally checking on other Alliance members' activities. Another three Alliance members appeared to be filling backpacks with water and food, and lying next to them were piles of linked chain.

For the first time, Bridger and Rachael felt like they didn't belong. The developing scene was totally alien. Hang and Tunes hurried over to join them, and the foursome greeted each other and then continued watching the choreographed movement.

Dread addressed the group from atop the southern rim of the crater. "I'm expecting guests at any moment. About twenty minutes ago a car stopped, the driver got out, and he surveyed our handiwork. Then he drove back toward Camp Sherman. It's only a matter of time before the cops arrive."

As the lanky college student talked to the Alliance members, Sasha joined the 11th Streeters. She hugged each of the Camp Dogs, and then taking a step backwards, spoke to them. "Thanks so much for your help. You made everything so easy for us."

She looked down at the road and then back to them. "Now is the time for you to leave. If you hurry, no one will ever know you were here."

Tunes didn't hesitate, quickly responding, "I'm staying. What can I do?" The other Camp Dogs all observed Tunes and then each other. No words were spoken.

Rachael faced Sasha and replied next. "We're all staying. Tell us how we can help."

The pretty activist wiped tears off of her cheeks and grabbed Hang and Tunes by their arms. She took a few steps backwards and pulled them with her. Stopping, she pointed to a STRONG member who was creating a pile of gear. He wore a red T-shirt, drawstring peasant pants, and his blond hair was in a man bun. "Hang and Tunes, your man is Runner. He's in the red T-shirt. Go over to him and he'll tell you what to do."

Next, Sasha took Bridger and Rachael over to another Alliance member, who was stuffing a backpack with food. "Arrow, these two wonderful Camp Dogs will help you." She examined her new helpers one more time. "You're now part of my support group. We're a team, and we work as one. Arrow will tell you what to do."

Sasha hugged Rachael and Bridger one more time before she left and returned to her climbing gear. She hoisted her pack onto her shoulders, picked up her helmet, glasses, and gloves, and disappeared over the crater's rocky rim.

Arrow viewed his helpers. "We've got to hurry. Everybody needs to be at their trees before the cops arrive. Bridger, grab the chain. Rachael, grab that pack." He pointed to a bulging daypack. "Okay, follow me."

Arrow scampered over the rim with the Camp Dogs right behind. They headed for the tree Sasha was now standing next to. As the threesome hurried down the slope, each of their steps produced a little cloud of dust, and by the time they reached their climber, the dust covered their feet, ankles, and lower calves.

Bridger glanced over at the other Camp Dogs, who were with Runner. Tom Weber was their climber, and Bridger noticed he was already ascending the tree. Again, the inchworm movement occurred. One leg extension, then a pause with hands moving upward. Then a pulling motion, using arm strength to raise him a little more. Then another leg extension pushed Tom higher, followed again by the pause and the pulling motion. He was moving upward about two feet with each cycle. Looking past Tom, Bridger saw another group with a climber in motion. He viewed Sasha again. She had attached something to her foot. Above her head, a metal, two-handled device was secured to the rope. At head height, a small rope was attached to another old-looking metal piece. Bridger, recalling his conversation with Hang the night before, viewed Sasha's climbing hardware more closely.

"Hey, Arrow, what are these metal gadgets I'm seeing?" Bridger pointed to the climbing gear. As Arrow explained the gear functions, Sasha climbed up the rope, mimicking Tom Weber's technique. Rachael and Bridger leaned backwards, tilted their heads, and watched her slowly rise up to the tree's lowest branches. The climbing rope dangled beneath her. Arrow held it in one hand, keeping it slightly taut. He looked at Rachael, and pointed to the mound of shiny chain next to her.

"Could you circle the tree with the chain, and unlock the combo lock? The number sequence is scratched on the back. Just add one to the second digit of each number pair." The young militant smiled. "Pretty tricky, huh?"

Rachael ringed the tree with the chain and returned to where the others stood. They all watched the rope being pulled upwards. Looking up, the trio saw Sasha peering over the side of her hammock and retrieving her climbing rope.

Arrow called out, "Do you need anything?"

"Yep. A sixteen ounce, double shot cappuccino would be great."

Her humor allowed the three to laugh and release some built-up tension.

"Coming right up, boss. Oh shit, Sasha. I left the espresso machine at home."

All four young people laughed again.

"You good, anyway?"

"I am. Do your thing down there."

The ground crew leader observed his team. "All right, students. Here's the drill. If the bad guys are here, we all chain ourselves to the tree. Here's how you chain yourself up."

He made a loop of chain on the ground and stepped into the middle. He then bent down, pulled the loop up to his waist, and holding it in place, sat down.

"Voilà!"

"Well done, Arrow. You made it seem easy."

"The trick is getting us all chained up next to each other."

Arrow stood up, dropped the chain, and stepped out of the loop. He then made three consecutive loops on the ground. "Care to join me?"

Rachael answered, "Why of course."

Arrow stepped into his circle, Rachael followed, and Bridger took the last ring. They all reached down simultaneously and pulled the chain up to waist height. With some wiggling and squirming, the chain tightened up around them, and then they simultaneously sat down together. Arrow exclaimed, "Beautifully done, team. I'm a lucky boy with you two at my side. One last thing. In this position, Bridger, you'll have to reach over, pull the chain taut, and padlock us in place."

"Got it, Captain."

The threesome reversed the procedure and freed themselves of the chain. Arrow spoke again to the Camp Dogs. "The tree sitters are our lookouts. They'll tell us when the cops are coming." Picking up his backpack, Arrow leaned it against their tree. Continuing, he said, "It's loaded with food and water. Also, there are light blankets in there, a tarp, some headlamps, playing cards, and some books and magazines. Now here's the bottom line. When Sasha alerts us, we chain up. Dread has a bullhorn up there, and he'll give us instructions. We basically sit on our rears until Dread tells us differently."

As if on cue, Sasha called out, "Here come the bad guys, people."

A metallic, echo-like squeak reached them from above, and the Alliance leader's mechanized voice called out to them. "Chain up everyone."

Sasha's support team chained up and sat down at the base of their tree. They leaned back and felt the strength of their host. Rachael closed her eyes and imagined the big tree's power flowing into her. She reached out simultaneously for Bridger and Arrow's hands. All three young people sat, holding hands, and watched a dust cloud moving in their direction.. As the cloud grew nearer, they could see a mini caravan was creating the swirl of dust. The sound of gravel crunching beneath moving tires reached them. The vehicle procession began to slow and then stopped about forty yards from them. The dust began to slowly settle, revealing the cars that created the disturbance. Rachael squeezed her compadres' hands and thought to herself, *nope, this isn't just a simple little camping trip.*

CHAPTER 33

Brian Larson received an interesting phone call at 6:30 a.m. from his friend, Jack Smith, who suggested he visit the Big Eddy Rise as soon as possible. Jack's message was somewhat cryptic because he wasn't sure exactly what he'd witnessed, but the store owner was certain it was illegal, and a big news story was probably waiting to be sniffed out. Brian loved how Jack got dramatic, but he was a little skeptical of his tale. Ropes dangling from tree branches aroused the news anchor's curiosity, though, so he called Cassie Williamson, his co-anchor/weather reporter, and convinced her a drive out to Camp Sherman could provide newsworthy material. Cassie lived in Sisters, not too far from Brian's house. It took him only a few minutes to drive over to her place. She saw Brian arrive and left the house before his Subaru Forester came to a stop by her mailbox.

Cassie opened the passenger door and called out "shotgun" before seating herself in the vacant front seat. Brian glanced over at his co-worker, smiled, and handed her a thermos cup of coffee he had brewed for her. He knew she liked her coffee strong with cream added to it.

"Here you go, partner. Thanks for coming along on this early morning jaunt. I hope we can find some news at the end of the trail."

"Me too, although I'm not sure if I'll be fully awake at the end of the trail. This coffee should help, though. Thanks."

She lightly patted Brian's driving arm in a friendly manner. Brian regarded Cassie and, raising his eyebrows, smiled at her.

Cassie was one of the reasons Brian loved his job. She had a very friendly, casual manner about her, and luckily for him, Cassie had a dedicated work ethic; no task was too small or too daunting for her. She had an Asian mom and an Anglo father who had served in the U.S. military. Cassie was smart, humorous, and attractive too. She was tall with a slender, hourglass figure. Dark hair surrounded her high cheekbones and beautiful dark eyes. When she smiled and laughed, she engaged anybody who was close at hand.

The Subaru continued west. The two reporters rode in silence, drinking their coffee and slowly waking up. Cassie studied Brian, who was now glancing at his phone, checking out news reports from yesterday, and driving with one hand. His coffee rested in the cup holder between their seats. She had a crush on her co-anchor, but did not divulge this to him. He'd just recently divorced and was not looking around yet; Cassie respected this. She would know when his mood changed and make herself available then. This guy was special, and Cassie didn't want to be just the rebound girl. She hoped for something more significant than just a quick fling or one night stand.

Brian was thirty years old and worked out regularly. He was about six feet tall, a few inches taller than herself, which she liked. They looked good together when they stood side by side in front of the camera. Brian had thick blond, somewhat wavy hair worn pulled back in a short ponytail. When he donned a hat, he would often untie his hair and tuck it behind his ears. His facial features came right out of "Portrait 101." Everything fit together nicely. He was more pleasant to observe than ruggedly handsome. His eyes were bluish gray. His nose was straight but not sharp and his chin had a squareish look, but avoided a chiseled appearance. Brian turned the Subaru off of Highway 20 and headed directly to Camp Sherman.

"What intrigued you so much about Jack's call?" Cassie checked her wrist watch and noted it was 7:15. "We don't normally go out on dates this early."

Brian peeked at Cassie and grinned. "We should. You look great in the morning. Do you just wake up looking good like this every day?"

Cassie laughed. "You're sure easy to please. No, seriously, Brian. What's up?"

"Well, the thing which really interested me was the ropes Jack mentioned. He said there were several ropes dangling down to the ground from some of the big trees' upper branches, and he mentioned some ropes running from a few big pines up to the summit of Big Eddy Rise."

"That does sound weird. Maybe we've got some tree climbing going on in our forest."

Brian thoughtfully considered Cassie. "Could be. I've never seen anybody scale a tree using ropes. This could be interesting. Anyway, we'll know pretty soon what's happening."

As Brian stopped his rig at the three-way, he noticed a cloud of dust settling out on the road ahead of him.

"Looks like we've got company this morning."

He passed through the intersection and eventually caught up to the churning ball of dust. Brian eased the car back just a little to lessen the dust's effects.

Occasionally, through the light brownish cloud, he glimpsed a white truck with Stihl chainsaws, bars down, racked along both sides of its bed. There must have been eight saws of varying bar lengths, with two saws really standing tall. Brian knew this rig. It belonged to his softball/VFW buddy, Dennis Stafford.

"I wonder why Dennis is driving his crummy out here at this hour. He's got some salvage logging going on right now, but nothing else."

Like any good newsman, Brian kept abreast of local happenings. Not much was missed by him.

Cassie responded, "I think we'll find out pretty soon. Dennis's brakes lights are glowing red."

Brian slowed his Subaru to match Dennis's speed, and eventually the two rigs came to a stop, one right behind the other.

The windless early morning caused the dust to slowly settle, and as it did, normal visibility returned. Brian and Cassie stepped out of their car, closed the doors, and peered forward.

"Holy shit! What's going on here?"

In front of the crummy were two parked cop cars: an OSP Charger was sitting behind a Jefferson County Sheriff's rig. The all-white Ford F-150 with its Sheriff insignia on the doors sat quietly in front of the caravan. No one other than the reporters exited their rigs.

"Grab the mic, Cassie. Is your phone completely charged?"

The young reporter opened the rear door of the Subaru and picked up the station's microphone. She also checked the battery level on her phone. As she did this, Brian also checked his.

"I'm in the nineties."

"Good, so am I."

Cassie walked around the car and handed her co-anchor the mic.

"Okay, partner, let's find out what's happening here." They both walked toward the other vehicles.

As they approached the crummy, all the truck's doors opened, and the logging crew got out. They peered up at the Big Eddy Rise hillside. A chorus of "boos" drifted down to them followed by a rhythmic chant: "Stop the greed. Save the trees. Stop the greed. Save the trees."

The chant continued for several rounds, then ended. More booing followed. Soon, drum beats started drifting down from above. One of the younger loggers eyeballed the others and asked, jokingly, if anyone wanted to dance. He didn't get any takers.

Dennis saw the reporters, and the threesome merged.

"Hey, it's my first baseman."

Dennis Johnson reached out his hand to Brian and Cassie in a friendly greeting. The logger glanced over at the police cars that now had officers stepping out of them.

"I believe we've got an impromptu softball practice about to start, or possibly, an AFW picnic is getting under way. Did you bring a side dish, Brian?"

"Nope. I'm totally out of the loop on this one," Brian said with a smile and then added, "Do you know what is going on?"

Dennis scanned up the hill at the groups of young people sitting at the base of several trees. A few of the sitters were creating the drum rhythm they heard. Then he observed the hammocked tree sitters, one of whom was also drumming. He turned back to the reporters.

"I believe we're looking at a 'stoppage of work order' for me."

"You have a logging show right here?"

"Yep. I own all these big trees." He gestured at the big Ponderosas.

"Really?"

"Yep, really, but it doesn't seem like I'm going to be cutting any trees down in the near future."

Brian and Cassie stared up at the occupiers. Brian thought about the region's local history, and knew a "first" was happening right here, right now.

Brian ventured, "Dennis, has this ever happened in Central Oregon before?"

"No, I can't remember anything like this," Dennis responded.

"Me neither."

Deputy Sheriff Johnny Edwards and State Trooper Alec Mills joined the threesome. Johnny was a redheaded, light-complexioned, freckle-faced, thirty-year-old who looked like he just turned eighteen. His trim, youthful body had added a few extra pounds after college and he now displayed a soft late-twenties appearance. The deputy was in summer attire. A short-sleeved shirt rested beneath his vest, and a white straw cowboy hat was perched on his head. The Jefferson County Sheriff badge logo adorned both of his shoulders as well as his truck. OSP Trooper Alec Mills, on the other hand, was still a gym enthusiast and his appearance showed it. Dark hair, dark eyes, and a dark 24-hour stubble were his trademarks. He managed to keep off the fat and maintain a youthful body by working out. Completing the package, a broad shouldered upper torso and narrow waist were followed by two strong legs. He was also in a short-sleeved uniform. His shirt and vest were blue and he wore his State Trooper's Mountie-style hat. The two officers approached their friends.

Trooper Mills spoke first as he greeted the small group. "Is this a private AFW meeting I've stumbled into?"

Brian responded first, "Dennis and I were just discussing possible reasons for our meeting, and were hoping you could shed some light on what's going on."

Johnny joined into the conversation and with a smile said, "I'm afraid this isn't an AFW meeting, my friends."

All of the men standing in the small circle were members of Bend's AFW post. Johnny and Alec had been regular Army, while Dennis and Brian were in the National Guard. All four men served in Iraq, and Alec also had completed one tour of duty in Afghanistan. The young men knew each other very well.

Brian spoke to the officers. "Well, gentlemen, what do we have here?"

Trooper Mills turned and gazed up the hill, then returned his attention to the group.

"I think it's pretty straightforward, Brian. This appears to be an act of civil disobedience and Dennis, I bet you're the cause of all this ruckus."

The logger laughed. "You're probably right, trooper. You know me; my middle name is 'ruckus.'"

Everybody present grinned at the response. Dennis's logging crew had gravitated back to the crummy. They'd fetched thermoses and sandwiches from the cab and now, most were sitting on the lowered tailgate, drinking coffee, talking, and eating their sandwiches.

The young logger who earlier asked for a dancing partner walked up to the road's edge right in front of the Big Eddy Rise, and was taking pictures with his cellphone. He was ignoring the boos directed his way. The logger took a step off the road, trying to get closer for a better shot. From the hill's summit a screeching, metallic sound issued forth as the bullhorn was turned on.

Dread's amplified voice reached the road. "Not one step further, brother. This land is under the protection of the STRONG Alliance and you are trespassing. Step back onto the road."

The young logger hesitated and looked back to the officers. Johnny waved him back and verbally told him to get back to the crummy. Alec and Johnny's demeanor immediately changed, and the two officers excused themselves.

Alec said, "For right now, I'd like all of you to stay back here by the crummy. I'm not sure where this is going. Brian, don't try any reporting until I give you the 'okay.'"

"I hear you, trooper. Good luck."

Brian observed the automatics holstered on his friends' hips. Both wore 40-caliber Glock pistols. On each gun, the hammer was in the firing position, held in place by a leather strap that could easily be unsnapped. Johnny's hand came down to his pistol and felt for the strap and hammer. Reassured his piece was ready, if needed, he moved his hand out away from his gun. Trooper Mills paused at his cruiser, and reached in through his open window, removing some binoculars from the dash. He and Deputy Edwards both moved to the sharp bend in the road and stayed on the roadway. Alec viewed the scene through his glasses.

"I don't see any guns, but look at those closest pines. The ones with the wires looping from them up to the summit."

He handed the glasses to Johnny. The Alliance was showering the officers with boos, and the drumming started up once again. Now the "Greed" chant was syncopated with the African drumming.

Johnny took the glasses away from his eyes. "Looks like dynamite bundles."

"Yeah, I thought so, too."

Dread was watching the officers through his own binos and could tell they'd found his insurance policy.

The screech once again rang out. "That's right, gentlemen. If anyone sets foot onto our property, one of those trees will be chopped in half by an explosion, and the top portion will come falling down onto the road."

As the Alliance leader spoke, he held up the blasting box, which at the moment had all three wires attached to it. Officer Mills looked at his friend, Deputy Sheriff Edwards, and then back up the hill. He cupped his hands around his mouth and shouted up to the young activist, "If you and your associates voluntarily leave this site, now, the charges against you will probably be minimal. If we have to arrest you, the DA will seek much harsher indictments."

Dread miced the bullhorn again. "The only way we'll leave this site is when our demands are met."

Trooper Mills glanced over at Deputy Edwards and grinned. "Now we're getting somewhere. Don't you agree, deputy?"

Edwards laughed, removed his hat, and dried his forehead with a bandana he had just retrieved from his back pocket.

Replacing his hat, the deputy quietly said, "Your negotiating skills are textbook. I'm expecting a positive, quick cessation of these illegal activities at any moment."

The two law officers smiled at each other. Then Trooper Mills gazed back at Dread. "What would your requests be?"

The young activist pointed his bullhorn down the hill at the officers, and detailed the Alliance's demands. "We need a legal document, signed by the Deschutes National Forest Director, the Governor of Oregon, the Superintendent of the Oregon State Police, and the Jefferson County Sheriff stating the forest surrounding us will not be logged. Pretty simple, officer. All the Alliance needs is the termination of this logging effort, and we'll peacefully leave this site."

Officer Mills glanced at his friend. "Well, do you want to drive out to the highway and contact dispatch, or do I get to?"

"You go ahead. I'll hold down the fort. Looks like we've got some serious young people here." Deputy Edwards thought for a moment and then continued. "You know, we'll need to blockade the road. Maybe down by the bridge turnout, and about ten yards back from here. Pass that on to my office. Technically, I'm in charge right now. The sheriff's down in Las Vegas for his annual convention. Have Rose send a deputy out here with the barricades and have her call in another deputy for an extra shift so patrols are covered."

"Okay, Johnny. You're beginning to sound like the next sheriff of Jefferson County." Both friends laughed at this.

Trooper Mills shouted up to Dread one last time before he departed. "I'm going to pass on your request, young man."

Alec thought to himself and then spoke again, "I'm Officer Mills; who am I speaking with?"

The leader responded, "My friends call me Dread, Officer Mills."

"All right, Dread. When I return, I'll have some information for you from my supervisor." The two law officers returned to their vehicles. Dennis Stafford approached them and stood with his friends.

"Well, Dennis, I think your work here is done for the day. It's a little too dangerous for you and the crew to stay around, so I'm asking you to officially leave. Sorry, but the logging is the issue here, and your presence might set something off."

"I totally understand, Alec. You know I was up all last night because our youngest had the stomach flu. At dawn, she finally fell asleep. Then, when I got out to the crummy, it had a flat tire, and now this."

Johnny regarded Dennis. "I'd say, strike three, you're out, big fella."

All three friends laughed, glanced at the ground, and shook their heads slightly in disbelief. Regaining eye contact, Dennis continued. "Yeah, you're right. Well, officers, good luck with this mess. Let's keep in touch."

"Certainly. Oh yeah, how's Suzy doing?"

"Really well. She's not sick anymore and hell, she got to sleep in this morning. I should have, too. See you later, gentlemen; it's time to get the boys back to Sisters."

He turned and walked back to his rig. The big diesel engine came to life and, with a few back and forth movements, turned itself around, but instead of moving forward though, the crummy backed up to Alec and Johnny. The crew cab's window slid down and Dennis smiled at the officers.

"The boys want to say good-bye to the tree huggers."

Dennis winked and backed his vehicle up to the bend. All the windows rolled down in the truck as it stopped, and four arms extended out and upwards with middle finger salutes for the occupiers. The Dodge's horn honked several times, and then the truck drove slowly away. A series of boos followed the rig as it left.

Alec and Johnny regarded each other, and Deputy Edwards spoke. "Is this going to be fun?"

"Probably not fun, deputy. Interesting and trying are words which readily come to mind. I hope unexpected and dangerous are not adjectives that will later describe this scene. Anyway, I'm off. I'll talk to your dispatcher before I call mine."

"Thanks."

"Certainly, boss. Adios."

Trooper Mills turned his rig around and headed for Highway 20. He waved at Brian and Cassie as he passed them. Alec thought to himself as he came to the three-way stop, *what will Salem think of this mess?* Well, he'd soon know.

Dennis Stafford sipped some coffee out of a thermos cup as he headed for Highway 20. *What had Dad said? "If things appeared to be too good..."* Well here is another situation supporting his belief. Dennis decided to call his mom and put the Seneca rebooting on hold. He grabbed his phone and punched in her number.

CHAPTER 34

Brian and Cassie noticed the sun's midmorning brilliance. It was warming up. Both reporters shed their sweatshirts and walked up to the deputy.

"We'd like to get an exclusive, Johnny. Do you mind if we try?"

"No, no, go ahead, but you know, if they say 'No thanks,' just let it go. Don't try and manipulate them into anything. If they talk with you, and you sense them getting agitated, just excuse yourselves, and get away. This is serious. I don't want you getting hurt."

Both reporters nodded their heads, showing their understanding of the situation. Brian looked at his co-anchor. "Are you ready, partner?"

"Certainly am. Got all our technical gear right here." Cassie held up her phone and the fake mic. "Let's get this interview done and canned."

They both walked up to the road's edge and Brian hollered up to Dread. "We're reporters from Bend's local station. Could we interview you about the STRONG Alliance and your goals?"

Dread was prepared for reporters, and the whole Alliance group knew what to say and, more importantly, what not to say.

He keyed his bullhorn again. "Certainly, but your reporting needs to be accurate or this will be our last discussion."

Arrow, Rachael, and Bridger relaxed and let go of each other's hands. The temperature was rising, and they'd all started to sweat. Arrow called up to Sasha, asking her how she was. She answered back that she was beginning to melt, but was staying hydrated and liberally applying the sunscreen. The ground crew started drinking water, too, and began sharing an apple. A scrub jay noticed this and was hopping closer and closer to the trio. Bridger was saving some apple for their visitor.

Dread called down. "Runner, would you meet the reporters and take care of our commitment to our fans?" Most of the Alliance members smiled at his humor. Runner unhooked the chain and stood up.

"Hook things back up, Hang. Duty calls."

He shifted his weight from foot to foot, waiting for the circulation to come back, and waved for the reporters to come up the hill and meet him. He moved over to the middle of the ridge and waited. The interviewers joined him and all three shook hands.

"I'm Brian Larson, news anchor for Channel 19, Bend, Oregon and this is Cassie Williamson, my co-anchor. We'd like to ask you a few questions." He reached over, took the prop mic from Cassie, and smiled at Runner. "We're a low budget station."

He pointed to his partner's phone and continued. "We'll get all this on Cassie's phone, and just pretend with the mic, but I assure you this is all serious and legit. We have a strong local following and your message, our interview, will be picked up by bigger stations. It may even make national news tonight. We're a sister station to national cable channel WNN."

Deputy Edwards was getting warm and thinking about moving out of the sun. He'd have to send for camp chairs and shade awnings. He watched his friends interview the occupier. They talked for about ten minutes. Then the reporters shook the young man's hand and returned down the hill. Runner walked up the hill and began talking to Dread. Edwards walked to Cassie and Brian, and standing in the gravel road, the three spoke to each other.

"We can't really talk here, Johnny. I don't want the Alliance to think we're best of friends."

Edwards responded, "I totally understand. Hey, do you have some extra water? I forgot to bring some with me."

"You bet. We'll give you what we've got. Well, I hate to leave you by your lonesome, but we need to get to the station. Adios, deputy."

"Bye, amigos, nice knowing you."

Cassie walked back to the Subaru and grabbed the two waters they had and returned, giving both to Deputy Edwards.

"Bye, Johnny."

"See you, Cassie. Thanks for the water."

The two reporters hopped in the Subaru, buckled up, and turned around. "This is big, Cassie, really big." Brian could hardly contain himself. "A real, serious, work-stopping, tree sit-in. With dynamite. Oh my God! This has never happened out here before. I mean, down in the Redwoods, yeah. But not here."

His partner put her hand on Brian's arm. "Whoa, big fella, settle down. No cardiac arrests before the station's parking lot, okay? Breathe slowly now. In one, two, three, four. Out one, two, three, four. In one, two, three, four. Come on, big boy, you can do this."

The young news anchor reached for his phone. He needed to call Channel 19 news' two other employees, the director and camera man, plus give the owner/producer and sometimes director a call, too. Everyone would need to meet at the station to discuss how to deal with this story. Technically, Brian was just the station's news anchor, but in reality, all of Channel 19 followed his cues and trusted his news sense. Even the owner followed his anchor's lead and deferred to his judgments. The Subaru passed through Sisters and continued on to Bend. Cassie checked her watch. It was straight up noon. She'd already put in six hours, and for nutrients she'd consumed one coffee. Hopefully, they'd stop for a bite to eat before returning to the station. Cassie thought about the occupation site they'd just left. This news was going to shake things up considerably around here. *Hold onto your hat, Central Oregon. This is going to be a wild ride!*

Deputy Edwards found some shade and was sitting on a rock under a big pine, sipping on a water bottle while peering up at Big Eddy Rise. Dread called down to his Alliance members, and three young people joined him at the summit. The seasoned deputy mused about the situation. *How long is this going to last? Could it get any hotter out here?* Johnny laughed at this thought. *Yes, it's going to get hotter.* Two ravens lit in the tree above the redheaded peace officer. They called out their arrival and cleaned their beaks on the branch they landed on. Looking up the hill, they noticed some activity and decided to investigate further. The birds jumped off their perch, showering the deputy with brown, dead pine needles, and flew up the hill. Brushing off needles from his uniform, Deputy Edwards watched them alight in a tree next to the summit. Once again, they announced their arrival and began cleaning their beaks.

CHAPTER 35

Woody and Karen Thompson were sitting outside on the deck in their comfortable, cedar Adirondack chairs enjoying a beautiful sun-drenched late afternoon. The wooden porch had a southwest exposure, and its thermometer read 81 degrees. The canopied portion of the deck containing their picnic table and barbecue was beginning to look inviting to them, but their desire to soak up the last remaining rays of the day prevented them from moving.

Karen glanced over at Woody, who was watching the backyard bird feeders with binoculars. The feeders hosted some evening grosbeaks and a couple purple finches; an acorn woodpecker would occasionally rock the boat as it alighted and pecked away at the suet. The yellow of the male grosbeak, mixed with the purples from the finches, provided a colorful moving canvas for the Thompsons' enjoyment. The stark black and white of the woodpecker only heightened the beautiful hues, making the scene even more entertaining. As she gazed at her husband, Karen was pleased. After so many years, he still was active and regularly exercised. He wore a broad brim tightly woven straw hat, a lightweight, light-colored long-sleeved shirt, shorts, and sandals. Woody's hair was long. In its present ponytail, it reached down past his shoulders. He was big boned with an able-bodied physique. Broad shoulders were followed by a narrow waist that was complemented by strong, nicely proportioned thighs and calves. He regularly fought off the extra pounds, but like most people his age, he had lost some ground over the years. Karen thought he was probably fifteen pounds heavier now than when they'd first met. His slightly receding hairline was hidden by his hat. Woody's rimless glasses rested on a straight nose above a full mustache. The years had created slight jowls that rounded over his small chin. His mustache mostly hid the jowls, which he secretly appreciated. Woody enjoyed smiling and laughing, and those actions had etched numerous lines onto his face.

Karen herself was much like Woody in her body's transition. She also had gained about fifteen pounds over the years. She was big boned and strong for a five foot, one inch woman. Karen wore her wavy brown hair in a shoulder length cut, which allowed her to occasionally enjoy pulling it back into a ponytail. She had a small mouth beneath a straight nose. Her brown eyes were surrounded by laugh lines, which she enjoyed defining as often as possible. Both Woody and Karen were watching the birds gorge themselves at the feeder and were trying to convince each other about who filled the bird feeder last. Due to a keener memory, Karen had the upper hand, which totally rebuffed Woody's inane, defenseless comments.

Sitting on the barbecue's small end counter was a plate holding several chicken and prawn kabobs Woody had put together for their dinner. Both the bird watchers were waiting for their hunger to develop before firing up the gas grill. The slider was open to the couple's TV room and Woody noticed the national news had just begun. The Thompsons were watching more news of late due to the nation's new president, whom neither of them liked or trusted. To them, he appeared to be like a loose cannon bent on destroying the many positive, recent achievements gained by the previous administration. They had become addicted to watching this new president, as so many Americans had, and tonight was no different than any other. They left their sunny perches and moved into the TV room, sitting down in front of their flatscreen. Allen Rodrigues, their favorite news anchor, was greeting his viewing audience. WNN, a national cable station, provided the Thompsons with the kind of news they could appreciate. It was strong on politics, human interest, and environmental reporting. This format was just what they liked to watch. Allen Rodrigues was talking, and the camera showed the news desk and his upper torso.

"We've got White House news tonight that reaches across the country and changes the playing field for the western states' timber industry. President McDonald signed an Executive Order yesterday suspending all federal logging regulations in our National Forests. How this will eventually change logging is vague, and what regulations have actually been affected is unclear. For instance, does the Endangered Species Act fall within the jurisdiction of this decree? At any rate, this is an unprecedented move which has many industry leaders excited about the possibilities."

At this point WNN switched to a feed showing a Boise-Cascade CEO being interviewed about the decree.

Woody regarded Karen and exclaimed, "This is total insanity. It's total bullshit, Karen. All this means is there'll be more and more logging done in old growth stands. I can't believe this."

Karen reached over to Woody's arm and patted it lightly. "Steady, there. It just sounds like another presidential decree the courts will strike down."

A commercial break allowed Woody to light the barbecue and start warming it up.

As he sat back down, Allen Rodrigues said, "We have more related stories that may depict where Western logging could be headed. A recently appointed federal judge from the Ninth Circuit Court of Appeals in San Francisco just struck down several lawsuits filed by environmental groups regarding a timber sale in Central Oregon. Citing the presidential decree, Judge Olson stated there were no grounds for the suits and consequently, the litigation lacked validity."

WNN again switched to a feed showing an interview with a Northwest representative of the Sierra Club, whose organization was one of the petitioners the court had ruled against.

Karen stared at Woody grimly. "Well, it looks like McDonald has done it again by creating a new front for people to battle over. He's amazing."

Woody went outside and placed the kabobs on the grill. He turned the burners down and returned to his chair next to Karen's.

"This really pisses me off. These battles have all been fought before and put to rest thirty-plus years ago. Now he's going to start everything up again."

The commercials ended and WNN's cameras moved back, once again showing all of Allen's desk and his backdrops.

"Another related story comes to you from one of our sister stations. This one, Channel 19, is located in Bend, Oregon. Channel 19 news reporter and evening anchor Brian Larson had an exclusive interview with a group of young people who are stopping a logging operation near Camp Sherman, Oregon, by occupying the site and refusing to leave. This is the same logging site that prompted the Sierra Club's suit, which today was struck down by the Ninth Circuit Court of Appeals."

Woody and Karen regarded each other in disbelief. They both loved the Camp Sherman area and the Metolius River that ran through it. They'd spent many days camped along the river's banks and underneath those beautiful old tree canopies.

"This cannot be happening!" exclaimed Woody.

Karen got up to check their dinner's progress. She turned the kabobs and basted them with olive oil. Returning, Karen saw two people standing in a Ponderosa forest on the TV screen. One person, the reporter, held a mic up to a young college student who stood somewhat uncomfortably in front of the camera.

He had been asked who their group was, and what their objectives were. Woody's eyes moved past the threesome to the forest's edge.

"Oh my God, Karen! It's Big Eddy Rise. I've been right where they are. I really don't believe this. Who would want to cut those trees down?"

Karen once again reached over to Woody's arm. This time she gently grasped his forearm and squeezed. "Relax, sweetheart. Something will stop this from happening. Actually, these kids are doing that, right now."

The young man standing next to the Channel 19 reporter began to talk. "We're the STRONG Alliance from Corvallis, Oregon. STRONG is an acronym for 'Save the Remaining Old Natural Growth," and we intend to do that. We'll occupy this site until we're assured by state officials the logging has been cancelled."

Brian spoke now facing Cassie's phone. "Some Alliance members are tree sitting in hammocks and others are chained to the base of several trees."

Cassie used the zoom on her phone for some close-ups of what Brian described. She chose the closest occupier's tree. This particular Ponderosa had only Alliance members protecting it. She then panned back to Brian, who asked the occupier about the danger of someone getting hurt here due to the presence of explosives.

"The dynamite we've positioned in several trees is meant to deter the logging activity, not hurt people. The Alliance feels very strongly these old growth trees must be allowed to live out their natural life cycle. There are plenty of second and third growth tree stands in Oregon which can be harvested. These old giants are not needed by the timber industry. The dynamite simply is an exclamation point our group is using to thwart this forest's destruction. We certainly don't wish to touch it off and most certainly do not intend to harm anyone. But, if we are not taken seriously, and someone attempts to force our removal before our demands are met, then they can expect an explosive situation."

"Thank you for your time and thoughtful answers." Brian turned to face his partner's phone, then, upon reflection, turned back to the Alliance member. "What's your name? I think our viewers would like to know."

Runner eyed Cassie's phone. His uneasiness had dissipated while talking to Brian. "My Alliance friends call me Freedom Runner, Runner for short."

"Well, thank you, Runner, for allowing us to interview you."

Cassie panned the area once ogain. This time she caught Dread at the summit holding up the blasting box. She slowly moved back to the original group of tree sitters. At that point, the feed was cut. Allen Rodrigues shifted his view away from the large paneled screen behind him and returned his gaze to the camera.

"Again, that was an interview from Camp Sherman, Oregon. This logging site occupation is still under way as I speak. One wonders if this kind of civil disobedience will become more common because of President McDonald's Executive

Order. After our break, we'll return with weather, and once again the West Coast has some startling news for us."

The Thompsons wanted to dine alfresco, so at this point they turned the TV off and went outside to the grill. Woody lifted the barbecue's cover and turned the kabobs. They seemed just right, so he removed them, placing the skewered entrees onto two ceramic plates.

"Come and get it."

He moved the plates onto their shaded patio table, where a green salad already waited. Karen spoke to him. "I'm fixing us some double vodka tonics, dear. I could use one after the dismal news we just heard. How about you?"

"Double my double."

"I think you might die from that, Woody. I refuse to assist in your suicide."

"Well right now I almost wish I was dead. Thank God for those college kids. They're showing some real balls, doing what they're doing. I hope their occupation works. You know, I should call Bridger up and ask him if he knows anything about those Alliance kids.

"Not now, let's have a drink and eat our dinner first."

They sat down under their patio's awning and dined. The kabobs were cooked just right and all the greens came from their garden. The feeders had shifted crews. Now a small flock of chickadees, nuthatches, and ruby crowned kinglets had taken over. These small birds flitted about nervously and were entertaining the Thompsons. A couple rufous sided hummingbirds joined the avian mix and were zooming around their own feeder. Occasionally, they aligned their feathers just right with the sun's rays, allowing the brilliant iridescence of their plumage to burst out. Woody was thinking about calling his old buddies, Hops and Doc, to see if they'd heard about the Metolius occupation. He'd do it right after speaking with Bridger. Woody hoped his grandson's acclimation to campus life was going well. *Heck, how could it not be?*

CHAPTER 36

THE FRONT DOOR SHUT BEHIND TARRI MCGRATH as she called out, "I'm home. Does anybody care?"

A voice responded from the living room. "No, but come on in anyway, and you'd better hurry because the Cassie/Brian show just hit the airways."

Tarri left her coat on a peg in the entrance hall, and as she walked to the commons room, her ponytail bounced and swayed behind her. She quickly found her overstuffed leather recliner, but before sitting down, she kissed her partner of ten years, Wendy, on the cheek and asked how her day went. Tarri got a "not now" look from Wendy, who was an avid fan of the Channel 19 evening news. She didn't want any trivial talk to interrupt her Cassie/Brian time. Wendy's no nonsense, response to Tarri encouraged a smile and laugh from the Sisters Ranger District's manager.

"Oops, didn't mean to break your concentration."

Wendy, hearing Tarri's quip, smiled and laughed also. "I'll tell you about my day after the news."

"Did I miss anything?"

"No, your timing was perfect, except for the 'How'd your day go' thing." The two women regarded each other with an affectionate, appreciative gaze, and then returned their attention to the flatscreen.

Brian Larson was reporting local news. Cassie Williamson sat to his left and helped his segment by offering applicable comments and sidebars about the news story as Brian reported it. If Cassie was reporting on a piece, the roles would reverse. The two co-anchors enjoyed playing off each other's dialogue. Brian had just finished detailing the occupation of Dennis's logging site by showing his personal interview with Runner. He glanced over at Cassie and continued.

"This kind of activism has never happened in Central Oregon before. The Oregon State students involved in the tree sit-in are dead serious about their demands. We'll need to follow this story very closely, Cassie."

She regarded him and smiled. "Oregon State, stepping up your game! Go Beavs!"

Brian laughed at this remark and shook his head. He returned his attention to the camera. "I'm sure we'll get a few calls from viewers about those thoughts, Cassie."

"That's great. Open dialogue is the foundation of our democracy. I'm glad Channel 19 can help promote the democratic process."

Wendy and Tarri liked Brian and Cassie's broadcast style. They appreciated the humor the two reporters injected into their shows, and the occasional departure from mainstream, journalistic professionalism didn't bother them at all. They appreciated the two young reporters' enthusiasm and their dedication to a newscast filled with Central Oregon content.

Channel 19 cut to a commercial segment, so Wendy got up and retrieved two Porters from the fridge. She returned to the TV, and handed Tarri one of the ales. Coinciding with the beer handoff, the Channel 19 news anchors reappeared on the screen. This time, the camera moved back, allowing for an expansive view of the studio. Cassie and Brian sat behind a large desk with straight lines and a glossy, reflective finish. Panels surrounded the desk, blocking the view of the anchors' legs. Both reporters appreciated this. They could sit, relaxed in their chairs, and not have to think about proper etiquette. Behind the co-anchors was a large, multi-screened board depicting familiar Central Oregon scenes. These pictures would periodically change during the newscast and, if possible, display an image that was pertinent to the news story. Three Sisters was currently displayed.

Brian observed his partner. "You've got some scary weather news for us, Cassie. What's going to happen?"

The camera backed out and followed Cassie as she stood and walked over to her green screen. Channel 19 had taken a feed from the National Weather Service and was going to run it. She stood before her weather board, which now just showed the state of Oregon.

"This is really incredible, Brian. We've had some strange weather in Oregon lately, but nothing like this."

"Central Oregon, batten down the hatches because we're going to get the mother of all storms hitting us in the next week."

The green screen came to life showing an enlarged view of North America. It depicted Canada, the United States, and Mexico, and the shot also extended out into the Pacific for a couple thousand miles. On the weather board, the jet stream motion was shown by moving arrows. Its upper flow came across the northern Pacific into the Gulf of Alaska, then, sitting off the coast about one thousand miles, it plunged south all the way to Central Mexico. At about Puerto Vallarta, the jet stream looped back north and passed just to the west of the Pacific Coast states. This was a huge, tight loop that rarely developed in the upper air current. At its upper extension, the arrows turned east and flowed across northern Canada. Sitting practically stationary, a large low hugged the Canada/U.S. border. Its air flow was counter-clockwise, and it was drawing warm, moist air up from the Gulf. What was alarming for Oregon and Washington was the high developing in central Mexico. It was predicted to move up the coast, slowly being pulled by the jet stream. Cassie's graphics showed the cyclone moving up the West Coast, eventually reaching Oregon and Washington's latitude. With the high located off the coast, and the much larger low in place inland, the two cyclones' wind patterns would merge together over Eastern Oregon and Washington. With this convergence, both systems' prevailing winds would be moving to the south. The Cascade Range to the west and the Rockies to the east would form a perfect funnel for the winds to shoot through and would amplify their force considerably. Cassie stood back from the board, allowing the viewers a full visual of the two rotating systems.

"You know, Brian, I'm not a meteorologist, but even I can see the severe storm that will be generated by this pattern."

Brian's tinny voice came from off camera. "Not a good thing to mention while doing your weather segment."

Cassie smiled at the camera and without missing a beat replied, "My bad, Brian. But you can see what I mean. The graphics are self-explanatory." The green screen shifted focus and depicted wind strength data, and the dark-haired weather reporter continued. "Here are the National Weather Service's predictions: Sustained winds of around 50 to 60 mph and gusts possibly reaching 75 mph. These levels are below hurricane strengths, but still can cause problems for us, like power outages and loss of property."

Cassie's board went back to the weather map portraying the high and low weather systems. She looked back to the camera. "It seems like Central Oregon can't catch a break right now. When we return, we will have more local news about potential earth-shaking problems."

Channel 19 went to commercial break, and Cassie rejoined Brian at the anchor desk.

"Thanks a lot, smart guy."

He began to laugh uncontrollably. His co-anchor gave away her true feelings by laughing, too.

"I couldn't help myself, Cassie. It was too perfect. I mean the weather lady flat out admitting she knows nothing about predicting the weather."

The young reporters laughed until tears ran down their cheeks. Cassie regained her composure first.

"Well, if you hadn't piped up, it could have passed right over some people's heads."

Brian deadpanned his next comment. "I don't think so."

This created another round of laughter.

"Hey you two, ten seconds!" Their camera director was counting down the seconds until live shooting. Brian quickly viewed his tablet to see what story followed. It was the geology piece he'd put together a few days earlier.

He got the "live" cue from the director and began. "A geologist from our local Bend OSU campus has informed Channel 19 that numerous quakes are occurring under Mt. Hood, and to a lesser extent, clusters of smaller tremors are happening beneath Mt. St. Helens, too. These quakes have been noted for a month by recording instruments OSU has placed on both mountains. What is interesting to the OSU scientists is the similarities between the Mt. Hood tremors and the quakes noted beneath Mt. St. Helens just prior to its eruption in 1980. Here is the interview Channel 19 had with Professor Anderson of the Bend campus."

As the interview was shown, Cassie and Brian observed each other and smiled. Brian spoke first, "Well, this show is almost a done deal. Good job tonight, partner. This was fun. Hey, I'm thinking about running out to the logging site tomorrow; want to come along?"

"Sure do. Wouldn't miss it for anything."

"Good. I'll pick you up around 8:00."

"Thank you, God. Our last date was really a bit too early."

Brian noticed the camera director counting down, and checked his tablet again. "Well, Central Oregon, our newscast is finished for tonight. My partner and I would like to thank you for tuning in, and we hope to see you tomorrow evening."

As the camera backed out, Cassie smiled and waved as Brian turned, facing her, and with audio off, asked what pizza they should order for the crew; this caused Cassie's smile to broaden even further.

Wendy and Tarri were still laughing and talking about Cassie's weather story when the show ended. After rehashing the scene, their talk turned to the impending storm. Wendy looked at Tarri.

"That's a pretty good blow coming our way."

"Yeah. Right before it hits, we should move the deck furniture into the garage, but you know, for the most part, we're pretty safe from windstorms. If we had some big trees close to us, I'd worry more, but we don't, so we'll be all right."

Wendy thought for a moment. "What about those tree sitters? I wonder what will happen to them."

"I don't know. I'm sure somebody will give them a heads-up. What a wild ride it would be, up in one of those giant old trees while it swayed back and forth in a big wind. This storm would certainly test your inner strength."

Tarri thought some more about the tree sitters and the coming storm. *Yeah, I'm sure somebody will give them a heads-up.*

CHAPTER 37

A BIG CROWN VIC PULLED IN BETWEEN TWO OTHer state vehicles and parked in its reserved space. The head cop of Oregon, State Police Superintendent Philip Ross, turned off the cruiser's engine, and leaving his trooper hat and sunglasses on, opened his door and stepped out of his car. Ross still drove the Ford Police Interceptor. He'd found one in mint condition and purchased it himself. The state repainted it for him at no cost, and the deep blue car with its stylish golden yellow stripes appeared brand new. Its big 250 horsepower V8 engine was powerful, and could get the heavy police car up to speed quickly. OSP had recently switched its fleet over to Dodge Chargers. They were fast and nimble, but lacked the street presence of the Crown Victoria. The superintendent parked at the Center Street lot. It was a short walk from there to the Capitol building, where he was to meet with the governor.

Philip Ross was 5' 9" tall and had a stout, strong physique. Broad-beamed would aptly describe his stature. His haircut was a military-style flat-top, matching his squareish head. He was clean shaven, had a pleasant smile, and when he donned his trooper's hat, he looked like the tough, professional officer that he was.

The superintendent was wearing his short-sleeve uniform shirt and was glad of it. The OSP uniform was dark and readily absorbed the sun's warmth. Today's heat required short sleeves and a wide-brimmed hat.

Ross quickly reached the Capitol and mounted the initial flight of steps, heading for the large, front doors. On the first landing, he stopped and gazed up. The huge marble-faced building was impressive. In the bright sunlight, the structure's sheen was almost blinding. Perched on top of the Capitol stood Oregon's Gilded Pioneer. Ross entered the building, glanced up at the beautiful murals, and took the right stairway up to the second floor. His meeting with the governor was in her working office, which sat behind her receiving room. He walked around the circular table in the outer room and through the large double-doored entrance into the governor's back room. The floor to ceiling wood-paneled walls subdued the light somewhat, but gave a rich feel to the room. The green patterned rug added to the earthiness and the wooden furniture furthered the ambiance. The governor, Sarah O'Connell, sat at an elongated table next to the fireplace. Sitting with her were Oregon's attorney general, Robert Smith, and the governor's chief of staff, Laura Roberts. They had all seated themselves at one end of the table and greeted Philip when he entered.

The OSP superintendent walked over to the trio. "Hello, governor, Laura, Robert. How are you?"

Ross extended his hand to the three officials and sat down next to Laura. She was a middle-aged native Oregonian who'd grown up in Portland. Laura was African American, with full bodied, wavy hair that extended to her shoulders. She wore a lightweight, cream-colored pantsuit to help mitigate the heat. Governor O'Connell was wearing a mid-calf skirt with a light yellow blouse that had an exaggerated collar and cuffs. Her brown hair was straight and cut in a chin-length bob. Her facial features were sharp, but pleasant. Attorney General Smith was wearing a short-sleeved light tan shirt with an orange tie held in place by an OSU Beaver clasp. He resembled a senior partner in a large law firm. His gray hair was parted on the side and closely trimmed. His hairline defied his age, remaining true to its youthful margins. All the sitting officials offered their greetings to Superintendent Ross. With the OSP boss present, the meeting commenced. Governor O'Connell spoke first.

"Well, superintendent, tell us about the logging site occupation. I watched the news last night and was dismayed by the report. What's really happening out by Camp Sherman?"

"Honestly, I don't know much more than you. I've talked with the trooper who made the initial contact with the occupiers. In a nutshell, they're an activist group from Oregon State who go by the moniker STRONG Alliance. They appear to be all college kids, and my trooper counted about twelve individuals. No guns were observed, but dynamite was placed on several trees close to the road. Their position is pretty straightforward: try to log the site and they blow up the trees. Several kids are sitting up in other trees, and more kids were chained to the bases of those same trees. They'll leave the site peacefully if we can guarantee no logging will occur there."

"Really, there's dynamite strapped to trees?" the governor asked.

"It appears so."

The governor regarded her attorney general. "Okay, Robert. What's your take on this?"

"Well, these activists are in serious legal trouble. Lots of felony issues here, unpermitted explosives in our forests being one of them. Blocking a legal workplace activity is another. If we dig further, I'm sure there'd be many more legal infractions."

Governor Sarah O'Connell thought to herself for a moment before asking no one in particular, "Where'd this logging activity originate? Forests like these have not been logged in Oregon for decades. What's changed?"

Attorney General Smith spoke again. "This is not state land, Sarah. This is National Forest, so it was, I believe, a Deschutes National Forest decision. Normally the feds communicate with us about their logging activities. They respect our rules and we observe theirs. None of our people heard anything about this logging sale. It pretty much came out of the blue. Apparently, something has changed."

Governor O'Connell's chief of staff entered into the conversation. "We know what happened, people. Our new president is what's changed. I'm sure you all saw or heard about his Executive Order, which basically shelved all logging regulations on federal lands. I don't think the feds care about our logging rules anymore."

Smith spoke to Roberts' statement. "You could be right, Laura. My office will need to make some phone calls and dig into this before anything can become clear."

The governor spoke again. "Okay, so what's the bottom line here? Who's now responsible for this mess?"

Smith responded. "Historically, the feds will not come in and police a problem within our borders, even if technically, it's on their lands. They expect us to take care of our own state."

"Okay, everyone. It's in our lap. So what should we do?"

Laura Roberts jumped back in. "I don't think we want to be the tough guys here and go in swinging. These are college kids, and even with dynamite, the public will see them as just young adults, not hardened militants bent on hurting others."

"Are you saying we should do nothing, Laura, so we don't appear to be bullies?" the governor asked.

"No, I'm not saying to do nothing, but I am saying we could look bad if we're too strong armed in our response."

Superintendent Ross had been listening, and now chose to reenter the conversation. "From a law enforcement perspective, we need to contain the situation. There should be 24/7 monitoring of the site. Roadblocks need to be set up and maintained to keep the public away from the dynamite. Dialogue needs to continue between us and the occupiers. You know, there's a practical side to the occupation resolution. If we keep the site contained, these kids will run out of food and water, and they'll have to quit their sit-in eventually, due to lack of sustenance."

The governor's chief of staff spoke again. "I think you're right. We could simply keep up communication with the young people, governor, always seeking a resolution. You'd look good with this response. A few timely media conferences explaining what we're doing will keep the public happy, and when the occupiers run out of food and give up, we'll arrest them and charge them appropriately."

Superintendent Ross was contemplating the governor's office. The sunshine entered her space through the veranda windows and lit up the conference room. The governor's podium and formal desk sat across the room from the officials, and Ross thought before all this mess would go away, O'Connell would be using those two pieces of furniture a few times. Official papers would need signatures and the public informed before this problem would be solved.

Governor O'Connell focused on Superintendent Ross. "Philip, I'd like you to go out to Camp Sherman and keep a close eye on this situation. This is too important for any simple miscommunication or mishaps to occur."

"Certainly, I'll drive out there tonight and stay at Black Butte Ranch. From there, I can easily drive over to the occupation site."

The governor regarded her colleagues, appreciative of their calm, mature professionalism.

"You know, we haven't touched on one aspect of this scenario that's personally very important to me."

Laura Roberts observed her boss. "Sarah, you were voted into the office of governor by a huge majority. Your personal feelings in regards to Oregon are important to this state's citizenry. What's important to you is probably very important to many Oregonians."

The governor smiled and continued, "This state stopped cutting old trees many years ago for numerous reasons. I believe most people simply enjoy their beauty and the healthy forest they represent. I feel exactly the same way. Camp Sherman is a beautiful mecca in the middle of our state, and I don't want it to be logged over like the rest of our forest lands. How can we stop this logging effort?"

Robert Smith felt compelled to answer the governor. "The State of Oregon has logging regulations in place, but right now, I'm not sure if we can change anything. This is federal land and the courts seem to be upholding McDonald's decree. I'll investigate various avenues, but don't hold your breath waiting for positive results."

O'Connell spoke again. "I think we all know what our immediate needs and responsibilities are. Let's all keep in touch on a regular basis. Robert, keep me abreast of our legal moves to thwart this logging site. Superintendent, call me tonight after you've visited the occupation. Go ahead and talk with the activists if you feel ready for the conversation. Our official response to their protest is it's an illegal act and should stop."

"Of course, governor. I'll contact you tonight."

"All right everyone, let's talk daily. I hope the next time we all get together we will be talking about the peaceful resolution of this occupation and the logging show that never reached fruition."

Everyone said their good-byes and headed off to their respective responsibilities.

OSP Superintendent Philip Ross walked down the Capitol steps and headed for his parked car. He'd have to contact his aide, Lieutenant Peters, so he could make the Black Butte Ranch reservations. Right now, he'd go home, let his wife know of his plans, pack his bags, and head for Central Oregon.

This time of year, especially with an Indian summer happening, the Metolius River area was a special place. The days were hot and the nights cool. Philip liked to play golf at Black Butte Ranch in the fall. In the late summer, the mountains looked rugged without their snowy cover. The jagged rims and summits really defined the volcanic peaks and hinted at their catastrophic origins. The superintendent knew golfing was probably not in his itinerary for this trip, but hopefully, before he returned to Salem, he could get in eighteen holes. This go-round would be serious work with no time for recreational indulgences.

Waiting out the occupiers was the simplest solution. It offered the least chance for confrontation. He was not too concerned about the State of Oregon's response to the occupation. Unfortunately, there was another piece to the puzzle needing to be accounted for. What would the federal government's reaction be to the activism? The superintendent hoped Attorney General Smith was correct in his speculation, and the feds would not get involved. That would be the best scenario. Philip Ross reached for his cellphone and dialed up his personal aide. *Time to get things moving.*

CHAPTER 38

The long, narrow Cabinet Room was filled to capacity. All the U.S. Government department heads were seated around the huge conference table that appeared to take up most of the room's space. Sitting behind and within arm's reach of their bosses were deputy secretaries, personal aides, or departmental chiefs of staff. The cabinet secretaries were conversing with each other. There was a feeling of foreboding in the room.

The top officials had been communicating with each other during the last few weeks, and they'd noticed several unnerving patterns occurring within their respective governmental departments. The secretaries decided this cabinet meeting would provide the perfect forum for disclosing their recent discoveries. It was somewhat ironic the meeting's agenda focused on governmental budget reductions and departmental downsizing. What the secretaries had recently unearthed was directly related to the gathering's theme. An unofficial, impromptu vote elected Secretary Billings as the spokesperson for all the agencies. After numerous private meetings with the departmental bosses, Billings had a good grasp on the perceived problems, and was ready to address President McDonald. In doing so, all the secretaries hoped the president would get on board and assist them in achieving his mandated federal cuts. Billings was hoping his presentation would be well received by the president and not dismissed.

Russel Nelson and Preston, both dressed in their white jackets, black slacks, and black leather shoes, rolled two serving carts up to the Cabinet Room hallway doors, which at this moment were still open. The carts were laden with carafes filled with iced lemon water. Each pitcher had condensation on its sides, and legs of water began running down their exterior surfaces.

Preston glanced over at Russel. "I wish I had a glass of this lemon water right now. It is a hot and humid D.C. day, brother."

Russel anxiously looked back at Preston and nodded in agreement.

At the Cabinet Room doorway, they were stopped by a Secret Service agent. They now waited for a cue from the agent for them to enter. One guard peered into the room, and then turning, motioned them in.

Preston regarded Russel and grinned, "Well, my man, welcome to the Big Time. Park your cart at the end of the table, near the window. Just place the water vessels on the table about four feet apart from each other. You copy, big fella?"

Russel nodded at Preston.

"I like it better when you talk to me, homie." Preston could tell his charge was nervous. "Come on, man. This is a walk in the park. Follow my lead."

The two White House servers entered the Cabinet Room. Russel parked his cart as directed next to the room's East Wall, and briefly gazed out at the Rose Garden. He then focused on his task. The room was crowded, so he carefully worked his way to the front of the conference table and placed the lemon water appropriately. He took in the whole scene while placing the carafes. There were lots of blue and gray suits on display with American flag lapel pins in place. Only two chairs were empty. The president was not in attendance yet, nor was his chief of staff. Russel looked down the full length of the wooden table to the far wall at the end of the room. There, a fireplace was centrally positioned with busts of Washington and Franklin to either side. The floor was covered with a huge, burnt red carpet adorned with a field of evenly spaced yellow stars. Behind Russel was an open doorway. It appeared to lead into a secretary's office. He thought the room that now contained the most important members of the president's team seemed extremely official and diplomatic. It was easy to imagine influential national and global decisions originating from this space. Preston caught Russel's attention and signaled for their departure. Both young men wheeled their carts into the hallway and headed for the kitchen.

Preston examined Russel, smiled, and shook his head. "Man, you is star struck. I looked over at you, and your mouth is on the floor. Your eyes big as silver dollars."

Russel smiled sheepishly. "I was a little shocked by all the people power and grandness of the room. It just kind of froze me up for a second."

"Yeah, it can happen. Especially at first. Remember, they just people. Most don't know it, but that's what they are, just people."

Russel and Preston returned to the ground floor kitchen. It was their break, so they headed for the small lounge next to the kitchen to "hang" and snack on whatever the cooks had prepared. No more official tasks awaited them. They were basically on call now. The cooks would have them do some prep work or general cleaning if they weren't summoned for other duties. Russel liked this job. It was exciting to be in the White House, and everyone he worked with seemed really pleasant. He looked forward to whatever job came next.

President McDonald and Henry Graham entered the Cabinet Room through Janet's office. McDonald noticed Secretary Billings and Interior Secretary Rice standing and talking next to the Franklin bust. They noted his arrival and took their seats. Secretary Billings sat across from and to the left of the president, while Rice sat on the president's right, two spaces removed. Between Rice and McDonald sat the Secretary of State and Graham.

McDonald started the meeting. "Good morning, ladies and gentlemen. I'm sure you all got our meeting's agenda. We're gathered here to review your departmental goals of reducing budgets, cutting jobs, and eliminating unnecessary regulations. You all know these edicts were the foundation of my presidential campaign and were embraced by the American people. Also, these departmental reductions will help me in my personal goal of beefing up our armed forces. The monies you slash from your agencies can be used to build a stronger, more aggressive military force. Okay, secretaries, that's our agenda. My chief of staff will take charge of deliberations now. I'm looking forward to hearing about your agencies' success in regards to the budget cuts."

Henry Graham was startled by McDonald's coherent, to-the-point introduction. *Maybe he won't "lose it" today.* He cleared his throat as McDonald eased back into his chair and began scrolling through his phone.

"Good morning, secretaries. Let's get right to this. Secretary Rice, how is your department progressing with downsizing?"

The uncomfortable feeling in the room was heightened by this first inquiry, and could be physically felt. The silence became noticeable to all as the Secretary of State scooted backwards, allowing Rice and Graham eye contact.

"Well, Graham. My department is having mixed results."

Most of the people sitting at the table, including Secretary Rice, were Washington outsiders who knew little about their departments, and even less about how to direct and control them. The strings to pull and channels to utilize for completion of even simple inner agency tasks were unknown to them.

"I'd say some departments are responding and some others are not. Many of my sections, like BLM, USGS, and the Bureau of Indian Affairs, have simply stonewalled me. They won't return emails or phone calls. Often, I hear about computer viruses affecting their communications. The assistant secretaries of my agencies are basically just passing on these excuses to me, and not doing anything to remedy the problem. Really, Mr. President, I think a complete shake-up of my branch, starting with the firing of all assistant secretaries, is in order. I believe these professional government officials are at the crux of the problem, and they don't want to facilitate your mandates.

"Now, on the other hand, some of my agencies are in compliance. For instance, the National Park Service seems to have done your bidding, sir. Although this has caused considerable damage, I believe, to your administration. My department, to date, has received several million complaints from park users, either by email, phone calls, or personal letters. Personnel cuts in the parks this summer caused huge lines while visitors waited for services. These lines became intolerable. Also, people were constantly made to wait or turned away from reserved rooms or campsites because they weren't ready for new arrivals. Hell, Mr. President, we got over 200,000 complaints about the one-ply toilet paper our bathrooms are now stocked with! This kind of voluminous public displeasure is a black eye for your administration."

President McDonald was reading news reports from the previous evening's broadcasts, and hadn't heard what Rice said. Henry Graham swiveled his chair around and discreetly nudged McDonald's leg with his foot. McDonald peered up at Graham.

"I think Rice has made several important points, Mr. President. The stonewalling by his assistant secretaries and the bad press caused by our poorly equipped National Park Service are disadvantageous to our overall administrative goals."

The president's gaze moved to Rice. "I agree with Graham's remarks, Rice. What do you propose we do?"

"Well, Mr. President. I suggest we allocate more monies to the Park Service and start weeding out of my agency the middle management people who are undercutting your goals."

The president examined his phone and now studied Rice. "This sounds like a serious problem. Let's meet later and develop some strategies. Graham will arrange a meeting."

"Certainly, Mr. President."

Henry Graham mentally sighed with relief. He never knew what McDonald would say or do in these meetings. Several times he'd just ranted on about personal agendas, completely diverging from the gathering's goals.

He centered himself, and continued addressing the secretaries. "Let's hear from the Department of Transportation. Secretary Redding, how has your department fared in cutting regulations and your overall budget?"

At this point, Secretary Billings made eye contact with Redding, and receiving a nod of consent, cleared his throat and spoke to Graham and President McDonald.

"Excuse my interruption, Graham, but I've been asked by my fellow secretaries to address the president about our mutual difficulties regarding these budget and regulation cuts. Mr. President, all of us have been comparing notes, and what Rice just described is what we're all encountering in our respective departments."

Graham realized the meeting held a hidden agenda that neither he nor the president was aware of.

He once again bumped McDonald's leg, gaining his attention. "Mr. President, Secretary Billings has some important information for you."

McDonald visibly seemed annoyed at this second interruption, and Graham hoped he wouldn't lose the president to some personal venting. Happily, Graham noted the president's harsh expression becoming more receptive. McDonald looked across the table at Billings and in a flat tone asked, "What do you have to say, secretary?"

"Pretty much the same message Secretary Rice shared. My agencies for the most part, are ignoring your budget requests. Like Rice, it's hard to nail down where the problems are because of poor communication. If I don't personally go to a department and sit with my assistant secretary, demanding to see proof of job layoffs, budget cuts, and regulation deletions, I'll get no information whatsoever."

President McDonald gazed at Billings with disdain. "That seems to be your job, secretary. I'm sure this is more difficult than what you expected, but so be it. Roll up your sleeves and slug it out with your employees."

Billings was annoyed by McDonald's callous and condescending remark and responded, "Mr. President, I don't have enough fists to slug it out with all my agency heads and all of their immediate subordinates. This is a total mutiny we are dealing with, and a well-planned one, too. Our departments are picking and choosing divisions that will and will not comply with your agenda. By doing this they are, in a subversive manner, turning American sentiment against your administration. I'd like to highlight one of my agencies, which has complied with cutbacks and layoffs, to help illuminate what I've just noted. The Forest Service has totally reined itself in, but in doing so, it completely angered the summer visitors and campers who use our National Forests. The Forest Service shut down numerous campgrounds this summer due to lack of funds and personnel. They kept open the campgrounds associated with National Monuments, but of course, these sites were a mess because of the lack of employees. My department, just like Rice's, received several million complaints from Americans whose vacation plans were erased or hindered by our budget cuts. This kind of publicity you don't need, President McDonald."

The president had drifted once again back to his phone, and had to be prompted by Graham. McDonald looked at Graham, who was looking at Billings, and followed Graham's gaze back to Secretary Billings.

Sensing something needed to be said, President McDonald asked, "What do you suggest we do, secretary?"

"I suggest we revisit these 'across the board' cuts, and give monies back to agencies that offer direct services to the American people, like the Park Service and the Forest Service. All the department heads present, Mr. President, could give you the same scenario Rice and I have presented, and they all have agencies within their structures that have high public visibility. These departments need to continue in the manner the public is accustomed to. If they don't, the voting citizenry of the country will not be supportive of your administration. Lastly, Mr. President, I strongly urge you to roll up your sleeves, visit all of your departments, and start rolling the heads of personnel who are stonewalling and derailing your wishes."

Secretary Rice was inwardly smiling and applauding Billings' choice of words. President McDonald returned to his phone, and while Billings was finishing his address, McDonald visibly stiffened and lurched forward in his chair. Graham noticed his boss's erratic behavior and studied the president closely.

"God damn those hippy-dippies!" McDonald glared at Graham with a crazed expression. "Shut down this meeting, Graham." He inspected Billings. "Billings, I want you in my office, pronto!"

He then locked eyes with the Secretary of Defense, then the Secretary of Homeland Security, and ordered them to follow Billings into the Oval Office. President McDonald rose and headed there also. As he left, he told his chief of staff to join him, ASAP. Graham visibly shook his head with frustration at this disruption. He clumsily thanked everyone in attendance for coming, and said they all would receive transcripts of the meeting in the near future. He then excused himself and headed for the president's office via Janet's office. As he walked to Janet's office, Graham thought, *what's next?* He considered the repercussions this scene would create in the national news. *McDonald really is a loose cannon. Controlling this guy is impossible.* Chief of Staff Henry Graham continued toward Janet's door at the south end of the Cabinet Room.

CHAPTER 39

All Ray Billings could do as he passed Janet's desk was glance at her and shake his head in disgust. He then continued into the president's office and waited for him to enter. He stood calmly by the president's desk. McDonald burst into the office.

"God damn it, Billings. What's going on at my logging site?"

Secretary Billings had no idea what the president was referring to.

"I'm not sure, Mr. President. What have you heard?"

"What have I heard? Don't you watch the news?"

The secretary had spent a very pleasant night dining with Janet at Murphy's and hadn't seen any national news.

"I didn't see the evening news last night, sir."

As Billings spoke, the Secretary of Defense, Tom Hastings, walked into the room with the Secretary of Homeland Security, Janice Logan, on his heels. Right behind them was Henry Graham. All four officials stood near the presidential desk for a moment, then Graham took control.

"Let's all sit on the couches." He motioned to the sofas, centered in the room.

"Janet," McDonald yelled.

"Yes, Mr. President." Janet came to the doorway.

"Have a dozen ham and cheese sandwiches sent here with some coffee."

"Certainly, Mr. President."

As the five government officials sat down, their paths crisscrossed over the Presidential Seal of the United States of America. The eagle's one-eyed stern gaze inspected the room where many important national and international decisions had been made. Graham and the president sat facing the three secretaries seated across from them. The president still registered a crazed expression on his face, and barely could control himself.

"Damn it, Billings! I've got tree huggers stopping one of my logging sites in Oregon. I just saw the news on my phone. All the national media outlets are reporting on it."

"Like I said, Mr. President, I missed the news last night. What did you learn from your phone?"

"Nothing I wanted to. Are any other sites being stopped by these hippy-dippies?"

Billings inwardly groaned at this question. *Well, the shit is going to hit the fan now.*

"Mr. President, there are no other sites."

The president's face became visibly red. His eyes narrowed as he venomously spoke to Secretary Billings.

"What the hell do you mean, there are no other sites?"

Billings took a deep breath, steadied himself, and calmly replied. "Sir, it appeared prudent to try one logging show first, and then wait to see what kind of response followed."

McDonald aggressively stared at Billings. His face became a deeper shade of red, and his voice ratcheted up a notch.

"Billings, if I'd wanted 'prudent' behavior, I would have appointed someone wearing a skirt, named Prudence, to be my Secretary of Agriculture. What part of numerous logging sites didn't you understand?"

"At the time, it seemed…"

"Enough of your excuses, Billings. You're dismissed. I need to confer with my team about how we can rid ourselves of these damn tree huggers. I'll get with you very soon, and we'll review your management skills regarding running the Department of Agriculture."

McDonald then motioned for Billings to leave with a dismissive sweep of his hand. Billings got up, and said his "good days" to the others. He turned his back on the president and left the Oval Office. As he neared Janet's desk, he stopped and regarded her. She gazed up at him with a sympathetic expression on her face and reached out for his hand. She gave it a reassuring squeeze, then mouthed "sorry." Billings mouthed back, "I'm quitting." Janet gave him a smile, then a double-thumbs-up approval. She tapped her wrist and quietly said, "Murphy's at five." Billings nodded and as he turned to leave, Janet handed him a folded note, cryptically adding, "You can't open it till you're in your limo, driving away from here."

Billings crossed his heart with his index finger before turning and walking to the West Wing main entrance. The attending Marine let the secretary outside, and opened his Continental's door for him. Billings eased back into the rear seat as the Marine shut his door.

"Where to, Mr. Secretary?"

"Back to my office, Jimmy. I have some packing to do."

"Going on a trip, sir?"

"Yes, I am. An overdue one."

"Traffic's light today, Mr. Secretary. We'll be there in no time."

"Great, let her rip."

Billings, true to his word, opened Janet's note as he rode to the Whitten Building. He read her message, refolded the note, and placed it back into his pocket. As he viewed the D.C. streets out of his limo, a smile lit up his face. Janet requested the secretary bring an overnight bag with him to Murphy's. She'd said a toothbrush and p.j.'s were all he needed because she'd provide everything else. The secretary continued smiling as he gazed out his window. *Wasn't that just the way life worked? One venture ends and another begins.*

CHAPTER
40

SECRETARY HASTINGS AND HOMELAND SECURITY

Secretary Janice Logan viewed each other with concerned expressions. They both liked Billings; he was a team player who could be trusted, and both secretaries knew the president's slightly veiled threat meant Billings' days were numbered. The president continued venting after Billings' departure.

"That screw-up has messed with my plans, big time." McDonald glared at Hastings and Logan. "I don't need any more assholes on my team like Billings."

Logan thought to herself the tree huggers, not Billings, seemed to be "messing" with McDonald's plans, but realized a logical interjection, rebutting the president's railings, would only create more irrational behavior, possibly directed at her this time. The president was still visibly angry.

"I want these..."

A knock on the Oval Office's hallway door announced the arrival of the sandwiches. Graham called out, "Come in."

Russel Nelson, followed by Preston, entered the Oval Office carrying serving trays over their shoulders. Preston's tray was filled with sandwiches and Russel carried the coffee.

McDonald saw the food and continued with his emotional outburst. "I want those hippy-dippy, Oregon tree huggers off my property, ASAP!!! Any way we accomplish this is fine with me."

Graham nervously studied the president. McDonald's rambling in front of the service staff was a basic Oval Office "no-no." He loudly interjected, "Excuse me, Mr. President. Let's refrain from discussion momentarily while we fill our coffee cups and grab a few sandwiches."

The volume of Graham's comment startled McDonald, who stopped talking due to the outburst. He observed the concerned expression directed his way from his chief of staff and mentally assessed his behavior. Noting the servers placing coffee and sandwiches nearby, McDonald realized his breach of security etiquette and discontinued speaking. His eyes drifted to the young servers and realized both were men. *What doesn't Peterson understand? Didn't I just talk to him about my wait staff interns? This is not what I meant by "well-proportioned eye candy."*

The two young men picked up their trays and left the Oval Office. In the hallway, Preston looked over at Russel.

"Whoa! Looks like the boss is a little disturbed. I hope we don't get any more calls from him, today. Hey, brother, aren't you from Oregon?"

Russel nodded his confirmation at Preston.

"Well, let's not let 'the man' know about it. If he did, you might be disappearing someday soon."

Russel laughed at Preston's joking. "I might need to go into hiding. You got a spare room?"

"Nope. If I aid and abet you, homie, I might end up missing, too."

Both young men smiled at each other's humor as they returned to the kitchen.

President McDonald, after several bites of his sandwich and some coffee, began to relax and regain his composure. The three remaining officials began discussing possible ways of removing the site occupiers. Secretary of Defense Tom Hastings mostly listened to the discussion, trying to get a feel for the others' true intents and their strengths and weaknesses. He was career military and had retired as a General in the Air Force. He'd left active duty ten years ago to pursue a consulting career, which aided large international corporations with their physical security. President McDonald had offered him his present position and Hastings jumped at the chance. The secretary was a soldier's soldier, an extreme hawk who truly believed military conflict was the best way to solve problems. President McDonald's administration appeared to be the perfect fit for him. McDonald mentioned many times while campaigning that the U.S. Government had become soft and needed to act more decisively and aggressively in solving international disputes. Hastings agreed completely with this sentiment and eagerly joined McDonald's cabinet.

Secretary Hastings was six feet tall, slender, with sharp facial features. His eyes were dark, his face clean shaven, but often showing a four o'clock shadow. He still wore a military style crew cut that lessened the graying appearance of his temples. He was decisive and straightforward in his discussions to the point of being rudely blunt at times.

As Hastings listened to the Secretary of Homeland Security and McDonald talk, he knew none of them had a clue as to how one could roust the occupiers. It was comical to him seeing the lack of experience exhibited by the present administration.

After hearing all the previous dialogue, it was apparent Janice wanted no part of this shit show and was directing all thoughts away from her department.

"Mr. President, this problem seems to be in the FBI domain. It's on federal land and I believe the FBI has trained personnel who can deal with this kind of situation," Secretary Logan suggested.

The FBI reference noticeably agitated the president. "Those liberal, Demo loving shitheads would only sabotage and hinder my objectives. I don't trust them any further than I can throw them, and don't bring up the CIA either. They're just as bad as the FBI. What a waste of taxpayer money. Those two organizations only work for the Dems, and even then, they're a total waste of money and time."

Secretary Logan did not want her department involved in this skirmish. She was already taking incredible heat about the administration's stance on immigrants. Her ICE arrests and Border Patrol Officers were constantly drawing the ire of the ACLU and other human rights organizations. The media were regularly knocking on her door, forcing her on a daily basis to defend her department's procedures and national intent. One more questionable situation was not appealing to Logan at all.

"Mr. President, my department is severely burdened with addressing your mandates on immigration. We are maxed out with guarding the borders and arresting immigrants, and Mr. President, I don't feel any of my personnel are well suited for a possible conflict in a forested area like we're talking about."

McDonald was beginning to lose patience with Janice's hedging and sidestepping. "Your personnel are extremely capable of..."

At this point, Secretary Hastings had heard enough, and felt it was time for some decisive, realistic dialogue.

"Excuse me, Mr. President, Secretary Logan. May I make a few suggestions?"

Chief of Staff Henry Graham exhaled with relief and smoothed some wrinkles on his gray suit with his left hand.

"Let's keep the Department of Homeland Security out of this, Mr. President. Logan has plenty on her plate as is, and frankly, there's a negative connotation existing in regards to her department and their efforts. No, you do not need Homeland Security to help police this situation, sir, and I agree with your assessment about the FBI and the CIA. They can't be trusted."

President McDonald observed Hastings. "Finally, someone I can work with. What do you suggest, secretary?"

"Well first, Mr. President, let's excuse Secretary Logan so she can go back to running her department."

President McDonald nodded and then dismissed Secretary Logan with a curt thank you and a wave of his hand. Secretary Janice Logan stood up, barely containing her smile of relief as she left the Oval Office. Logan wanted nothing to do with this new mess of McDonald's.

As the door closed behind the Secretary of Homeland Security, the Defense Secretary continued. "There are numerous military solutions to this problem, Mr. President."

McDonald's demeanor visibly changed with the mention of "military." He leaned forward, his face brightening with interest and curiosity.

"Do you mean like the use of Delta Force or a Seals Special Ops mission?"

Hastings inwardly smiled at this question. "No. I don't think this situation requires such specialized forces, Mr. President. I think regular service members could handle this situation."

At this point Chief of Staff Henry Graham entered into the conversation. "Mr. President, I might suggest a wait-and-see attitude here. This appears to be an occupation by college activists and not hardened eco-terrorists. Usually, sir, this kind of situation is dealt with by the local, state officials. We wouldn't get involved to any great extent. We'd have open dialogue with the governor about the occupation, share resolution ideas with her office, and offer any assistance requested."

"Hell, I don't want to work with Oregon's sorry-ass governor. We need to circumvent her. How can we sidestep the liberal skirt?"

President McDonald was looking directly at Secretary Hastings when he asked the question.

"It's easily done, Mr. President. I have numerous connections in the military who owe me favors, and we can very discreetly get your bidding accomplished, but I agree with Graham if we fly in now, throwing punches at a bunch of defenseless college kids, we'll seem like bullies taking on the little guy."

"Defenseless? Hell, the report I saw said they have dynamite in place ready to use."

Hastings continued. "Let's get some confirmation on explosives, Mr. President, and in place, ready to use, is not the same as blowing things up. It even looks good for the occupiers if the explosives are present and they're not touching them off. They come off looking resolute, but patient and mature. The American public likes that approach."

Graham jumped back into the conversation. "After some investigating, let's reconvene again and share notes about this occupation."

McDonald wasn't liking this wait-and-see attitude. He'd been pretty excited about Hastings' initial mention of the military solution, and now it appeared everyone was backing off.

"I'm not going to sit on my thumbs for long, Graham. Hastings, I want those hippy-dippies out of there!"

"Mr. President, when we convene next, I'll have several military options for you to think about. During our recess, I'll be contacting a couple of ex-colleagues who I think can help us."

"Great, Hastings. You've said what I want to hear. Possible quick solutions. Not this wait-and-see crap. Wait-and-see doesn't get the job done."

After picking up another sandwich and taking a bite, the president continued. "All right, gentlemen, let's get this moving."

Graham and Hastings departed the Oval Office, the chief of staff heading down the hallway to his work space, and Secretary of Defense Hastings heading for the West Wing's North Entrance and his waiting limo. He had no intention of putting together a military operation meant to bust a bunch of college kids. Killing young people was not going to be found on his résumé. No, he'd just let all this hype dry up and blow away. McDonald would be off on some other tangent by tomorrow anyway, and would probably forget about his tree huggers.

President McDonald sat alone in his Oval Office, finishing off his ham and cheese sandwich. It was after four, and soon he'd retire to his second floor residence to begin watching the evening newscasts. He regarded his sandwich and thought about the servers who delivered it. They were not what he'd asked for. He'd have to talk with his chief usher once again, and hopefully, the man could get it right this time. Anybody was replaceable. He might have to make Mr. Peterson aware of this.

CHAPTER 41

IT WAS 6:00 P.M., AND A JEFFERSON COUNTY patrol car headed for the southern roadblock. Oregon State Police and Deschutes and Jefferson County deputies set up two roadblocks, which they were manning 24/7. Also, right below the Big Eddy Rise, OSP Superintendent Ross positioned a surveillance post next to the Metolius River. Whoever manned this site simply surveyed the cliff and the opposite riverbank with the intent of containing the occupiers and keeping them from replenishing their water supply. Tonight, the Staters had "river duty" and the north roadblock, and Jefferson and Deschutes County deputies were responsible for the southern barricade. More troopers were added to the Bend and Madras outposts. The occupation responsibilities had stretched the region's manpower allocations too thin, but now, with the addition of more personnel, OSP could comfortably hold up its end of the occupation surveillance and continue with its regular Central Oregon patrols. Jefferson County and Deschutes County threw in together, and their combined forces allowed them enough deputies to fulfill their containment responsibilities and continue on with normal police work. After it was all said and done, the various police departments felt their control of the occupation site was doable and could proceed smoothly.

The OSP boss had visited the occupation site early and communicated with the occupiers. While talking with Dread on the Big Eddy Rise's southern slope, Ross discerned the young man's resolve. The superintendent respected the dreadlocked college student and what his group was doing. He knew civil disobedience was a natural response to perceived oppression, and was thankful he was dealing with such a mature group as the STRONG Alliance.

He delivered the governor's response to the Alliance's demands. He also reported Oregon was trying to dissuade the federal government from this logging endeavor, and this was true to a certain degree. Unfortunately, all of the state's inquiries about the logging show were ignored by Washington D.C. When Attorney General Smith contacted Steve Johnson, the Deschutes National Forest Director, about the logging activity, Johnson deferred matters to Secretary Billings' office. When Smith contacted the Agriculture Department, he was completely ignored. No one returned his overtures. The frustrated attorney general contacted Governor O'Connell, telling her Washington apparently wasn't going to cooperate with Oregon in regard to resolving the logging issue. With no resolution from the McDonald administration forthcoming, the State of Oregon continued with its "wait them out" strategy. This was not what O'Connell had hoped for, but those were the cards she was dealt.

The Alliance had occupied the logging site for a week, now. The State Police continued with containing the area, and were satisfied to wait and watch. The governor and Ross felt another week of occupation would probably deplete the group's food and water, forcing the Alliance to surrender and give up the occupation.

A routine developed on the hill. One groundkeeper from each occupied tree would visit the rise's summit several times a day and bring back food and water to his or her group. Each time, a new individual was used for these food runs, which allowed for all the Alliance members to get up and move around. This procedure helped alleviate boredom, and seldom used muscles got a minimal workout. Along with food being delivered three times a day, the tree sitters' honeypots were lowered and cleaned out daily by the Alliance member who'd ascended to the summit. After the groundkeeper returned, the tree sitter would retrieve their honeypot by rope. It was usually accompanied by another freshly cooked meal.

Dread never left the summit. He occasionally communicated directly to the Alliance using his bullhorn, but most information was relayed via groundkeepers. He made a show, periodically, of holding up his blasting box whenever it appeared law enforcement was observing him. The lanky militant did all the cooking for the group. Delicious aromas drifted down to the south roadblock guards, who joked about a food cart out of sight in the Big Eddy bowl.

The occupiers' routine was aided by the rainless, mild Indian summer. The days went by with regularity as the ground team, when not occupied, read, played cards, wrote in journals, or simply napped during the day. At night, drumming, chanting, and singing filled their time. Each group had a lantern, so illumination could be produced if required.

Dread built a fire each evening, and one member from each tree was allowed to join him around the campfire. This group would drum and smoke pot while they conversed and played their music. This occupation was, by far, the Alliance's easiest, most stress-free act of defiance. They all, to a person, felt the fake dynamite's presence had restrained the local law enforcement's efforts, gaining for the Alliance a freedom of movement they'd never experienced before.

The activists were somewhat concerned by the depletion of their food stores, and the apparent lack of legal success in stopping the logging show. Usually, lawsuits by conservation groups would allow them to quit a site, but to this point, nobody had heard about litigation. For the moment, though, the occupation was proceeding better than expected, and the group's mood was extremely hopeful and confident.

CHAPTER 42

DEPUTY HENDERSON'S CHEVY CAPRICE PATROL car created a billowing mass of dust as it proceeded to Deputy Edwards' position. His Jefferson County pickup was parked just behind the roadblock fencing, and Henderson could see Edwards leaning up against the left fender of his vehicle while he viewed the occupation site through a pair of binoculars. He brought his cruiser to a stop, and opening the door, stepped out of his vehicle into an unusually gray early evening. Deputy Edwards turned and faced Henderson, nodding his head in greeting. Before walking back to meet his "relief," Johnny dropped his binoculars on his pickup's front seat. The two law officers merged together with a handshake and verbal hellos.

The dark clouds and low light subdued the forest's colors. As Deputy Henderson surveyed the forest, dull greens and oranges were predominant. Manzanita leaves were dark green and the dusty forest floor appeared brown versus light tan. There wasn't a breath of air flowing through the tree canopies, and this left their branches and needles frozen into place. The entire forest was eerily quiet. There were no crows or Steller's jays talking back and forth, and even the ever present, always in motion squirrels were absent. The Metolius River's continuous voice seemed to be shouting because of the weird silence. Henderson viewed the occupiers' location and noted Dread's campfire smoke drifting straight up from its source.

Deputy Henderson spoke to Edwards. "Wow, this is a little quiet."

"Yeah. It's been like this for about an hour, now. Must be the quiet before the storm."

"Yep. Supposed to hit about ten o'clock tonight. Brian and Cassie said on their late night show it was going to be a doozy. I hope they're wrong."

"Me, too."

Deputy Edwards gazed up into the gray sky, and then panned the still forest once again. He looked back to Henderson. "Nothing unusual happening on the hill. The kids left their trees about an hour ago. They should be returning pretty soon with their grub. Anyway, it's been a long shift. I'm heading for Sisters and a dinner date. You know, if the wind gets too bad tonight, you should leave the barricade and head back to Metolius Meadows. You'll be safe from falling branches there."

"Good idea. If it gets dicey here, I'll move out."

Edwards thought some more. "Now that I'm thinking about it, whoever has the bridge barricade could move into the nearby big parking lot. It should be safe from potential wind damage, too."

"Good advice, partner. I'll give them a call, and mention what you said."

"Okay, deputy. I'll leave you in command of this logistically vital surveillance point. Hold down the fort. See you at about six o'clock tomorrow morning."

Deputy Edwards returned to his truck, got in, started the engine, and pulled a U-turn. As he drove past Henderson, he gave him a casual salute, then continued on toward Highway 20. Looking in his rearview mirror, the deputy's gaze fell upon one of the tree stands, and he could see a sitter's silhouette on the edge of his or her perch. *Shit! I wonder if they know about the coming storm.* He checked his watch. He was going to be late for his dinner date in Sisters with his wife and kids. He hadn't spent real, quality time with his family for quite a while. He thought once more about the tree sitters. *They've probably experienced bad weather before, and are prepared for such occurrences.* Johnny checked his watch again and unconsciously drove faster.

CHAPTER
43

Deputy Henderson radioed his OSP counterpart at the bridge barricade and they talked storm strategies. After the discussion, he settled back into his seat with a pair of binoculars and began his watch. A few occupiers returned from the summit with dinner for their teams, and after a while, several more young people moved back to the summit and disappeared into the crater. Henderson knew drumming and singing would soon issue from the hillside, and actually looked forward to it beginning. The African beat produced by the occupiers mingled with the forest, and the large tree trunks softened and muted the rhythms, making them even more primal and authentic. As he watched the hillside, darkness fell, and the only light came from numerous lanterns the tree sitters were using and the orange-yellow glow thrown off by Dread's campfire. The smoke was now tilting in a southerly direction as a slight breeze had developed. The drumming slowly made Deputy Henderson drowsy, and after a while, the law officer's head fell backwards, resting upon his cruiser's front headrest. He fell asleep.

The young activists spent the night quietly. The summit group drummed for a couple hours. Then, around nine, everyone returned to their trees, leaving Dread to tend the fire and eventually fall asleep next to the warm embers. All the groundkeepers unlocked their chains and removed themselves from their bondage. They rolled out Insulite pads and bedded down for the night. The tree sitters bundled up in their hammocks. All of them noted the unusual stillness of the evening and the lack of movement from their trees. The big Ponderosas had stood silent and still since dusk. All the activists, plus Deputy Henderson, slept peacefully, and didn't notice the wind intensifying.

As the high pressure cell slowly moved northward, its wind rotation began pulling in colder marine air. This atmosphere was now mixing with the warm air produced by the large, low pressure cell to the east. The meteorological conditions aligned perfectly, causing the air temperature to drop drastically and the predicted gale force winds to develop. By the time Dread woke up, his fire coals were sporadically hissing from the large drops of rain hitting them. The winds were already reaching 40 mph, causing the old growth Ponderosas to creak and groan as they rocked back and forth. Tree hangers were sprawled in their hammocks, wedging their feet tightly against one branch while grasping the other hammock limb with their hands. The large trees would tilt crazily in one direction until the trunk's tensile strength overcame the wind's force. Then they'd rebound back to their normal, at rest position, only to surpass this point and continue on. With the wind continuing to add energy to this cycle, the back and forth motion became even more pronounced and frightening.

Sasha, Climber, and Tom struggled to stay in their roosts. Climber and Sasha attempted to gear up and descend, but they'd waited too long. When they knelt in their hammocks to put harnesses on, they'd been tossed off balance, and both had nearly toppled out of their roosts. All they could do now was lie flat in their perches, bracing themselves against the trees' swinging motion.

As the wind quickly intensified, all the support teams arose and watched helplessly from the ground as their sitters struggled to stay aloft. Dread ran down from the summit, quickly realizing the dire straits his tree sitters were in. He stood underneath Sasha's tree and stared up. As he peered upwards, rain came down in monsoon torrents, drenching all the activists. The creaking noise created by the swaying forest was frightening, and the wind rushing through the canopy produced a deafening roar. It was hard for the Alliance members to communicate with each other even though they stood in close proximity. Dread, soaking wet, shined his light up into Sasha's tree. His beam highlighted hundreds of large rain drops as they plummeted to the ground. He could see her body's indentation in the hammock, and her hands clutching the branch in front of her.

Dread shouted up to her, "Don't try and come down." The wind ripped Dread's words from his mouth. He shouted again. "Tie yourself to the tree trunk, and wait out the storm." The expression on his face was one of fear and frustration. "Sasha, can you hear me?"

The groundkeepers saw a quick thumbs-up sign flashed to them, and then Sasha's hand rapidly resumed clutching her branch. Tree trunks were pushed to their limits by the storm's strength, and their canopies were covering twenty-plus feet as they swayed back and forth. The ground crews were pelted by cones propelled downwards by the combined forces of gravity and strong wind, and those hitting the Alliance members' exposed skin inflicted painful cuts and contusions. Dead branches were beginning to crash down around the occupiers. Their defenseless position was becoming an obviously dangerous situation. Rachael had a large cut on her forehead where a cone had struck her, and bloody rainwater ran down into her eye and onto her cheek. Red hair was plastered to her head and drenched clothes clung to her body. Dread assessed her and the others and yelled for them to get up to the summit.

He called up once more to Sasha. "Hold on, Sasha. Don't give up."

Next, the Alliance leader ran over to the other tree hanging sites, and dismissed all the ground crews to the summit. After sending all the ground crews up the hill, he hollered at Climber and then to Tom, giving them the same directions that Sasha received.

Water dripped from Dread's beard and hair as he ran for Big Eddy's summit. A large branch crashed to the ground directly in front of him, and he jumped over its still rocking shape. His clothes, like Rachael's, were drenched and clung to his body. The sloping hillside now had large rivulets of water running down it, turning the forest floor into a goopy slurry, and as the occupation leader ran up the incline, he slipped, falling head first into the muddy slope. He quickly regained his footing and continued on, now with mud dripping off his clothes and face.

After Dread clambered over the wet basaltic rim, he saw the Alliance members clustered in groups of twos and threes, holding tarps over their heads. The elk tent had blown over and lay on the ground. He joined the nearest group, and found himself with Bridger, Rachael, and Tunes. The coed's cuts had stopped bleeding, but now she was shaking uncontrollably. Wiping water and mud from his face, the Alliance leader voiced what everyone was thinking.

"Shit, they could all die out there in this storm. I can't believe this is happening. For Christ sakes it's September, not December or January. Sasha is strong, but God, this is unbelievable."

Bridger put his arm around Dread's shoulder and pulled him close. "The storm will blow through and everyone will make it."

The four young people knew his words were really a veiled prayer, and all remained silent.

Rachael continued shaking. Her wet shorts and T-shirt were not providing insulation, and she was losing body heat. Dread regained his composure and began thinking about immediate needs. He bolted from the tarp and submerged himself into the collapsed tent, reemerging with damp sleeping bags, several wool blankets, and thermorests. As he passed the others, he tossed them two or three of his possessions. He also gave each group instructions to reposition themselves near the lee side of the crater's rim. The occupation leader returned to his group and moved them to the basaltic wall. They scooted the tarp under and over them and placed an Insulite pad beneath them. Next, they clumsily draped a damp sleeping bag over their legs and upper bodies, and, holding the upper portion of the tarp close to their heads, tried to create an airtight space. Rachael was put in the middle as all the young people crowded together. Their combined body heat slowly warmed up the bag, heating the air trapped beneath it. Rachael soon stopped shaking, slipping into an exhausted sleep. All the occupiers began to doze off only to awaken when an extremely loud wind gust passed overhead. The entire encampment slept fitfully, waking to the storm's ferocity and dozing during the quieter moments.

Deputy Edwards also hadn't slept well during the storm. His bed's headboard rested against a north-facing wall, and the noise of the wind hitting the outside wall was enough to keep anybody awake. Adding to his disturbed sleep was his concern for the occupiers. At 4:00 a.m., he rose from bed, dressed, and went into the kitchen. The storm's bravado had abated, and now only minor gusts of wind passed over and around his home. He brewed some coffee, filled a thermos, and quickly ate his cold cereal. After rinsing his bowl out, Edwards made several ham, chicken, and Swiss cheese sandwiches, and put them in a paper sack along with some bananas. He was out the door and on the road by 4:30 a.m. His departure time would have him arriving on site about dawn.

The road from Bend to Camp Sherman at 4:30 in the morning was mostly empty. A few long haul rigs passed by, going in the opposite direction with marker lights lit up. Not many passenger cars shared the road with the Jefferson County patrol truck. Johnny pulled off Highway 20 and continued on. He slowed down when he neared the Meadows and peeked into the entrance road of the small housing development. Henderson's car sat parked next to the outgoing curb. Edwards turned in and drove past the patrol car, noting his counterpart was asleep. Turning his vehicle around, Johnny pulled to a stop behind the deputy's car. Before he opened his door, he grabbed a spare cup, filled it with coffee, and retrieved a sandwich from his bag. He carefully walked over to Henderson's rig, trying not to spill the coffee. After quietly setting the coffee on top of the cruiser, Edwards rapped loudly on the window. Henderson lurched forward, grabbed the steering wheel with both hands, and looked out his window with eyes swollen and red from lack of sleep. His cruiser's electric window slowly slid down. Johnny spoke to his tired fellow law officer. "Good morning, deputy. Your surveillance skills are a credit to the Jefferson County Sheriff's Department."

"Knock it off, Edwards. I just sat through the 'night from hell' out here! Down by the occupation site, branches were falling all over the place, and I heard one big tree snap off and hit the ground with a hair-raising crash, right next to my cruiser."

Johnny handed Henderson the coffee and sandwich as he spoke. The exhausted deputy gratefully accepted them.

"Thanks, deputy. Anyway, I got out of there about midnight, and made it back here."

"What happened to the kids?"

"I don't know. The rain was coming down in sheets, and visibility was really bad. I saw one or two flashlight beams bouncing around in the forest but really, I couldn't see squat. When a falling branch landed right in front of my cruiser, I left and drove here."

"Okay, okay, let's go check on our young activists."

At the three-way, Johnny rolled through the intersection and sped on. The dull gray light of dawn was filling the forest with subdued visibility as his truck drove over small downed branches and around some of the larger ones. The road was littered with Ponderosa cones, which crunched loudly under the truck's tires as his rig moved forward. An eerie quiet once again prevailed in the forest. Edwards' heart was beating faster as he neared the occupation site, and a slight sheen of perspiration formed on his forehead, which he dried off with a swipe of his forearm. *This does not look good*, thought Edwards as he slowed down his truck where their barricade had once been. The wind had blown the roadblock over and busted it apart, scattering pieces of white wood all over the road and nearby forest floor. The early morning light was beginning to materialize. When Johnny gazed up the hill, he could barely make out the profile of Big Eddy summit. He stopped his truck, set the emergency brake, grabbed an eighteen-volt flashlight from his passenger seat, and stepped out onto the road. The crunch of his boot on the gravel startled him. The forest's quiet was unnerving. Henderson pulled up behind and joined him. He also held a flashlight.

No Alliance members could be seen. The forest floor was covered with branches and pinecones, and a shallow, elongated pond had formed at the road's edge where there was poor drainage. Deputy Edwards shined his light up into the closest trees, which he knew sitters occupied. Nobody was in sight, although he thought there were bulges showing in both hammocks. He then directed his beam further up the hill to the last sitter's tree. Johnny caught his breath. A body was hanging by a short rope from one of the tree's branches. He ran up the hill, slipping and falling on the slick, hillside surface. Edwards, with his heart racing now, and covered with mud, stared up from the base of the tree at its lower limbs. He saw Sasha, motionless, hanging by her lanyard. The lanyard was attached to her waist harness, and the other end of the rope was tied off to a stout branch. Her body, with its upper torso and legs sagging downward from the lanyard's fixed position, looked like it was skewered in the lower back by a huge, invisible sword, and was now held up for all to see. Her motionless, ragdoll appearance was frightening.

Deputy Edwards cupped both hands together and hollered up to the summit. "Dread, come down here! Bring your climbing gear!"

Edwards continued shouting until he saw a head pop up above the rim and look down his way. He then shouted out once more, pointing up to Sasha. Her lifeless body slowly rotated in a slight breeze that had just developed.

All the Alliance members were stiff, sore, cold, and half asleep as they were rousted by the faraway shouts. Hang heard the alarm first and scanned down the hill. His eyes followed the deputy's gesture, and seeing Sasha hanging from her tree, the tall, lanky college student yelled for everyone to wake up, then bolted over the crater's rim. He slipped and fell his way down the slope to the big Ponderosa tree, coming to stand next to Edwards, who was giving directions to his partner.

"Go back to Camp Sherman fire hall. The EMT numbers are on the front door, posted in one of the window panes. Get them here. Call the numbers, and let the phone ring until someone answers it. If you get a recorded message, call back again and again until someone answers. We need help, now!"

"Copy that, deputy."

Henderson slipped and fell his way back to his patrol car. After leaning outwards from their perches and seeing Sasha, the other tree sitters descended to the ground and immediately ran over to their fellow occupier's tree.

Deputy Edwards was questioning Hang. "We need to get her down. Do you have some climbing gear nearby?"

Hang stared up at Sasha. Her climbing rope was hanging down to the ground within arm's reach. Her perch was the closest to the forest floor, resting no more than thirty or forty feet above the ground. The catastrophe had quickly woken him up, allowing his mind to race through numerous possible scenarios. He thought about his gear up at the summit and the rope dangling next to him.

"I'm going up old school."

The young college student grabbed the rope with both hands and pulled himself upwards to about a foot off the ground. Then, he moved quickly up the rope, hand over hand. About halfway up, the thin climbing rope cut into his hands and drew blood, causing him to wince with pain each time he pulled upward, but Hang never slowed or considered stopping.

By now the entire Alliance had joined Deputy Edwards and was watching Hang ascend the rope. As Hang got near Sasha, she groaned in pain. He looked down to the Alliance members.

"She's alive!"

The group below hugged each other and vocalized their relief. Rachael found Dread and tightly held his hand as they watched the rescue unfold. The tree sitter's black hair hung down, pointing to the group below as a breeze rocked her gently from side to side. Hang grabbed onto the hammock's branch and pulled himself onto the platform. Kneeling, he assessed Sasha. She had a large contusion on her forehead, lacerations on her cheek, and blood still dripping slowly from her face. He quickly pulled up the climbing rope and tied a friction knot onto the lanyard, then wrapped the rope once around the large limb where he knelt. This wrap would provide the needed brakeage on his descent system.

"She's coming down."

Hang retrieved a knife from his pocket and cut the lanyard. Sasha swayed a little to the side, but didn't bounce noticeably when the lanyard's tension was released. He then lowered her to the ground. Several Alliance members retrieved Thermorest mattresses from the summit along with some wool blankets. Sasha's body was placed on the insulation, and all the occupiers crowded around her. Dread knelt in the muddy soil next to her. With a frightened expression on his face, he held Sasha's hand. Edwards pulled the blankets over the still activist's body and began checking for her vitals. She was cold to the touch, too cold. He then probed for a pulse, but couldn't find one. Next, he checked for breathing. None was apparent. *Oh shit! This is really bad.* Deputy Edwards immediately started resuscitation.

Dread looked on in horror and disbelief. "I thought she was alive."

"She will be, don't worry, she will be."

Dread's tears began blurring his vision. He blurted out, "What can I do?"

Deputy Edwards was completing a session of twenty heart compressions, and glanced over at Dread.

"Is she your girlfriend?" Dread nodded confirmation. "Hold her hand. Tell her you love her, you need her, and not to leave you. Just keep talking to her."

Johnny quickly gave Sasha two breaths, and resumed chest compressions. He could feel the crunching movement of at least one broken rib as he continued resuscitation. He gave her several more breaths of air. As he continued doing CPR, two large ravens flew into Sasha's tree and nervously sidestepped back and forth on a branch that held her hammock in place. They watched Hang as he lowered himself, foot by foot, down the rope. The pain from his cut hands was almost unbearable now, and whenever he grasped the climbing rope tightly, he wanted to scream out. The ravens looked from Hang down to the assembled occupiers, and started their chuckling, raspy clicking talk. One of the big birds tilted its head back and squawked loudly. Both ravens gazed south down the road at several approaching vehicles. The emergency lights of the Camp Sherman ambulance flashed red and white. It was followed by two patrol cars. The caravan stopped quickly at the road's bend. The two ravens cocked their heads from side to side as they watched people emerge from the rigs. They again squawked loudly, then lifted themselves upwards with several wing flaps and flew to a nearby tree.

While officers quickly left their cruisers and rushed to the rescue site, two EMTs jumped out of the ambulance into the early morning light, and, opening up their emergency vehicle, grabbed a gurney from its recesses. They, too, headed for the crowd of people. As the first responders arrived, Deputy Edwards was listening for air movement at Sasha's nose. Suddenly, the young college student gasped and coughed, which was followed by an agonizing groan of pain. The deputy looked down at the pretty, African American woman's face as her eyes fluttered open. A tear fell onto her cheek and he wiped it off with his thumb, leaving a muddy smudge on her face. Edwards sat upright on his knees and viewed the Alliance members.

"Make room for the medics, people. Get out of the way."

Dread, still holding Sasha's hand, focused on Climber. Dread's vision had cleared, but tear trails nevertheless ran down his cheeks. "You're the man, now. I'm going with Sasha. She needs somebody with her."

Climber nodded in agreement, and searched for Runner. The two quickly conferred and then quietly walked to each Alliance member, giving them instructions. Sasha lay on the ground, regaining consciousness with Deputy Edwards attending to her.

A medic knelt next to Edwards. "I'll take over, now, officer."

The other EMT arrived with the gurney. Deputy Edwards stood and took a few steps backwards, allowing the medics to assess the young activist's condition. OSP Trooper Alec Mills and Deputy Henderson came to stand near the EMTs, ready to assist if needed. Deputy Edwards, wiping tears from his face, joined them. As all the first responders congregated, they didn't notice the Alliance members drifting off and the tree sitters regaining their perches.

After assessing her condition, one of the medics focused on the police officers. "She's stable enough to move. Let's do it."

The other medic looked into Sasha's eyes and carefully patted her shoulder. "Everything's going to be fine, young lady. We are going to put you on our gurney and transport you into Bend. You'll be good as new in no time. All right, gentlemen, on my count. One, two, three, lift."

All the officers and Dread helped raise the injured coed off the ground and onto the stretcher. Another blanket was quickly put over her as one medic checked her pulse. The other EMT talked quietly with Dread.

"You're welcome to ride with us, young man, but if things get critical, you'll need to sit back and let us work. You can trust us. We know what we're doing."

The lanky college student nodded.

The EMTs placed Sasha into the ambulance and locked her gurney's wheels. Trooper Mills pulled Dread off to the side as the paramedics hooked Sasha up to their monitors.

"Dread, you'll need to stay in the hospital. Do not leave. If you do, there'll be a warrant issued for your arrest. Consider the hospital a house arrest situation. Do you understand?"

The young militant once again nodded his head in understanding. After speaking with Mills, Dread contemplated Deputy Edwards and his eyes began to water. Edwards' eyes met the bearded occupier's gaze. Dread walked over to the Jefferson County deputy sheriff and hugged him. They embraced for a moment, then separated. As Dread wiped tears from his eyes, Officer Mills escorted him to the ambulance's rear door. He regarded the Alliance leader with his long dreads and wet, muddy clothing.

"Do you have any cash for food?"

"No."

The OSP trooper retrieved his wallet from an inside pocket and handed Dread forty dollars.

Dread reluctantly accepted the money and said, "This is just a loan, you know."

Mills smiled at Dread. "Yes it is, and I know you're good for it."

The ambulance engine started, and one of the EMTs helped Dread up into the rig. Back doors were shut, and with red and white lights flashing, the rescue vehicle drove off toward Bend.

Mills focused on Deputy Henderson. "Would you go with them, deputy? Stay at the hospital until a trooper relieves you."

"I'm on my way."

Henderson drove off down the gravel road in Highway 20's direction. Deputy Edwards gravitated toward the bend in the road and stood there looking up at the occupation site.

Trooper Mills joined him. "Good work, deputy."

Edwards surveyed Mills. "What a way to start the day."

The trooper could tell his friend was mentally exhausted from his ordeal.

"Why don't you go into Camp Sherman and start some trouble?"

Edwards regarded Mills and laughed. "You want me to get some espresso coffees, don't you?"

Both officers began to laugh.

"Yes, I do, deputy, and get some scones while you're at it. Be sure and find some crotchety old local before you leave, and tell them how much you love Jack's espresso machine."

The two friends continued to laugh. "Sounds like a plan, trooper."

Edwards turned away from the occupation site and headed back to his truck. "Hey, deputy."

Edwards stopped, turned back around, and faced Mills.

"I want you to know you're one of the reasons I can do this job. I'm proud to be serving alongside of you."

Johnny Edwards smiled at his friend, and turned back to his rig. He started his truck, turned it around, and headed off to the Camp Sherman store.

Officer Mills returned his gaze to the hillside and the occupiers. After all the happenings, not much had really changed. The site was a little messier now. Branches littered the slope and a couple Alliance members were traversing the hill, picking up their windblown gear. About the only real difference was a new hill boss. Trooper Mills continued to view the logging site. *What the hell?* He went back to the Charger, retrieved his binoculars, and, returning to his previous spot, raised the glasses to his eyes and adjusted them. *Holy crap! Unbelievable!* The trooper lowered his glasses and smiled. *Hurry back, deputy. I've got something you'll want to see.*

CHAPTER 44

Deputy Edwards didn't find any locals to goad into a discussion about Jack's espresso machine. He felt somewhat unfulfilled about this as he stopped his truck behind the state cruiser and washed down a bite of lemon–poppy seed scone with a gulp of his mocha. Mills stood over by the road's bend, and upon hearing the truck, looked back and waved Edwards over to his position. The trooper held his binoculars in his hand, and waited for his friend to join him. Edwards rejoined Mills and handed him an espresso and scone. In return, he received the glasses.

The sun had risen above the treetops, and the day was heating up. Johnny was wearing his wide brimmed cowboy hat and sunglasses. He removed and pocketed the glasses.

"Take a look at the dynamite trees, deputy."

Johnny raised the glasses to his eyes and focused on the closest tree and its bundle of explosives. He then scanned the other trees with their dynamite packages. Dropping the glasses from his eyes, and viewing the hill without them, Edwards slightly shook his head in disbelief. "I'd say things have drastically changed, trooper."

"I agree. Those bundled flares don't offer the occupiers much protection."

Johnny responded, "Nope, they certainly don't. I'm sure your boss would like to know about this new development."

"He probably would, deputy. Yep, I foresee a radical shift in our strategy. Maybe even some arrests occurring within a day or two."

"That seems likely to me. I'll hold down the fort, if you want to talk with your boss," Edwards offered.

"Yeah, I do. He also needs to know about Sasha and Dread. I'll go run him down at Black Butte. See you in a couple hours. How you fixed for grub?"

Deputy Edwards thought for a moment. "Fine. Got some sandwiches and fruit."

"All right, next time you see me, I might be accompanied by the superintendent."

"Okay, I'll keep myself awake, and looking ever vigilant."

"Perfect, deputy."

Mills walked back to his rig, turned it around, and headed for Black Butte Ranch.

Deputy Edwards watched the Alliance members picking up their gear and organizing the hill. Climber was retrieving downed blasting wire. Johnny decided to pick up pieces of the barricade, and after gathering together several boards and stanchions, he fabricated a makeshift roadblock. It would have to do until another one was moved onto the site.

All the Alliance members were somber, and didn't talk much with each other. Sasha's near death was still very present and real. They all quietly got their positions in order, hung or laid out sleeping gear to dry, and pretty much thought about their occupation in a less positive manner. They could see two of their blasting wires were blown down by the storm, but one still remained in place. This provided them some protection. They could not see the flare bundles had been exposed for what they really were. Consequently, they still believed they held the upper hand, when in reality, their bluff had been revealed and no longer protected them.

Several groundkeepers were now moving up the ridge, and Deputy Edwards knew cooking aromas would soon be reaching him as the morning meal was fixed by the young occupiers. He returned to his car, kicking cones off the road as he walked along. He reached into his truck, fetching his espresso and his scone. Leaning up against the hood of his rig, Johnny began drinking his coffee and dining on pastry. The sun rose higher, the day grew warmer, and the hillside routine returned. Deputy Edwards, unlike the young occupiers, knew their days were now numbered, and very soon this occupation would be over.

CHAPTER 45

Superintendent Philip Ross sat on his deck overlooking Black Butte Ranch's golf course and the North Sister. Defining his horizon, the stark, snowless summit rose abruptly up into the blue sky. He held a cordless phone in one hand and slowly ran the other over the short stubble of his crewcut. He'd soon be talking with his boss about changing strategies regarding the Big Eddy Rise occupation. Trooper Mills divulged information that totally changed Ross's opinion of their present wait-and-see tactic. The lack of explosives and the close call with the tree sitter made him consider removing the occupiers rather than outlasting them. *No time like the present.* He punched the governor's office number into the phone and waited for her secretary's greeting.

Governor O'Connell sat at her desk with her chief of staff, Laura Roberts. Roberts had pulled a chair up close to the governor and they were discussing Oregon's budget shortfall and several possible remedial measures. None of them were particularly attractive to Oregon voters so their conversation dealt with how these strategies could be bundled, allowing voters agreeable options. All the windows were opened in the office, allowing a slight breeze to cool the ladies. They both wore lightweight blouses, skirts, and sandals.

The governor's desk phone blinked and she answered her secretary.

"It's Superintendent Ross, governor."

"Put him through, Susan."

"Hello, superintendent. How did you fare last night?"

"I was fine, governor, but we almost had a fatality at the occupation site."

"What?"

"One of the students fell out of her tree and was caught at the end of a tether for a period of time. She died on site, but was revived by a Jefferson County deputy. She's now in the Bend hospital with her boyfriend. We have both of them under guard at this moment."

"Oh my God, Ross. Is she going to make it?"

"I believe so. I haven't spoken with a doctor, so I'm just speculating as to the prognosis."

"Just a second, superintendent, Laura Roberts is right here. I'm going to put us on speaker phone."

Ross could hear the governor filling Roberts in on their conversation. When she finished, Ross interjected, "Also, governor, the dynamite bundles are actually flares that were painted to look like explosives. Last night's wind and rain exposed them for what they really are."

At this point, Ross decided to forge ahead with his new opinion about the occupation strategy.

"Given these new developments, governor, I suggest we arrest the occupiers quickly and remove them from the site. There is no threat of explosives, and I certainly don't want another injury on my watch."

Governor O'Connell and Laura Roberts conferred about this new plan as the OSP boss listened in. After some debate, both O'Connell and Roberts agreed with Ross.

"We'll have a press conference tomorrow, superintendent. In it, we'll explain the reasoning behind our strategy shift. You should be good to go after we've shared this news with the state's citizenry."

"All right, governor. I'll get all the pieces into place for the occupiers' arrest. It won't take more than a day or two."

"Good, superintendent. Laura or I will call you after our news conference, and we'll expect the arrests to occur the next day or the day after."

"Good luck with your news conference, Governor. I'll be waiting for your call."

Governor O'Connell and Laura talked some more about the news conference. They felt public sentiment would be open to removal of the students now that one nearly died while occupying the site. Laura left the governor and headed for her press secretary's office, where she would help prepare the address the governor would give.

Philip Ross once again gazed out at the golf course and thought about playing eighteen holes, although he had a few responsibilities to deal with before it could happen. First, he should visit the occupation site, appraise the situation, and talk with the new Alliance leader. Then he needed to contact Peters, getting him moving on arranging the "arrest" details with Jefferson and Deschutes Counties. He'd also ask Peters to set up a golf date three days from now with a tee time of 5:00 p.m. By five, the day's temperature would have dropped, allowing for a comfortable eighteen holes, followed by a late dinner at the Ranch's restaurant.

Ross found his trooper hat and Crown Victoria keys, and headed out the door. It was time to have a talk with the young occupiers about their immediate future.

CHAPTER 46

Cassie was drinking coffee from a thermos cup Brian had given her after she settled into his Subaru. Once again it was a dark, rich roast with cream, just the way she liked it, and her co-anchor also threw in a homemade scone with the deal, a bacon and cheese masterpiece that Cassie couldn't get enough of. She playfully thought about what she would do to get more of the scones. She leaned over subtly and checked the paper bag for another one.

Brian noticed Cassie inclining in his direction, and caught the scent of her shampoo. It had a nice coconut and vanilla aroma he liked. "What do you need, partner?"

She thought of several things instantly, but decided to be professional. "Just checking for more scones. It was delicious. My compliments to the chef."

"Yeah. It's an old family recipe handed down from generation to generation, which I just found online. Pretty good, huh?"

Cassie smiled at Brian. His hair was pulled back into a ponytail. He wore dark glasses, a T-shirt, shorts, and sandals.

"They're damn good. I'd do anything for another one of those."

Brian thought about her choice of words and smiled to himself. *What was she thinking?* Her dark, straight, thick hair was recently cut into a bob. The style accentuated her high cheekbones, making her exotically handsome.

Oh boy, thought Brian, *she is so beautiful.* He felt a tingle in his groin. *Better stop this line of thought, right now, brother. You've got work to do. Say something!*

"Hey, your storm was incredible last night. You were spot on with your weather report."

Cassie laughed. "Well, the National Weather Service was spot on."

"I hope the activists fared all right."

"Me too. We should know pretty quickly."

Brian pulled off Highway 20 and headed in Camp Sherman's direction. At the three-way, he noticed a Crown Vic ahead of them.

"Looks like we've got the superintendent up front. I hope it's not a bad omen."

"Probably not. He's been visiting the site pretty regularly. I assume it's another routine, hands-on type appearance by our head cop."

Brian inspected ahead of the old cruiser and saw two other rigs parked near what appeared to be a roadblock, badly in need of repair. He stopped his Subaru behind the Crown Vic. Both he and Cassie donned wide-brimmed hats, grabbed their phones, and stepped out into the bright, mid-morning sunshine.

Superintendent Ross left his vehicle, and looking back at the two reporters, waved hello. He turned and continued walking to where Deputy Edwards and Trooper Mills stood. His trooper called out a greeting, "Hello, superintendent."

Ross joined the officers, and Mills gestured up to the Rise. "Things are pretty much back to normal. The kids did their breakfast routine and policed the hill of storm debris. From the looks of it, everybody is a little subdued and just passing time, right now."

Philip Ross removed his hat, wiped the perspiration from his forehead with a scarf that he'd retrieved from a side pocket, and repositioned his hat onto his head. The superintendent appeared to be all "business" this morning.

"Trooper, I'd like you to accompany me up to the summit. We need to talk with our young activist about his options."

"Be glad to, sir."

Ross focused on Edwards. "Keep your eyes open, deputy. If you see anything suspicious, give us a holler. We're on channel 21." All three officers checked their personal radios.

The two OSP officers started up the Big Eddy Rise and were immediately met with a chorus of boos and chants.

"Stop the Greed, Save the Trees," echoed through the forest.

Both troopers eyed the groundkeepers as they passed by their sites. They noted confusion on the young people's faces. Looking upwards, they saw Climber holding up his blasting box, which still had one wire connected to it. He keyed his megaphone. "Stop there, officers. One more step and I'll blow up the tree."

Ross and Mills didn't hesitate and continued up the rise. They occasionally kicked a cone to the side while walking around manzanita bushes and stepping over downed branches.

The groundkeepers and tree sitters were conversing with each other about the apparent perplexing change in police tactics. While monitoring the OSP movement, they began cinching up chains and placing thermorests under themselves for more comfort.

Climber held the blasting box to his side as the troopers warily climbed over the crater's shallow rim. Mills looked around the campsite at the elk tent, kitchen site, and fire pit. No one else appeared to be present.

"Anyone else in the crater, Climber?"

The young activist observed the two OSP officers and knew the end was near. "No, I'm alone right now."

Superintendent Ross addressed Climber seriously. "Young man, your dynamite turned into road flares last night, and you almost lost one of your friends to a near fatal accident. Thanks to a Jefferson County deputy, she is with us today. I've talked with the governor and my orders are to remove your group from this site in the next few days. As it stands, if you and your friends leave this site peacefully, the governor will ask the local DA to reduce all charges against you to misdemeanors."

Ross was shooting from the hip here, but felt the governor would go along with these offers. Climber thought about the superintendent's words.

"You'll have to carry us off the site, sir. We won't walk off of our own free will. When the time's appropriate, I'll tell the tree sitters to leave their hammocks and join us on the ground. This will make things easier. We won't offer any physical resistance, but we won't help you arrest us either."

As Ross formulated his next statements, he surveyed the campsite again, noting the overall cleanliness and tidiness of the occupiers' stronghold. He was impressed with the Alliance's attention to detail and operational mode.

"I understand your position. We won't expect you to walk off the hill on your own. When you see the county jail bus arrive, that will be your cue of the impending arrests. So we can proceed with your arrest in a timely and organized manner, they'll be more deputies and troopers on site. After you've been cuffed and placed on the bus, you'll be taken to the Deschutes County jail, and what happens next is pretty much up to the judge and your legal team.

While the OSP officers were negotiating with Climber, Cassie and Brian talked with Edwards. They did an impromptu interview with the deputy, who detailed for them the early morning events, and the removal of Sasha by ambulance to Bend's hospital. Edwards pointed the flares out to his friends and noted "off the record" this was a game changer for the state's occupation strategy. The reporters thanked him for the interview and immediately decided to visit Sasha and Dread at the hospital. They said their goodbyes, and drove off to St. Charles Medical Center.

Mills and Superintendent Ross picked their way back down the hill. Again, they stepped over downed branches and around manzanita bushes. During their parley with Climber, several chipmunks had emerged from their burrows and now were scampering about. A few scrub jays also reappeared, hoping for a handout from the occupiers. Eventually, after enduring more verbal abuse, the police officers regained the west road and rejoined Edwards. Ross began formulating logistics as he left the Rise, and once he, Mills, and Edwards got back together, the superintendent started to articulate them.

"We need to get a new barricade in place, here, and I want another roadblock farther down the road by the southern bend. We've lucked out so far in regards to disturbances from tourists and news organizations. It's been a little strange we haven't been pestered by the lot so let's make sure some last-minute invasion doesn't screw up our arrests. I'll have those barricades sent out here this afternoon, Mills. I'd like you to supervise their placement."

"Will do, superintendent."

"Deputy Edwards, let's make this easy on ourselves. The Jefferson and Deschutes County Sheriff's Departments will maintain the river surveillance, and the Staters will control the roadblocks."

"Sounds like a plan, sir."

"Okay, gentlemen. I'll get the barricades sent your way. As we speak, Lieutenant Peters is taking care of the arrest logistics. We should be removing the activists day after tomorrow, or at the latest, the next day. I'll be better informed about our schedule after talking with Peters and the governor."

The OSP superintendent excused himself, and leaving the officers at the repaired barricade, turned his Crown Vic around and headed back to Black Butte Ranch. Ross needed to confer with his aide and then call the governor to relay the details. As he drove toward the Ranch, he thought about his 5:00 p.m. tee time scheduled in the near future. The weather was perfect: not a cloud in the sky and no apparent breeze. He hadn't played a round yet, and maybe these holes could be considered a celebration, a victory game. It appeared the Big Eddy Rise occupation was going to end peacefully. Hopefully—Ross wasn't counting his chickens before they hatched—but he couldn't think of anything that could derail the resolution discussed with Climber. Maybe he could get another round of golf in before he left Central Oregon. Another round would be icing on the cake. The Police Interceptor turned onto Highway 20 and Philip Ross punched the accelerator, allowing the big V8 to flex its muscles and propel him back to the Ranch.

CHAPTER

47

Cassie and Brian turned onto Highway 20 and headed for St. Charles Medical Center. Sasha was in the ICU there with a badly damaged lung, several broken ribs, mild hypothermia, and a severe concussion. They'd heard from Deputy Henderson via cellphone. Sasha's prognosis was good and a complete recovery was expected.

As the newscasters drove east, they decided there would be no interviews today. This visit was meant only to buoy the young couple's spirits and to offer them support in any way possible.

Brian considered the Three Creek Lake sign while driving through Sisters and then glanced at his co-anchor, who was perusing her phone.

"Hey, I know these work dates are fun and all, but would you like to go on a real date with me, sometime?"

Cassie thought for a moment, and responded. "Only if you promise to bring some more of those scones."

"It's a deal, and I'll even throw in some fruit like oranges and apples. Have you ever hiked Tam McArthur Trail? The trailhead starts by Three Creek Lake."

"Nope, I haven't, partner, but I really like hiking, so if that's our date, it sounds great to me."

"It's a fantastic hike. You get to the top and there's an overlook displaying the Three Sisters and a great northern view of the region."

"Really, Brian, all I need are the scones and you to make this date spectacular!"

Brian thought about this comment from Cassie. She hadn't been joking. *Does she really like me?* He continued driving to Bend as an old, familiar tingling revisited his lower torso.

"Can you make an early morning start tomorrow?"

"Sure."

"Well, let's call it a date, then. I'll pick you up around 8:00 a.m. with fresh coffee and a scone for your epicurean delight."

For a moment the two drove on in silence, both lost in thought, thinking about their hike. Eventually, the young reporters started talking about their workday. Cassie would go back to the station and put together their piece with Deputy Edwards and edit her weather segment. Brian needed to visit the local OSU campus and interview the geologist there. The professor had called yesterday and said more significant volcanic activity was occurring on Hood, and the blond news anchor wanted to have his interview ready for this evening's broadcast. When they reached Bend, Cassie asked to visit her favorite florist shop. She wanted to get Sasha some flowers. After the floral purchase, the reporters headed once again for the hospital.

The Bend traffic was moving slowly, and it took a while for them to reach St. Charles. They parked the Subaru and walked to the hospital's entrance. Brian thought about Sasha and her injuries, and wondered how Dread was doing. He also thought about the occupation site, and how things would be changing there pretty soon. The hospital outer doors automatically opened for the reporters. They headed for the reception desk and their unannounced visit with the two activists.

CHAPTER
48

CHANNEL 19 WAS ON AND TARRI MCGRATH AND her partner were watching their favorite anchors report the local news. Brian mentioned later in the show they would have a serious piece about the Big Eddy Rise occupation. Tarri's interest perked up upon hearing this message. Since the occupation had started, she and Steve Johnson, her immediate boss, had talked several times by phone about the young occupiers. They felt extremely fortunate the Alliance had stepped in and stopped the logging effort, and both were very thankful their loosely concocted strategy had worked. Neither of them had heard anything from Secretary Billings. Both felt they'd dodged a bullet.

Brian was engaging Cassie in conversation related to the recent windstorm. "Wow, Cassie, you sure nailed the storm's strength and ferocity with your forecasting last night."

Cassie regarded her co-anchor, then turned and faced the set's camera. "It was just as bad as the National Weather Service predicted, Brian. Several roofs flew off buildings in the area, and some outbuildings were torn apart. A few older houses and modular homes were damaged severely and one large, historic barn near Prineville was completely flattened. A few thousand people lost power in Bend and the surrounding area, but Central Oregon Co-op said almost all customers had regained their electricity and the rest would have service back by tomorrow morning. Honestly, we fared pretty well, considering the wind strength. The Weather Service is calling this event Central Oregon's 'Storm of the Century.'" Cassie looked back at her co-anchor.

Brian met her gaze. "It sure seemed like a beast to me. I didn't sleep a wink last night because of the wind noise."

"I didn't either, Brian, but really, the strongest part of the storm was to the west of us. It really hit the Black Butte, Camp Sherman area the worst."

The camera backed out, showing the anchor's desk and more of their backdrop.

Brian continued, "Speaking of Camp Sherman, we have a tragic story to relay to our viewers about the site occupation. After Cassie's weather forecast, Channel 19 will air an interview with Deputy Edwards of the Jefferson County Sheriff's Department, who arrived at the logging site around dawn this morning."

When the station went to commercial break, the two reporters talked about Sasha. She had been conscious and able to communicate with them during their visit, although at times she lost her train of thought and had to be prompted to continue her conversation.

On cue, the two anchors faced the camera and smiled. Brian flashed an expression of surprise at the camera and literally jumped upwards about an inch. He regained his smile and turned toward his partner. "I'm literally jumping out of my seat in anticipation of your weather segment."

"I can see that, Brian. I hope my reporting is worthy of your excitement."

The camera backed out and allowed a broader studio shot as Cassie walked over to her green screen.

"Did you see it, Tarri?"

Tarri McGrath glanced over at Wendy. "Cassie was playing footsie with Brian."

"Are you sure?"

"Yes, I'm sure. Brian flinched big time when she touched him with her foot."

Tarri started to laugh. "These two are pretty unpredictable as is. With a little romance thrown in, who knows what more will happen?"

"This could get really interesting. Fun interesting, if you know what I mean."

The two ladies looked at each other, and reaching for one another, held hands for a moment. Tarri returned her focus to the set as Cassie ended her weather spot and headed to the anchor desk. "Let's see if any more sparks fly."

The pretty, dark-haired anchor sat down, and Brian commented, "We're back to more boring, sunny, warm days and cool evenings. You've kind of let us down today."

"Don't give up hope, Brian. Who knows what next week will bring?"

The camera then moved closer, showing only Brian's face, which took on a somber expression.

"Early this morning, one of the tree sitters nearly died at the occupation site. Cassie and I interviewed Deputy Edwards about what happened. It was the deputy who brought the young activist back to life by administering CPR. The early morning storm blew her out of her perch, and she hung by a rope until Edwards arrived on site and noticed her body dangling from a tree branch."

Wendy and Tarri regarded each other in disbelief. Both women wanted the occupiers to succeed. This accident was tragic and frightening. They continued to watch as the station showed some of the interview with Deputy Edwards. At the remark about bundles of flares being exposed, Tarri once again gazed at Wendy with a concerned expression.

"Oh no! This could change everything!"

Right then, Tarri's cellphone went off, and she checked the caller I.D. It was her boss.

"Hello, Steve. Are you watching Channel 19?"

Director Johnson had been watching the news, and its content prompted his call to Tarri. "Yes I am. What an awful night for those kids. I hope Sasha is going to recover quickly, although it sounded like she was pretty banged up. Did you catch the part about the dynamite?"

"Yes. Wendy and I are sitting here not believing what we're hearing."

"I know, I know. It's all so tragic."

There was a pause in the conversation. Then Johnson continued speaking. "I think the kids will be arrested soon."

Tarri responded, "You're probably right. I really thought our plan was working perfectly, and those old trees would be saved, but I don't know now."

"We'll have to wait and see. Well, I just called to see if you were watching the news. I'm keeping my fingers crossed and hoping Sasha and these young activists make out all right. Hopefully, they can continue to stop the logging effort."

"They haven't been arrested yet. Maybe they won't be. Who knows, Steve, Salem might not want the trees cut either."

"That would be helpful. Well anyway, say hello to Wendy for me. I'm thinking positively and hoping for the best."

"Okay, Steve. Thanks for calling. Bye."

While Tarri and Steve conversed, Brian finished his segment about the occupiers, and the station went to break. Tarri turned off her phone just as Channel 19 came back on the air. The camera moved back, showing all of the anchor desk and the multiscreen background where a recent picture of Mt. Hood now filled the screens. Its stark, jagged arêtes and peak composed most of the shot. Brian began his story about the volcano's recent activity.

"Our last segment tonight revisits OSU's geologist, Professor Anderson, who has more startling news for us."

The show now aired Professor Anderson's interview. It was shot in the scientist's small faculty office. He was shown sitting at his desk surrounded by bookshelves filled with various publications. Besides mentioning quakes beneath Hood and St. Helens, and their continued increase in numbers and strength, the professor also talked about a bulge forming in Hood's blown-out, partially cratered summit. He noted this was exactly what St. Helens did before its catastrophic explosion. When Brian's interview ended, the camera pulled back and once again showed Cassie and Brian sitting next to each other.

"Does the OSU scientist believe an eruption is imminent?"

"Well, it's a possibility in his opinion, Cassie. If things continue as they are, then Professor Anderson believes Mt. Hood will certainly have a significant volcanic event, but conversely, if all these symptoms subside, he feels nothing will happen, and we'll be off the hook."

The camera moved in for a close-up of the two reporters. Cassie and Brian turned and were now observing each other.

"Well, I guess it's a wait-and-see situation."

"Yes it is. We'll be keeping in close contact with Professor Anderson."

The two reporters looked back to their camera.

"Well, thanks, Bend, for joining us tonight. We'll see you tomorrow with all the latest and most important news for Central Oregon."

The camera backed out as Cassie waved. Her co-anchor watched her, talking in a serious manner.

Wendy regarded Tarri. "I'll bet he's giving Cassie a little feedback about her foot flirting. What do you think, Tarri?"

Tarri looked back at her partner, and nodded her agreement. "Yeah, I'd be saying, 'what took you so long?'"

Both women laughed.

Tarri continued, "Hey, the evening news is getting a little too serious. I'm not sure if I need a beer, or some overly caloric food right now."

"I've got a great suggestion. Let's have both."

The two ladies turned off their flatscreen and headed for the kitchen. Soon, they were on their deck with dark Porters and a tray of munchies nestled between them. They sat overlooking the Three Sisters and Broken Top, and offered a toast to the young activists who had stopped the Big Eddy Rise logging. Tarri hoped a miracle might materialize and continue to stop the logging activity. She took a sip of her Porter and quietly gazed at the mountains.

CHAPTER

49

IT WAS 7:00 P.M., AND THE PRESIDENT HAD retired for the evening after eating a five-course meal in his private dining room. The chef had prepared browned halibut with diced almonds and a lemon sauce reduction for the main entrée. While dining, McDonald sat in his favorite chair, and faced the room's lone fireplace and mirror, which hung above the mantel. The president enjoyed admiring his reflection whenever he sat or rose from dinner. A substantial, ornate chandelier hung above the table, providing more than ample light for his phone browsing. The highly polished mahogany dining table with matching chairs had place settings for four, but these seats were mostly ceremonial. McDonald usually supped alone. Occasionally, Henry Graham ate with him, but not tonight.

McDonald perused his phone while eating, mostly ignoring his service staff. His Secret Service detail had grown accustomed to his verbal flare-ups, and discreetly checked on his well-being whenever a vocal disturbance occurred.

After finishing his meal's last course, a dessert of strawberry shortcake topped with whipped cream, the president rose, primped in the mirror, and walked across the hall to his living room. His personal living space was comfortably furnished and cozy compared to the other White House rooms. It had a white marble fireplace on the west wall. Above it hung a picture of a thoughtful, uniformed General Washington posing by his writing desk. Two chocolate-colored leather recliners faced the fireplace, with an ornate wooden table positioned between them. A fire, laid with seasoned oak, quietly burned, adding warmth to the room. Walking past this cozy setting, McDonald sat down on an overstuffed fabric couch facing the east wall, which featured mounted 60-inch flatscreens. The continuous line of TVs was broken in the middle by the Yellow Room's doorway. McDonald didn't like this visual interruption, but since this was the only wall long enough for all the TVs, he lived with the door's distraction. A coffee table crafted in the eighteenth century sat before his couch, and end tables supporting Tiffany lamps flanked the large sofa. Deep pile, dark-colored, wool throw rugs were placed throughout the room in well-trafficked areas, adding to the rich ambiance of his living room.

As McDonald sat down and stretched out his legs, resting his feet on the coffee table, his hard, leather-soled shoes immediately scuffed the ancient table's surface. He was unaware of or chose to ignore the scratches his heels created in the old table. Picking up his remote, he turned on each flatscreen to the preset evening news channels. The president enjoyed watching an array of network telecasts. This allowed him to keep abreast of the "libs'" messages so he could attack them in an informed manner. WNN with its Hispanic anchor, Allen Rodrigues, riled him to distraction, and his nightly tirades often targeted this network.

The president recorded all the shows he watched, and the remainder of his evening would be spent viewing and dissecting each network's telecast. He would write memos about specific segments, noticing the reporters who were responsible for the various pieces of journalism. During this nightly ritual, his phone sat idly next to him, recharging.

As McDonald viewed his screens, Allen Rodrigues's voice caught his attention. WNN's anchor had just mentioned Oregon's governor by name. The president quickly muted the other TVs and focused on WNN's news story. The screen showed a close-up of the newscaster as he continued with his report.

"Oregon's Governor, Sarah O'Connell, said today in her public news conference the state's logging site occupation would soon be over. A young tree sitter nearly died last night after falling from her platform. She dangled from her roost by a rope for most of the late night and early morning. The Governor felt the time was right to end the occupation and return the area to normalcy before anyone else was injured."

McDonald jumped to his feet with clenched fists raised above his head and whooped in excitement. "Serves the little hippy-dippy right for messing with my logging site!"

One of the Secret Service guards quietly opened the living room's hall door, and noting the usual scene, slowly closed the door and regained his position.

President McDonald was ecstatic about this news, and was about to call Graham when Rodrigues mentioned Secretary Billings' name. This also caught the president's attention. *What has this asshole done to gain national attention?* He leaned forward on his couch in anticipation.

"WNN has just learned the Secretary of Agriculture, Ray Billings, has tendered his resignation, citing an inability to work with President McDonald. Billings felt it was best to resign his office and move on."

McDonald stood up and shook his fist at the flatscreen.

"You bastard! How dare you sucker punch me?"

Once again the hall doorway slowly opened and then quietly shut. With a reddening face, the president sat down and reached for his phone. Allen Rodrigues continued talking about Secretary Billings' resignation, and then noted the other secretaries who'd recently quit their positions. As McDonald scrolled through his contact list, he stopped for a moment and mused. He placed his phone back on the couch. *This is perfect. Billings was a pain in the ass and he just saved me some work. Firing the asshole could have been messy. Now, I can hire a new Agriculture Secretary, one who can follow orders, and get some more of my logging operations going. Well, thank you, ex-Secretary Billings. Take your sorry ass back to Texas and may all your oil wells be forever dry!* McDonald was beginning to really like the evening's news.

He looked back to WNN's newscast and noticed the screen now showed Rodrigues talking with another young newsman who sat across from him at the anchor's desk.

"It's good to have you back with us, Steve."

"Thanks, Allen. It's always my pleasure to be here."

The two reporters' physical appearances were strikingly different. Allen's dark complexion, neatly combed and parted hair, and rimless glasses depicted the serious, intellectual side of reporting, while his youthful political reporter's short, gelled hair, reddish cheeks, and full Van Dyke beard portrayed the eager, daring, investigative side of the news business. McDonald instantly didn't like this young "punkish" reporter, and continued sitting on the edge of his couch while the newsmen conversed.

"Your investigation into ICE arrests produced some startling information, Steve."

"Yes, it did, Allen. Not all states have seen the same amount of increased ICE activity. Actually, a large disparity exists between the states in regards to these arrests and detentions."

"What exactly have you discovered?"

"Well some states, like Texas, which has a large immigrant population, have had no increase in ICE activity, while others, like Oregon, have seen huge jumps in arrest numbers."

"That's an amazing revelation. What states have seen the most significant rise in immigrant detentions?"

"Well, Oregon, Washington, California, Massachusetts, New York, and Maine have all seen incarceration increases near or above 1000%."

"I see a direct correlation between blue states and heightened ICE activity, Steve."

"Yes, the blue states have been hit the hardest with immigrant arrests and deportations, while the red states have seen little change in their migrant populations."

"This seems to depict political favoritism, and there could be huge constitutional and ethical questions raised because of this apparent one-sided policy. Are you sure your data is correct?"

"Certainly. Arrests are public record, and I simply compared data from previous months to develop this story."

"If what you've reported, Steve, is in fact actually happening, then this information could be very damaging to the McDonald administration."

"Yes it could, but we must remember all I did was uncover data suggesting possible political manipulation. There could be other factors I'm not aware of which generated these numbers."

"Hopefully, we can get some clarification regarding your findings from the present administration. Thanks for your good work and reporting. I'll be looking forward to your next segment with us."

"It's always a pleasure to be here. Thank you."

At the end of Steve's segment, WNN went to commercial break. McDonald dumbly stared at his flatscreens, somewhat stunned by the piece he'd just viewed. *Shit was going to hit the fan now.* He reached for his cellphone, and as he picked it up, a knock came from his hallway door. A Secret Service agent announced a staffer's entrance. Preston entered the living room and greeted the president. McDonald stared at Preston grimly.

"Just checking on your fire, sir."

Walking over to the fireplace, Preston picked up the poker, repositioned the burning logs, and added another piece of wood. As he turned from the fire and headed for the hall door, he looked back at the president.

"Would you like anything from the kitchen, sir?"

McDonald continued watching WNN commercials. "Yeah, send up a few ham and cheese sandwiches on white bread."

"Certainly, Mr. President. They'll be brought up right away."

The young man left the living room and headed for the domestic stairwell. As McDonald watched more news, his cellphone announced a caller, Henry Graham.

"Yeah?"

"Are you watching the news?"

"What do you think?"

There was a long pause. Then Graham continued, "What's with the ICE arrests occurring only in blue states?"

This direct inquiry startled and agitated McDonald. He stood up and began pacing back and forth.

"The arrests are happening all over the place, Graham. This is just Demo bullshit. It's the same old liberal crap that's always thrown at us."

There was another drawn-out delay in the conversation. "Okay, let me word it another way, Mr. President. Why have the arrest percentages only increased in blue states?"

Another pause occurred, this time created by McDonald. His anger had reached the boiling point, and the president began talking to Graham with an elevated tone. "It's a little plan created by Secretary Logan and myself. We wanted to put the hurt on those liberal candy-assers."

The chief of staff frowned and held his phone away from his ear. "You should have consulted with me, or at least informed me about your scheme."

"Hell, Graham, I can't talk to you about every little thing I'm doing in regards to running this country."

"Well, this 'little thing' is going to be huge news tomorrow. It will be labeled 'Presidential Abuse of Power.' Your enemies don't need any more fuel right now, and this information will just aid their efforts.."

"Well, get to fixing this for me. Develop some news which creates somebody else hatching this arrest stuff. Hell, it's your job, Graham, so get moving on it!"

Another long pause punctuated the phone call. "Mr. President, there might be too many loose ends…"

McDonald's attention had drifted back to WNN when the commercials ended, and Allen Rodrigues was now engaging his viewing audience.

"We'll leave you tonight with a peculiar development occurring in several adjacent states out west. Idaho, Wyoming, and Utah citizens have noticed caravans of FEMA trailers traveling through their states into remote areas late at night."

The president began to get edgy while watching this story develop, and sat back down on the edge of his couch.

"Graham, I'll get back to you tomorrow. Meet me in my office at nine, and we'll scratch out a strategy to make this ICE thing go away. Direct your efforts to solving this problem, and stop complaining about it!"

White House Chief of Staff Henry Graham noted silence on his phone. This told him his conversation with the president was terminated. He thought about his boss's lack of tact and his incessant rudeness. *What a jerk.* He'd meet with McDonald in the morning and hopefully something could be done to right the ship because a few more screw-ups like this would see the end of this administration. Graham wondered how many other vengeful schemes the president had created without his knowledge. One thing was certain, McDonald was so clumsy and brash with his plotting that any plan he developed would eventually be uncovered.

The president sat transfixed while watching Rodrigues report on the last story. The anchor was continuing with his segment.

"The FEMA trailer caravans disappear into isolated military reservations. WNN has received a video from a Wyoming resident who flew her personal drone over one of those reservations. I believe that you, like myself, will find the drone's discoveries to be curious and worthy of explanation."

McDonald audibly groaned. He was sure his chief of staff would hound him about this revelation tomorrow, along with pestering him about the ICE strategy. A knock on the hall door drew McDonald's focus away from the news. Another intern had replaced Preston for the evening, and now entered with McDonald's sandwiches. The president noted with satisfaction his server was a well-endowed young lady wearing a skirt and white uniform top. He directed her to the coffee table. As the young woman bent over and removed the sandwiches from her tray, McDonald checked her out. She straightened up and, looking at the president, asked, "Do you need anything else, sir?"

"Yes. Would you bring up some medium roast coffee? I feel like working late tonight."

"Certainly, Mr. President. It won't take but a moment."

The young lady turned, and McDonald watched her leave the room. *Now, she's more like it.* He was thinking about her return as he triggered "play" on his DVR remote. He now watched the drone's flight. It flew over sagebrush for a moment and then hovered above what appeared to be an empty internment camp. A razor wire fence created a huge, rectangular compound. Guard towers were evenly spaced around the encampment's perimeter, and neat rows of FEMA trailers surrounded several large centrally located buildings. The drone flew to the end of the compound and back, showing about a thousand white trailers within the fenced enclosure. As the drone retraced its flight back across the sagebrush, the video ended. Allen Rodrigues's face once again filled the screen and he continued with the news story.

"As you can see, the FEMA trailers appear to be part of a large, vacant internment camp. Who the camp is for is a mystery. WNN contacted the Pentagon and Homeland Security Secretary Janice Logan about the camp, but no information from either source was forthcoming. We'll keep searching for answers and hopefully this mystery will be solved soon."

The camera backed out, showing more of WNN's studio, and Allen Rodrigues bid his audience a "good evening."

The president threw his DVR remote onto his sofa, bouncing it off the couch and onto the floor. He stiffly leaned back into the couch. *Tomorrow is going to be a real pain. I need to contend with Graham first, and get him working on smokescreens for the media. The news about the ICE arrests and now these God-damn camps is going to need immediate attention.*

After he got Graham moving, the president would busy himself with finding a new Secretary of Agriculture. He needed somebody tough and loyal who could quickly get some new logging sites open in Oregon. If McDonald conferred with some of his old timber industry cronies, he felt sure they'd know just the person for the job.

As the president thought about tomorrow's schedule, another knock announced someone's entrance. He glanced at the door from his couch as the young coed entered with his coffee.

"Ah yes. Bring it right over here, young lady."

CHAPTER 50

Henry Graham left his office and checked his watch. It was straight up 9:00 a.m. He headed down the long West Wing hallway toward the Oval Office. Last night's newscast had created quite a stir on Capitol Hill. Not only had everyone become aware of and disturbed by the ICE arrest disparities, but the empty, isolated internment camps had created an even bigger clamor. *What was McDonald thinking?* Graham ran his fingers through his unkempt hair, making it even messier. He arrived at the president's doorway, and a Secret Service agent announced his entrance as he let Graham in.

The chief of staff found the president sitting on the couch, scrolling through his phone. The president looked up. "Good God! Do you ever look in the mirror?"

He ignored the insult and sat across from his boss. The two men said nothing for a moment, and simply regarded each other.

"Well, Mr. President, the news about the empty internment camps overshadowed the ICE 'arrests' reporting. Could you explain these camps to me?"

McDonald didn't like Graham's leading question or his tone. "They're no big deal. Don't make them into a problem."

"The people on Capitol Hill think they're a problem, sir, and these congressmen need to be our allies if we're going to get any work done. Did you and Secretary Logan create these camps, and if you did, what are they for?"

The president sat staring at his chief of staff. He was becoming angry, and now, not only did he not like Graham's tone, he also didn't like where the conversation was going.

"Hell, yes. Logan and I created the camps. We're preparing for possible terrorist attacks within our borders. Remember me? I'm the guy who's tough on terrorism. I need to look tough, Graham. These camps show I'm ready to take charge of any domestic attack we might encounter."

The chief of staff looked up at the Lincoln portrait, hanging across the room from him. Lincoln's steady, strong gaze returned his overture.

"Mr. President, these encampments don't appear to be designed for terrorists, unless an army of several thousand jihadists attack us all at once. No, they suggest the internment of groups of people, possibly an ethnic group or a religious faction you might target. This concept is not well received by elected officials, nor by most of our country's voting populace."

"You're beginning to sound like some left-wing weakling, Graham. Of course they're meant for groups of people. If any camel-jockey attacks our country, I'm going to fill those camps with Muslims until the fencing is bulging and near bursting. This will give the remaining unincarcerated ragheads something to ponder. They'll think twice before helping their brethren attack and kill rightful U.S. citizens."

McDonald was now standing and his voice rose to such a level, it caused his hall sentinels to check on him. He waved them off and stood glaring down at his chief of staff aggressively.

"Don't question my actions! I'm the Commander in Chief. If I've screwed up, you need to make my problems go away. That's why I hired you."

There was a long pause as the two men stared at each other.

"Mr. President, you either need to throw a punch or sit down so we can continue this conversation."

McDonald glowered at Graham for a moment, then returned to his couch and sat down.

"All right, sir, let's think about how we're going to fix these 'screw-ups.' Denying their existence is an impossibility, and creating some stories that make them seem like benign situations of no importance won't fly either. Creating a scenario portraying each activity as a product of miscommunication between you and others seems to be our best tactic. Although this solution requires an individual or individuals to perjure themselves. Finding someone who is willing to do your bidding may be difficult."

"Graham, it doesn't need to be difficult. Shit, let's just find some under-secretary in the Homeland Security Department who's in debt up to their ears, and make them a deal. If they'll be our fall guy, we'll make them rich. Maybe they'll do a little jail time. Hell, I'll pardon the asshole when nobody's looking and they'll be a little worse for the wear, but a lot richer."

The chief of staff couldn't believe what he'd just heard. *Am I talking to a Mafia don, or the president of the United States?* He sat quietly for a moment, collected his thoughts, and then addressed McDonald. "I don't know how we'd locate such a person, Mr. President."

"Get the Pinko FBI on board or the Demo-loving CIA. They've got the personnel to find our man."

"I don't think they'll assist you, sir. Your relationship with those departments is pretty shaky. They'll just blow smoke in your face."

"Well, shit, there's more than one way to skin a cat. Let's get Hastings on board and have him use Military Intelligence to gather the information we need. Hell, it'll work just fine."

The White House chief of staff looked over at the Oval Office desk. Its polished surfaces and carved eagle looked stately. He thought of other Presidents who had sat at the presidential desk: JFK, Lyndon Johnson, Ronald Reagan, Bill Clinton...*Had they ever asked their chief of staff to bribe people?*

"What are you gawking at, Graham?"

He returned his gaze to the president. "Nothing, sir. Just thinking about strategies. I'll try and locate a friendly under-secretary who will confirm whatever story we'll float. If I can't find somebody, then Defense Secretary Hastings will be our next option. I'm sure he can locate a vulnerable minion for us."

"Good, good, that's what I need to hear from..."

"Knock, knock."

The two men looked over to Janet's door. She stood in the doorway and waited for their attention.

"The Secretary of the Interior is on the line wishing to talk with you, Mr. President."

"What does he want?"

Janet left for a moment and then returned. "He wants to know if you have assigned a date and time for his meeting with you regarding downsizing his department. He mentioned Graham hasn't contacted him and wondered if you forgot about the appointment, or if you no longer wanted to meet with him?"

The president regarded his right hand man, who responded, "He's referring to our last full cabinet meeting, sir, and the stonewalling most secretaries were experiencing within their departments."

The president looked back to Janet. "Tell Rice to be here tomorrow at 10:00."

"Certainly, Mr. President."

Janet returned to her office and McDonald contemplated Graham.

"You'll need to remind me about what Rice is concerned with, but not right now." The president checked his watch. "I've got a full plate so let's call this meeting over. You're going to find a patsy for us, ASAP. Let's get this mess behind us, quickly."

"I'll do my best, sir."

"Do better than that, Graham. We don't want any screw-ups."

Graham couldn't believe what he'd just heard. "Certainly, sir. I'll be in contact with you very soon."

McDonald rose and moved to his desk, where he sat down and looked at his phone.

Henry Graham quietly left the Oval Office and headed straight down the hall to his working space. Partway down the corridor, he stopped, turned, and stared back at the Oval Office doors. Two Secret Service personnel stood, resolutely guarding the entrance. Just then, he realized those doors would never open for him again. He was quitting. He'd turn in his resignation tomorrow and be out of Washington D.C. by the next day. Graham was not going to be a party to this circus any longer. Entering his office, he grabbed his car keys and sunglasses, and thought about heading over to Murphy's. It seemed like the perfect place to have lunch and celebrate his governmental departure. *How did that song "The Gambler" go? Well, it was clearly time for him to fold 'em. Hanging around this administration was like playing Russian roulette; sooner or later, you were going to lose.* Soon to be Ex–Chief of Staff Graham headed for the North Entrance. Without looking back, he left the West Wing and his political career.

McDonald sat at his desk perusing his phone. He looked up and noticed Graham had left. *Good, I have more important matters to contend with.* The president began to recall Secretary Rice's rebellious Interior Department. He'd meet with him tomorrow. They'd map out an attack plan, and then put it into motion. *Those lifer, government parasites won't know what hit them. They've never seen or met anything like 'Slice and Dice' McDonald. Battling with Interior Department employees sounds like a great way to spend a couple days.*

McDonald also needed to find a new Secretary of Agriculture. He wanted to hit Oregon hard with his logging agenda. A smile spread across the president's face. *Hell, I'll get a dozen logging operations going all at once. If need be, I'll send military detachments to each logging site. Those boys will keep the tree-hugging activists at bay. The hippy-dippy liberals out west won't be stopping any more of my clear-cuts.* McDonald rocked back in his desk chair and contemplated the ceiling chandelier. The sparkles emanating from the cut crystals mesmerized him. *Nope, nothing will stop me now. I'll have my way with Oregon's old growth forests.*

Part Three

The Silverbacks Take Over

CHAPTER 51

Woody was driving over to his friend Hops' house. Hops lived on several acres overlooking the Nehalem River Valley. His real name was Steve Williams, but his friends usually referred to him as Hops because of his fermentation practices, which produced some excellent IPAs. The road was winding and uneven, causing Woody's truck to bounce and lurch from side to side as he traveled along.

He soon was motoring through dairy acreage. The pungent smell of cow manure and methane wrinkled his nose. This had been a rare year for the dairy farmers because their pastures' growing season had been incredible. The fields had already been cut twice, and a third cycle was producing more grass. The dairymen were letting the cattle have their way with the last pasture growth. The Indian summer would eventually abate, causing the grass to become dormant, but for now, the Holsteins' bulging udders seemed to show an appreciation for this year's extra grass.

Woody crossed the North Fork and continued on. Another five minutes, and he'd be arriving at the "Brew House," as he liked to refer to Steve's home site. His thoughts revisited last evening's newscast, and once again he felt angry about what was reported. Not only was McDonald continuing with his vengeful, racist form of governing, but the tree stand occupiers appeared to have lost their battle. It seemed like the state of Oregon was going to arrest them sooner than later. He and Karen had felt helpless and small as they watched the night's broadcast. The obvious, retaliatory ICE arrest news was disturbing and the reported internment camps were frightening to the Thompsons. The ramifications of these events pointed to a racist, police state that Karen and Woody wanted no part of.

An early morning, local newscast shed more light on the Big Eddy Rise logging site. An anonymous source told a Portland station the young OSU activists would be arrested tomorrow and be lodged in the Deschutes County Jail. Logging would probably start right after the Alliance was arrested, possibly the next day or the day after. On a brighter, more hopeful note, the same show offered some good news discussing a possible legal injunction that would halt McDonald's Executive Order. A high-profile group of attorneys had filed another suit. This litigation attacked the decree as being unconstitutional. Their premise suggested the Executive Branch of government could not negate the Legislative Branch's laws by simply creating and signing an Executive Order. This was abuse of the "Separation of Powers" concept created by the Constitution, and the Ninth Circuit Court of Appeals had promised an early ruling on this case, possibly rendering a decision by next week. It would be incredibly good news if the court struck down McDonald's Executive Order.

The big Titan turned onto Hops' driveway and continued uphill to the level parking pad. His friend's property had a great view of the river valley. The mountainous ridge sitting on the north side of the flood plain was a spectacular visual bonus, with Onion Peak, a partially treed outcropping of volcanic rock, sitting directly opposite from Steve's property. Its domed configuration always drew one's attention. Actually the view wasn't what drew Hops to this location. It was the sloping, southwest-facing orientation of the land that attracted him, and he had taken full advantage of this inclination. His house was powered by a solar panel array, and of course, he also nurtured a large trellis system for Oregon Cascade hops on the property's warm hillside, along with an extensive garden system.

Woody smiled to himself as he drove up Hops' driveway. He couldn't remember who had suggested a monthly men's group gathering, but the creation of the ritual was well received by all those participating. Each month, one of the friends would sponsor the get-together. The host was responsible for several things: fixing his companions dinner, informing them about some interesting subject or situation he researched, and decorating a laptop or desktop monitor with an outfit depicting a well-known personality. This character could be fictional or real. The ritual of embellishing the computer screen occurred because one of the attendees lived in Colorado, and Skyped his presence to the gathering. The host transformed the computer and Dakota, their Colorado friend, had to determine who the character was. The friends would all offer clues until Dakota guessed correctly and identified the new persona. Somehow, the silliness of this endeavor struck a resonant chord with the friends, and they totally enjoyed playing their roles.

Woody's oldest friend was the Colorado participant. He'd known Dakota since fourth grade. Their friendship was still going strong after nearly sixty years. They'd lost track of each other for a while, as young adults often do, but then reconnected in their later years. Tom Pathways, or Dakota, married and raised a family with his wife Sharon outside of Denver. Sharon had worked as an RN and Tom was a tattoo artist who owned his own shop. All their children graduated from high school, started families, and now lived near their parents, giving Tom and Sharon the opportunity to enjoy being hands-on grandparents. Just recently, Dakota had retired and passed on the shop to others, but he still kept in close contact with the tattoo artists and enjoyed visiting the old shop, seeing what new tats had been created, and seeing how everyone was faring.

Dakota continued on in retirement with his other artistic passion, painting on canvas and producing surreal and abstract art pieces. He also continued with his shamanistic life. Tom was part Chickamauga Cherokee, and early in his life had been mentored by an Oglala Sioux shaman in the spiritual ways of the Lakota peoples. Now, Dakota facilitated a local following and maintained a parcel of land high up in the Rockies where Vision Quests and Sun Dance Ceremonies were held. People from all over the United States would come to his gatherings and participate in Lakota religious rites. Over the years, Tom, Sharon, and their children had helped, and were still helping, many individuals learn about and live in the First Peoples' philosophical ways.

Woody reached the level parking area and stopped next to Doc's old Mercedes diesel. Woody had met Doc when Doc was a med student and Hops' roommate at the University of Oregon. Back then, he was a skinny young black man full of energy and intelligence. If Doc read something once, he'd remember the complete text, word for word, the next day. He blazed through med school, married, and opened a small clinic in Northeast Portland. Later, Doc opened another clinic in Southeast. He and his wife eventually bought a home in the Eastmoreland neighborhood. Doc would split his efforts between the two nearby clinics. Dr. Edward Wilson, as he was known by his patients, and his wife never had children. She spent her free time running charitable functions and attending prominent social gatherings. About ten years ago, Doc's spouse met a younger physician and changed addresses. This caught him by surprise and hurt terribly. He sold both clinics, and moved down to the beach near Woody and Hops and his old firefighting friend Ranger. It took several years for Edward to recover from his loss. After he reclaimed his life, the county allowed him to open a nonprofit medical clinic in Nehalem, Oregon. Most of his patients were uninsured locals. The community and Dr. Wilson's patients greatly appreciated his efforts. The clinic, open Friday through Sunday, received volunteer assistance from RNs and a PA who lived in the area. Also, he began writing a fictional piece about a young black boy growing up in Portland during the '50s. His initial writings had been well received by those attending his readings. Between his clinic, close friends, and writing, Doc's retired years had become very comfortable and rewarding.

Next to Doc's Mercedes was an old Ford F-150 pickup that had resided on the coast for too many years. The dark blue paint had faded, rust now etched its outline, and numerous dents gave it a three-dimensional appearance only an old work truck would have. This vehicle belonged to Ranger, a close friend of Doc's, and now a good friend of Hops and Woody. Ranger retired from the Marine Corps in his forties. He'd served in the Vietnam War and returned stateside after the campaign to help train young Marines at the Corps' Military Base in Twenty-Nine Palms, California. After fifteen years of instruction, he retired as a Captain. Ranger returned to Oregon looking for work. He met Doc while employed by the Forest Service. Doc had taken a hiatus from his medical profession and joined a smoke repelling crew based out of Cave Junction. Ranger was on the crew, and the two men became fast friends. Edward returned to his medical practice after several years of firefighting, while Ranger moved on to the north and began smoke jumping in Alaska. He met and married a Native Alaskan and they raised their two sons together. Ranger's wife had died ten years ago of congestive heart disease and he still grieved for her. He remained very close to his two boys. Both young men joined the military after high school and now belonged to elite, clandestine units. Neither could talk with their dad about their specific missions. He didn't see or hear from his boys for long periods of time, which caused him some anxiety, but as Ranger often said, he's glad his sons are keeping the bad guys at bay so all of us can have our freedoms.

Eventually, Ranger's knees gave out and jumping was not possible anymore. He returned to Oregon and settled on the coast. Upon retirement, the ex-Marine immediately got busy developing a line of firefighting tools that quickly became the gold standard of the industry. He'd used enough tools while fighting fires to know what designs worked best. He took his experience and creativity, and developed equipment that outworked all the competition. All the hot shot crews based in the West bought his tools, and he eventually developed a profitable cottage industry. His business totally interested him, kept him busy, and provided a little spending money after all the bills were paid.

Woody parked his rig. He left his truck with a small cooler in hand that held a six-pack of Pilsner beer. This was a most sacrilegious act on his part. Hops' house was strictly ale territory, but a concession was granted for Woody. His friends all turned their collective noses up at his Pilsners, feeling such brews were only for lightweights, AKA Bob Thompson.

As he reached the front door, Woody thought about his earlier encounter with Hops' wife Susan when he left his house. Susan passed him in his driveway carrying several bottles of home-brewed ales and a cribbage board. She'd laughed as she passed Woody and said her husband had a great presentation to share about the heritage of Black Angus cattle. Susan mentioned being on the edge of her seat, last night, as she listened to Steve practice his informative lecture. When she entered Woody's house, she glanced back over her shoulder and called out this research was even more thrilling than her husband's previous dissertation about Jersey dairy cows.

Woody was still smiling to himself as he walked through Hops' open door. He could hear laughter and conversation coming from the house's west-facing rear deck that partially overlooked Onion Peak. It was a warm, clear, late summer evening, and the men gravitated to the sunshine. Passing by Steve's laptop, Woody regarded the screen and laughed out loud. Not only was his bearded friend, Dakota, grinning at him while holding a marotte and wearing a jester's hat, complete with bells, but the computer itself was embellished with a dismembered Raggedy Ann doll. The separated pieces were taped to the screen in a fairly rational manner. Her red bangs were affixed to the top of the screen with her pigtails draped down its sides. The doll's dress covered the keyboard, and her legs, extending downward, were taped to the keypad's front edge. Raggedy's two arms were attached lower down on the screen and now rested on top of her dress as if she were clasping her hands together on her lap. Dakota was totally enjoying the moment.

"Hey, I'm turning the table on you guys tonight. Who am I?"

Woody thought for a scant moment, "A really weird Santa Claus?"

"No way, man. Think about it."

Dakota pumped his marotte up and down several times and shook his head, causing his jester bells to tinkle.

"This is a tough one, Dakota. I don't know, a Bourbon Street reveler during Mardi Gras?"

"No, no, Woody. Think about what you've seen on TV."

Woody thought the clue was a little too vague to be helpful, but good naturedly guessed again. "A contestant on the *Gong Show*?"

"Oh shit. You're not even close. Get me to the other guys."

Woody picked up the laptop and carried it out onto the deck.

"By the way, Dakota, your red hair is beautiful in the late afternoon sunlight."

Woody found a shaded spot on the deck behind the south wind screen, and positioned Dakota so he could see the entire deck.

"Hello, gentlemen. Were you ignoring Dakota on purpose?"

His friends contemplated him. Doc spoke for the group. "Of course we were, but since you've brought him outside we'll socialize with the little upstart. You do realize he's turning the table on us, and trying to best us at our own game?"

"Well, yes I did notice he was a little demanding tonight, and dressed kind of weird."

Hops joined in. "That's what we all noticed too. Hey Dakota, your red and white horizontally striped stockings really define those gnarly old legs of yours."

Dakota pumped his marotte up and down again, and jingled his bells. "I've got it. I'm Waldo from the 'Where's Waldo' books."

The four men chorused, "Nope, try again."

"No way, I'm Waldo, right?"

Ranger offered the next clue. "Your red bangs and pigtails are very becoming, little one, but you should take better care of your clothing; it's a little raggedy for such a nice, young lady."

Dakota radically pumped his marotte up and down. "This was way easy, fellas. Did anybody keep track? I've only gotten three clues, although technically, Ranger's comments could be construed as two, spliced together like they were, but as it is, drum roll please."

The four friends began drumming on whatever surface was within reach.

"I'm Raggedy Ann Doll, right?"

Woody gave Dakota the double thumbs-up sign. "Damn, you're good."

"Well yeah, but now it's your turn. Nobody's guessed who I am yet."

Doc considered the computer screen.

"Dakota, we can see you. You're a court jester. Why do we have to 'guess' at your identity when we literally can view your image plain as day?"

"Well of course I'm a court jester, but whose court jester am I?"

Doc continued on. "There were dozens of well-known jesters throughout history. You'll need to give us a verbal clue since your marotte and hat are pretty generic."

"Okay, if I must, I can oblige you. I'm the Fool's fool, the Clown's clown, the..."

Woody blurted out, "You're McDonald's court jester!!!"

Dakota's grin got even broader. "Give him a Kewpie doll!!"

"I had it at Fool's fool, Dakota. Nobody else fits that expression better than our sitting president."

Woody's comment set off a lengthy, emotional, and animated discussion among the five men about the recent political news, ICE arrests and internment camps being in the forefront of their railings. The friends were all left of center with their politics. Doc could be the most philosophical about things. Ranger had a militaristic side that conflicted with his general left-leaning social views. Hops was almost socialistic in his beliefs, and Woody wasn't too far behind him.

The discussion eventually left politics, and drifted this way and that. Growing seasons were discussed along with a critique of this year's salmon fishing on the Nehalem River. Doc mentioned how the ales were mighty tasty, but at the moment, he really needed some proper food to sustain himself. This prompted Hops to begin delivering his researched material about Black Angus genetics.

"Okay, okay. Before I fire up the 'barbie,' I've got some interesting information for all you carnivores."

Woody remarked, "I was given a sneak preview by Susan. The Black Angus is my favorite bovine, so you can bet I'm all ears."

Ranger studied Woody. "You've got a favorite bovine?"

"Yep. Black Angus are the best range cow for Eastern Oregon and their meat is well marbled, yet fairly firm."

Ranger and Doc exchanged glances and shook their heads good naturedly.

Doc joined in. "Well, Hops, enlighten us about Woody's favorite ruminant."

Dakota's tinny voice emerged from the laptop. "Could you guys speak up please or pull me closer to the podium so I won't miss anything. Also, are we talking about cows?"

Hops lowered his head slightly, and raised his hand in a stop motion. "Please, please, gentlemen, enough banter. Let me start my discourse."

Everyone became respectfully quiet.

"The Black Angus cow is distantly related to the Scottish highland cattle, which have existed since the sixth century A.D. Any questions?"

Woody responded, "No, pretty clear. Go on."

"Presentation concluded, gentlemen."

Woody exclaimed in dismay, "That's it?"

"Well, yeah, Woody. Wikipedia didn't have much information on the subject. How would you guys like your steaks?"

Hops dramatically ripped a towel off a platter, which rested on the deck's picnic table, exposing four thick-cut New York Steaks. As his guests called out their favorite doneness levels, Woody sat glumly, staring off across the valley.

"That's it? Really, you couldn't find any more information? Hell, I knew everything you just said back in fourth grade."

"How do you want your steak cooked, Woody?"

"Oh yeah, rare for me."

"Good, you guys want one well done, one medium, I like mine medium rare, and one rare. Sorry, Dakota, but understandably I'm not cooking one for you."

"I totally understand. I'm cooking my own steak as we speak."

"Well gentlemen, it'll be medium rare all the way around. You've made this very easy for me."

There was good natured ribbing and complaining directed at Hops regarding his "one size fits all" cooking style, but no one really minded. He was the chef tonight and everyone gladly followed his rules.

The men sat at the picnic table and drank their beers while general conversation once more developed. Ranger moved Dakota over to the table so he could hear and contribute to the discussions. Hops busied himself with cooking the steaks and slicing up late summer watermelon. As the sun got closer to Onion Peak, the men's group had about one hour left of direct sunlight. Woody brought up the imminent arrest of the tree sitters. None of his friends had heard the early morning broadcast about the occupiers' incarceration. The conversation focused on the valiant effort the young OSU students had put forward. The group lamented about the storm and Sasha's near death. All the men realized the logging site was a result of the McDonald administration's attempt to meddle in Oregon's business. His presidential order dropping logging regulations wasn't well received in Oregon and in particular, the men's group hated the intrusion caused by McDonald's Executive Order. Most Oregonians were outdoor enthusiasts who greatly appreciated the old trees and their primal ecosystem.

All the friends disapproved of the "monoculture" approach to logging often practiced in Oregon. The homogenous stands of trees eventually created a biodiversity desert when compared to the natural ecosystems they replaced. On the coast and in the Cascades, the deer and elk initially benefitted from logging sites. Being browsers, they found lots of new food sources from the plants that established themselves first after a clear-cut, but when the replanted seedlings reached the height of about eight to ten feet, the tightly packed new forest didn't offer much sustenance for any animal, and the elk herds and deer needed to migrate to other areas for food.

Hops called out, "Come and get it" as he lowered a platter of steaks onto the picnic table. He followed this gesture with a large bowl of sliced watermelon and another bowl of mixed greens from his garden, and lastly, forks, knives, and various salad dressings were placed before everyone.

"Dig in, gentlemen."

This remark was followed by thank-yous and numerous "my compliments to the chef" type statements. Woody eyed the laptop and noticed Dakota taking the first bite of his barbecued steak.

"Bon appétit, Dakota."

Dakota responded, "Back at you." He waved his skewered bite of steak at his friends.

Woody watched his friends sitting around the picnic table and eating dinner. The conversation turned to college football. Oregon State was playing Colorado tonight and the men would soon retire indoors to watch the game. The Pac-12 offered up an unusually early conference game, which was well received by fans, but not so much by coaching staffs.

Woody was in a reflective mood, and noted how all his friends had slowly yet distinctively aged over the years. Doc had never gained much weight and remained skinny. His short-cropped, curly black hair was tipped with gray. His beard was totally gray and his dark skin seemed to have lightened over the years. His clothing always appeared to be a little baggy on him. For his age, he was still very nimble and moved easily. His bespectacled face at times could have an intense look, but often it wore a smile directed at whomever he was conversing with.

Ranger had aged the most. He was the oldest of the group, having just turned seventy-two. He had dealt with several serious medical issues within the last few years that had caused him to age quickly. He'd gained weight due to a prolonged period of immobility and now walked with a slight limp because the additional pounds were aggravating his injured knees. His hair was short, parted on the side, and now tinged with gray. He wore old-school dark-rimmed glasses that rested on a straight, pointed nose. Ranger loved to talk and share stories, and he, like Doc, often smiled and laughed while conversing.

Hops was in the best shape of all the friends. He, like Doc, hadn't gained much weight since high school. He was well built with broad shoulders and narrow hips. Steve's hair was steel gray and his short beard followed suit. A pair of reading glasses hung around his neck. Hops enjoyed lively intellectual conversation and could hold his own when talking about most any subject. He especially enjoyed talking about brewing beer and crafting wine.

Dakota was the artist of the montage. His entire head was covered with long gray hair. His beard rested on his chest, and his hair hung down to his mid-back. Dakota's round nose held up black-rimmed glasses, sitting in front of small, dark, piercing eyes. He ate ample helpings while dining. Over the years, the calories burned while exercising hadn't exceeded the calories gained from eating, so Dakota had gained a little weight, but his additional pounds didn't slow him up. He still worked out regularly, and like all of the close friends, he loved to converse.

The friends were all enjoying their steaks, melon, and salad. The sun was touching Onion Peak's summit and the temperature was quickly dropping. The others hadn't noticed Woody's unusual silence. When he commenced talking, they all took note because of the seriousness of his tone and facial expression.

"You know, those Alliance kids showed lots of balls by stopping that logging show. I really admire what they did."

"I do too, Woody. What's on your mind?" Doc asked.

"Well, I wonder if I have as much balls as those OSU kids."

Doc contemplated Woody. "Well there were about a dozen of those kids, and even taking into account the two females in the group, that still leaves a ten to one ratio, so I'd say, no you don't have as much balls."

Hops laughingly interjected, "Doc, I think Woody has something serious to say, and even though your levity is greatly appreciated by myself and possibly others, let Woody continue in a receptive atmosphere."

Ranger and Dakota began to laugh quietly while Doc and Hops smiled.

Ranger said, "I think Woody is suggesting he should take over the occupation of the Big Eddy logging site."

Everyone observed Woody with humorous, curious expressions on their faces.

"Well, yes I am. I think it's something needing to be done by somebody, and why not me? I hate clear-cutting and its greed-head approach to forest management. I have always enjoyed camping and fishing in the Metolius forest, which this logging effort threatens, and I totally hate McDonald, who is obviously behind this forestry scheme. Who better to continue the civil disobedience and blocking of this logging show?"

The four friends viewed Woody in disbelief. Woody continued speaking. "I don't know. Maybe I could sneak to the top of the Big Eddy Rise, hang out up there with guns, and tell anyone who tries to start logging that I'll shoot at them. I've got a shotgun and deer rifle. If I was a logger and saw a gun pointed at me, I'd move away and not try to cut any trees down."

Hops went into the kitchen and retrieved one of Woody's Pilsners from the refrigerator. He poured it into a chilled pint glass and, returning to the picnic table, handed it to Woody. "Here, have a sip and reflect upon what you've just said."

The sun went down below Onion Peak. The shadows crossed the valley floor, creeping up Hops' hillside. The friends didn't notice the low light and chill accompanying the early evening.

"I have thought about it. The Rise is like a fort. There's a bowl at the top with a protective rim of basaltic rock around it. Nobody could get at you if you defended yourself. Hell, all I'd have to do is control the site for a couple weeks, and you know, just sit up there looking all serious. Eat up my food and water and then give up when I run out of grub. By then, shit, who knows what will have happened? McDonald could be fighting impeachment battles and incapable of continuing on with his shenanigans. I'll be arrested, put in jail, let out on bail, and return home to wait for my arraignment. McDonald's stupid Executive Order will be proven unconstitutional by then. My illegal logging site occupation will be dismissed by the court because there'll be no grounds for legal action."

Everyone sat quietly and observed Woody.

Doc spoke up. "You really have given this some thought."

"Well, I have, and I'm thinking about doing this. There's a short window of opportunity here. The activists are probably going to get arrested tomorrow. Right after the arrests, before the loggers start cutting down trees, I'm going to get on the site and take over. I found my old bullhorn that I used at track meets. It still works. With it, I can make my intentions known to the authorities. I'm just going to pretend like I'm going camping, tell Karen I'm off to the Blitzen River for some serious early fall fishing, and sneak up to Big Eddy Rise when nobody's looking. I'm telling anyone who shows up there's a new sheriff in town and the loggers better stay clear of my forest."

Hops spoke to Woody. "This is pretty crazy, big fella. It all sounds fairly benign the way you're describing everything, but seriously, you could get shot and killed. 'Those who live by the gun die by the gun.' I'm pretty sure that's a direct quote from John Wayne."

Everyone laughed nervously at Hops' humor.

Doc added, "There are too many unknowns, Woody. I mean there are a lot of people who disagree with eco-terrorism, and what you're proposing is eco-terrorism, plain and simple. You can't expect the same response from the law that the OSU students received. Their dynamite was meant to blow up a few trees, but your rifle is meant to harm or kill people. Totally different ballgame with a whole new set of rules."

"I'm telling you guys this Rise is like a fort. Nobody is going to try and get me."

Hops spoke next. "Woody, you'll eventually fall asleep. While you're blissfully dreaming, somebody could simply walk up the hill and get the draw on you, and in the process, if things went bad, you could get killed."

"Well, if there was more than me on the hill, we could always have a pair of eyes watching our surroundings."

The meaning and gravity of Woody's words weren't lost on his audience. Dakota's voice resonated from the computer.

"You want us to join you on the site and help stop the logging operation?"

Woody contemplated all his friends. "I guess I'm suggesting all of us could take over the Big Eddy Rise for a couple weeks and bluff our way through the occupation."

A very unusual silence befell the men's group. All of the old friends were lost in thought and retrospection for a moment. Whole lifetimes of passive behaviors were critiqued, mental notes were reviewed about paths not taken, and 'if I'd only done this' moments were revisited. The silence continued until Doc spoke again.

"I really appreciate what you're suggesting, Woody. I just don't know if I could participate in something which could harm others."

Woody responded, "I understand your position, Doc. I don't think I could shoot somebody either, but like I said, this would basically be a bluff, and one we'd carry out for just a couple of weeks."

Hops jumped in. "You can't have an occupation site filled with guns and not expect somebody to shoot at you. If shooting starts, somebody is going to get hurt. You could plan to give up, but before you waved the white flag, you or one of us could be dead. Also, what if the officials don't want a surrender situation? What if they want to just plain eliminate the tree huggers and make a statement?"

Dakota had been listening to the discussion and had soul searched his opinions about activism and the human spirit's need to defend good from evil. He'd noted his vote was often his only response to the "wrong" that threatened his beliefs. This understanding was disconcerting to him and inspired his immediate words. The tinny sound of the laptop speaker drew everyone's attention.

"Each and every one of us has led community-oriented lives. We've always done things for the good of our friends and neighbors. Doc, you were a family practitioner. Woody, you taught school. Hops, you were a veterinarian, and Ranger, you served our country in the military. We all helped others and were role models. I don't think doing the right thing and modeling correctness is enough sometimes. Ranger, you know more about this than the rest of us. I know we all have felt at times civil disobedience is the only language registered by some aggressors. Hell, I think back to all the marches we've participated in and the causes we've stood up for. I also notice how complacent we've become in our old age. Our present presidential administration is a threat to our beliefs, and the world's well-being, as far as that goes. The logging show near Camp Sherman is just one small example of McDonald's disregard for what most people want, but it's our 'small example.' It's our chance to locally stand up to McDonald's disrespect and make a statement. I know each of us has said, 'I should have done more,' or felt like we should have stood taller and stronger when resisting some form of aggression. Well here's another 'wrong' we can either passively vote against come the next election, or we can say, 'Hell no, not on my watch, and never, ever in my backyard.' We can stand up to and push back against this disgusting administration and its equally repulsive little schemes."

Woody spoke in response to Dakota's declaration. "Would this lengthy rhetoric be a 'sure I'll help you, Woody' type of answer?"

Dakota's hairy bespectacled face broke into a smile, and glancing downwards, he shook his head from side to side. His tassel bells jingled slightly.

"Yes it is, dumbshit. Do you only understand a literal yes or no answer?"

Seeing Dakota flick Woody some shit slightly relaxed the friends, making them smile and laugh.

Dakota continued, "I'm pretty sure I could shoot at someone if they were trying to kill me. Hell, my ancestors did a lot of shooting at Anglos in uniforms. I can probably do the same."

Doc reflected some more about his own thoughts and Dakota's. "I'll help with the occupation, Woody. I won't hold a rifle or shoot at anyone, but I can assist in any other manner. Obviously, if medical attention is needed, you'd want me there."

Woody sniffled a bit and wiped a tear from his cheek. The tinny sounding speaker once again was activated.

"Oh God! He's going to cry! Would somebody give the big baby a hanky? Preferably one that's been used!"

All the friends including Woody started to laugh. Hops found a used dinner napkin and handed it to Woody. He grabbed it and mimed wiping his tear away.

Ranger had not entered into the conversation. He'd just been listening and assessing his friends' dialogue. He knew his sons would be proud of him for standing up to the McDonald administration. They were U.S. soldiers, but both boys detested their Commander in Chief. Ranger also knew his friends were not a fighting force he'd normally engage in combat with. They weren't skilled in warfare, nor did they have the mettle for it. You could train soldiers to fight and increase their fighting spirit, but this transition wouldn't occur with his friends. No, the Big Eddy Rise would provide the safety these would-be warriors needed, and Ranger felt with his expertise, he could keep them alive for at least several weeks. He entered into the conversation. "I'm getting pretty chilled, gentlemen; let's go inside and continue our discussion."

It was now almost dark, and a few tree bats were flying around the deck picking off the insects that were attracted to the light. All the men moved into Hops' living room and sat down near the TV. The living room overlooked the now dark river valley through three large floor-to-ceiling panes of glass. The room had a beautiful Southwest décor, complete with Navajo rugs on the floor. Beaded, knotty pine wainscoting covered the walls to the four foot level, and the ceiling was completely overlaid with yellow pine tongue and groove boards.

Each men's group member held a new beverage, which they'd all grabbed while passing through the kitchen. Casual remarks were now being made about the soon-to-begin OSU/Colorado football game. Ranger nestled into a beautiful Amish style chair, upholstered with a wool Navajo printed fabric.

"I've listened to all of your frank comments and opinions, gentlemen, and I feel everyone here is being fairly reasonable about your assessments. From a military standpoint, the Big Eddy Rise is a very defensible fortress. A properly trained group of soldiers with the right armaments could stop any ground assault easily, unless large numbers of troops were committed to the skirmish. That's not likely to happen. I have the weaponry we'll need, but don't have the necessary manpower."

The group of men observed Ranger with quizzical expressions. Dakota's new perch on a book shelf provided a perfect view of the scene.

Woody exclaimed, "What do you mean, Ranger?"

"Well, none of you have been trained to use weapons, and none of you have been in combat. Being shot at brings out the worst or the best in people. In a skirmish, you hope for the best because the worst requires lots of body bags."

Doc spoke to Ranger's comments. "Don't try and sugarcoat our decision, Ranger."

Ranger laughed at Doc's jest. "Well, Doc, a little reality check is always prudent. Anyway, the site's perfect. I've got the weapons, but you guys are untested. I think Woody's right, though. We would be basically bluffing our way through a few weeks, and then our best option would be to give up. Our sword and shield rattling will just make law enforcement think twice before trying to remove us. I believe the state will once again take the wait-and-see tactic regarding our occupation and just sit by until we run out of food. Woody, I might regret this, but you can count me as 'in' with your little logging site take-over."

Everyone knew Hops didn't commit one way or another, and unintentionally, they all turned their gaze in his direction. Hops felt their anticipation and responded, "I'm not sure if I can go along with this, fellas. It seems like there's so much to lose if everything goes south. Possible jail time being the least of the potential ills. I've worked so hard to be where I'm at, enjoying my retirement with my wife, kids, and grandkids. It actually would seem a little selfish on my part to run off on some macho, eco-terrorist exploit and leave all my loved ones in shock wondering if I'll ever come home."

Dakota spoke for all the friends. "I totally know where you're coming from, Hops. I had all those thoughts, and it's cool with me if you don't want to participate. I can live with your decision. We all know you'll be constantly sending good thoughts our way."

Everyone echoed Dakota's comments. They even proffered an impromptu toast to their host and "good ol' common sense."

Woody checked his watch and was glad to see it was game time. The evening's serious discussion had taxed all of the friends emotionally, and a little diversion was called for.

"Hey, it's game time. Let's table this discussion for a while. Think about it some more, and revisit it after the game."

Everyone agreed with this sentiment and positioned themselves in comfortable chairs or on the couch facing the TV. Hops brought a couple platters of fruit, crackers, and cheese from the kitchen. The laptop's speaker once again drew everyone's attention.

"Well, amigos, I'm going to say adios. Woody, call me early tomorrow and let's talk some more about occupying the site. Sounds like we have to get right at it. Go Buffs!"

"Will do, Dakota. Go Beavs!"

Everyone started clamoring their good-byes to their friend.

"Sleep tight, Raggedy."

"Are you going to meet with Raggedy Andy after the game?"

Dakota gave his friends the middle finger salute, and grinning their way, shut off his computer. Hops jumped up and did the same with his laptop. He quickly regained his seat as the Pac-12 opening began broadcasting.

Oregon State won its first regular season game by defeating the Buffs in Boulder. It was a major upset to start the football season off with, and the men's group broke up on a jubilant note. Woody made plans to talk with everybody early in the morning because if the group wanted to access the site easily, they needed to perfectly hit the window between the STRONG Alliance arrest and the start of logging.

All the friends said their "good evenings" and headed home. Woody flashed his lights at Susan as she passed him heading the opposite direction. Susan arrived home and told Hops how she'd beat Karen's ass by grabbing two games out of three in cribbage and how much she enjoyed watching the Beavers get a win. She'd asked Steve if he would retire with her, but he responded by saying he was going to watch the replay of the Beavers game. It was slated to air in about half an hour. Susan kissed her husband good night and went to bed. Hops went into the liquor cupboard, fetched a favorite single malt of his, and poured himself a two-fingered draught. He dripped a few drops of water into his drink and sat down in his favorite chair, which rested in front of his flatscreen. His thoughts were not on the upcoming rerun.

As he drove home, Woody devised a plan allowing for his departure from home without arousing Karen's suspicion. He'd determined a straight-up, transparent disclosure of his plan to his wife was a bad move. No, a simple deception was best here. He rarely tried to hide anything from Karen, but this situation was so radical and filled with possible problems Woody didn't want to awaken his wife's emotional side and her potentially angry response. Woody concocted a men's group, early fall road trip in his recently, renovated Chevy step van to the Steens Mountain area. The friends would camp near the summit and hike down into the Blitzen River Valley for some catch and release fly fishing. The glaciated valley would be the perfect spot because cellphones didn't work in this isolated locale, so the lack of communication wouldn't startle Karen.

When Woody got home, he and Karen conversed in the living room for a while before going to bed. They talked about the game and Woody's road trip. Karen decided to go visit her mom in Portland for a few days and then verbally mused about paying a surprise visit to Bridger. She was a little peeved at their grandson, and felt like dropping in and giving him a little motherly roughing-up over his reclusive behavior. The Thompsons retired, both thinking about their separate trips.

CHAPTER 52

Hops sat down in front of his TV. He placed his whiskey glass on the chair's flat, broad armrest and scrolled through the channels until the OSU/Colorado replay appeared. Hops muted the sound and, picking up his drink, took a sip of the aged single malt. *What were his friends thinking?* Steve couldn't believe, at their age with so much to lose, they were willing to get killed or jailed to stop the logging of the Metolius tree stand. He, like them, loved the Ponderosas of Central Oregon. Hops, Woody, and Doc had spent many days fishing the Metolius. Back before fly fishing had become popular, the trio had caught their share of rainbows, browns, and bull trout out of the stream. The river was one of the most pristine, clear, and cold trout streams Steve had ever fished. *Shit, those guys are actually going to occupy the site.*

Hops reviewed Woody's statements about the legality of the Executive Order and its imminent demise. Woody was right. The Ninth Court would probably nuke McDonald's dismissal of logging regulations. It made total sense. Why it hadn't already happened was the real mystery. Without the Executive Order, the logging would be halted. The site ran along the banks of the Metolius, which held one of the few healthy populations of bull trout left in Oregon. This fish was on the Endangered Species List so any possible disturbance to their habitat would torpedo the project that threatened them. The Big Eddy Rise logging site was just such an endeavor. So in a week or two, this logging show would be illegal and the occupation of the ground wouldn't be necessary. *Christ, these guys are really pissing me off.*

Steve knew the Big Eddy Rise geography very well. He had camped in the upper bowl a few times, and realized it was fort-like. He agreed with his friends' assessment; it was easily defensible. He took another sip of his whiskey and watched Oregon State's big halfback bowl through the Colorado defense and into the end zone for a TD. *What an unstoppable force this guy was going to be.*

Hops continued thinking about his friends' plans. The cessation of McDonald's decree and the defensibility of the Rise seemed to suggest their possible success. The big unknown would be how the state of Oregon would treat this new, more militant occupation. Steve thought they'd probably use the same "wait-them-out" strategy that was employed against the OSU occupation. *Why force the issue? When the Ninth Court weighed in, everything would be a moot point anyway.*

How they would be treated by the state after their assured arrest was another unknown. If no shots were fired, and they surrendered voluntarily, the state would probably be lenient. He couldn't imagine the state going for the jugular with this scenario. The men had no prior records. They were responsible and productive citizens. Hops felt even an overly zealous DA could be handled with a good legal defense team. The friends had enough money to pay for one. *Damn it! What am I going to do?* Hops already knew the answer to this question. He took another sip of his drink, and watched the big halfback score another touchdown. *Nobody's going to have an answer for this guy.* He thought about last year's Civil War football game, and how this young man had dominated. Carry after carry, he had gained yards, gotten first downs, and eventually scored touchdowns. The Ducks couldn't stop him. *This could be his breakout year.*

Steve relaxed in the old, Amish style wooden chair. He took another quaff and held the liquid up to the light for a better view. The drink had a burnt brown color. There were a couple sips left and he was going to savor this smooth, lightly peated whiskey to the last drop. Hops thought of several decisions he'd made, nixing options because of their possible negative consequences. Many of these resolutions he had grown to regret. He tilted the glass back and finished the last of his drink. Next he grabbed the remote, but before turning off the TV, watched an Oregon State defensive back snag a poorly thrown pass and take it in for a "pick six." Hops turned off the TV and the living room lights. Leaving his glass on the kitchen counter, he headed for bed. *I'll have to call Woody early, and tell him I'm on board.* He quietly opened his bedroom door and slipped into the dark room.

CHAPTER 53

Woody had been on the phone most of the morning. Before Karen got up, he'd talked with Dakota and Ranger, and about 7:30, Woody received the call he'd been hoping for—Hops contacted him, joining the occupation. This meant a lot to him and he told Steve so. Everyone who needed an alibi agreed Woody's road trip/fishing trip ruse sounded good. It would give them roughly two weeks before spouses began to wonder and worry. Hopefully, it was all the time they'd need.

Dakota packed his bags and took an early flight out of Denver. Upon arriving in Portland, he'd catch the return run of the Nehalem Valley's PDX bus. It would drop him off about a quarter mile from Woody's house at the local Shell station.

Karen left for her mother's assisted living residence at 10:00 a.m. She hoped to have lunch with her ninety-two-year-old mom at their favorite restaurant, The Ringside, at about 1:00 p.m. She'd given Woody a kiss on the cheek, and reminded him to be careful about snakes. Woody mentioned his snakebite kit, AKA Doc, would be with him and she shouldn't be concerned. Then Karen gave him a big hug and said she wouldn't worry because he usually made good decisions that kept him out of serious trouble. Woody noticed she emphasized serious. He had responded by saying he'd keep his troubles in the mild to problematic range, and totally avoid the serious category. Karen hugged him again and left for Portland. Woody walked Karen out to her car, and as he returned to the house, wondered which level of "trouble" a civil disobedience, eco-terrorist, logging site occupation would fall into. He closed the front door and concluded it rested in the problematic zone, so everything was good.

Ranger arrived at Woody's at about 10:30. The two sat at his dining table and discussed strategy. They both agreed the first important goal was to access the rise without causing a confrontation. Their timing should provide the needed stage for an easy, trouble-free takeover. The STRONG Alliance was being arrested, probably as they spoke. If they arrived early tomorrow morning, they'd beat the loggers to the site. Both men thought the logging company would give the area at least a day's rest before jumping in. The friends felt the only troublesome unknown was whether a residual roadblock would still exist.

Ranger felt a disguise would be best for them. Something that wouldn't alert a possible barricade sentinel to the trouble that had just arrived on the scene. He knew Woody had recently refurbished a 1970, Chevy P10, step van, and it was housed next door in his garage/workshop. Ranger suggested with a little modification the old van could loosely resemble a TV crew's news vehicle. Woody balked at the use of his van. He'd just put a year into its restoration, and the old parts rig had just received its third and final coat of paint. The retired teacher felt the mint condition, step van was worth about $15,000 now, and he was in no hurry to mar or disfigure his newly finished creation. Ranger continued arguing for the van's conversion. He felt a news station's satellite rig would allow them the best chance of getting close to the site without being discovered. Then they could easily unload their gear and position themselves on the Rise's summit.

Woody and Ranger walked over to the shop and entered it through the side door. When the lights came on, the vintage truck seemed to sparkle in the fluorescent lighting. Woody had done an excellent job of restoration. The short-chassis rig was a large, rectangular box with an extremely blunt hood. Most of the engine housing was in the cab of the vehicle. It had slider doors for both driver and passenger, and two rear doors that were hinged on the sides and swung outwards. Two, large, rectangular windshield panels appeared to be perfectly vertical. The friends walked over to the van and slid open the driver's door. A metal dash with simple gauges rested behind a large, inclined steering wheel. This model was a three-speed manual with a floor-mounted gear shift, and a straight six engine. This power train was sufficient for a short-chassis model. Ranger hadn't seen the finished product. He was really impressed with his friend's handiwork and congratulated him on his restoration efforts. This embarrassed Woody somewhat and he sheepishly thanked Ranger for his compliment.

The ex-Marine stood back from the step van and simply considered it for a moment. He then checked out the shop and noted all the machinery it held. In particular, he regarded Woody's industrial size acetylene torch set-up.

"You know, this could easily be made to resemble a news van. I mean, not really, but we could do a few modifications, suggesting a news rig, and let the viewers fill in the details. You know, Woody, like a magic act. Whoever views your van will want it to be a news rig, and will see one. This deception could give us an advantage if we need one."

"I'm not following you, Ranger."

"Well, we'll never be able to make your van look exactly like a contemporary news rig, but if we throw some black striping on it, with station lettering, like Channel 45, Burns, OR, and affix some old TV satellite dishes to the top, whoever sees it just might think it's a news van."

Woody stared at Ranger, somewhat alarmed. "How would you affix the satellite dishes?"

"We'd have to drill a few holes through the ceiling for tie-down bolts. I'm thinking no more than six holes."

"Holes through the ceiling?"

"Yep, I think so. Can't glue the dishes on. Probably not enough curing time for the adhesive. Hey, Woody, don't worry. We'll patch everything up, good as new, after the occupation."

Woody viewed his freshly painted step van. "And the stripes?"

"Glossy black enamel would be best. A couple stripes of different thickness running around the truck would look good. On the sides we can break the striping with Channel 45 Burns, OR, lettering. Probably, place the Channel 45 above the Burns, OR, and slightly tilt the lettering toward the front. It will look pretty classy."

Ranger had a mind's eye vision of the newly created news van, and was pretty pleased with his creation.

"Glossy black paint?"

"Yeah, yeah, that would be best. Hey, again, not a problem, Woody. After we leave the occupation site, and get your van home, we'll just throw some Z-lack paint on the black enamel and whitewash it. Heck, we'll probably need another two coats of your finish paint, but if all of us help you, it would just take a couple days to get your van back into shape."

Woody thought for a moment. "Maybe we could just rent a news van."

"Not likely, and we don't have the time. Your rig could be converted by nightfall. Time is of the essence, amigo. If we're going to be on the Rise by eight tomorrow, we need to be on the road by three in the morning."

Woody thought Ranger's disguise logic was prudent and his van did seem to be a perfect fit. After they unloaded their gear, they could just park the rig down the road by the bridge. It would be fine there.

Woody had just mentally worked through his concerns when Doc and Hops walked through the shop's side door. Hops greeted his friends.

"Hola, compadres. What's up?"

They walked over to where their friends were standing. The two men shared the strategy with the new arrivals, and, even the ever-questioning Doc appreciated the scheme.

Ranger pointed out the two tasks needing completion: mounting the dishes and striping the van's sides with the news channel's moniker situated appropriately. The ex-Marine volunteered to position the dishes. Woody offered to be Ranger's gofer, and Doc and Hops by process of elimination ended up with the striping job. Hops took off to get several old satellite dishes, which resided behind his garage, some tag board from the Nehalem arts and crafts store, and tape and paint from the lumberyard.

After he drove off, the three men found tape measures, a felt marker, and a chalk box on the woodworking side of the shop. Once they determined a good measurement point on the van, they laid out the two horizontal stripe locations. Next, the chalk box lines were added, and they were ready to begin taping.

The three men completed their task, and since Hops hadn't returned, started talking about essentials for the occupation. The food would be basic: potatoes, rice, dried fruits, and canned vegetables would suffice. They figured four gallons of water per person would be required. The group then thought about armaments. The friends had shotguns and big game rifles they could bring. Ranger remarked he had that area covered, but didn't comment further. Although the weather was still Indian summer–like, everyone knew this wouldn't last much longer so it was decided tents with rain flies were needed. In general, the men chose to consider this a several-week-long camping/hunting trip into the back country, and to pack accordingly.

Hops showed up with his list completely checked off. His vehicle rolled to a stop in front of the shop's bay doors. Woody opened both doors, letting in the sunshine, and the men grabbed the items they would be working with.

Hops had retrieved three dishes. Ranger liked the arrangement of three dishes even better than two. Doc began taping the van while Hops, using a utility knife at the woodworking bench, began cutting out of the tag board a "Channel 45" template. This would produce a somewhat crude signage, but it was a one-shot affair and nobody expected artisan quality.

Ranger and Woody found a ladder and several drop cloths. They'd also fitted a half-inch drill with the appropriate bit. Woody carefully placed the doubled-over drop cloths on the roof's surface so it wouldn't get marred. With each hole drilled, the retired teacher visibly cringed. Having noticed this, Ranger became somewhat dramatic and exaggerated while drilling. This increased his friend's anxiousness, and Doc and Hops stopped their work just to watch Woody's uneasiness. Ranger would groan and swear while drilling through the metal roof, cursing the dull bit and the roof's seemingly tempered metal. He would dramatically plunge through the roof with the bit and rout out the hole by running the bit back and forth several times before moving on to the next bolt location. This last gesture, routing out the hole, sent the retired teacher into fits. He blurted out words of caution to Ranger, reminding him of the bolts' actual diameter. Doc and Hops were totally amused by the whole scene. Once, Woody turned and faced them. The two bystanders immediately spun around and pretended to be searching for something on the nearest bench while hiding their laughter from their friend.

Partway through the morning, a break was called, and all the friends joined together on the shop's floor. The dish installers inspected the painting crew's endeavors, and were impressed by their straight taping job. They commented Hops had missed his vocation. He could really cut out tag board accurately. Woody mentioned quality tag board etching was a sure sign of an excellent elementary teacher in the rough. Hops ventured instructing a classroom of young people seemed somewhat daunting, and was glad his accurate use of a utility knife had not influenced his career choice.

While the friends bantered and admired each other's accomplishments, Ranger had sidled over to the paint spray cans and hid half of them away. Later, while the group enjoyed some coffee and day-old scones, he quietly talked to Doc. Their other two friends conversed about the upcoming occupation and last night's ball game. Woody mentioned to Hops that Dakota would call for a ride in the late afternoon and someone would need to oblige his request. Ranger and Doc ended their clandestine conversation and rejoined their friends.

After the men finished the pile of scones and their coffee, they returned to their work. Woody and Ranger carefully climbed onto the roof to finish the bolt holes. They had cut gaskets out of an old inner tube so the satellite dishes would mount securely, and once they were satisfied with the bolt hole alignments, Woody climbed off the roof and entered the van. He was to tie down each dish by cinching the nuts onto the bolts. Everything progressed along without any hitches until Doc called out there wasn't enough paint to finish the job. An additional problem emerged when Hops mentioned he'd bought all the enamel the lumber store stocked, and whoever got more would have to travel to Tillamook, requiring a round trip of about an hour and a half. For some reason, Woody was shackled with this responsibility by his friends, who all offered unwavering rationales as to why they shouldn't make the drive. Doc and Ranger didn't have enough gas, and Hops had already been a parts gofer. The retired teacher had good-naturedly shouldered the burden and driven off to Tillamook. Ranger walked out to the shop's driveway and watched the Titan reach the paved road, heading for Tillamook. He returned to the shop.

"All right, gentlemen, now the real work begins."

Hops was the only remaining person who had been left out of the loop. "What do you mean, the real work?"

"Time to cut a hole into Woody's van's roof."

"What?"

"Yep. We need the 'unknown' to be on our side. Whenever you engage in a military operation, you don't want your enemy to know all of your possible moves. You want them to assume the usual, and you want to execute the unusual."

"Okay, Rambo. Why the hole in the roof?"

"It might be our best escape route if we're detected and cornered. They'll expect people coming out of the doors, and the roof egress may give us a slight edge."

"Having to exit the van via the roof doesn't sound advantageous to me, Ranger," Hops pointed out.

"No, it probably doesn't, but a surprise departure route just might save our asses."

Doc joined in. "Woody will be really pissed about a hole in his roof."

"Hey, he won't know about it until we get back, and then I'll weld the roof back into place, grind it smooth, and paint it for him.

Hops suggested, "Hell, maybe he'd like a moon roof in his rig, and we'll have already provided the rough opening for him."

The friends laughed together. Doc continued, "I really think that's unlikely, people, and he'll see the hole when he gets back with the paint."

"No, he won't," Ranger replied. "I'm going to cut it out and leave two tiny uncut metal hinges. If need be, one good kick will dislodge what's left in place. I'll duct tape Woody's Mariners flag over the escape hatch. It will cover my torch work, and he'll think it's totally cool to have his flag hanging up there."

The three friends gazed at each other and thought for a moment. Then they grinned. Hops spoke first. "Totally going to work. Let's get to it."

Doc laughed and shook his head. "I don't know about 'totally going to work' but once it's done, there's no amount of crying Woody can do that will change anything."

"That's the spirit, Doc. You guys wheel those tanks over here next to the van, and I'll get to cutting."

The two men did as instructed and moved the bottles. They also uncoiled the dual hose from the cart. Ranger placed the ladder once again onto the van's side, and cushioned its rails so they wouldn't scratch the van. He climbed on top and reached down for the acetylene torch. It was passed up along with the striker. Doc tossed up some gloves, goggles, and a leather apron.

"Make sure my bottles are open."

Hops checked the valves and gave Ranger the thumbs-up. The ex-Marine struck the gas and then, adjusting the oxygen supply and gas levels, got the color he wanted. He bent down over the roof, and the sound of metal being torched, accompanied by acrid smoke, began filling the shop.

Doc glanced over at Hops as they watched from the shop's floor. In a serious tone he said, "Awfully nice of Ranger not to scratch the side of Woody's van with the ladder."

Hops replied in a somber voice, "Yeah, really thoughtful of him. I think Woody would totally appreciate Ranger's concern for his van."

The two men laughed heartily and continued watching the torch dissect the van's roof. Ranger stopped for a moment and held the torch to his side. "Would you guys open the bay doors again, and get a draft going through the shop? We don't want Woody to smell my handiwork."

Both men did the metal worker's bidding and returned to their observation point. After about fifteen minutes of cutting, the ex-Marine shut off the oxygen and the gas. "That should do it."

He checked out his job and then handed everything back down to his ground support. Ranger left the roof and moved the ladder back to the shop's wall. Finding some duct tape, he removed the Mariners flag from its place of honor above the main workbench. He entered the van, felt the metal with his hand, and finding it cool enough, taped the pennant over his new egress route.

"There, nobody will be the wiser, gentlemen. And who knows, this egress might come in handy."

Their work was basically finished until Woody returned, so the three friends ventured into the Thompsons' kitchen and began making lunch from the refrigerator's offerings. They found some watermelon and a bunch of grapes. To this, they added cheese and crackers; several wimpy Pilsners were also procured from the bottom shelf. Hops smiled and mentioned, "You'd think he'd have some real beer on hand for his friends to drink."

Doc and Ranger championed Hops' comment. The three were about to give Woody a verbal thrashing when he entered the kitchen carrying a sack filled with aerosol paint cans.

"How'd you guys do while I was gone?"

The three men dropped their heads down, observing their food, and hid their spontaneous smiles. Ranger recovered first and looking up said, "Really well. We just need some paint and we'll finish the job in a jiffy."

The other men regained their composure and regarded Woody. Doc spoke. "Want some grub?"

He held up a platter of cheese and crackers and nodded at the watermelon.

"Sure, looks great. Has Dakota called yet?"

Hops answered, "Nope."

Woody checked his watch. "He should be calling pretty soon. It would be cool if the van was finished so he could be the first to see our makeover."

Doc and Hops stood up and grabbed the paint can sack.

"Let's get this done, partner," Doc directed.

"I'm totally with you, Van Gogh. Let's put the last brush strokes on this van's ol' sides."

The two men left their friends grazing and headed back out to the shop.

After Woody had eaten for a few minutes, his landline rang. "That's probably Dakota."

He picked up the receiver. "Hello, no, you've got the wrong number."

Woody hung up. Ranger laughed and waited for the next call. He'd seen this scenario before. The phone rang again. Woody retrieved the receiver, and before he got it to his ear, Dakota's voice was heard. "I know you're there, Woody. Come and pick me up, asshole, before you irritate my inner beast."

"With whom am I speaking? Is this Dakota?"

"No, Woody, it's your dead mother who wants to check your diapers. Yes, it's me. Now come and get me, dickwad!"

"You know, Dakota, please and thank you go a long way when asking for a favor."

"Please and thank you, Ms. Landers. Now, come and get me, asswipe, before I forget my manners."

"I somehow think you've missed my point. Nonetheless, I don't want you to continue creating the embarrassing scene which, undoubtedly, is evolving at the gas station. Ranger and I will be there soon."

Ranger had been smiling during Woody's conversation. The phone was hung up, and the two men headed for the old Ford and the Shell station. They quickly arrived at the station and parked by the convenience store. Dakota saw them and waved. Woody contemplated his oldest friend. His long gray hair was pulled back in a ponytail. He wore sunglasses, tank top, cargo shorts, and a wide-brimmed straw hat. His beard rolled down onto his chest. He looked like an old wizard on vacation waiting for something magical to happen. Woody approached his friend and they laughed while hugging each other.

"Good to see you, Dakota."

"Likewise, ol' buddy."

Dakota glanced over at Ranger, who sat in the truck, and called out, "Hello, Ranger."

Ranger gave Dakota a wave and responded, "Come on, Dakota. We need your artistic eye critiquing our creation."

"Oh yeah? Well I'm all about critiquing someone else's work. Let's go."

The two men got into Ranger's truck, and all of them returned to Woody's. The truck came to a stop in front of the right shop door, and the three disembarked.

Ranger, knowing what was to come next, purposely parked behind the empty bay door. Woody asked his friends to wait outside while he checked on their project's progress. He entered the shop. The stripers were standing back from the truck, admiring their work.

"You guys finished?"

Doc answered. "It's a done deal, Woody."

"Dakota's here. I'm going to back the rig outside, and let him view our masterpiece in the sunshine. Raise the door for me, Hops."

Hops pushed the open button, and the door lifted up. Woody started the van. He found reverse and backed it into the daylight, coming to a stop next to the audience. A whistle of appreciation from Dakota greeted the rig as it came to a stop. Their friend did a 360-degree walk around the step van, returning to his place of origin. All of the friends stood together regarding their finished project.

"I'd say you have all missed your calling. You should be restoring old vehicles full time. This is beautiful."

The friends audibly sighed in relief. Their job passed Dakota's critique, and since he owned an artistic eye, they felt their efforts were validated.

"I've never heard of Channel 45 before, but I'm sure its Eastern Oregon's very best, and probably a great news organization. Also, I think Central Oregon will soon know more about Channel 45. Am I correct in my speculation, gentlemen?"

Woody answered for everyone. "You're spot on, ol' wise one. More precisely, Central Oregon will know at the latest about our Burns station by this time tomorrow."

All five men walked around the van together, noticing the striping job in the sunlight, and the various orientations used by the satellite dishes.

"May I suggest one final touch to your canvas?"

Everyone stopped and faced Dakota.

"We'll need to paint the dishes a generic white color. The grays and black don't look professional enough for this vehicle."

Ranger and Woody regarded each other. They'd completely overlooked the obvious regarding their efforts. Ranger focused on Dakota. "Apparently, we needed your expert eye evaluating our work. We totally missed that."

Woody exclaimed, "I've got several cans of white Kilz in the shop. They'll easily cover up those dark colors. Let's get on it, Ranger."

The retired teacher drove the van back into the shop and the bay door closed behind it. As Woody stepped out of his van, he considered Ranger. "Hey, was it your idea to hang the Mariners flag on the ceiling?"

Ranger slightly stiffened at the inquiry, but quickly realized its benign nature and relaxed. "Yep. Nice touch, don't you think?"

"Yeah. Great idea. I like it up on the roof. It looks cool."

Ranger somewhat nervously repositioned the ladder so the roof could be accessed again. Doc, picking up on his friend's anxiety, and realizing its source, jumped onto the ladder before Woody could. He laughed and said a real painting pro needed to finish the dishes. Woody deferred to his friend's desire and felt himself lucky because he didn't have to climb up on top of the van again. Doc and Ranger stood on the van's roof together and Ranger quietly said, "Quick thinking, my friend. That was close."

Doc smiled back at Ranger. "No need for Woody to be distraught, now. Let's allow him a few more days of ignorant bliss."

"Right you are, my good amigo. Right you are."

Ranger slapped Doc on the back and the two men turned their attention to their task. They didn't worry about the overspray since the van's white and the Kilz pigment were so similar, and as the ex-Marine pointed out, the van would get another paint job when they returned home. The Kilz was fast drying and a couple coats later, their job was finished.

The five friends all joined together on Woody's back deck in the late afternoon sunlight. Soon, the sun would be below the trees that lined the backyard's western boundary. The large, green space invited the men to play bocce ball, but they were all business while they sipped on their Pilsners. They discussed the needed occupation items, and all agreed once again each person should be responsible for two weeks' worth of personal food and equipment. Doc said his good-byes first, and headed over to his clinic. He needed to put together a complete medical bag, prepared for any possible emergency. Ranger left next. He talked about gathering together the needed armaments their standoff might require, and about having a bag of tricks at their disposal. He seemed really pleased to be preparing for a possible mini war. Hops was the last to leave. He only had to get together his personal stuff. He asked Woody about what guns he was bringing, and after hearing the response, thought he'd duplicate the effort. The retired teacher reminded his friend to hide the weapons and appear to be packing for a fishing trip. Following that recommendation, Hops said his goodbyes and left.

Woody and Dakota made a list of essentials for the two of them. Dakota basically had only packed his clothes and brought a sleeping bag with him. The two men headed for the store and bought the food they needed. On the return trip, they stopped to pick up the pizza awaiting them at the local pizzeria. Back at Woody's, they ate their pizza and talked about the Big Eddy Rise and the Metolius area. Dakota wasn't familiar with the river or the Ponderosas found on its banks. Woody described in detail the Rise's bowl and how fortress-like it was. They both felt the van's conversion was the answer to a quick and safe access to the hill's summit. Before turning in, they packed everything into three large travel bags. Woody showed Dakota his Browning 12-gauge shotgun and his Savage/Fox 30-06 scoped deer rifle. They checked out the safety mechanisms and how to load both guns. Woody found two boxes of goose shot for the shotgun and several boxes of ammo for his deer rifle. They placed everything into the van and locked up the shop for the night. The two men came back inside, and noting the time, decided to turn in.

Before retiring, Woody wrote Karen a note, and left it on the dining table, knowing she'd see it there. He told her not to worry about snakes and the like. He'd have a great time fishing with his friends, and he loved her very much. Also, Woody mentioned whenever there was cell reception, he'd give her a call. After placing the short letter onto the table, Woody reflected upon the note. Except for the endearing comment, there wasn't a lick of truth in the rest of the message. This was a little disconcerting to Woody, who normally was totally upfront with Karen. There would be "hell to pay" for this little excursion. He only hoped some kind of divine intervention would save his ass from Karen's wrath. After thinking about a godly "saving grace," he pretty much left his worries behind.

Bob Thompson retired to his bedroom and nestled into his pillow-top, queen-sized mattress. He reached over to his bed stand and turned off the light. As he drifted off, he thought of the early start, and how accessing the Big Eddy Rise would be memorable even if it wasn't really very eventful. *You don't need action-filled drama to make something interesting,* thought Woody as he fell asleep.

CHAPTER 54

Ranger drove home from Woody's. He'd navigated Highway 101 and turned west on Nehalem Road. Just before the ocean, he took a right and maneuvered his way up the hill on a one-lane, asphalted, potholed road until he reached his house. It was a log cabin that he built on a westward slope, facing the ocean. From his living room, he viewed the Pacific through old spruce and cedar trees, and at night, he could hear the breakers fall onto the sandy beach below his perch.

When the Pacific storms of November and December hit the coast, Ranger would sit in his easy chair by the living room windows and watch the big trees rock back and forth in unison while the storm's weather pushed on them. He'd gaze upon the big breakers pummeling the shoreline through sheets of wind-driven rain. Ranger knew these massive fronts once had been the ultimate test for early coastal explorers. He appreciated the ancient navigators' bravery and skills and admired their accomplishments, given the horrendous conditions they'd faced.

After parking his rig, the ex-Marine walked into his entryway and placed his hat and coat on wall pegs. He climbed down the steps into the daylight basement. The stairwell walls were tight-knot tongue-and-groove yellow pine. Ranger had finished them with three coats of semi-gloss, and the entire basement area was walled with this yellowish wood. Its light color helped brighten up the potentially dark space.

As Ranger reached the stairs' landing, he opened the doorway immediately to his left and entered his personal armory. He turned on the overhead lights and viewed his weapons room. The knotty pine walls glowed yellowish-orange in the fluorescent lighting. Three walls were lined with shelving and locked gun cases, and a long, wooden workbench was connected to the fourth wall. Here, Ranger loaded rounds and tinkered with his weaponry. The shelves were filled with various sized plastic totes with labels affixed to their fronts. About twenty boxes sat waiting to be opened. Any small army would be satisfied with Ranger's stash of armaments.

Before he started gathering together the essentials, Ranger looked past all his sundries and noted the pine boards on his walls. In less than a day's time, he was going to defend a stand of trees from chain saws, and this forest was composed of the same species of tree that produced these beautiful planks of wood. This irony was not lost on Ranger. He shook his head slightly in wonderment. *How the priorities of life change with the accumulation of experience.* Ranger felt humbled by his choice to defend the old pines. Something about the decision felt terribly right to him.

He unlocked one of the gun cases, and pulled out from it five CZ Czech rifles. They'd been built right before the collapse of the old Soviet Union. Ranger had bought a case of the ARs from a friend, and he still possessed five weapons, a thousand rounds of ammo, and ten magazines. He pulled back the bolts and checked for rounds. Then he put all five rifles into a large military duffel bag. He went to a tote and retrieved the magazines and ammo from it. They also went into the duffel bag.

After several hours of thoughtful planning and packing, Ranger had four bags filled with weaponry and military survival gear. He had packed all the essentials he could think of to protect his friends from harm, and defend the Big Eddy Rise from a potential military assault. Hopefully, he hadn't forgotten anything or lacked something he needed. Only time and retrospection would determine the answer to those thoughts.

Ranger put all of the duffels into the back of his truck and closed the canopy's overhead gate. He locked it and returned to the house. After another hour of packing personal items, he placed his gear next to the front door.

His alarm was set for 2:00 a.m. He hoped events wouldn't get complicated for his friends, and everyone would return home safely. Unfortunately, unlike his amigos, Ranger knew how weapons always complicated whatever transpired. Hopefully, just this once, their presence wouldn't claim someone's life or create an unwanted mishap. Ranger reached over and turned off his reading light. He fell asleep quickly. He slept soundly, much more so than his four friends, who spent their night and early morning hours tossing and turning while anxiously dreaming about what tomorrow might bring.

CHAPTER
55

THE SMALL CARAVAN ZIGGED AND ZAGGED ITS WAY along Highway 22 between Hebo and Grand Ronde, Oregon. Woody and friends had left his house at 3:00 a.m. and now traveled in tandem. Ranger followed the step van in his Ford pickup, with Doc riding shotgun. They had moved down the coast and across the Tillamook Bay lowlands, and now were heading east through the remnants of an old temperate rainforest. The moon was half full and when the tree canopy allowed, the road lit up with the night orb's reflective light. Woody had turned the van's headlights off several times and driven solely by the moon's glow. His friends oohed and aahed at the road and forest's magical appearance when lit only by the night sky. Hops sat in the passenger seat. Dakota sat in a cushioned bar stool jerry-rigged into position directly behind the engine housing. With the stool sitting just so, Dakota sat behind his friends and could see out through the van's front windows. Ropes held the stool's legs tight to the engine cover, but Dakota had to keep himself upright by grasping the front seats with his outstretched arms. A bean bag chair had been placed in the van for a more relaxed ride if the stool occupant tired and needed a break.

The men gradually woke up as they traveled. They'd finished their coffee and the sandwiches Woody fixed for them, and were now spending their travel time conversing. Doc and Ranger, following behind the van, were reminiscing about their smoke-jumping days. Woody, Hops, and Dakota's conversations drifted back and forth between the occupation's unknowns, sports, and politics. At the moment, the three friends were verbally attacking the McDonald administration's atrocities. They found ample room for outrage in his immigration policies and were now reviewing the news about the ICE scandal.

The two vehicles' headlights pierced the early morning darkness. Ranger tried to hang back a bit so his lights didn't constantly shine into Woody's rearview mirrors. Occasionally, the ex-Marine would creep up close to the van, and his lights would pan across the panel truck's rear doors. The new striping job would be illuminated for a few seconds and then would darken again as Ranger's beams shifted away from the Chevy. Ranger would slow up again if this happened and let Woody get further ahead.

There was no traffic on the road at this hour. The log trucks hadn't started moving yet, nor had the flatbed rigs hauling alfalfa. The tourists and casino gamblers who also frequented this corridor were all still in bed so the new, soon-to-be, Big Eddy Rise occupiers had the road to themselves.

Ranger's headlights were slowly rounding a tight corner when he noticed Woody's rig at a dead stop directly in front of him. He stomped on the brakes and came to a halt, inches from his friend's newly painted black bumper. Doc's hands held tightly onto the dash in front of him, and, after the old truck came to a stop, he turned and viewed Ranger.

"Well, if I wasn't already awake, this little maneuver would certainly have done the trick."

Ranger responded, "No shit! That jolted my senses upright. I wonder what the problem is. I hope it's not engine trouble. Mechanical problems would put a 'wrench' into our timeline."

Ranger turned on his emergency flashers. The two men exited their truck, and both walked along the van's left side, gaining the driver's door. Woody slowly slid the door's window back. As they looked into the cab, he pointed over to the right of the van. His eyes were silver dollar size and the expression on his face was one of wonderment.

"Look at the cat!"

Doc and Ranger carefully peered around the van's hood, noting the road's shoulder. A big cougar sat, gazing back at them. Its tail twitched rhythmically behind it. The cat rumbled a guttural greeting, and all the men sat or stood statue-like as they watched the magnificent night prowler. The cougar appeared to be in no hurry to depart. Its big yellow eyes stared at the van. The men and cat were so close the animal's whitish whiskers could be seen and its nostril movements observed as it scented the night air. The van sat in an open canopy area with the moon's light illuminating their location. Woody reached over and turned off the rig's headlights. In the moonlit arena, the two factions, human and cat, watched each other. The puma's tail continued flicking back and forth. Doc and Ranger's adrenaline began to pump into their systems and their arm hairs began to lift.

Without glancing at Ranger, Doc said in a whisper, "This is unbelievable."

No one spoke in response. The mountain lion sat on its haunches and observed the five men for a few more seconds. The forest behind the cougar was a mosaic of dark greens and black tree trunks. The secondary canopy growth was dense. The cat sat before a trail that broke through the greenery's thick wall. The big animal stood up, and still contemplating the men, leaned forward and down. She reached out with her large, front paws, and in one continuous movement, the cougar stretched and yawned at the same time. She regained her upright stature. With her tail curving gracefully upward, the cougar turned and walked back into the forest.

Woody spoke first. "Did I see what I saw?"

Hops answered. "Totally happened. It was really incredible."

Dakota voiced his thoughts, "Pretty good sign. Doesn't get much better than that."

Woody responded. "Signs, like in telling us something, like an omen or foreshadowing?"

"No, like a blank blackboard with no chalk in the tray. Kind of like you, Woody. Jesus, Hops. Why is he driving?"

Hops was laughing now. "I don't know, Dakota. I guess since it's his van and he has a valid driver's license, we just let him drive."

"Well, I'm checking his license in the daylight."

Woody remarked, "Hey, I was just using good communication skills and 'feeding back' my interpretation of what you said, Dakota. Anyway, did you get any kind of vision when you saw the cougar?"

"Oh my God! Please, someone save me. No, I didn't get a vision, Woody. The cat was just a big rabbit's foot. A good luck sign. A confirmation of what we're doing."

Woody started laughing so hard, tears began rolling down his cheeks. Dakota joined in with his friend's laughter, and Hops just shook his head at their bantering. *This could be a very long ride.* Monitoring the conversation, Ranger and Doc were amused by their friends' verbal playfulness.

Ranger spoke to his friends, "Aside from the comic routine, we just witnessed something special. Don't think I've ever seen anything like it. I believe you're right about a 'good sign,' Dakota. I'm feeling pretty confident about our plan because of our friend's little visit. Anyway, let's get moving before someone comes around the corner and smacks into my truck. Our cat's visit won't be much of a defense in the reckless endangerment litigation that would surely follow such an accident."

Ranger and Doc returned to their truck, and Woody started the van up and pulled away from the cougar's trailhead. He ran through the gears and once again was navigating the curves of Highway 22.

The two vehicles passed through Salem as dawn arrived, and just east of the city limits, Ranger's lights flashed high then low several times. Woody pulled over near the men's correctional center and waited for Ranger. The ex-Marine stopped behind the van. He left his truck, walked over to the van, opened the back doors, and stepped up and into the cargo bay. He dropped a duffel bag on the van's back deck.

"Time for your first class in CZ rifles, gentlemen."

Hops spoke to Ranger. "I've shot those before, Ranger. They've got the adjustable rear sight, right, and the safety lever is on the right side?"

"Yep, them's the ones. This couldn't have worked out better. Since you know the weapons, you can drive while I fill Woody and Dakota in on the finer points of these rifles. Doc's going to drive my truck since he doesn't need to know how to use the weapon. How about you guys switching places?"

Woody and Dakota sat in the back, near Ranger, and Hops moved to the driver's seat. He started the van and headed up the hill. Hops ran through the gears, finally shifting into third after the Chevy reached the summit. He checked the rearview mirror and saw the F-150 directly behind him. In the dim light of early morning, the two vehicles headed for the Cascades.

Woody glanced over to his deer rifle and the shotgun cases lying across the van from him, against the rig's wall. Ranger noted his friend's gaze and the questioning look on his face.

"Woody, your bolt action 30-06 will be no match for the M4s we'll encounter in any military assault. You might as well have a slingshot. For every shot you get off, ten will be coming back at you. Trust me, amigo, we need to fight fire with fire."

Woody nodded his head in agreement. "All right, Ranger, you're the man. Tell us about these bad boys."

The two students sat cross-legged in the van's cargo area facing Ranger, who sat on the bean bag chair. All three men rocked back and forth with the old van as it proceeded east. Ranger fetched three AR rifles from his military bag. He handed his students each a weapon. He then retrieved magazines and ammo from the duffel bag. Next, he showed his friends how to load the magazines with cartridges, and how to insert the clips into the guns. They pulled back the bolt and loaded a bullet into the chamber. Next, they reversed the process, leaving an empty chamber and clipless gun. The ex-Marine showed them the location of the safety lever. It also chose the preferred firing mode: semiautomatic, short burst, or automatic. Ranger finished his lesson by instructing on how to use the weapon's sights properly. Although the sight system was basic, Ranger took no chances with assumptions, and drew a picture for the two men, showing proper alignment of front and rear sight features. Then he talked about misalignment and drew several pictures demonstrating improper aim and how you could correct your shot by raising or lowering the rifle's butt on your shoulder. Woody and

Dakota aimed their rifles at various features inside the van, developing a better feel for the weapon and its nuances.

The three men didn't notice the van reduce speed as it climbed up into the Cascade Mountain Range, nor its increased rocking as it followed the Santiam River's course. When Hops drove the van past the summit, near Hoodoo ski resort, and continued on to Central Oregon, the two men handed their weapons back to Ranger.

"Well, gentlemen, I hope you enjoyed your intro to Czech assault rifles. They're the best you can have. They rarely 'jam up,' they're balanced nicely, and their sights are easy to use. Hopefully, you'll never have to shoot one. Any questions?"

Both men assured their instructor they'd gotten everything. Ranger then asked Hops to pull over at the nearest wayside, and told Woody and Dakota to fill up all the banana magazines with cartridges. Right before the downslope adjacent to Suttle Lake, Hops pulled over and stopped. The old Ford mimicked the maneuver and came to a halt next to the van.

The pullout rested directly above Suttle Lake's western end, providing a panoramic view of Central Oregon. The sun, now above the horizon, cast an orangey-yellow early morning light. The men gazed east and saw Black Butte standing in front of them. Right before the old volcano was the turnoff to the Metolius. Their destination was less than an hour away.

Ranger pushed open the back door and turned back toward the three men. "Start looking for my lights to flash on and off after we go through the three-way stop near Camp Sherman. I'm searching for an abandoned summer home's garage to stash my rig in. Hopefully, one's available. If I'm flashing my lights, come to a stop. We'll need to transfer my gear to the van before I hide my truck away."

Woody responded, "Copy that. See you in the big trees."

Ranger left the step van and rejoined Doc in his truck. The two vehicles departed their lofty perch and headed down the Cascades' lee side. Doc continued driving and Ranger rode shotgun. The two vehicles drove toward the rising sun and the Metolius River. The ex-Marine's thoughts drifted about, but always returned to the task at hand. He hoped their occupation would start easily and end easily. *They'd soon know about the starting part.* The sun rose higher as the vehicles neared the Metolius River turn-off. It was shaping up to be another hot day.

CHAPTER 56

SUPERINTENDENT ROSS STARED UP AT THE YOUNG activists chained to several trees. True to Climber's word, the tree sitters had lowered themselves to the ground about an hour ago, and now sat with their ground crews chained to the big trees. It was near eight in the morning and already the old forest was beginning to heat up. Ross lifted off his trooper hat and wiped the perspiration from his forehead with his paisley bandana. He viewed his preparations. Everything appeared and felt right. Climber had come down from the summit earlier and joined one of the ground crews. Ross noted for the first time since his arrival, the Big Eddy Rise didn't have a waft of smoke drifting upwards from the summit's bowl. The sight was a little strange. It actually seemed unnatural now to have a smokeless sky above him. All the occupiers were quietly waiting for their arrest. No drumming or chanting was reverberating through the old growth stand, and the activists seemed subdued and saddened by their apparent failure. Ross observed all the groups and noticed the students quietly conversing or not talking at all. One couple, a redheaded girl and a pony-tailed young man, was holding hands and her head rested upon his shoulder. They seemed content to simply await their arrest. Superintendent Ross turned and watched his law officers as they prepared to handcuff the occupiers. He was chagrined by the lack of manpower available and hoped the procedure wouldn't take too long or be too strenuous for his men.

The previous forty-eight hours had put quite a strain on local law enforcement agencies and had totally derailed the incarceration of the STRONG Alliance. The 3rd Street U.S. Bank in Bend had been robbed two days ago at 8:00 a.m. A bank manager and a few tellers were surprised by three gunmen dressed as local air conditioning repairmen. Their AC system had gone down the day before, and the repairmen had arrived the next day, right on schedule. They had been let into the bank by the manager. From that point on, it became a serious bank robbery.

Tellers were duct taped and positioned in a back room with a guard, and the manager was forced to open the vault and teller drawers. After the robbers sacked up their loot, the bank manager was seated with the others, and all the employees were then bound together so they couldn't move. Their cellphones had been collected and the bank phone lines had been compromised. The robbers had then let themselves out the front door and driven off.

Late-arriving employees found their fellow workers trussed up in the conference room. The police were summoned to the bank at roughly 10:00 a.m. By then, the robbers had been gone for an hour.

The Deschutes Sheriff's office and the OSP were both contacted and arrived at the crime scene. Since Ross was in the area, he shared command of the investigation with Deschutes County Sheriff Evan Ryerson. It seemed to be the perfect robbery. Besides the AC units not working, the branch manager, upon further investigation, found the surveillance cameras had been disabled so there were no pictures of the thieves. They had worn gloves, and most assuredly, they'd stolen the repair van they drove off in. This didn't leave the investigating officials much to go on.

Sheriff Ryerson and Superintendent Ross were about ready to downsize the investigation and get onto other business when a patrol car called dispatch with the location of an apparently broken down AC repair van east of town on Knox Road. This part of the Bend area was a mix of housing developments, one- or two-acre lots, and larger parcels of land still being used for agricultural purposes. Ryerson and Ross had both driven to the site and inspected the rig. Nothing unusual appeared to have happened, except the getaway vehicle had run out of gas. A quick check of nearby domiciles had produced no clues or information, so an extensive search of the area seemed essential, and one immediately commenced. Deschutes County deputies joined the OSP troopers in a house by house, building by building, shakedown of the region. As of yet, the robbers had not been found, and the manhunt continued.

Almost all of the law enforcement officers in the area were now preoccupied with finding the thieves. Superintendent Ross knew his aide, Lieutenant Peters, had set in place the logistics for the occupation arrests. Everything was set to go. The Deschutes Jail and the correctional center were ready for the large influx of people, and the jail's prisoner transport bus was at their disposal. The robbery had postponed the occupation arrests by twenty-four hours, but Ross felt accomplishing this task sooner than later was paramount. The governor expected the resolution of the standoff to have already occurred and was waiting for her OSP boss to call so a press conference could ensue. Ross had deliberated with Peters about the lack of available manpower, and in the end, it was decided to proceed with arresting the students using a small, senior, well-trained group of deputies and troopers. Lieutenant Peters would continue monitoring the manhunt and Superintendent Ross would manage the student arrests. Both Jefferson and Deschutes County Sheriffs had given Ross a couple well-qualified deputies, Johnny Edwards being one of them. These law officers, coupled with several OSP troopers, would be the personnel Ross had at his disposal.

The superintendent felt slightly uncomfortable with this situation. It was barely enough manpower for the arrests. Each student would be physically carried to the county's bus, and this alone, in the midday heat, would be taxing. He was not concerned about firepower. The students would not resist and need to be subdued by his officers. This fact was reassuring given the limited numbers of personnel doing the arresting. Ross surmised the deputies and troopers would need to take their time, stay hydrated, and rest whenever it seemed appropriate. Both he and Peters mused by the end of the day, there'd be some tired enforcement personnel and a bunch of students incarcerated and waiting for their defense attorneys. All in all, though, both law enforcement officers felt the arrests could be done safely.

The OSP boss looked back at the Deschutes County prisoner bus. It was parked right behind the road barricade and sat ten yards away from the bend in the road where he now stood. Parked behind and across the road from the bus were a half dozen patrol cars. At the moment, all the officers were talking strategy and gathering together the needed essentials. It had been decided that the OSP troopers would work as a group and the deputies would do the same. Ross noted Deputy Edwards and Trooper Mills were present, and he had confidence in these men, knowing they were capable officers. He had not met several of the other deputies and troopers present. Mills was taking command at this point, and all the men were readying themselves for the job. The superintendent could see bolt cutters in hand and zip ties being distributed, and a deputy had just fetched two stretchers from the county's bus.

Ross was a little concerned about the roadblocks farther away from his present position. He'd removed his security from these points to fill his manpower needs. Without guards at these locations, anyone could come down the road. This hadn't been a problem in the past, since it appeared most people on their own volition chose to stay away from the occupation site. Superintendent Ross returned his gaze to the young OSU students. It was about time to commence the arrests. He turned back to Officer Mills, gained his attention, and waved him over.

CHAPTER
57

Woody peered into his rearview mirror and noted Ranger's beams signaling him to stop. They'd passed through the three-way and gone by several summer homes. The vehicles stopped adjacent to a rundown, derelict-appearing house that seemed to be what Ranger needed. Woody glanced into his side mirror and saw the ex-Marine walking over to a slightly skewed, separate garage, which, like the cabin, had seen better days. Ranger pulled open the large, single door and peered inside. After a moment of inspection, he pulled the door completely open and returned to his truck. As he neared his rig, Ranger thought about the daylight and how they didn't want anybody catching them stashing the Ford in the old, abandoned garage. Woody, Hops, and Dakota left the van, and with Ranger and Doc's help hastily transferred all of the gear from the truck to the Chevy. Everyone was somewhat startled to see all the equipment Ranger had stashed in the old Ford. They carted four bulging duffel bags and numerous backpacks between rigs, and Dakota, after toting a particularly heavy duffel bag to the van, regarded Ranger.

"Hell, what did you put into these bags? This one felt like it actually did have the kitchen sink in it."

Ranger replied, "Hopefully, I've got everything we'll need and then some, but let's not talk about it now. We need to hide my rig before anyone sees us."

Ranger nosed his truck into the tilting garage and closed the door behind him. He leaned a piece of old roof shingle against the door before he returned to the van. When he reached the Chevy, he opened the driver's door and asked if he could take the helm. Woody accommodated his request and moved into the passenger's seat. The van was completely filled with backpacks and duffel bags now. The men had piled gear into small mounds to make seating areas. Before Ranger sat in the Chevy, he took a moment to take in their surroundings and listen to the Metolius River. It was about nine in the morning. Bright sunlight streamed through the forest. The river gurgled and splashed its way past the old summer home, and several crows, sitting in adjacent trees, called back and forth to each other. *It's fish or cut bait time. I guess we're all going fishing.* Ranger sat in the driver's chair, shut the side door, and started up the engine.

"All right, gentlemen, we're going to rock and roll now. I'd like you all to grab a rifle and chamber a round."

All the men viewed each other questioningly. Doc voiced the group's concerns. "Are you expecting trouble?"

"Nope, but we need to be prepared for it."

The interior of the van became very quiet as the men contemplated the request.

"Come on, fellas. Don't get cold feet now. Lock and load; be prepared for the worst and expect the best. Let's go."

Ranger worked through the gears and headed for the Big Eddy Rise. His friends found their rifles and prepared them for use. The van passed by the last summer house and a section of raggedy woods, which was in need of Forest Service management. Ranger checked his mirror and noted in the distance a boil of dust billowing up behind him. He rounded a corner and immediately came upon an unmanned barricade. Ranger said to no one in particular, "This isn't good." He stopped the van within a few feet of the roadblock. Both he and Woody looked down the road to the next corner.

Woody exclaimed. "Holy shit! You're right. This is totally not good!"

The other men stood up and peered over the engine housing at the road's visual terminus. They all noticed numerous patrol cars and an official-appearing bus parked at the next bend. The ex-Marine got out of the Chevy and motioned for Woody to do the same. They walked up to the temporary barricade. Ranger observed the far-off scene through a pair of binoculars he'd grabbed from the van's dash. For a moment he watched the arresting activities proceed. No law enforcement officers had noticed their arrival as they all faced away from the men's position. He handed the glasses over to the retired school teacher, who in turn watched the occupation arrests begin.

"Well, this might change our game plan, Woody."

Woody mumbled an agreement and continued viewing through the binos.

Inside the van, Hops, Dakota, and Doc were also watching the officers arresting the STRONG Alliance members. Their view was not as clear as Ranger's and Woody's, but they could make out groups of uniformed officers walking up to the students.

Doc spoke to his friends. "That's a whole lot of 'public servants' at work. It might be a good time to put this vehicle in reverse and quietly depart."

His audience nodded their approval. Hops hung his head out the driver's window and conveyed Doc's thoughts to Ranger. The ex-Marine was about to respond when he looked past the van at the dust now settling behind them. The image of a dark blue Dodge Charger was beginning to emerge. It had stopped about a hundred feet behind the van. As the dust settled even further, the emergency lights atop the car became apparent.

Ranger studied the OSP cruiser. He quietly remarked to himself, "Well, shit's going to hit the fan now!"

He glanced over at Woody, who was viewing the patrol car, too. The retired teacher returned Ranger's gaze with an expression of utter shock on his face.

Lieutenant Peters had been following a dust cloud for several miles. He was driving to the Big Eddy Rise with good news for his boss. The bank heist thieves were cornered in an old barn near Powell Butte, and had given up without incident. Peters left the scene about an hour and a half ago, and had just now caught up to the lead rig's dusty path. As he trailed the vehicle, he saw, through the dust, the rear end of what appeared to be the jail bus, but when he rounded the last corner, the dust had settled enough for good visibility and he noticed the bus now looked more like a TV station's satellite rig. *This was not going to be helpful.* He reached over and turned on his rollers. *I need to get this crew turned around and headed back to Camp Sherman, pronto.*

Ranger saw the trooper's lights go on and went into automatic. "Woody, grab the roadblock. We're going to swing it off to the side."

"Don't you think...?"

"Now, Woody! Don't talk. Just do it!"

Alarmed by everything, Woody was beginning to tremble, but he grabbed his end of the barricade and pulled it to the road's edge. Ranger lifted up his end and pivoted it across the road. Then he hollered at Woody, "Get in the passenger seat."

Woody did as he was told. He sat down and faced his friends. "We're so totally screwed!"

Ranger jumped into the driver's seat, started the van, and punched the accelerator. Gravel flew away from the rear tires, showering the road behind the rig with a barrage of pebbles. Woody stared at Ranger and frantically yelled over the engine noise, "What's the plan?"

Ranger didn't respond immediately. He was surveying the scene ahead of him. He took in the jail bus, the half dozen squad cars, and the groups of law enforcement officers standing near the base of two trees. He also noted a barricade just before the bend in the road. There appeared to be a lone officer standing just inside the roadblock. Ranger felt more than saw a relatively straight route from the road's bend to the summit of Big Eddy Rise. He aimed the van at the imagined path.

"Plan? Plan, I'm working on one."

The van was now going about thirty miles an hour with a huge cloud of dust following. Lieutenant Peters was totally blinded. He hit the siren and followed slowly behind the dust ball.

Superintendent Ross looked back at the siren's sound and saw what appeared to be a news rig running down the road at a dangerous pace. All the hill's participants were now watching the white satellite van bear down on their location. Officer Mills and Deputy Edwards studied each other with questioning expressions. There had been no news coverage problems during the entire occupation, and what was rumbling in their direction, right now, appeared to be just that. As Ross began moving aside from the van's course, he noted an arm and hand emerge from the van's passenger's side, frantically waving him away from his position.

Ranger steered straight for the hill. All of his friends were holding tightly onto some part of the van's interior, peering forward with various expressions of concern on their faces. Hops, Doc, and Dakota seemed somewhat in control of themselves and already resigned to their imminent, clumsy entrance. Woody, on the other hand, seemed petrified.

Ranger spoke loudly. "Doc! You'll need to find the bullhorn. It's in the top of my green pack. Everyone else, grab your weapon and don't let go of it."

As Ranger spoke, the Chevy step van lunged forward off the gravel road and became airborne. It passed over the side ditch and nosedived into the slope beyond the corner. The sound of splintering wood, crunching metal, and flying gravel filled the ancient forest. A discerning ear might have caught the high-pitched scream emanating from Woody's vocal cords as his van flew through the air, but probably not; the whining engine noise most likely drowned it out. Ranger downshifted into second and punched the accelerator.

At the last moment, Superintendent Ross leaped to the side and rolled out of harm's way. From his prone position he'd watched the van fly above and past him before it rammed into the hillside.

All the Chevy's occupants lifted slightly off their perches as gravity pulled their projectile back to the slope's incline. The passengers were thrown forward and then tossed backwards as their ride bucked several times while moving up the slope. Only Ranger, white knuckling the steering wheel, remained in place. He looked ahead for his path. He downshifted into first and half throttled the van. This kept the engine from lugging, and the old rig continued gaining ground on the summit. Ranger shouted back at his friends as Ponderosa trunks passed dangerously close to the rig's sides.

"Doc, grab the stepladder along with your bullhorn."

Woody had been tossed back into the cargo area with the first major bounce, and now retrieved his rifle. He sat with his back against the van's wall and glanced up at the Mariners flag. A corner of duct tape had come loose, and part of the pennant hung down. Woody noticed in the newly exposed roof an unusual scar in the metal. Before he could ponder the blemished surface, the van lurched dramatically to the side, rolling him over and into a mass of gear.

Ranger swerved to miss a big Ponderosa. There was a wrenching metallic sound as the big tree ripped off the driver's side mirror. The van was losing momentum, and the back wheels were beginning to lose traction. The Chevy moved past both law enforcement teams and their correlating clusters of site occupiers. They all seemed transfixed by the absurd action passing by them. Deputy Edwards' eyes tracked the vehicle as it drove past, and his head swiveled slightly as he held onto his zip ties and bolt cutter.

Ranger sensed the Chevy wouldn't go much farther before it bogged down. Choosing his spot, he twisted the wheel sharply to the left, and three fourths of the way through the turn, jammed on the brakes. The van skidded around the last portion of the maneuver and came to an abrupt stop.

The old rig hadn't quite finished moving, though. The drastic turn left it on two wheels, balancing with its uphill side leaning up the slope. For a second, the old rig rested and then, like a tired beast, the Chevy rolled over onto its side. A rush of air pushed dust outward and upward from the overturned rig. For a moment, the forest was completely silent.

The inside of the van was a jumble of bodies and gear. Everything not tied down had fallen to the Chevy's right side, and lay in tangled heaps. Somehow Ranger, as the van capsized, maneuvered his body's position so he now stood securely on the passenger seat's inboard edge, holding onto the steering wheel, which now was above his head. Looking over and down, he jumped off the seat and landed on the van's side amongst the piles of gear and his friends. He quickly noted nobody had broken bones or was bleeding, and everyone was still holding their rifles. Doc had found his bullhorn and held it at ready. The stepladder was nearby.

"All right. No time for tears. We need to flex our muscles. Hops, Woody, use the van's hood for cover and point your guns at the state cops. Dakota and I will point our weapons at the county deputies. Doc, you need to mount the ladder and speak over the van to whoever is listening. Tell them we're in charge now. They need to raise their hands in the air and back down the hillside to their vehicles."

Ranger surveyed his friends and took a deep breath. "We're in charge, amigos. We've got the high ground and they're vulnerable. These guys will know that. Act like you know it too."

Next, Ranger reached down and ripped off the Mariners flag, exposing his torch handiwork. He punched out the roof panel with one powerful kick, and taking hold of Dakota's shoulder, he pushed him through the opening. Woody examined the hole in his van's roof.

"What the hell! How did the..."

Hops grabbed Woody's arm and pushed him out the escape route and directed him to the van's front. Simultaneously, four Czech CZ barrels emerged from around the van's perimeters and found their targets. Almost as quickly, a bullhorn was keyed and Doc's voice addressed the law officers.

"Everyone freeze! Raise your hands in the air and listen up. There's a new sheriff in town!"

Trooper Mills was in a half crouching position, standing next to two other OSP officers. They all held the same unsure, defensive posture. Mills hadn't thought to drop his possessions and unholster his weapon. Everything happened so quickly, and appeared more comical than threatening. The trooper looked over at Deputy Edwards. Edwards was in a half crouch, too. His team had also been caught off guard, and still held bolt cutters and zip ties in their hands.

The STRONG Alliance members were just as surprised by the situation as the peace keepers, and were viewing each other with apprehensive expressions. Intuitively, they all knew the situation had transcended to a new level that was not to their liking. Climber and Runner were already making eye contact and using primitive hand gestures to communicate with each other about the Alliance's next move.

Superintendent Ross viewed the scene from the road. It was blatantly obvious his contingent of officers was in serious trouble. They were all out in the open, targeted by gunmen who held the high ground and were protected by the overturned van. One wrong move and his officers could be shot down before they had a chance to return fire or seek the safety of a tree trunk.

Trooper Mills assessed the situation. He saw two AR barrels pointed at him. The nearest Ponderosa was ten feet away, and five college students sat on the ground chained to it. He slowly began raising his hands into the air. The other troopers and deputies followed suit.

Ranger, noting his targets raising their hands, asked Hops what he was seeing. He replied the troopers were surrendering. Ranger, without taking his eyes off the deputies, gave Doc more directions. All the activity and commotion following the van's crash caused Doc to forget to tell the police to back down the hill. Ranger noted this.

"Doc, on my cue, tell them to walk backwards down the hill with their hands in the air. They should go to the closest cruiser, face us, and leave their hands up. Assure them we don't want to kill anyone. We're here to continue the occupation of this logging site and will surrender the site when we're assured of its safety."

The ex-Marine then turned his attention to the nearest deputy. Edwards and Ranger warily inspected each other. "Deputy, I'm going to take you as a hostage. In deciding your next actions, please consider your family and friends. This site occupation is not worth your life. I promise to let you go in a couple hours if you cooperate."

Deputy Edwards nodded his head to show his comprehension of Ranger's remarks.

"I need you to unbuckle your holster belt with one hand, leave the other raised, and let your gun fall to the ground."

Deputy Edwards followed Ranger's instructions.

"Do you have an ankle holster?"

Edwards shook his head from side to side.

"Now, take several steps toward me. Do not get between me and your fellow officers."

The deputy took three steps in Ranger's direction.

"Okay, Doc, relay my message."

Doc repeated the occupiers' newest demands. The bullhorn's metallic sound drifted through the forest. All the law enforcement officers commenced walking backwards down the hill. They reached the ditch together and carefully walked up onto the road. Superintendent Ross moved back to the closest cruiser and faced the Big Eddy Rise with raised hands. Lieutenant Peters had previously joined him. They both awaited the arrival of their fellow officers.

Peters spoke to Ross. "Jesus, we got caught with our pants down."

Ross looked at his close friend blankly and simply shook his head in disgust. "In forty-some years of law enforcement, I thought I'd seen everything. I stand corrected."

The bullhorn was keyed one more time. Doc explained a deputy would be held hostage while the van's gear was transferred up the hill. He would be released after all the equipment was moved. No one was to leave the front of the cruiser until given the "okay" to do so.

Ross focused on Peters. "They've got Edwards as their hostage."

"He's a seasoned, smart deputy, superintendent. He won't make any rookie mistakes. Edwards is just the guy you'd want in this position."

All of the law officers made it to the patrol car and now stood facing the rise with their hands up. It was a grim and embarrassed group of officers.

Ross spoke to his men. "This was my fault, people. It's all on me."

Ross's words trailed off, and all the officers continued watching the movement above them.

The sun had risen to near midday height. The cloudless sky was robin egg blue, and a slight breeze bent the smaller Ponderosa pine branches. The Metolius

River could be heard in the stillness of the moment. A few yellow-rumped warblers and pine siskins checked out branches for insects, and some scrub jays flew from tree to tree in search of prey. Chipmunks reemerged and were now actively scurrying between manzanita bushes. Several of the law officers glumly watched the forest creatures' activities while the others simply viewed the hill's newest occupiers move their equipment.

Climber and Runner determined the Alliance needed to quickly and quietly depart the scene. Climber notified the third group of Alliance members of their intent to abruptly leave. All the occupiers unchained themselves and, leaving all their gear behind, slowly started walking to the Metolius. Ranger noticed this, and considered it a good response by the young students. Climber's plan was to access the river, then follow the streambank to the pull-off where their bus was still parked. The Alliance members moved from tree to tree as individuals or in groups of two. They all reached the river together and made their way downstream to the bus. Upon reaching the old bus, Climber reached under the front wheel cover and retrieved a magnetic metal key box. He removed the key and unlocked the bus's door. He also noted Bridger's Jetta still sat parked next to the bus. The young occupier looked around at his fellow Alliance members and did a mental headcount, coming up short.

"Hey, where are the 11th Streeters?"

Runner focused on Climber. "I told Bridger and Rachael about our plan. I thought they were right behind me."

Another Alliance member joined in. "They were, but then Hang and Tunes joined them. The last I saw of them, they were near the summit's top, and appeared to be going into the bowl."

Climber responded, "Okay, okay. Maybe they chose to join the new group. Anyway, we've got to move on. Everybody climb on board. Let's go home."

Climber closed the bus doors behind the last Alliance member and, taking the helm, started the engine up. A small report startled some nearby jays and a puff of blue smoke wafted away from the tail pipe.

Runner called out to Climber, "Should we go into Bend, and see about Sasha and Dread?"

He thought for a moment, then responded, "No. Our rig's too recognizable. We'll go home and figure out what to do from there. If need be, I can drive back tomorrow and check on them."

Climber left the dusty, log-enclosed parking lot and headed the old bus for Corvallis. The Alliance had lost their battle to protect the old growth, but, he thought to himself as the bus turned onto Highway 20, *another, more aggressive, fight to save the old trees has just begun.*

CHAPTER 58

HOPS AND RANGER STAYED WITH THE VAN WHILE their other friends began transporting gear up to the bowl. Ranger stood just past the van's rear. He could observe the law officers down by the cruisers, and they could see him. He held onto Deputy Edwards' right shoulder with his left hand, and pointed his CZ at him with his right. Hops, still using the van for cover, pointed his rifle down to the road. In this manner, the two men kept the police at bay while their friends transferred gear.

Hang and Tunes grabbed Bridger and Rachael as they were following Runner's directions. Bridger hadn't seen his gramps when the men escaped from the van. He and Rachael were slowly moving to the river when their friends caught up to them. The four young people conversed behind a giant Ponderosa trunk. Hang told Bridger his dad, Hops, and possibly Doc were part of the van's crew. From their safe vantage point, the four students saw Dakota lug a duffel bag and backpack up to the Rise's bowl. Bridger and Hang immediately decided to go up to the summit and meet with Woody and his friends. Tunes and Rachael hesitated for a moment, thinking about other recourses, but after further thought, chose to stay with their friends.

The foursome maneuvered their way back up the slope and slipped into the bowl from the south side. Dakota left for another load just prior to their entrance, leaving the camp site empty. Apprehensively, the young friends stood near the tent and waited for the arrival of the next equipment bag. Under one of those duffels would be Gramps. The first load to arrive was carried by Dakota. He dropped his bag and, glancing up, saw the young people.

Oh shit! It's Bridger and Hang. Woody didn't say anything about this. Seconds later, another bag arrived, hoisted by Doc. He dropped his burden. As he straightened up, Doc followed Dakota's gaze to the students. Upon seeing Bridger, he cocked his head to one side and said, "Bridger, what are you doing here?"

"Well, Doc, I was about to ask…"

Just then, a third duffel bag appeared. A verbal grunt accompanied it as the bag landed atop the basaltic rim. Everyone watched Woody as he scrambled over the lip, regained control of the parcel, and delivered it to the encampment's center. Woody scanned the camp. His eyes eventually found the young OSU students.

"Holy shit! Bridger, what are you doing here?"

Doc responded, "That seems to be the prevailing question, Woody. Dakota and I will continue our Sherpa mission while you determine the answer to the unanswered query."

Dakota and Doc studied each other, smiled, and shook their heads as they left the citadel. Both men cautiously walked back to the van.

Doc said, "Apples don't fall far from the tree."

"It would appear you got that correct, my friend."

Woody examined his son, then Hang and the others. He recognized Rachael and Tunes from the Corvallis apartment. His view returned to Bridger. His grandson wore river shoes, dirty cargo shorts, a tank top, and appeared to have not bathed for a week. Woody, with a slight smile on his face, spoke quietly to his son. "How are your classes going?"

The obvious lightness of this inquiry lessened the tension everyone was feeling.

"No classes as of yet, Dad, but I'm acclimating well to campus life."

Woody raised his eyebrows and nodded his head up and down several times. The three bystanders could sense grandfather and grandson were reconciling in their own way. With two sentences, the pair reconnected and showed respect and forgiveness for each other. Woody and Bridger took several steps toward one another and embraced.

Bob Thompson spoke again to his son. "You are such a dumbshit. What are you doing here?"

In an aside, Hang spoke to Tunes and Rachael quietly. "We've progressed from 'what are you doing here' to 'Dumbshit, what are you doing here?' I sense definite headway being made, don't you?"

The three laughed softly as grandfather and grandson hugged. The two men separated and Woody eyed Hang. "Is this how you interpret 'You two take care of each other'? Did I literally have to say, 'and keep him out of trouble'?"

Hang laughed and shrugged at Mr. Thompson's remark. "You asked the impossible, Mr. Thompson. You know how hardheaded Bridger is, and in my defense, I was doing my best, and as you can see, he still has all his fingers and toes."

Woody and Bridger walked over to the others. Woody gave Hang a hug and squeezed both Rachael and Tunes' hands. He stood back from the young people and was about to speak when Bridger blurted out, "Gramps, why are you here?"

Woody took a deep breath and responded, "I'm not sure. Well, yes, I am. I'm doing the same thing all of you did; my friends and I aren't going to let this logging happen."

"But Gramps, you've got guns. You could get killed."

"I know, I know. Everything appears really complicated now, but...Bridger, I need to help unload the van. I love you very much, but I should help my friends right now."

Tunes spoke up. "We can help, too, Mr. Thompson."

Woody intuitively responded to him. "No, no, you can't. Stay inside the bowl. This is our thing now. Stay in the bowl and don't show yourself to the police."

Woody hugged Bridger again and then left for the overturned van. The four young people watched Mr. Thompson scamper over the basaltic rim and disappear.

Rachael took Bridger's hand and squeezed it. "I can see where you get your strength. Your gramps doesn't wear a superhero uniform or look like one for that matter, but he is one just the same."

Bridger gazed at Rachael appreciatively. "I think you're right."

Hang voiced a thought that needed to be broached. "Hey, everybody, what are we going to do?"

Rachael responded, "I don't know. Let's wait and see where things are going. I'm not sure what I want to do."

Tunes didn't say anything. He had his earbuds in and was just listening for now.

Bridger spoke next. "I agree. Let's just hang and talk with Gramps after they've got all their gear up here and everyone is present. I'm really not sure what I want to do, either."

The four friends found some water bottles and some cold leftover rice and bean burritos. They retired to the shady side of the tent and waited for the day's events to play out.

Bridger and friends watched as the Big Eddy Rise's bowl received four army duffel bags and roughly a dozen packs of various sizes and shapes. Woody brought the last load up. It included his two personal bags, one of which he placed in the shade, away from the other gear. Everyone gathered together at the rim and peered down at the Chevy van.

Doc was climbing up the stepladder with the bullhorn in his hand. He keyed the horn and spoke to the deputies and troopers below. "Thanks for your patience, gentlemen. We're almost finished with our transfer. We'll be letting Deputy

Edwards go momentarily, but we need you to accommodate us once more. Please move your vehicles back to the next bend in the road, and in the future, do not trespass between here and there unless we agree to your passage."

Superintendent Ross spoke to his contingent. "All right, officers, it appears we've been dismissed. Let's move back to the corner. No heroics, people. They've still got Deputy Edwards."

All the law enforcement personnel got into their cruisers and began slowly backing up to the ninety-degree bend. The jail bus pulled forward and then backed into an ATV road. From there, it turned left and followed the other vehicles in retreat.

Hops and Doc slowly walked up the rise. Doc carried the stepladder and bullhorn while Hops carefully backed up the hill with his CZ pointed downhill. He was watching Ranger more than observing the county police cars. The ex-Marine let go of Deputy Edwards' shoulder.

"Thanks for your trust, deputy. Your calm behavior helped keep everything under control. One last thing. I watch the news, Edwards, and know you saved a young girl's life not too far from where we're standing. Please accept my gratitude for your service."

Ranger's words surprised Deputy Edwards. He turned and studied Ranger. Standing before him, pointing an AR rifle at him, was an aging man. His short gray hair was somewhat greasy, his scruffy gray stubble needed trimming, his black-rimmed glasses, sitting atop a pointed nose, needed cleaning, but yet, he stood before Edwards with confidence and in total command of the situation. Edwards actually felt safe standing next to his adversary.

"Who are you?"

Ranger focused on Edwards. "Just an old man doing what he thinks is right, deputy. You're free to go. On the way down the hill, you can pick up your weapon. Grab the belt by one end and don't touch the pistol."

The holstered Glock lay where it had dropped, and Edwards bent over and lifted it up by the buckle end of the belt. He continued down the Rise and crossed the roadside ditch. It was about a quarter mile to the corner where all the cruisers were now parked. It was midday and Johnny found his kerchief and mopped his forehead with it. Most of his shirt had sweated through with perspiration, and the slight breeze cooling him off felt good. He stopped walking for a moment and turned back to the hill. He saw Ranger, holding his AR at the ready, turn, lower the rifle, and climb into the summit's bowl. Left on the hill was an old, overturned Chevy step van and various sundries the Alliance had abandoned. Ropes hung from the trees, chains girthed the tree trunk bottoms, platforms still remained aloft, and numerous personal items like daypacks, books, water bottles, and blankets lay at the bottom of several old Ponderosas. After thoughtfully viewing the hillside, Edwards turned and once again faced the far off bend in the road. *What had Mills said, seemingly so long ago, now? "I hope unexpected and dangerous are not words used to describe this scene." Well, Trooper Alec Mills, I believe those thoughts aptly depict our present situation.* With Trooper Mills' omen in tow, Edwards continued walking to the cruisers.

CHAPTER 59

Ranger climbed over the bowl's rock perimeter and joined his friends. He noticed a larger than expected cluster of people near the elk tent. *Now, this is a surprise.* He recognized Bridger and his best friend Hang standing next to Woody.

The ex-Marine spoke to Bridger. "Well, hello, young man. What brings you to this neck of the woods?"

"Hello, Ranger. I think the same thing that brought you here."

The ex-Marine walked over to Bridger and gave him a handshake accompanied by a half hug. He extended his hand to Hang. Then, he inspected Rachael and Tunes. "I think some introductions are in order, Bridger. Would you do us the honor?"

Bridger introduced his new friends to everyone. After the introductions, Ranger became preoccupied for a moment. He surveyed the campsite, noting all the gear left behind by the Alliance. He glanced over at the basaltic wall. "Dakota, take your CZ and these binoculars, and position yourself on the wall where you can observe our police friends. Let me know if they move in our direction."

As Ranger spoke, he retrieved some binos from one of his personal packs. After passing off the glasses, Ranger rejoined his friends. He surveyed the college students. "What are we going to do with all of you?"

Woody spoke up. "They need to get going, Ranger. I don't want any of them involved with this takeover." The retired school teacher thought for a moment. "Karen would kill me if I let Bridger or Hang stay, or for that matter, let any of these kids stay here."

Doc eyed his friend straight-faced and responded, "In regards to Karen, Woody, I think you're already a dead man. You'll need to come up with another rationale for your decision."

Everyone present acknowledged Doc's dry humor with a smile. An "ahem" was uttered by Tunes. "I'm going to stay on the hill, gentlemen. There are only five of you. I don't think you have enough people to keep this site safely patrolled at night. There's enough food and water left behind by the Alliance to sustain me for a while, so here I am at your service."

Hang jumped into the conversation. "I'm staying, too."

"No you're not, Hang. I can't let you."

"Mr. Thompson, please stop. You've been my mentor, my father, since I was old enough to know it, but you cannot tell me what to do now. I'm staying. Not only do I care about you, but I care about these trees, too."

Woody contemplated Hang's words and was, momentarily, at a loss for words.

Bridger and Rachael spoke simultaneously, "We're staying, too, Gramps/Mr. Thompson."

Woody was jolted back to reality by those words. "No, you are not. If anything happened to you kids, I…"

Ranger had been listening to and sizing up the situation while the others conversed. During their discourse, he had developed a plan suitable for all those involved, so he jumped into the mix.

"Hold on everybody, hold on. Tunes is right. We need more people to safely police our site. We've got three sides needing constant surveillance at night, and this requires more people than we have if we're not to become zombies due to lack of sleep. Also, we could use people on the outside, helping us if we need anything. Bridger, you and Rachael could be those people."

Ranger's proclamation got everyone's attention. He walked over to the same bag that produced the binos, and retrieved two walkie-talkies. He handed one to Bridger. "If you kids stay at the first campground past Camp Sherman, these will work. It's a straight shot from here to the campground. Where's your car, Bridger?"

"It's at the wayside, near the lower bridge."

"Is it still there?"

"I'm not sure."

"No matter. Do you have a credit card with you?"

"Yes."

"Okay, here's the deal. You need to get into Bend, with or without your car. Rent a rig. Preferably one with some cargo space. You can't drive your Jetta around now. Some knowledgeable cop will spot it and stop you for questioning. After you've got your new ride, come out to the campground and become wonderful, tourist type campers. We'll talk each day on channel 17 at 7:00 a.m. and 7:00 p.m. If we need anything up on the Rise or any information, you can provide it."

Woody thought about Ranger's comments and liked what he said. He reentered the conversation. "You need to call your grandmother immediately. She's planning an impromptu Corvallis visit tomorrow or the next day. When you talk with her, be prepared for hell's wrath. She's pretty pissed at you for not calling." Everyone smiled at Woody's comment. "Tell her whatever you must to keep her from visiting you in Corvallis. Oh yeah, don't mention me or my buddies. You didn't see us or know where we are. I told your grandma we went on a Blitzen fishing trip."

Ranger studied Woody and the college students. "Okay, we've got a plan, everyone. What do you think?"

He was greeted by nods of approval. Doc contemplated Ranger. "You're a fast thinker for an old fart, Ranger. Having people on the outside is a great idea. What do we do next?"

Ranger examined Dakota, who was looking through the binoculars at the moment.

"Are all the police still in sight, Dakota?"

"Yep. I counted nine to begin with and I still see nine."

"Okay, we need to get Rachael and Bridger out of here, now, before our friends, the police, start moving. All right, kids, you've got five minutes to get your plastic, cash, IDs, and anything else you might need for your camping trip. Let's move it!"

The two young people scampered over the volcanic wall and within a couple minutes returned with a wadded-up tent containing everything they needed. As they crossed the encampment, their tent trailed several lines on the ground. A couple still held on to ground pegs.

Ranger inspected their bundle and smiled. "Nice job. Tidy those lines up a bit. I don't want anybody tripping on them. Okay, we're going over the wall behind the big Ponderosa." Ranger motioned to the only tree near the summit's wall. "Then we'll access the stream bank and follow it to your rig. Hopefully it's still there. If not, you'll be hitching a ride into Bend."

Bridger quickly hugged Woody. "I love you, Gramps."

Rachael did the same. Without any more discussion, the three were over the wall and gone.

Woody wiped tears from his cheeks as he stood, awkwardly facing the direction of their departure. Doc walked up to Woody and stood next to his close friend.

"It's a good plan, Woody. They'll be safe in the campground, and who knows, their proximity might save our bacon sometime down the road."

Woody nodded his agreement. Doc turned away from Woody and surveyed Hang and Tunes.

"You guys are something else. At your age, I couldn't have done what you just did."

Both Hang and Tunes bowed deeply and majestically toward Doc.

Hang spoke, "I hope our service is worthy of your compliments, Sir Knight."

Hops laughed. "This is getting pretty deep, gentlemen, and I'm wearing low-cut running shoes, so please, enough of the B.S., okay?"

This brought a needed bit of mirth to the gathering. Doc looked around the campsite and over at Dakota.

"Is everything still copacetic with our peace officers?"

"If you mean, 'are they still just hanging around and not menacing us,' then yep, everything is still cool."

"Okay, let's tidy up the Alliance gear. Sort out what we can use from what we can't. Pile up the unusable stuff by the far wall and stow the functional gear in the tent. Also, we should get our own tents pitched and think about tonight's dinner."

Everyone began moving about, fulfilling Doc's directions. Hops relieved Dakota from guard duty. Dakota joined the others and the camp policing continued. Soon, a small pile of unneeded items emerged and numerous tents were positioned around the bowl's interior.

Doc was inspecting a stash of foodstuffs, thinking about the evening cuisine, when Ranger hoisted himself up and over the north wall. He appeared no worse for wear and smiled at his friends.

"Mission accomplished, gentlemen. Our young accomplices are heading for Bend as we speak."

The new occupiers of the Big Eddy Rise found themselves grinning at each other and spontaneously applauding Ranger's declaration. The tensions of the day's turmoil were beginning to abate. Woody, noticing an opportune moment, left his tent-raising task and walked over to the pack he had placed in the shade. He carried it over to the fire pit and pulled from it a small cooler. Dakota knew what to expect. He'd helped his friend pack the night before. He went and sat down upon a basaltic rock near the cooler and awaited the unveiling.

"Come one, come all. I believe it's time for some reflection, good cheer, and good drink." Woody pulled two six-packs of Pilsner cans from his cooler.

Ranger and Doc glanced at each other and smiled. Doc turned away from Woody and spoke quietly to Ranger, "Damn Pilsners. We need to talk to this boy."

"We already have, Doc. It's of no use."

"You're right. The man's awfully stubborn."

They joined the others. Woody passed the beers all around and raised his can into the late afternoon sky. "Here's to our successful day, and to what will be the equally successful occupation of the Big Eddy Rise."

All the men raised their beers into the air and championed the toast. They took a ceremonious drink of their Pilsners. Doc thought to himself. *You know, this beer really isn't too bad.* He took another sip and regarded Woody. *Maybe I could learn to like it.*

CHAPTER 60

THE TROOPERS AND DEPUTIES WATCHED THE RISE become motionless. They'd seen Ranger enter the bowl. They continued watching a little longer and after a while concluded the new occupiers were settled in for the night. The sun was getting low, and for the first time this fall, Alec Mills noted a chill descending on the forest. He walked over to his cruiser and found his uniform coat lying on his front passenger seat.

Deputy Edwards rejoined his comrades and answered all their questions. He'd decided not to retell the personal conversation between him and Ranger. It didn't seem pertinent, and also was somewhat embarrassing. Superintendent Ross called everyone over to his Crown Vic and commenced strategizing.

"It seems our new sitters are done for the day. Seems like the summit's going to be their campsite. We need to have a different roadblock scenario in place immediately. I want a stop just downriver from Camp Sherman. Let's put it in place right past the first campground. Another barricade needs to be just upriver from the fish hatchery. That takes care of the lower road. On this side, we'll have a...what kind of weapons did they have?"

Mills spoke up. "Looked like AK-47s to me, sir."

"Edwards, can you confirm that?"

"I think so, sir. The magazine looked like an AK-47's. Really, I mostly just noticed the barrel, and they all pretty much look the same."

Several of the officers laughed at this remark. One gave Edwards a friendly shove.

"Anyone notice optics on any gun?"

Several negative responses answered this question.

"All right. We'll set up another roadblock just past the last summer home between here and the three-way. I believe our previous location by the lower bridge turnout will still be appropriate. About how far is the blockade from the summit?"

Mills answered. "About a thousand yards, superintendent."

"Good, that will work. Deputies, for now, you'll take the lower river road positions. Nobody drives below the summit. Troopers will take care of the upper road's positions. Okay, gentlemen, one last thing, when you get into position, turn all civilian vehicles away from your location. Inform the drivers about our various roadblocks. If asked about your blockade, tell whomever it's in response to the logging site occupation. No more details should be offered."

Everyone nodded in agreement.

"Okay, people, let's get moving."

It took the law officers a moment to determine who would be where, and then deputies and troopers departed. Ross, Peters, and Mills found themselves alone at the bend. Mills chose to guard their present location. All three troopers, now, had their uniform coats on as the temperature continued to drop. A pair of ravens landed in a tall Ponderosa near the OSP officers and were cleaning their beaks on branches while they watched the men.

Superintendent Ross talked to his officers. "This could get dicey, Peters. I want a command center set up in view of the summit, but out of range."

Mills responded, "Those AKs can lob a round this far, but their accuracy at this range is nil."

"Okay. Peters, set up our site right here. I want shade awnings, porta potties, and a trailer. I also want a bulletproof barricade positioned where the road bends next to the hill. Drop it back about twenty yards. We need a honey bucket and shade at this location, too. Get us a SWAT team transport for running personnel back and forth between here and there. Now that I'm thinking about it, put a bulletproof barricade around our command center, too."

Peters interjected, "The occupiers told us to stay back here, sir."

"I know, but we're pushing back, Peters. I want a closer observation point, and these people need to know we're serious. Seeing a barricade and a SWAT rig rolling back and forth several times a day will convey our message."

Peters took a deep breath and exhaled slowly. "I agree with your response, Phil. We need to be aggressive with this bunch."

Ross regarded Mills. "Well, trooper, how things change. One minute we're finishing up a job, and the next, we're starting all over again."

Mills eyed his boss and smiled. "Just keeps you on your toes, sir."

"What do you think about our planning?"

"Sounds good to me, sir. Although I'm wondering if we might need some forest patrols? The woods, for the most part, are pretty open and allow for good visibility, but there is one section of dense vegetation near Camp Sherman someone could move around in, and not be seen."

Ross thought about Mills' comments. "You're probably right, trooper. We'll have an officer sweep said area periodically."

Ross contemplated the Rise's summit. A smoke column rose up into the early evening's sky. He smiled to himself. *Is this a comforting sight or just a nagging reminder of problems?* He turned to Peters.

"Let's go, lieutenant. There's a lot to do before tomorrow's sunrise. Good luck, Mills. You know this is a different animal we're dealing with. Is your assault rifle in the trunk?"

"Yes, sir."

"Well, please avail yourself of it. We'll see you in the morning, officer."

Peters and Ross walked to their patrol cars. The superintendent remarked, "See you back at Black Butte, lieutenant."

Without looking back, Peters waved his acknowledgment, got into his cruiser, started the engine, and headed off to the ranch. Ross did the same. As he drove through the old growth forest, he thought about his celebratory golf game. *It will have to be postponed.* His next thought was about his overdue phone call to Governor O'Connell. *This is not what she's expecting. A trip into Salem is probably forthcoming.* The Crown Vic continued on to Black Butte. The OSP boss felt a soak in his hot tub, which overlooked the Three Sisters Mountains, was in order, and a double vodka tonic should probably accompany his leisure moment. Tomorrow was a new day, and the superintendent hoped it would be less stressful and more predictable.

CHAPTER
61

THE NEW OCCUPIERS WERE FINDING PLACES FOR their equipment and gear, and the old elk tent became the depository for most of these items. Hang and Tunes, along with Hops' help, were heating the leftover burrito fixings. Hops produced a small brick of cheddar cheese and was grating it. Woody and Dakota laid a fire and lit the mix of needles, cones, and tree limbs. A nice blaze was warming the early evening air. Ranger was cruising the summit's perimeter, searching for possible defensive problems. He was standing, assessing the closest Ponderosa, noting this area's weakness. A slight ditch started at the summit's northwest quadrant, then moved away and downward from the bowl, and where the trench met the gravel road, it was about six feet deep. A culvert had been placed at this point to facilitate runoff. At the top of the ravine sat the Ponderosa Ranger was inspecting. It was about ten yards from the summit's wall. You could tell the tree received more water than neighboring trees because its branch system started closer to the ground and, in general, more needle clusters held onto the limbs. The ex-Marine was concerned about the ditch, the tree's trunk, and the limb foliage providing a screen for an aggressor. He couldn't change the ditch or trunk, but intended to quickly eliminate some of the lower branches and needles.

Ranger returned to the bowl's mess area when someone yelled, "Come and get it!" Woody replaced Doc at the southwestern wall's sentinel position, and Doc joined everybody around the fire. There was plenty of daylight left so no lanterns were lit. The older men and their young brethren commenced eating the warm burritos and consuming some wine that Hops had brought.

The two ravens who witnessed the law enforcement dispersal were now perched in the same Ponderosa that Ranger had just inspected. They sidestepped back and forth on an upper branch and cocked their heads downward, examining the scene below. The forest became eerily quiet. Off in the distance, some Steller's jays started loudly screeching. Their racket was joined by nearby crows, who began cawing aggressively back and forth to each other. Ranger noted this crescendo and got up to investigate the possible cause for the disturbance. As he walked over to the basaltic wall, the ravens above the encampment started squawking, adding their voices to the already loud chorus of disturbed bird calls. Ranger reached the wall and gazed out into the ancient forest. As he viewed the trees, numerous birds could be seen taking flight. The camp ravens clumsily flapped wings several times and lifted off their perch. For a moment, Ranger wondered about what he was seeing. The Ponderosa tops were quivering as if the bases of the trees were being shaken. As he watched, the tree trunks themselves began to erratically move.

Woody called out from behind Ranger, "Wow! Do you feel that?"

The ex-Marine felt tremors developing beneath his feet and their intensity began to grow, causing him to grab the basaltic rim to steady himself. The earthquake's strength continued to magnify. Ranger surveyed the forest and watched the big Ponderosas perform a clumsy, unchoreographed dance. Trees swayed back and forth in all directions. The ground beneath the behemoths actually rolled in a wave-like motion. Ranger held tight to the rock to maintain his footing and spread his feet farther apart for better balance. Back at the fire pit, sparks were flying from the jostled-apart fire, and all of the men had either been knocked off their perches or voluntarily left their rests and were now sitting on the ground. Nobody tried to stand up. A horrendous, frightening, grating sound arose from the ground, and the bedrock lurched drastically upward, throwing Ranger off his feet. After the massive slippage, the tremors began to subside. A couple minutes passed and then all ground movement abated. The men looked at each other with various expressions of surprise and fear.

Dakota spoke up. "That was some conversation the Great Spirit had with us!"

Hops stood up and righted his chair. "Yeah, I hope the message was something like, 'Hey, you boys are doing a great job and I applaud your efforts.' What a monster earthquake. It would be fine with me if I never feel one like it again."

A number of Amens followed Hops' exclamation and the men began to put their camp back together. Hang and Tunes got up and started pushing pieces of the fire back into the pit area.

Doc was setting everyone's chairs back up, and brushing off uneaten portions of burritos. The men began repositioning themselves around the fire pit.

Woody picked up his CZ rifle and returned his gaze to the cruiser and the surrounding area. Ranger revisited the fire pit. The forest became quiet again and the Metolius River could be heard splashing past the base of the Big Eddy cliffs.

Ranger spoke to his friends. "Holy smokes. What's going to happen next? Okay, gentlemen, let's try and refocus. Earthquakes notwithstanding, our defenses here are pretty good. There are perfect rifle ports on the summit's rim. Couldn't be in better locations. Each vantage protects a quadrant of the hill. The riverside isn't a concern. I've got a plan for it, which won't require constant vigilance."

Ranger pointed at the closest Ponderosa. "Our one problem is the big boy over there. We'll need to delimb the lower portion of the tree. Right now, it makes a perfect blind for possible intruders."

Hang spoke up. "I've got all the climbing gear required, Ranger. We might not need it, though, depending upon how the branches are spaced."

"Excellent, Hang. Let's check out the situation after we eat. The pruning needs to be accomplished tonight. I've got a handsaw that will cut right through those branches."

Hang left the fire pit to find his climbing gear, and the other men continued finishing their burritos.

The fire's smoke drifted straight up again as the evening colors began to transform the forest. Soon, Hang and Ranger would be delimbing the old tree, and night lookouts would be chosen. The occupation transition of the Big Eddy logging site was complete. There was indeed a new sheriff in town, but what this really meant remained to be seen.

CHAPTER 62

MOST OF THE NEW OCCUPIERS SLEPT FITFULLY during the first night of occupation. Ranger, Hang, and Tunes were the last to retire. The three men delimbed the bottom branches of the problematic Ponderosa, and on the lowest, uphill branch, Hang attached a motion detection, battery-powered security light. It hung below the adjacent basaltic wall, ensuring the occupiers' movements wouldn't set it off. The three men bedded down around midnight. Hops volunteered to take the first watch and was to be relieved by Dakota at 2:00 a.m. There wasn't much to guard against. A lone patrol car sat off at the farthermost bend with one trooper in attendance. He mostly stayed within an arm's reach of his vehicle, and posed no threat to the occupiers.

All the men rose around six or six-thirty the next morning. They'd poked their heads out of the various tents and slowly gravitated to the fire. Ranger brewed some coffee, which was eagerly accepted and slowly consumed. There were enough burrito fixings left over for another meal. The occupiers ate their food and drank their coffee while the sun rose higher above the horizon. The forest's denizens began to move about just as the evening's chill began to wear off. Once again the pair of ravens joined the group and took up residence in the now pruned Ponderosa.

Ranger finished his burrito and cleaned his plate with a dirty towel. "All right, gentlemen, let me have your attention please."

They all stopped their eating and conversing to gaze at Ranger.

"There's lots to be done today, my friends. I don't know what the authorities will decide to do with us, but we're going to be prepared for everything. I've got numerous little projects for everybody. First of all, before anything else, we require another guard on duty. We need somebody at Dakota's location at all times, but another person needs to be watching the other quadrants, and for now, that includes the river side, too. So, Doc, you're the man for right now. Just spend your time equally among all three sites and let us know if you see anything develop. Even one person moving around is important. It doesn't matter if they seem to be a fisherman or hiker, let us know about them."

Doc nodded his head in agreement with Ranger and finished off his burrito and coffee.

"Woody and Hops."

Woody responded with a smile. "Yes, Captain Ranger, sir."

Ranger responded, "Such enthusiasm warrants a special, most important, project, and one is on the docket: a latrine needs to be constructed."

Most of the occupiers laughed and smiled at this bit of gamesmanship.

Hops eyed Woody. "Way to go, smart ass. Don't worry, I'll be supervising your efforts and you'll create the best commode ever."

More smiles and light ribbing from the audience followed these comments. Ranger continued on. "I noticed an indentation in the ground behind the large boulder near the river wall. Probably a good spot to dig a pit. You could also fashion a privacy wall by using those long branches by the fire pit and some of those small tarps in the elk tent."

Hang walked over to where Ranger suggested building the latrine. "You know, guys, this hole wasn't here before. This was flat ground. I stowed all my climbing gear here, and there wasn't a depression present when I stashed my equipment."

Ranger walked over with Hops and Woody and observed the indentation.

Woody spoke up. "Totally weird. I wonder what we'll find with our digging."

Hops joined in. "Only one way to find out." He handed his friend a short shovel. "I'm going to gather together our partition material."

"You were serious about the supervisor stuff, weren't you?"

Hops laughed. "No, I'll be digging in a minute, just as soon as I get the tarps and branches together."

Ranger focused on the young men. "I've got a special project for you guys. This will take you back to grade school, and your days of modeling clay during art class."

Hang and Tunes smiled and looked at Ranger.

Tunes spoke first. "Sounds like great therapy. What's the project?"

"Well you're going to sculpt C-4 explosives into shapes similar to pinecones."

Their expressions changed from mirthful curiosity to trepidation. Hang spoke to Ranger. "Is this safe, sir? I mean what if we drop it or something?"

"Don't worry, gentlemen. It's perfectly benign as it is. Follow me."

Ranger led the two young college students over to one of his duffel bags. As he went, he stooped over and picked up a big Ponderosa pinecone. He rummaged around in his bag and pulled out eight bars of plastic explosives. After grabbing a couple dinner knives off the mess counter, the three of them sat down and the ex-Marine began detailing what he wanted.

The sun rose higher in the sky and the temperature warmed up. Dakota and Doc, standing guard duty, continued with their watch, and the remaining occupiers moved on with their projects. Woody was dutifully shoveling out the latrine pit. A small mound of soil lay off to the side of the two-foot deep hole that was enlarging with each shovel stroke. He jabbed the shovel downward and felt it hit rock. He reinserted the blade and encountered the immovable object again. Probing some more, he found a leverage point and pushed downwards on his shovel handle. A basaltic chunk of rock partially exposed itself. Woody reached down and physically removed the rock. The grayish-black angular piece of basalt joined the dirt pile. Woody resumed digging and once again struck rock. He duplicated his previous efforts, and a second block of basalt joined its mate. Woody was beginning to sweat. He wiped his brow with his shirt sleeve, and while he inspected his progress, he cocked his head to one side and curiously examined a small, cone-shaped hole at the bottom of his diggings. It was mysteriously becoming larger as he gazed at it. He got down onto his knees and bent over his project to get a better look. The indentation was getting even bigger, and he could see dirt and rock pebbles fall into a small black hole centered in the middle of his pit.

"Holy shit! What kind of Indiana Jones stuff is this?" Woody looked over at Hops, who was emerging from the tent carrying two small blue tarps. "Hops, get over here. You won't believe this."

He joined Woody and the two men knelt at the rim of the hole, watching the magic unfold below them.

"Unbelievable, Woody. Let's get at this."

Hops picked up another shovel and the two men started moving more dirt and rock. They exposed a mosaic of basaltic pieces, piled around and on top of each other forming a plug in a basaltic rock hole. Woody removed one large chunk near the side wall, and with a rumbling crash, the remaining boulders fell into a dark void below them. A plume of dust and stale air rushed out of the hole. The two men examined the hole in disbelief.

"Holy shit, Hops. What have we found?"

"Hey, Ranger, get over here, pronto!"

Ranger looked up from where he was helping fashion C-4 into pinecone shapes. He joined his friends at the hole. "Very nice, guys, I ask you to create a latrine, and I believe you've excavated a septic system. It appears I need to be more careful in how I phrase directions."

Both Hops and Woody smiled at this comment. The three men then gazed down into what appeared to be a basaltic chute that narrowed at the bottom. The tube was about three feet in length and the bottom's diameter was about two feet.

"Time to do some spelunking, my friends. Let's get our headlamps and go exploring."

The men departed and quickly returned with headlamps in place. Ranger returned carrying a length of rope, and Woody brought an eighteen-volt flashlight back with him. The ex-Marine attached the rope to the nearby boulder. Hops dropped a pebble into the darkness and a slight "thunk" quickly followed.

"Good, it's not too deep."

Ranger tied a few knots into the rope for handholds and tossed the coil down into the cave.

"How deep do you think it is?"

"Probably not even eight feet."

"Well, let's go. Who's first?"

Hops volunteered and with some help from his friends got himself into position to descend into the darkness. He lowered himself into the hole. His headlamp beam easily illuminated the floor below.

"It's only about six feet down."

Hops felt a rubble of rock as his feet found the cave's floor. He gained his balance and shined his lamp's beam around the cavern.

"Incredible. You guys won't believe this! Get down here!"

His beam highlighted dust particles still settling out of the air from the entrance collapse. The cavern appeared to be about six feet high and about twenty-five feet in diameter. Somewhat in the center of the cavern, about ten feet from Hops, a thick pillar of basalt appeared to help hold the ceiling in place. The roof support was about eight feet in diameter. To add to the intrigue of the scene were various sized vessels placed on the cavern's floor. They seemed to be woven of organic materials and were basket-like with lids.

"Hurry up, you guys! This is amazing!"

Hang and Tunes joined the above-ground audience and helped Woody and Ranger descend into the hole. The two men joined Hops on the cavern's floor. The light from all their headlamps completely illuminated the space.

Woody spoke first. "This is way cool! Total Indiana Jones stuff."

The three men shined their lights onto the cave's walls and noticed primitive artwork depicting teepee villages near mountain ranges, rivers, fish jumping over falls, and various other animals such as bear, cougars, ravens, and deer. The men then shined their beams at the baskets. They walked over to them, and gently lifted lids off the containers. The baskets held stashes of obsidian rocks, sandals, already fashioned spear points, and various sizes of arrowheads. Near the baskets were bundles of stiff, dried out deer hides, and several bunches of straight, barkless juniper tree branches.

Hops called out to the ground crew. "Somebody get Dakota down here!"

Tunes went and relieved Dakota of his position. Dakota peered into the now partially illuminated hole beneath him.

"What's up? What did you diggers find down there?"

Woody shouted back, "It's a Native American cave filled with all kinds of stuff, Dakota. Get down here!"

Dakota stood up with a serious expression on his face. He retrieved a leather pouch from underneath his shirt and after pulling its strap up and over his head, he held it before him. He thought solemnly about the sacred site his friends had found. Opening the pouch, he drew pinches of tobacco out and tossed them in four specific directions around the cave's opening. He replaced his pouch and lowered himself into the cavern.

Dakota reached the cave's floor and Woody handed him the flashlight. "Take a look around."

Dakota shined the flashlight's beam on the walls and at the various baskets. He walked over to one basket and reached inside. He pulled out small bundles of sagebrush ends. The tiny leaves were dry and crumbled easily.

Dakota viewed the men with a serious expression. "Well, you guys have done it now. We're all dead men."

Woody glanced over at Dakota with an expression of concern on his face. "You're kidding, right?"

Dakota returned Woody's gaze. "Of course I'm kidding, Woody."

All the men laughed at Dakota's response. Woody became less apprehensive and laughed also. They began moving about and examining more items. Woody moved around to the backside of the column and immediately, an echoed "holy shit" bounced back to the men; then he quickly reappeared.

"There's a body back here. Really. It's like mummified."

Dakota removed his pouch again and followed Woody as he led the way behind the column. There on the cave's floor, lying on a woven mat, was the dried body of a person. It was surrounded by baskets, carved figurines, wooden bowls, antlers, and various other animal accessories. Dakota offered more tobacco to the Great Spirit. All the men joined Woody and Dakota.

Hops spoke. "This is getting a little eerie. Don't you think?"

Ranger addressed his comment. "Yeah, it's not every day you find an undisturbed crypt while you're out camping in the woods."

While the others inspected the mummified ancient body, Woody was surveying the area. His beam located a smaller, secondary tunnel branching off from the cavern. He stooped over and started walking down the tunnel. The ceiling dropped lower to where Woody had to begin crawling. His headlamp lit up the area in front of him. The tunnel jogged left and when Woody rounded the corner, he abruptly came to its end. A pile of basaltic rocks formed a closure to the crawlspace.

Woody began pulling rocks away from the rubble wall until a ray of light shone through. He pulled a few more away so he could clearly see out of the small opening. Directly ahead of him was the Ponderosa Ranger and Hang had delimbed. Woody became excited about his discovery. *There's actually a secret passage from the summit. How cool!* He wriggled his way around so he faced the larger chamber and headed back to his friends.

Dakota noticed a breeze coming through the cavern. "Did you guys notice air movement in here when you first entered the cavern?"

Hops replied, "Nope. The air was pretty stale and stagnant."

"Well, there's some now."

Ranger took note of the conversation. He also noticed the airflow and Woody's absence. "Maybe our missing compadre can help us solve this riddle."

As if on cue, Woody made a timely entrance into the cavern. He straightened up and walked over to his friends.

"This is pretty cool, guys. There's a tunnel leading to an opening adjacent to the Ponderosa you trimmed, Ranger. It's partially blocked by rocks. I opened it up a little. Looks like our stronghold has a secret entrance."

Ranger responded to Woody's exclamation. "Show me the way, partner."

The two men left the others and retraced Woody's route. The ex-Marine looked out the small portal.

"This could be very helpful. Damn! This place is full of surprises. I'm feeling pretty good about defending ourselves, Woody. Nobody has a clue what we've got up here."

Ranger's words buoyed Woody's spirits. "Yeah, this place is like an old castle, filled with secret chambers and passages."

"Yes it is, my friend, yes it is."

The two men returned to the large chamber and their comrades, and Ranger suggested they all go topside.

Hang reached down and one by one, helped the older men out of the cave. The sun was nearly overhead now, and things had warmed up. Ranger gathered everyone near the campfire ring. He called Doc over and spoke so Tunes could hear him.

"This changes a few things, gentlemen. Not only does our fortress have stout walls, it has a basement built like a bank vault. Plus, we have a secret entrance.

The immediate change I foresee is our sleeping arrangement. We'll bed down in the cavern. It will be the safest place for us, and this gives us an incredible advantage because we're the only ones who know about this tunnel system. It could be our saving grace. Okay everyone, we need to refocus. Now, back to what we started doing this morning. Woody, you're still on latrine duty. Find a suitable site, and make us a commode. Hops, you're going to construct an access ladder for our bedroom. You'll find rope in one of my duffels. Lash together some of those bundled-up limbs and make us a stout ladder. Okay, Hang and Tunes, we're back to our project. Doc and Dakota, if you want a break from guard duty, switch out with Woody."

The two men viewed each other with acknowledging smiles.

Dakota called out, "I'm good, Ranger."

Doc immediately followed Dakota's cue. "Me too."

"All right then, back to work. Oh yeah, Woody, would you go below and button up your spy hole?"

"Certainly."

Woody let himself down the rope, and walked around the central pillar. He avoided looking at the ancient American, and crawled back to the tunnel's end, closing it up. On his return trip, when passing by the mummified corps, he again averted his eyes. The long gray hair, sunken cheeks, and eyeless sockets scared Woody somewhat and gave him the "creeps." *Am I really going to sleep down here next to a dead person?* Woody grabbed hold of the first knot on the access rope and pulled himself upwards. He wasn't feeling so good about their new sleeping arrangements.

CHAPTER
63

CASSIE WILLIAMSON SMILED AT BRIAN AS THE two sat before the camera waiting for their cue. It had been a busy day for the two reporters. Cassie interviewed numerous people at various locales about the Big Eddy Rise logging conflict. She'd readied her weather segment and done another interview with Dread and Sasha at St. Charles Medical Center. This piece was a filler, and if time allowed, it would make the show. Brian was reporting about the Big Eddy Rise's takeover by eco-terrorists, and also had an interview with Deputy Edwards ready to air. Professor Anderson had been interviewed again. Interspersed between these various pieces were stories about Bend's baseball team, the Elks, some data about an increase in local building, and a human interest piece about a ninety-eight-year-old quilter who lived in Sisters.

Cassie studied the show rundown and softly whistled. "We're loaded tonight, Brian. Got your skates on?"

Brian lifted his left foot up for Cassie to see. "Nope, partner, got my slaps on. How about you?"

Cassie mimicked his action and showed Brian her sandaled foot. The two young reporters had told their viewing audience they'd be wearing pool shoes, AKA sandals, during airings until the next serious rainfall of the fall season arrived. The station had positioned a low mic that caught the slapping sounds the sandals made as the young reporters moved around. Feedback from recent polling had showed this bit of silliness was a big hit with the station's audience.

Brian was cued by their director, and now both he and Cassie sat smiling looking at the camera. Cassie's black bangs had recently been trimmed and ended right above her dark eyebrows, and Brian wore his blond hair pulled back into a ponytail.

Wendy sat in front of the flatscreen with her feet on a small ottoman. It was seven o'clock and Channel 19 news had just commenced.

"Hurry up, Tarri. The news just started."

Tarri came in from the kitchen carrying a platter filled with fruit, cheese, and crackers. She gave Wendy a quick kiss as she passed by and sat down. Tarri kicked off her shoes and also positioned her feet on a small ottoman.

"What's happened?"

"Nothing yet. Your timing couldn't be better."

The two women watched as the camera moved in for a close-up of Brian.

"An incredible story developed this morning at the Big Eddy Rise. As local law enforcement began arresting the STRONG Alliance members, a van filled with gunmen broke through a roadblock and crashed halfway up the hill."

Wendy reached over, took Tarri's hand, and held it while she contemplated her partner with an expression of disbelief on her face.

Brian continued. "The gunmen took Deputy Edwards of the Jefferson County Sheriff's Department hostage for about an hour while they moved equipment from the overturned vehicle to the summit's bowl."

The camera backed away from Brian, allowing the viewers to see Cassie, who observed Brian seriously. The background panels now showed a scene of the Big Eddy Rise.

"At this point, Channel 19 does not know what happened to the STRONG Alliance members. It appears they're no longer present at the site. When we return from break, I'll have an exclusive interview with Deputy Edwards, who will shed more light onto this developing situation."

Channel 19 went to commercial break.

"Holy cow. What will happen next out there?"

Tarri let go of Wendy's hand and grabbed her phone. She called Steve Johnson. Steve was eating outside with his wife and sons when she called. Seeing the caller ID announcing his co-worker, Steve answered the call.

"Hello, Tarri?"

"Are you watching Channel 19?"

"Nope. I'm dining alfresco with the family. What's up?"

"Eco-terrorists have taken over the Big Eddy Rise. Brian's reporting on it right now."

"Really?"

"Yes, really, Steve. I can't believe it."

"Okay, I'm going to say thank you and get the laptop out here on the picnic table. Thanks for calling. Bye."

Director Steve Johnson retrieved the family's big screen laptop from the kitchen and positioned it on the picnic table so everyone could see the monitor.

Steve called out to his family. "Well, ladies and gentlemen, steady yourselves. We've got some serious breaking news happening."

The Johnsons watched in silence as Channel 19 came back from break with the Deputy Edwards interview.

The serious nature of the lead story made Tarri and Wendy forget about watching for flirtatious moments between Brian and Cassie. Both the women felt the sandal gimmick had been created by the reporters just so they could "play footsie" more easily.

Deputy Edwards described the site takeover in a professional manner. He was asked by Brian what the gunmen were like.

"There was a lot of gray hair, ponytails, and salt and pepper beards. I'd say all of the men were pushing seventy. The man who took me hostage was a serious, calm, experienced individual. It felt like he had dealt with volatile situations before. Anyway, I'm glad to be here, talking with you, Brian. It was a scary experience I don't want to repeat."

"You seem to be getting all the super serious jobs up there, deputy. First the storm and Sasha's near death, and now you're taken hostage."

Deputy Edwards laughed at Brian's comment. "You know, I'm thinking about changing jobs pretty soon. Coffee barista is looking pretty darn good right about now."

The interview ended with Brian recapping the day's events on the Big Eddy Rise.

The camera pulled back, showing Cassie and Brian sitting behind their desk. The back panels showed a sunny view of Hosmer Lake.

"Well, Brian, it seems like we've got some deadly serious 'silverbacks' flexing their muscles up there at the Metolius logging site."

"I agree, Cassie. Of course we'll be watching this story closely. What have the Weather Gods cooked up for us?"

"I think our sandals are staying on for at least another week, Brian."

Cassie hesitated just a moment and smiled at Brian. Both reporters faced each other. A slight upper body motion by Cassie betrayed her efforts to regain her sandals before walking over to the weather board. The camera pulled back as she did her weather segment. Cassie noted the regional dryness, but mentioned next week a low could cross the Cascades and give Central Oregon its first normal, autumn bath. She continued with her forecast, noting the next day's predicted weather and detailing in length the region's extended forecast.

As Cassie returned to the anchor desk, Brian held a cold copy in his hand, just given to him, off camera, by the station's owner.

"Holy trembles! What will happen next? This is breaking, breaking news, Bend. Just minutes ago, an earthquake rocked the Metolius River area. Our station just received a phone call from the Camp Sherman store owner, Jack Smith, who described his store as a total wreck. All of the shelved merchandise and foodstuffs were knocked onto the floor and the store experienced numerous breaks in its water pipes. Jack was knocked off his feet by one extreme jolt, and basically crawled to a safe location under a countertop to wait out the earthquake. That's all we've got right now. Cassie and I will get on this story immediately, following tonight's show. We'll have more details in tomorrow's report."

Cassie commented, "Where do we go from here with the evening's newscast, Brian? These events are all so incredible and nerve-wracking."

Brian held up the rundown notice and replied, "We'll just continue with our show, Cassie. Nobody said this job would be easy."

Cassie smiled at Brian and voiced her agreement. Brian jolted to the side just a bit before starting his piece about Bend's minor league baseball team.

"Did you see what I just saw?"

Wendy had not missed Brian's response to Cassie's footmanship. "Yes I did. Looks like our young lovers aren't going to let us down."

Cassie responded, "No, they're not. Good God. What an incredible newscast, and I'm wondering what will happen out by the Metolius next? We've had tree sitters, now gunmen, and the quake sounded like a pretty intense, scary rumble."

"This is becoming totally surreal. I have no idea what's going to happen next."

Wendy arose and got both of them a locally brewed ale from the refrigerator. As she sat back down, the local news returned. The camera moved backwards, even further, allowing the back panel to be completely seen. It showed a partially completed house. Cassie reported on increased building and employment in the area. After the previous segment, Brian left the show's script and leapfrogged to the Professor Anderson piece. Time was running out and the station's owner/producer wanted the geologic story to finish the evening's broadcast. The professor noted conditions worsening on Mt. Hood and in his opinion, a major event was forthcoming. At the end of the Anderson tape, the camera returned to Cassie and Brian.

Cassie commented, "Well, Bend, get ready for more incredible natural phenomena, all brought to you free of charge by Mother Nature herself."

The backdrop now showed a picture of Mt. Hood. Brian and Cassie smiled and waved at the camera as Brian signed the team off the air. The last sight of the two reporters before Channel 19 broke to commercials was Brian once again jolting to the right as if shocked by an electric current. This time Tarri caught the symptomatic lurch by Brian.

"Did you see the flinch, Wendy?"

Wendy had her beer bottle raised and had missed the last flirtatious endeavor. "Nope, I missed it. Who initiated things?"

"It was Cassie again."

"Our young lady needs to develop some professionalism in my opinion."

"Yeah, but her lack of 'on air' etiquette sure makes things interesting."

"You're right. What was I thinking?"

The two women left their flatscreen and moved into the kitchen with their beers. Wendy sat at the counter on a stool and watched Tarri prepare a salad for dinner.

Wendy mused aloud. "I hope things don't get too crazy up on the Metolius."

"Me too. It's time for the occupation to get resolved. Hopefully, the Ninth Court will put an end to this McDonald nonsense and nobody else will get hurt."

Wendy added. "I wish the Ninth could put an end to McDonald. That would really solve a lot of problems."

"Yes it would."

CHAPTER 64

PRESIDENT MCDONALD AND HIS SECRET SERVICE contingent left the West Colonnade and entered the West Wing. He was scrolling through his smartphone as the procession neared his office. McDonald had spent the previous evening dining with the Mexican President and the Canadian Prime Minister. Following their lavish meal in the State Dining Room, the two statesmen and their wives attended a ball in the East Room honoring their diplomatic visit. Tuxedos and floor-length gowns were the required dress. Finely faceted, jeweled necklaces and bracelets sparkled and shone under the large East Room chandeliers. President McDonald had a beautiful escort whose jewelry outshone the competition both in size and brilliance. McDonald felt young and giddy with his lovely eye-candy date holding onto his arm. Uncharacteristically, he made the rounds and conversed with many of the ball's attendees.

The White House kitchen created all the hors d'oeuvres for the gala and also supplied the serving staff. Russel Nelson and Preston, among others, were chosen to serve at the event. They carried trays of appetizers from guest to guest and switched things up occasionally by serving champagne to those who preferred the bubbly over the bar service.

Preston and Russel enjoyed working together. They would keep an eye out for each other and one would get the other's attention if a humorous scene was occurring nearby. The two had similar senses of humor, and noting the obscure oddities of the diplomatic world kept their job interesting. Preston got Russel's attention focused on a group of tipsy women who stood together, admiring each other's jewelry and casually conversing. One particularly inebriated lady was waving her champagne glass around as she talked and gestured. Preston sensed an accident in the making, so he'd alerted Russel. He was not disappointed. As the two young men watched, McDonald's date walked over and joined the group. In a dramatic gesture, the drunk attendee twirled around and playfully bowed to the young escort. In doing so, she splashed champagne onto several of her companions. There was a moment of silence, and then the ladies burst into laughter. Several servers converged on the women and offered napkins to those who were doused with drink. The ladies dabbed at the champagne and immediately started laughing and conversing again. Introductions and polite handshakes soon followed and the women continued on as if nothing happened. Russel and Preston exchanged mirthful glances. Russel gave Preston a double thumbs-up sign and the two men carried on with their responsibilities.

The ball continued on with a local D.C. band playing pop and light rock cover songs. Near midnight, the attendees began to call for their limos. They paid their respects to the honored guests and left the White House in small, friendly groups. The East Room quickly emptied.

Russel and Preston noticed the ballroom become vacant and walked over to each other. They were responsible for breakdown.

"Nice work, brother. You're becoming a first-rate White House staffer."

Russel responded, "I've only had the best of instruction."

"No need to flatter me. I..."

"No, no, I'm talking about the helpful cooks downstairs."

Preston gave Russel a shocked look and clutched his heart. "Man, you really hurt my sensitive side, homie."

"Don't take it personally, Preston. Those are some very knowledgeable people in the kitchen who know what they're doing. You've certainly augmented their..."

At this point, Preston retrieved a handful of ice from a pitcher and flung the cubes at Russel. Russel ducked, but a few chunks found their mark. Both young men laughed at their antics and started to shove each other. At that moment, the White House chief usher quietly entered the ballroom.

"Ahem, gentlemen."

Both Russel and Preston froze. They knew Don Peterson's voice.

"Are we breaking the room down and getting it back to normal?"

Preston responded, "Yes, Mr. Peterson. We're just letting loose of a little tension by playing around. We'll get right back to it."

"Good, Preston. You men need to clock out by 1:30."

Russel responded, "Count on it, sir."

"I am, Russel. I most certainly am." The chief usher did an about-face and walked out of the ballroom, hiding his smile from the young staffers.

Preston glanced over at Russel. "Okay, homie. We've got a deadline. Let's move it."

Preston and Russel went into action and commenced putting things away and restaging the East Room. Preston eyed Russel as they wheeled two large bus carts out of the ballroom. "Got time for a few games of pool after we clock out?"

"Certainly. I don't have any classes tomorrow. Are you going to cry again if I kick your butt?"

Preston laughed out loud at this remark and continued down the hall to the service elevator.

The president's guests and their wives stood outside of the ballroom in the hallway with McDonald and his escort. He offered his guests a few nightcaps and some after-hours talk pertaining to trade. The ladies, noticing a diplomatic moment in the making, offered their apologies and retired to their VIP quarters on the second floor. The Prime Minister's wife asked McDonald's date to join her, and the invitation was gratefully accepted. Two aides appeared from nowhere and brought their bosses expensive distilled liquors, originating from their respective countries. The three men sat in chairs next to the Green Room's fireplace, enjoying a small fire, and sipped on various cocktails.

McDonald steered the conversation to possible new trade sanctions among the three countries. His ideas had been politely rebuffed by his counterparts and by one o'clock in the morning, all three gentlemen realized nothing was to be gained by further conversation. The President of Mexico and the Canadian Prime Minister excused themselves and left for their sleeping quarters. President McDonald sipped on a Canadian whiskey and watched the fire's flames dance about. A White House server stood by a dry bar near the hall entrance. Secret Service agents stood guard at the entrances to the Green Room. McDonald dismissed the bartender, who asked the president if he wanted the liquor cart left behind. McDonald shook his head in response and the server left the room, pushing the cart before him. The president tossed back the last of the whiskey, set his glass down on the antique marble tabletop, and rose up onto unsteady legs. *No late night news shows for me.*

He crossed the hallway, slowly ascended the Grand Staircase to the second floor, and, turning right, walked to his master bedroom. He entered the room and for a moment looked indifferently at his bed. His young escort was sitting under the covers reading a magazine.

"Not tonight, honey." McDonald turned and walked into his bathroom, shutting the door behind him. The young lady, embarrassed and unsure of herself, rose from the bed and dressed quickly. She peeked into the hallway, and an agent motioned her to follow him. They rode the elevator down to the ground level. The two passed through the kitchen and walked up a short flight of steps to where a limo waited for her. The agent paid the young escort his respects and she drove away.

McDonald slept fitfully because of his overindulgence, and his foggy head hadn't cleared yet as he walked past the Cabinet Room to his work space in the morning. The president entered the Oval Office and sat down. He hadn't seen last night's news, and because of his tight schedule, couldn't watch his DVR recordings after he awoke. Whenever he missed the nightly news, McDonald became edgy, and the hangover was exacerbating his mood. He sat down at his desk and hollered, "Janet, get me some coffee and scones, ASAP, and what's first on my schedule?"

Janet came to the doorway. "Will do, Mr. President, and your first meeting is with Ted Horner."

"What the hell is our meeting about?"

"I don't know, Mr. President." Horner was McDonald's new chief of staff. He was a skinny, fortyish man with a weasel-like appearance and similar body movements. He had dark hair and eyes, and pointy facial features. He seemed to run whenever he moved. McDonald had encountered trouble recruiting a new chief of staff. All those he asked politely refused service, and, consequently, he borrowed an underling from his press team and told him he was acting chief of staff. Horner was the perfect choice for McDonald because he was a "yes" man and would never question the president's decisions. He also knew enough about White House internal workings to navigate his way through the maze and get a job done.

"When's our meeting, Janet?"

Janet responded from her desk. "In thirty minutes, Mr. President."

McDonald rocked back in his desk chair and began scrolling through his regular news sites. "Shit!"

"What, sir?"

McDonald ignored Janet's inquiry. He had just found Allen Rodrigues's piece discussing an upcoming Impeachment March. Rodrigues noted the rally was being promoted by the ACLU, AFL-CIO, NAACP, NEA, and a host of smaller organizations. The attendance prediction called for half a million participants.

"God damn it, that's absurd!"

"What, Mr. President?"

McDonald yelled at Janet, "Don't worry about it, Janet! If I want you, I'll holler out your name."

Janet rolled her eyes at his comment. *Yes, you most certainly will, Mr. President.*

McDonald continued perusing the news. He noted pieces about his meeting with the Mexican President and the Canadian Prime Minister. Speculation abounded about the possible new trade pact and what it would offer the participants. There were interviews with Graham about his quitting the White House team.

McDonald's already agitated state was becoming worse. His face was reddening, and his upper left eyelid developed a tic. The president, without warning, abruptly jumped out of his chair, yelled like a madman, and brought both fists forcefully down onto the top of his desk. Loose papers flew off the desktop onto the floor.

"Nooooo God-damn way!"

He picked up a glass paperweight and hurled it across the room. It smashed into the fireplace's marble façade and exploded into tiny fragments, which fell to the floor accompanied by shattered pieces of marble.

The Secret Service team stationed in the hallway burst through the doors with Glock pistols in firing position. They visually swept the room and, noting McDonald alone, nervously holstered their weapons. One agent asked McDonald, "Is everything all right, Mr. President?"

"Hell no, it isn't. Do you think I yell and break shit because I'm happy?"

"Well no, sir. I was just…"

"I don't need stupid questions, agent, Agent…?"

"It's Agent Thomas, sir."

"Well, Thomas, no more bullshit, dumb questions!"

McDonald waved his security back outside. The two men resumed positions outside of the Oval Office hall door. They looked over at each other in disgust.

McDonald yelled at Janet. "Janet, get Hastings on the line, and tell him to get over here, right now!"

Janet found Hastings in transit. "He's en route to the Pentagon, Mr. President."

"Well, tell him to turn his ass around and get over here."

"Will do, sir."

Tom Hastings was returning to his office from a meeting with Boeing's CEO regarding a large military contract. He was feeling pretty happy with himself about the deal he'd just brokered when Janet reached him. Now he sat reluctantly in his limo as it redirected itself to the West Wing. He'd heard McDonald yelling at Janet and was savvy enough about Oval Office interaction to know problems awaited his arrival. His Lincoln stopped at the West Wing North Entrance and a Marine opened his door. He was let into the lobby by another Marine, and he resolutely walked to the Oval Office. He entered the president's personal working space and found McDonald sitting on his couch, staring into space.

"Good morning, Mr. President."

"What is so damn good about it?"

Hastings sat down across from McDonald and waited for the ensuing tirade.

"Some shithead, hippy-dippy, silverback, rifle-toting eco-terrorists have taken over my God-damn logging site. Hell, we were just getting rid of those college brats, and now this happens. What the hell are silverbacks, anyway?"

Hastings had seen the previous night's news and was aware of what McDonald's rantings referred to.

McDonald yelled in Janet's general direction. "Janet, where are those scones?"

"They're coming, Mr. President."

"Well, hurry them the hell up!"

Hastings didn't know where to start with the president's outburst. He wasn't sure what McDonald wanted of him. He addressed the only apparent question the president mentioned.

"Silverbacks are older, dominant male gorillas, sir. Dian Fossey studied them at her site in Rwanda."

"Diane who?"

Hastings mentally shook his head in amazement at the president's apparent lack of knowledge.

"Not essential data, sir. Simply put, the media has classified your eco-terrorists as silverbacks because they appear to be older, dominant men."

"Well I don't care how dominant they are. I want them out of my logging site, pronto!"

Just then, Acting Chief of Staff Ted Horner entered the president's office.

McDonald glared at Horner. "What the hell do you want?"

Visibly shaken by this greeting, Horner mumbled a response. "We have a meeting scheduled, sir."

"Well, I'm busy now, Horner."

McDonald thought for a moment and, apparently changing his mind, motioned for his chief of staff to sit across from him, next to Hastings. Horner walked across the Presidential Seal and joined Hastings on the couch. He wasn't sure what to think of McDonald's conflicting remarks and request. He sat down quietly and determined to say nothing until spoken to.

"Where was I, Hastings?"

"I'm not sure, Mr. President, but you appear to be upset about the events at your logging site in Oregon."

"You're damn right I'm upset."

"Was there something you wished me to do relating to this problem?"

"Jesus Christ, Hastings, why do you think I called you over here?"

Hastings was becoming irritated with this childish dialogue. He reiterated his previous question. "Mr. President, what can I do to help alleviate your concerns?"

"Get rid of those eco-terrorists. I want them out of my woods."

Horner was beginning to understand the subject of the conversation unveiling before him. He, too, had seen the evening news and knew about the silverbacks.

Russel Nelson was pulling a double shift at the White House. An intern had called in sick and he'd been contacted personally by Don Peterson and requested to work the early morning shift. Russel agreed, even though he was tired from the previous evening's work and his late night pool games with Preston. He was currently a little nervous and excited at the same time as he was working the morning shift by himself without any immediate supervision. His first call to duty was McDonald's request for pastries and coffee. As he stood before the Oval Office doors with his tray, waiting to be ushered in, he reminded himself: *These are just people. They may not realize it, but they are, just the same.*

Hastings responded to McDonald's comment. "Getting armed men out of the woods could cause fatalities, Mr. President."

There was a knock on the door, and Russel entered the president's office. Hastings, looking at the president, raised his hand in a stop motion, but McDonald ignored him. "I don't care who dies! I want those silverback eco-terrorists out of my forest, dead or alive!"

Russel set the platter of scones on the coffee table between the three men. He rested the coffee carafe and cups next to the pastries and stood up by the end of the couch. "Is there anything else you need, Mr. President?"

McDonald appeared to be surprised by Nelson's request. He hadn't registered the young man's entrance, and only now noticed him.

"No, no, that will be all."

Nelson turned around and left the Oval Office. He found himself in Janet's adjoining room. The dark-haired, dark-eyed secretary glanced up at Russel and smiled. As she did so, Janet flagged Russel down by waving her hand in his path. He came to a stop by her desk. Janet leaned forward and spoke softly, "You need to leave via the hall doors. The same doors you entered through."

Russel groaned and physically slumped over a bit, hanging his head down. Resting his hands on Janet's desk to support himself, he shook his head in disgust. Janet patted his hand several times and smiled up at him. "Don't worry about it, darling. Just turn around and before entering the office, knock to announce yourself. Your knock will give the big blowhards enough time to stop talking, and then you just cruise out the front doors."

Russel smiled his thanks and followed Janet's directions. As Russel was ushered out by the Secret Service, he heard the president talk loudly to Hastings again. "That's what I want, Hastings! I want those silverback bastards out of my woods, dead or alive!"

The doors closed behind Russel as Hastings responded to McDonald. "I believe you're asking for a military solution to this problem, Mr. President."

"You're damn right I am."

Hastings regarded Ted Horner. "Ted, I'll need to talk privately with the president. Have Janet reschedule your meeting on your way out."

Horner did as the Secretary of Defense suggested and left the Oval Office.

"All right, Mr. President, the Joint Chiefs of Staff will never agree to our attack on the militants. So we're going to sidestep normal channels to set up this engagement. This plan should not be discussed with anyone else, Mr. President. Understand?"

McDonald nodded his head in agreement.

"I know a couple of active duty personnel who can help us achieve our mission. I'll need to contact them. How soon do you want the removal of our problem?"

"Yesterday! The sooner the better. Let's get rid of these hippy-dippies right now."

Secretary Tom Hastings thought for a moment about all the possible consequences that could befall him because of this yet-to-be-determined illegal scheme. In his opinion, the penalties ranged from losing his job to possible jail time. The thought of bombing and then routing out eco-terrorists with ground troops intrigued his military persona. It also excited his flag-waving, hawkish, anti-liberal, right-wing political side, too. If worst came to worst, Hastings knew he could vanish without a trace in the blink of an eye, avoiding any possible negative repercussions.

Secretary Hastings pulled from his suitcoat pocket a flip phone he'd purchased from a local grocery store. He laid it on the coffee table in front of the president.

"You ever see one of these, Mr. President?"

"Certainly, it's a damn phone, Hastings."

"Yes it is, sir. But this phone is a disposable phone. It has no contract and cannot be traced back to you. You buy them at grocery stores and purchase minutes for them whenever you want. I want you to have Janet get you one of these phones and set it up for you. Whenever you need to contact me about our plan to eliminate your problem, we'll talk using these phones. Do you copy me, sir?"

"Sure, Hastings. Is all this spy stuff necessary?"

"Yes it is, sir. Since the route we're taking to accomplish your goal is illegal, we'll need to be covert."

"Okay, Hastings. I'll get Janet on it this morning."

"All right, give me a piece of paper."

The president reached over to his desk for a sheet of writing paper and inadvertently grabbed one with the Presidential Seal as its letterhead. He handed it to Hastings. The Secretary of Defense wrote his name and cellphone number on the paper.

"When you get your new phone, add this number, and only this number, to your contact list."

The two men sat across from each other and said nothing. Hastings checked his watch and calculated the present times for Pacific Daylight Time and Mountain Daylight Time.

"I need to go, Mr. President. I've got a couple calls to make regarding our plan so things can get rolling. If all goes well, your little irritation could be gone by this time next week."

McDonald clapped his hands together in excitement. "That's what I needed to hear, Hastings. Some God-damn decisive action, producing immediate results. You're a good man, Secretary."

McDonald reached over and got another scone from the tray and poured himself more coffee. He offered the secretary a pastry, but Hastings rose instead and excused himself.

The Secretary of Defense headed for the North Portico. He called his driver while halfway down the hall, and when he departed the building, the Marine's uniform jarred his memory into motion. As his car pulled up, Hastings was lost in thought, recalling an isolated airbase near the DMZ he commanded some forty-plus years ago. The two men whom he'd soon be calling were young pilots then. They both owed their military careers to Hastings.

Hastings' car came to a stop next to him and a Marine opened the back door. The secretary seated himself and watched the door close behind him.

"Where to, Mr. Secretary?"

"Back to the Pentagon, lieutenant."

CHAPTER 65

Secretary Hastings looked out his Lincoln's tinted window as it headed south to U.S. Highway 395. The traffic was moving slowly and the adjacent city's profile was uninteresting. Soon, he'd cross the Potomac River and exit north to the Pentagon.

At the moment, the secretary was not thinking about his present job. His mind had drifted back in time, again, and he continued reminiscing about his first command. He was vividly picturing the small airbase just below the DMZ. It was Captain Hastings back then, and he was responsible for a quick-response "Sandy" team. His airfield had four Douglas A-1 Skyraiders and three HH3 Sikorsky Jolly Green Giant helicopters attached to it.

The Sandy missions were fairly basic. They offered downed airmen in enemy-controlled territories an escape plan. The Skyraiders would fly to the pilot's position and secure it from the Viet Cong or North Vietnamese regulars until a Sikorsky Jolly Green Giant could arrive on scene and pluck the aviator from the ground. The Douglas aircraft were well suited for these missions. They were heavily armored, carried an extensive arsenal of weapons, and could stay aloft for great lengths of time. Once the Sikorsky helicopter retrieved its airman, all three aircraft returned to base.

Under Hastings' watch, one Sandy rescue had gone tragically awry. Initially, the mission had gone well. The downed F-105 pilots had been successfully removed from a rice paddy/pond system they'd parachuted into. Tragically, as the rescue team departed, an enemy Zu-23-2 anti-aircraft battery opened fire on the three retreating warplanes. One of the A-1 Skyraiders was shot down and crash landed into the rice paddies. The plane came to rest within a quarter mile of the village that sheltered the farmers who cultivated the ponds.

After the remaining Sandy team had departed, the hamlet militia advanced on and surrounded the A-1 pilot. His Colt 45 was no match for the twenty-some attacking villagers who wielded AK-47s and machetes.

The original Sandy team, minus their downed plane and pilot, returned to Hastings' airfield and rebooted themselves. Two more Douglas airplanes and another Sikorsky lifted off the field and headed back north to retrieve their endangered colleague.

The aircraft arrived on scene and immediately one Skyraider attacked and destroyed the anti-aircraft battery with rockets and cannon fire. The other Douglas went for the small band of peasants that surrounded the crashed A-1 Skyraider. It became obvious the rescue mission was too late. In the midst of the village militia lay the decapitated body of the downed Sandy pilot.

Lieutenant Rodgers, one of the A-1 pilots, ordered the Jolly Green Giant airmen back to the base. Then he and Lt. Henry, the other Douglas aviator, commenced dispatching the fleeing villagers. Only a few militia members made it back to their hamlet.

What happened next was never recorded in a flight log book or any "after action report." The two airmen turned their assault on the defenseless North Vietnamese village. A My Lai type massacre ensued. Both Skyraiders depleted their armaments against the hamlet. Rockets, 250-lb. bombs, 20-mm cannon fire, and lastly, cluster bombs whose projectile pellets shredded the thatched roofed huts were used against the farmers. As the two Douglas aircraft flew away, the hamlet was engulfed completely in flame. Between the burning buildings lay dead or dying dogs, pigs, and most of the village's population. A few peasants escaped the massacre and returned slowly to the carnage, locating the bodies of loved ones and attending to the wounded.

Lieutenants Rodgers and Henry returned to their base, and were met on the tarmac by Captain Hastings. They debriefed behind closed doors with the captain and the Sikorsky crew. After they had been dismissed, their base commander retrieved from the two Skyraiders the film cassettes showing intermittent recordings of the massacre. He destroyed the tapes by exposing them to a strong magnetic field produced by the base's commercial-sized magnet.

When Captain Hastings wrote up his report, detailing the Sandy mission, he omitted any discussion of the North Vietnamese village. He only noted the successful rescue of the F-105 pilots and the loss of his base's airman. In this manner, Hastings saved Lts. Rodgers and Henry from an inevitable court martial and probable dismissal from the Air Force.

Secretary of Defense Hastings sat in his limo's black leather bench seat and gazed out at the mired traffic and Potomac River. It was time to call in his markers and receive some reciprocal help from Rodgers and Henry. He hoped both men would agree to his wishes. That would be the best case scenario. As the secretary mused more about possible ensuing developments, his black sedan moved slowly in the Pentagon's direction.

CHAPTER
66

SECRETARY HASTINGS' CAR EVENTUALLY PASSED A wreck on Highway 395, exited the interstate, and headed north to the Pentagon. After gaining entrance to the grounds, Hastings' driver parked in the limo's reserved slot. The secretary entered the building and, after several cordial hall conversations, reached his office. He walked over to his aide's desk and asked him to locate information about Lieutenant Rodgers.

"I'm not sure what rank he is now, but I've heard he commands a small airbase in Idaho. Get me his military record, too."

Hastings gave his aide more pertinent information about Rodgers, then entered his office. He sat down at his desk and waited for his aide to locate his man. It didn't take long. His landline's blinking light attracted his attention, and he answered the phone.

"I've got the information you requested, sir. Your lieutenant is a colonel now, and he commands Mountain Home Airfield in Idaho. It's just southeast of Boise by about forty miles. Do you want me to raise the colonel for you?"

"No, no, not yet. Where's he stationed, again?"

"Mountain Home Airbase, sir. It's near Boise."

"How old is the colonel?"

"Let me see...he's going to turn 68 in December, sir."

"How long has he held that command?"

"Looks like eight years going on nine."

"Okay, let's ring him up."

"Yes, sir."

Colonel William Rodgers sat in his office perusing base data on his computer. He was checking the airfield's fuel consumption for the last quarter and comparing it to the previous year's quarterly consumption. He'd been asked to tighten up base spending. The colonel couldn't change the price of aviation fuel, but he could reduce training flights and in this manner lower his fuel costs. He'd done just that in the last three months and was now checking on monetary results.

The colonel's office was noticeably bland. Not only was it furnished with Vietnam War era metal desks, chairs, tables, and filing cabinets, but the office lacked personal mementos. There was little indication of its occupant's lengthy military career, which spanned over forty years. Several personal pictures adorned the walls along with a number of historic aviation replicas. "A Higher Call" by John D. Shaw was centered on one wall. It was surrounded by numerous paintings and pictures of Douglas A-1 Skyraiders. Apart from the aviation pictures, the colonel's space was drab, military gray.

Colonel Rodgers was a stoic, pragmatic man who didn't need reminders of who he was or where he'd been. Mountain Home Air Force Base was his last assignment. Actually, Rodgers was surprised he still commanded the small airfield. He was well past military retirement age, and had not been asked to tender his resignation. Rodgers intended to hold his command for as long as possible. The base practically ran itself, and Rodgers enjoyed the military lifestyle. Nothing in the civilian world interested him as much as the Air Force and its airplanes. Playing golf and completing crossword puzzles didn't intrigue the colonel in the least.

Colonel Rodgers' desk phone's blinking light caught his attention. He picked up his receiver. "What is it, airman?"

"Well, sir. I've got the Secretary of Defense on the line. He wishes to speak with you."

Colonel Rodgers sat motionless for a second. He hadn't talked with Tom Hastings in decades. The emotions he now felt were a mixture of surprise, comradeship, and apprehension. *Why is Hastings calling me after all these years?*

"Any idea why he's calling?"

"No, sir. Nothing was mentioned."

"All right, airman, put him through."

"Yes, sir."

Secretary Hastings was informed by his aide Colonel Rodgers was standing by. Hastings pressed his phone's button. "Rodgers, Rodgers, are you there?"

"Yes I am, sir. How are you doing, Mr. Secretary?"

"Living the good life, Colonel Rodgers. Dodging political bullets now, but nonetheless, I'm liking the D.C. battlefield. And you're a full colonel now with your own command. Good for you, Rodgers. Seems like the military has agreed with you."

"It has, Tom. Is it safe to call you Tom, Mr. Secretary?"

Secretary Hastings laughed aloud at this comment, but also thought about the separation between Rodgers and himself and the intent of this phone call.

"Yes, it is, colonel. You know as of late, I've been reflecting about my career and thought about my first command. That was a long time ago and you were part of it. Our small airfield south of the DMZ was a pretty dicey situation. We were lucky no North Vietnamese regulars came after us. You were a good stick and reliable officer who made my job easy."

Rodgers thought about the Sandy missions he'd flown while under Hastings' command, some successful, some not. All were stressful, and Hastings had been a great CO to his airmen. Always supportive and understanding.

"Thanks, Tom. Now it's my turn to command a small airfield. It's kind of like a three-ring circus. You've got the pilots, the support personnel, and now the civilian employees. It can get a little messy at times."

"Yeah, we didn't have the civilians to deal with in Vietnam. I suspect not having them to trip over constantly made things much easier for me."

"You bet. They can be a pain in the butt. They've got a whole different work ethic and bitch about most everything."

"Well, colonel. Not everyone has the mettle for your job. My aide tells me you've been at it for eight years, so the responsibility of the command must agree with you."

"I enjoy it, Mr. Secretary. The base is small enough, allowing me to know all the pilots and most of the enlisted. It has a good feel to it."

"Our base below the DMZ was pretty small, too. Remember, we even knew the cooks' first names."

"Yes I do, sir. There were some real characters in that bunch."

"Any plans for retirement, Rodgers?"

"No, I don't have my retirement planned. I haven't given it much thought. They keep extending my duty contract and I'm pretty satisfied with what I'm doing."

Secretary Hastings felt it was time to get to the meat of his call. He injected some suggestive, threatening dialogue into the conversation. "Don't get caught with your pants down, colonel; a rejection notice can appear at any time at your age. I've seen it over and over again. Damn good airmen will be let go so younger officers can advance."

Colonel Rodgers thought about the advice and the subtlety of its tone.

"Thanks for the insight, Tom. I really should be making plans for civilian life. My head in the sand attitude is a little irresponsible on my part."

"Better late than never, colonel."

After pushing the retirement button, Hastings decided to get right to it. "Colonel, I've got a delicate situation on my hands, and I think you're the man to help me out."

"How so, Mr. Secretary?"

"Well, I've got a directive from the Oval Office for an airstrike near your base."

Rodgers couldn't imagine how Hastings' comment was applicable to his present geographic area. He ventured a statement trying to nail down what the secretary was soliciting.

"I assume this is not a training mission, Mr. Secretary."

"Correct, colonel. This is a strike against armed eco-terrorists in Central Oregon."

Colonel Rodgers immediately thought of the potentially illegal nature of this plan. "You know, Tom, an attack on civilians by one of my planes could be very costly to the pilot and myself. The Posse Comitatus Act could bite us in the butt and get us court martialed and jailed."

"I know, colonel. We're dealing with a delicate shade of gray here, but this strike is a direct request from the president. You know, colonel, I went out on a limb for you back in Vietnam, and I'm hoping you can reciprocate the favor. Orders will be following my request. The president and I are checking on strategies to use with the Joint Chiefs of Staff. There will be orders; we just don't know as of yet the pipeline they'll be coming through."

Colonel Rodgers thought about Vietnam and Hastings resurrecting his Sandy mission. *Some things never go away. I think I know where this conversation is going. I will soon be caught between a rock and a hard place. If I don't agree to Hastings' request, forced retirement seems imminent, and if I do agree to the secretary's plan, I could be court martialed and out of a job, anyway.* Rodgers decided to continue with the conversation and see where it led.

"Okay, Mr. Secretary. You've got my full attention. What exactly do you need?"

"Well, I need some intel in regards to the eco-terrorist location. Do you have the appropriate systems at hand?"

"Yes. We've got a number of drones on the base."

"Can you get thermal imagery?"

"Most certainly."

"Good. We need to know what their night security is like. Do you have F-16s at your disposal?"

"I've got a squadron assigned to me."

"Very good. We'll need one plane dropping a 'smartbomb' on a 'lit up' target sometime in the near future."

"I think I've got everything you need, Mr. Secretary. When do you want the intel?"

"The sooner the better, colonel. I'll have my aide send you some coordinates by this afternoon. Once you get them, get me the thermal intel about the encampment and its layout."

Colonel Rodgers decided to try for a long shot. "You know, Tom. This mission could cost me my career. You might suggest to the president a 'thank-you' is in order, say, a couple million thank-yous placed in a secure location with my name attached."

Secretary Hastings thought about Rodgers' request. *A payoff? Well, hell, the president and I are asking a lot of him.* Secretary Hastings felt Colonel Rodgers' request was warranted.

"I'll check into that, colonel. I can't speak for the president, but your request seems reasonable to me."

"Good, Mr. Secretary. Get me those coordinates and I'll get you your intel."

"Excellent, colonel, I'll be waiting for your information. Thanks for your help."

"Certainly, Mr. Secretary. I hope when we talk next, you can tell me about the president's response to my retirement plan."

"I'll work on it. Get right on gathering the intel. I need your findings sooner than later."

"Certainly, Mr. Secretary. Good-bye."

Colonel Rodgers leaned back in his gray desk chair. He scanned his room, noticing its starkness and lack of personality. *The military is and always has been my life. This mission could end my career. Secretary Hastings covered for me back in Vietnam. Do I owe him my job because of it?* The colonel continued dwelling on the conversation. *If McDonald sets up an offshore account for me, I'll provide the services Hastings asked for. If not, I'll politely refuse. Either way, I'll probably lose my job.* In one scenario, Rodgers would have a military pension, in the other, an offshore bank account. The latter possibility was more problematic, but any termination of his military career would be difficult for him. Rodgers would figure things out.

Secretary Hastings returned the receiver to its cradle. *Well, part one went fairly well. Is McDonald smart enough to part with a few million dollars in order to solve his problem?* The secretary buzzed his aide and asked him to get the phone number for and personal information about Lieutenant Henry. Part two of the equation was about to be dealt with.

CHAPTER 67

Secretary Hastings' aide had some trouble locating Lieutenant Henry's military record. For one, the lieutenant was now lieutenant colonel. He also had switched services and was now in the Army. Henry commanded a training center near Yakima, Washington. His base was affiliated with Lewis-McChord Military Base, and trained soldiers from all branches of the service. Not only could visiting troops get instruction at the base on new military hardware, they could also receive training on various assault strategies; everything from urban warfare to biochemical tactics was taught there.

When Hastings ended his conversation with Lieutenant Colonel Henry, the secretary said his good-byes, and hung up feeling good about his efforts. The lieutenant colonel seemed pleased and honored to be helping the president fight the eco-terrorists, and did not ask for any special favors in return for his services. The legality of the engagement was not brought up. Henry understood his soldiers were part of a clandestine mission that could not be addressed through normal channels. Furthermore, he was not concerned about initiating the mission without orders and trusted the secretary's assurances about them arriving later. Lt. Colonel Henry assured Secretary Hastings his men would be on site within forty-eight hours of their conversation, and the squad would consist of only seasoned, battle-tested regulars capable of handling any engagement. In response, Hastings relayed the troops would most likely be doing a body count following an air strike and not much more. Near the end of the conversation, the two officers' discussion focused on the soldiers' interactions with the onsite civilian forces. Both men thought their troops should offer assistance to the local authorities. They also believed any inquiries about the squad's presence should first be directed to Lt. Colonel Henry. He was to terminate the questions with a "need to know" statement, and if this tactic didn't work, the inquiry would be passed on to Secretary Hastings. He would deal with the questioning in a similar but more authoritative manner.

After his phone conversation with Henry, the secretary laid his flip phone onto his desktop. He had one more call to make. All the pieces were in place now, and two experienced, reliable men would be handling the actual assault. Hastings needed to pass this information on to the president.

CHAPTER 68

Hastings dialed the Oval Office. While he waited for his connection with the president, the secretary thought about the ensuing mission. *Hell, there won't be anything left of those old farts when the dust settles.*

McDonald was sitting behind his desk talking with Ted Horner and his press secretary, who had not been offered chairs, so they stood together beside the president's desk. They were listening to his ramblings and trying to create some diversions to place before the media and the American public. In this way, they hoped to transfer focus away from the president's failings and falling voter support. McDonald was currently assuring them he had a huge plan in the making, and when it "broke," it would silence the naysayers and bring back the public support he'd lost.

A blinking light drew everyone's attention to the desk phone. It was Janet's line.

"What is it, Janet?"

"Secretary Hastings is on the line, sir."

"Put him through."

McDonald dismissed Horner and his press secretary with a wave of his hand, and both men left the Oval Office. In the hallway, they looked at each other, realizing nothing had been accomplished in their meeting with the president. They decided to rendezvous after lunch in the press secretary's office to devise some smoke screens to help McDonald keep ahead of his many political and public adversaries.

Secretary Hastings received McDonald's abrupt greeting. "What do you have for me, Hastings?"

"Well, Mr. President, everything is set in motion. It will take a few days to become operational, but after that, we're good to go."

McDonald felt a rush of childish excitement. "Good man, Hastings."

"We'll need to meet this afternoon, sir."

"Of course, of course. I want to hear all the details."

"I'll be there at 3:00 p.m., Mr. President."

"Great, Hastings. I'll clear my schedule."

"One last thing, Mr. President."

"Yes, what is it, Hastings?"

"Do you have your new cellphone yet?"

"Well, no I don't, but is it of..."

"Have it up and running when I arrive for our afternoon meeting, sir. And yes, it is of importance, the utmost importance."

Hastings closed his flip phone and leaned back in his chair. Working with this man was like dealing with a teenager. Modern-day American history was about to be made. A military strike against American civilians within the U.S. continental borders hadn't happened, well, Hastings couldn't remember when it had occurred last. McDonald wasn't even aware of the significance of this event.

Hastings surveyed his schedule and saw he needed to change a photo op with Boeing executives to another time. He contacted his aide and got the rescheduling in motion, then ordered some food from the commissary. After perusing the first section of the *Washington Post*, trying to ignore stories dealing with the McDonald administration, Hastings turned to the sports section and began reading about the upcoming Redskins' home opener.

CHAPTER 69

President McDonald moved from his Oval Office desk to his couch and rested there eating a sandwich and drinking coffee. After talking with Hastings, the president was excited about his afternoon meeting with the Secretary of Defense. He was childishly curious about the tactics he'd soon use to take out the occupiers. His imagination was racing with "Hollywood" style scenarios when Janet came to the doorway.

"Mr. President?"

"What?"

"The White House chief usher wishes to speak to you about a scheduling change."

His expression noticeably soured when Janet mentioned the chief usher. *This guy is such a pain in the ass.* The president stood up and walked over to his desk.

He picked up his phone's receiver. "Yes?"

"Mr. President, I've got a scheduling change for you. Your working meeting with President Hernandez of Mexico and Prime Minister Elliot of Canada has been changed to 3:00 p.m. They both accepted invitations to speak at the AFL-CIO luncheon at noon today. Their aides assured me they could be at the White House at three for your meeting."

McDonalds's eye began twitching upon receiving this news. *Why in the hell wasn't I asked to speak at the luncheon? God-damn liberal union snots!* He was about ready to concede to the chief usher's request when he remembered Hastings' meeting.

"I can't meet with them at that time. I've got an important engagement with Secretary Hastings then."

There was an extended silence on the chief usher's side of the phone. "Mr. President, both countries' leaders are scheduled to depart tomorrow morning. This probably..."

"Well, they shouldn't have accepted the union engagement if they wanted to speak with me. Hell, have Robinson meet those two. He can handle that shit. You best get to rescheduling this for me. I certainly don't want to ruffle our visiting dignitaries' feathers."

"Certainly, Mr. President. I'll get ahold of the Vice President, immediately."

"Good, good, Peterson. I don't want any more interruptions today."

"Certainly, Mr. President. Good day."

McDonald hung up the phone without responding to the chief usher.

While he'd been talking with Peterson, McDonald had doodled numerous notes on the presidential letterhead paper on which Hastings had written his flip phone number. He'd absentmindedly written "kill the hippy-dippy, old fart, silverbacks" on one edge of the paper, and on the opposite side, next to the secretary's phone number, he wrote, "Hastings is a good man!" In the middle of the page, he'd scribbled notes about the meeting's rescheduling, mentioning both the new time and the date. McDonald had finished his notations with uncomplimentary thoughts about Peterson and union leaders. Upon completion, the paper became an incriminating scripture in numerous ways, one that should never have been created.

McDonald stood up and tossed his pen onto his desk. Rethinking his action, the president reached across his desk to grab the discarded pen. He fumbled the maneuver and the pen fell onto the floor from the back side of the desk. *God-damn pen*. When he scooted around the end of his desk to retrieve the writing utensil, McDonald's unbuttoned suitcoat brushed across the desktop. As it did, the open jacket pushed before it the incriminating note. It reached the desk's edge and fell off, doing a lazy, aerial loop before coming to rest, face up, on the discarded papers within the wastebasket. McDonald didn't notice the paper's descent, and upon retrieving his pen and resettling himself onto the couch, he reached for another sandwich and began perusing his phone. Hastings couldn't get there soon enough for him.

CHAPTER 70

McDonald sat in the Oval Office for a few hours viewing his phone and checking his favorite news sites for information. He became irritated by the mostly negative coverage of his administration by the media, and in particular the Impeachment March statistics were agitating him. The liberal media estimated roughly a million demonstrators had marched on Washington. McDonald found this number to be absurd and obviously inflated. Even more irritating was the reporting about the crowd's demographics. It appeared a larger than expected proportion was Republicans. *Totally concocted lies*, thought McDonald as he continued navigating his phone. A knock from Janet's doorway pulled him away from his phone.

"I've got the phone you asked for, Mr. President. I'll put it on your desk. There's a sticky note attached with your phone number written on it. They're simple to use. When 'America the Beautiful' starts playing, just open up the phone and you're immediately connected to your caller. To stop the call, just close the phone."

"Okay, Janet. I get it. Can't be too damn hard."

Janet returned to her office and wondered how long it would take before her boss needed her assistance to use the phone.

There was a knock on the Oval Office's hall doorway and Hastings was let in by a Secret Service agent. He walked over to the couch opposite from the president and sat down.

"Well give me the details, Hastings. I want to know how those old fart, hippy-dippies meet their demise."

Secretary Hastings was startled by this immature, callous response by the president.

"Well, Mr. President. It's relatively simple. We drop a bomb on the terrorists, blow them up, and send a squad of men in to finish them off and count bodies."

"That's it?"

"Yes, Mr. President, it is. The whole operation will probably last about fifteen to twenty minutes."

"Well, damn. In one fell swoop, I'll get my logging operation back, and public support will swing my way because of my decisive action against these silverback apes or whatever they are."

"I'm not sure of the politics, sir, but you'll definitely not have any more occupiers to deal with."

"Good, good, when does our attack begin?"

"I've got some intel to gather, and personnel needs to get into place, but I'd say within four or five days the attack can commence."

"Excellent. Can we watch in the Situation Room?"

"Probably, Mr. President. It requires a satellite or drone hookup, and we've got a drone at our disposal so we're probably good to go."

"Will it be a 'real time' feed?"

"Yes it will be, sir."

McDonald clapped his hands together in excitement. Hastings once again was put off by this show of immaturity and wanted to terminate his presidential meeting, but he had several more "points" to discuss with McDonald before he could leave.

"You'll need to set up an offshore account with two million in it for one of our players. That would be Colonel Rodgers. I suggest you do it. His part in our mission is instrumental."

McDonald stared at Hastings without speaking. His demeanor became noticeably cold and aggressive.

"Bullshit if I will, Hastings. Hell, I'm the Commander in Chief and he'll follow my orders to the last detail. I'm already paying his God-damn salary. I don't need to throw more cash his way for him to do his job."

Hastings looked back at McDonald and took a deep breath. "Mr. President, you really don't give him his orders. The Joint Chiefs of Staff do, and we've bypassed them. Also, sir, the American people pay Rodgers' wages, not you. These points aside, Mr. President, here's the reality of the situation. You're asking Rodgers to break the law and possibly throw away his military career. He knows this and is willing to take a chance with us if he's compensated for his efforts. You need to oblige him, Mr. President. I don't think we'll find anybody else to play ball with us."

Hastings and McDonald blankly stared at each other. McDonald flinched first.

"All right, Hastings. I'll set up the account. What's his legal name?"

"William S. Rodgers."

"Okay, I'll get my people on this right away."

"You'll need to, sir. I expect to be talking with Rodgers tomorrow, and the account needs to be functional by then."

"No way, Hastings. It will be in place with two million in it, but Rodgers can't access the cash until after the mission."

The Secretary considered this response. It appeared businesslike and he consented to it. "Seems reasonable, Mr. President."

"You're damn right it's reasonable. I learned a long time ago not to pay someone for a job until it's done."

"All right, I need to take my leave now. I've got another meeting on my schedule, and remember, we use our flip phones to communicate about this mission. Savvy, sir?"

"Yes, yes, Hastings."

Secretary Hastings stood up and without saying anything else, turned and left the Oval Office. McDonald was left by himself. He called out to Janet and asked her to get his mortgage company on the line. While he waited for his desk phone to start blinking, his hand reached over to the cushion next to him and upon finding his cellphone, he began scrolling through news sites.

CHAPTER 71

Agents Stone and Robbins were pressing buttons and contemplating screens in the back room of their White House office. All their surveillance monitors were controlled from there. The West Wing's camera system had gone down earlier, and they'd called up their usual repair technicians, but repairs were put off until tomorrow morning. Seemingly, numerous D.C. banks were having similar problems, and all the repairmen were out on call. Now, the Secret Service agents were attempting to correct the problem themselves, but with no success.

Stone looked over at Robbins, "We'll have to physically monitor the West Wing until tomorrow morning."

"Seems to be the case, doesn't it?"

"Yep."

"How many agents do you think we'll need?"

"Three should work. Two at main entrances and one rover."

"We'll be staffed pretty thin."

"Yep."

Agent Stone thought about the nightly task of retrieving West Wing wastebasket contents. An agent usually did this. He'd bring the trash back to their ground-level White House office and shred it.

"Should the rover pick up the trash?"

Agent Robbins thought about Stone's inquiry. "Nope. Their rounds will be interrupted, and they'll have to leave the premises to bring back the trash. We'll need to find someone else."

"How about buzzing the chief usher and nabbing one of his interns for the job?"

"Perfect solution. I saw Russel in the halls earlier. He's a reliable kid. I'll call Peterson and see if we can borrow him."

Russel, while sitting in the breakroom, was called to the chief usher's office. When he entered, Don Peterson was at his antique writing desk examining his computer screen. Russel could see the weekly White House Staff work schedule on the monitor. Peterson swiveled around in his chair and faced Russel. "Have a seat, young man."

"Thanks, sir."

"I don't like asking this favor of you, but I'm up the creek, so to speak."

"What do you need, Mr. Peterson?"

"Bottom line, I need you to work another shift for me. The Secret Service wants your help this evening with a minor task. They trust you and asked for your assistance. I hate requesting you to do three shifts in forty-eight hours."

Russel knew he'd be dog tired when he went to his morning classes the next day, but the thought of hanging around the Secret Service agents intrigued him.

"I can do it, Mr. Peterson. I could use a break, though, and some food. After that, I'll be good to go."

"Thank you, Russel. I'll call the agents and let them know you'll be available in about an hour."

Russel turned to leave the chief usher's office. As he opened the door, which led to the staff's stairwell, the chief usher called out his name.

"Russel, come on back here."

He walked back to the chief usher's desk, and Don Peterson pulled out his wallet, retrieving four tickets. He had season passes to the Redskins home games and these tickets were for the season opener. Peeling two tickets away from the others, he handed them to Russel.

"Thanks again for your help, young man. My wife and I will be in the other seats. Bring a friend and come join us."

Russel was speechless for a second. He'd never been to a pro football game before.

"This will be incredible. Thank you so much, Mr. Peterson."

"My pleasure."

The young intern once again headed out of the room. *Two tickets to a Redskins game, wow!*

As he opened the office door, he stopped and turned, facing the chief usher. "Is Preston working on Sunday?"

The chief usher scanned his screen. "No, he's not. Good choice. He's a big Redskins fan, and my wife and he get along fabulously. They're almost embarrassing to be around when they start in with their joking."

"Great, I'll give him a call."

Russel headed down the stairs to the ground floor and the kitchen where he'd avail himself of the food the cooks set aside for the staff.

Agent Stone walked into the kitchen and gave a greeting to the cooks, who all smiled back in return. He found his recruit sitting on a couch in the staff room with an empty plate next to him. He was scanning his phone and monitoring Facebook. The young intern looked up as Stone approached the couch.

"Hello, Russel. I'm Agent Stone."

The two men shook hands.

"Thanks for helping us out tonight."

Stone extended his arm, inviting Russel to join him. They headed for the Secret Service office. It was two doors down from the kitchen. Entering the Center Hall, the two turned left, passing by a few stately statues and presidential pictures, then quickly entered the Secret Service rooms. Agent Robbins looked up from a computer screen and greeted Russel.

"Hello, Russel. Welcome to the Secret Service. You're an agent for a night."

Russel smiled, "Glad to be aboard, sir."

The two agents grinned at his response.

"We need your assistance tonight because our surveillance is down in the West Wing. No big deal really, although it does throw a monkey wrench into our usual routine. We're subbing out one minor task to you so our agents can be freed up to monitor the building."

Russel, with a straight face, queried, "Do I need a gun, sir?"

Once again the agents smiled at his quip.

"No, young man, we don't want you to hurt yourself or any of us, for that matter. No, we'll carry the guns and you'll carry the trash."

Russel laughed and then gazed quizzically at Agent Robbins.

"That's the job, Russel. Every day, the wastebaskets in the West Wing are collected and their contents shredded."

Agent Stone opened a nearby door, turned on the lights, and allowed Russel to view their shredding machine.

"Not a very glamorous job, but a totally necessary one."

"No job is too small or unimportant for Agent Russel Nelson, sir. I'm ready to go."

Stone smiled and clapped Russel on the back. "You're a good man, Nelson. We're lucky to have you on our team."

Robbins brought out a large laundry cart from the shredding room and rolled it over to Russel.

"Okay, Agent Nelson, take this cart through the Palm Room and get started with your assignment. If someone's working late, just announce your entrance and continue on with your chore. Everybody expects their wastebaskets to be emptied, so your arrival will be anticipated. It could take you a couple hours to get all the baskets emptied. All right, Agent Nelson. Off you go."

Russel wheeled his cart out into the hallway and headed for the West Wing. He encountered a few Communications staffers working late, but as he continued on with his chore, nobody else seemed to be in the West Wing. Once he'd entered the main building, Russel checked out the Cabinet Room and the secretary's office space. He then entered the Oval Office from Janet's room and spotted McDonald's desk wastebasket. Walking over to it, he bent down to pick it up. The can was partially filled, and Russel's eyes were instantly drawn to an uncrumpled piece of paper lying on top of all the other severely crunched-up throwaways. He could read the writing on the paper and noted a phrase asking for the deaths of the silverbacks. Russel had been following the Oregon news, and knew all about the Metolius occupation and the silverbacks. It was an intriguing story that D.C. news stations were following closely. The young intern observed the surveillance cameras. Their small red lights were off. Impulsively, he reached down into the wastebasket and grabbed the paper, hastily folded it, and put it into his pants pocket. After dumping the wastepaper into the bin, and checking for more baskets, he quickly left the Oval Office. Russel pushed his cart down the southern hallway. *What the crap did I just do?* The new recruit checked out a small dining room and continued on down the hall. *I stole a piece of paper out of the Oval Office. Spies do this shit! What was I thinking?* Russel reached into his pants pocket and felt the folded paper. He started to pull it out of his pocket so he could place it in his bin, but just then a Secret Service agent rounded the corner and saw him.

"How's it going, Agent Nelson?"

Russel was caught off guard. "Um, um, pretty good, sir."

The agent noticed Russel's nervous behavior. "Everything okay, Russel?"

He collected himself and responded, "Yes, everything's just fine. You kind of scared me coming around the corner so quickly. It's a little eerie in here after hours."

"Yes it is." The agent seemed to think to himself for a second. "Hey, don't forget the bathrooms. They've all got baskets in them, too."

After he spoke, the agent turned to leave. As he did, he glanced up at the closest surveillance camera and saw its red light on, again.

"Well look at that. Our bugs are up and running again."

Russel viewed another camera and saw its indicator light was aglow, also. The Secret Service man glanced back at him. "Just keep doing your chore. You're halfway through already so you might as well finish."

Then, the agent headed down the hall in the opposite direction and Russel continued on, entering the next room and finding its wastebaskets. The West

Wing's security system was fully operational. There wasn't a chance now for Russel to return his presidential paper to his trash cart without his movement being recorded. He tried to calm his nerves. *It's okay, it's okay, Nobody saw me take it and nobody will miss it. It's just a piece of trash.*

Russel finished his rounds and took the cart back to the Secret Service office where Robbins and Stone were viewing the live West Wing monitors in the back room. Stone came out of the room and greeted Russel.

"Good job, young man. I'll have to take your Secret Service badge from you now. Your efforts are no longer needed."

Russel smiled and let go of his cart. "I'm actually a little glad I'm a civilian again. This job is somewhat nerve wracking. The West Wing is a tiny bit creepy late at night."

Agent Stone smiled. "Yeah, it is a little strange around here without the hustle and bustle of the daily routines playing out before you. Well, thanks for your efforts tonight, Russel. We appreciate what you did for us."

"I see you got your eyes back."

"Yeah, it was kind of weird what happened. The monitors just all of a sudden lit up. Robbins and I didn't do anything to aid the process."

Russel looked back into the observation room and noticed the monitors showing the space he'd just visited. Saying good-bye, he headed for the staff lounge next to the ground floor's kitchen. The young intern said hello to the cooks and entered the break area. His hand unconsciously found the folded paper in his pocket. *Hell, what was I thinking! This was a stupid, stupid thing to do.* He pulled his hand out of his pocket, and sat down onto the lounge's couch. *Well nobody saw me take the paper. I'm not going to get caught.* Russel picked up a copy of the *Washington Post*, and thinking about the Redskins tickets, he turned to the sports page and began reading about the season opener. He'd give Preston a call tomorrow morning and invite him to the game.

CHAPTER 72

A FEW MELODIC NOTES FROM "AMERICA THE Beautiful" emanated from the president's new phone and reached Janet's desk. *I wonder what that's all about.* She continued on with her work. Soon, she'd print out the schedule for McDonald, even though she knew he'd blow off most of the agenda and give the work to VP Robinson. *I really should make two copies and send one directly to the vice president.*

Colonel Rodgers had just finished talking with Secretary Hastings about the drone mission scheduled for the evening. Hastings liked Rodgers' punctuality and was pleased with the colonel's efforts. He decided to call McDonald and pass on the good news.

McDonald opened up his flip phone. "What is it?"

Secretary Hastings ignored the president's rudeness. "Colonel Rodgers has checked in. Our site intel will be gathered tonight."

"Who's Rodgers?"

Hastings shook his head in bewildered disgust. "He's the colonel who's going to drop our bomb for us."

McDonald sat up in his desk chair. "Can we watch the information being gathered in the Situation Room?"

"We could, Mr. President, but I don't want to. Activity in the Situation Room causes people to get curious, and we don't want any antennae pointing our way. I'll get the recon info from Rodgers and fill you in on the details, tomorrow."

"Damn good thinking, Hastings. I'll clear my schedule in the afternoon."

Hastings was about to cut the president off when he thought about the president's phone. "Do you have my number in your contact list?"

"No, not yet."

"Well, do it now. Where's the paper I put the number on?"

"Shit, Hastings. You sound like my damn mother! Your number's on my desk."

"Well, go get it."

McDonald stood up from the couch and walked over to his desk. It was bare of papers. The president stared at Janet's doorway and hollered, "Janet, did you take a paper off my desk?"

"No, Mr. President. I haven't been in your office today."

McDonald started searching on the floor around the desk and in the trashcan. Hastings heard the president yell at Janet and shook his head in disbelief. *Goddamn idiot!* McDonald walked through the Oval Office looking for his lost paper, but didn't find a trace of it.

"I can't find the paper, Hastings. You'll have to give me the damn number again."

Hastings thought a moment about the missing note. "Where did you last see it?"

"What the hell did I say, Hastings? It was on my desk. God damn it. It's just a piece of paper."

Secretary Hastings took a deep breath and forced himself to relax. "When did you last see it, Mr. President?"

McDonald was becoming very agitated over the paper nonsense. "Christ, Hastings." He forced himself to revisit yesterday's Oval Office happenings. The chief usher's call eventually resurfaced. "Peterson called me yesterday afternoon. I jotted some notes on your God-damn paper and left it on the desk top."

"Did you throw the paper into the garbage can?"

"Are you listening? I left the paper on my fucking desktop!! Who cares about the God-damn paper? Give me the number and I'll get it entered into the fucking phone!"

McDonald at this point was red in the face, and his eye tic came back, further aggravating his state. Secretary Hastings, sensing the president's crazed state, realized it was fruitless to talk with McDonald any longer. He gave McDonald the number once again, and curtly said his good-byes.

Hastings knew he'd have to sleuth out the missing paper on his own. His memory told him the paper had his phone number and name on it. Just his name and number could be enough to compromise his anonymity. *What did McDonald write on the damn paper?* The Secretary decided to call the Secret Service and get them to review yesterday's tapes from the Oval Office. Hopefully, this bit of detective work would clean up the missing paper situation. *McDonald probably tossed the sheet into the wastebasket.* Hastings walked out of his office and stood next to his aide's desk.

"Lieutenant, get the White House Secret Service team on the line for me."

"Certainly, sir."

He returned to his desk and waited for the connection to be made.

Agent Stone had just checked in when the secretary called. He told Hastings about the surveillance system going down, and when asked about any other irregular or unusual happenings, the agent mentioned Russel Nelson had performed the shredder pick-up. The secretary then inquired about Russel, and Agent Stone referred him to the chief usher for more information.

After talking with Don Peterson, Secretary Hastings knew about Russel's internship and his George Washington University dorm address. The secretary decided to investigate further by sending two Military Intelligence guys over to question the young college student.

Hastings left his office and once again spoke to his aide. "Lieutenant, send a couple of our M.I. boys over to the Foggy Bottom campus. They're to interrogate Russel Nelson regarding a missing Oval Office document. Have them go to his dorm room and question him there. If anything appears suspicious to our men, have them detain Russel and put him into the Quantico brig. That should put the 'Fear of God' into our young intern."

"What are you actually looking for, sir?"

"A sheet of paper with the Presidential Seal on it. It will have some notes scribbled on it."

"All right, sir. I'll get right on this."

"Excellent. Have our M.I. boys contact us after they've questioned Nelson."

"Certainly, sir."

After returning to his work space, he sat down on his couch. *This is already becoming messy. Working with McDonald is incredibly problematic. Hopefully this mission won't get derailed because of his ineptness.* Hastings momentarily fantasized about the mission's repercussions. He could see the newspaper headline in his mind's eye.

Eco-Terrorists Attacked by the U.S. Military

Such a read would certainly shock a few left wingers wide awake when they read their morning papers. The secretary picked up the sports section of the *Washington Post* and began scanning it again, searching for more Redskins articles. The secretary had endured a long, uninteresting baseball season, and feeling fall in the air made him anxious for the return of football.

CHAPTER 73

The lecture about the French colonization of Southeast Asia was one of Professor Susan Riley's favorites. It led into the broader subject of twentieth-century European world colonization, and this subject was the professor's area of expertise. Looking into the small lecture hall's amphitheater style seating, she found Russel Nelson, one of her favorite students. Surprisingly, Professor Riley found Russel asleep. As she watched, Russel's head slipped off of his hand and dropped suddenly, causing her student to wake up and look around sheepishly. *The young man must be burning the candle at both ends,* thought the professor. She averted her eyes and continued talking, noting in her lecture the importance of the area's raw materials to France.

Russel was awakened again by the commotion of changing classes. He groggily got his laptop packed up, left the lecture hall, and headed for the building's front door and fresh air. The warm, D.C. day greeted him as he reached the entrance steps. Russel donned his sunglasses and sought the shade provided by an old elm tree. Sitting down, he pulled out his cellphone. Russel once again tried to reach Bridger. It seemed like a month since they'd last talked. Before college started, the two conversed daily, and the absence of communication with his best friend was unsettling for Russel. He wondered why their contact had stopped. Not really expecting to reach Bridger, he pushed the phone's call icon. This procedure had been duplicated about thirty times in the past few weeks.

Bridger and Rachael were in the Sisters fly fishing shop, picking out some nymph patterns for fishing. The two had dutifully camped on the Metolius for several days now, and Bridger had decided to teach Rachael how to fly fish. They'd purchased a beginning fly fishing set from the Camp Sherman store, and Rachael had proved to be an apt student. The young redhead had learned the basic overhead cast quickly. Bridger loved watching Rachael navigate the river in her bikini and hip boots. The young college coed had mastered casting by ignoring Bridger's instructional comments such as "use more hip movement" and instead focused mostly on the fly's presentation, which indicated the worthiness of the cast.

After Rachael demonstrated good technique with the overhead, side cast, and roll cast using dry flies, Bridger decided to introduce drift fishing with nymphs. This had required a line change and some new patterns.

The two students, both wearing shorts and tank tops, had just left the fly fishing shop when Bridger's phone went off.

"Holy shit, Rachael, it's my second bestest friend Russel!"

Rachael noticed her boyfriend become visibly excited, and a smile crept across her face as Bridger answered the call and became animated.

"Russel, Russel! How are you, amigo?"

Russel was surprised he'd actually contacted Bridger. "Where have you disappeared to? I've called you a million times and gotten your carrier's stupid recording a million times in response!"

Bridger was giddy with delight, but was mentally brought down to earth with this question. *Shit, what should I tell Russel?* He decided to trust his old friend.

Russel sat on the college campus bench under the shade tree in Washington D.C. and absorbed his friend's story. It was utterly incredible. The STRONG Alliance, Rachael, the silverbacks, Mr. Thompson...it was like hearing about a Hollywood movie.

"You are totally lying to me, aren't you?"

"No, no, I'm not, Russel. It all happened and is still happening."

While Bridger was talking, Russel thought about his note, depicting the silverbacks' death.

"Crap, Bridger. I took a note from the president's office which mentions killing the silverbacks. Also, the president was talking with the Secretary of Defense when I was in his office, and I heard him say the same thing to him."

Bridger was stunned by his friend's comments. "Your note says the silverbacks are going to be killed?"

"Yes, and the president's conversation with Secretary Hastings said the same thing."

"Oh shit! I've got to tell Gramps."

"Yeah, I'd say the sooner the better."

Russel's thoughts were in imagination mode. He couldn't believe how surreal and serendipitous this conversation was. A slight breeze rustled the elm tree's leaves and slightly cooled him.

Rachael and Bridger had gravitated to the shade provided by the store's awning. Rachael stood close to Bridger while he talked. He put the phone in speaker mode so she could hear the conversation. Rachael got Bridger's attention by placing her hand on his forearm.

"Is Russel in danger? His note, it's like espionage. People get locked up for what he did."

Bridger stopped thinking about his gramps and the silverbacks.

"Hey, Russel. Taking the oval office note is pretty serious stuff. Does anybody know you took it, or have it?"

"No, well, I don't think so. The surveillance system was down when I grabbed it, and I haven't talked to anybody about it but you."

"Probably a good thing. Shit, you could end up in jail for stealing stuff out of the Oval Office!"

Russel felt himself getting nervous. He had pushed the reality of his deed into the recesses of his mind and now all the ramifications flooded back into his consciousness. He started to feel a little nauseated.

"I'll destroy the note today. Everything will be okay."

"Good idea. Well, Russel, I've got to get back to Camp Sherman. Sorry about cutting you off, but I'm worried about Gramps and the silverbacks."

"No problem. I totally understand. Hey, give me a call when you have service again. I want to hear about everything, okay?"

"Will do, amigo, adios!"

"Adios. Tell your gramps to be safe."

"I will."

Russel casually examined his phone as he mused about his conversation with Bridger. He thought more about the White House note in his laptop's case. Later tonight, he'd get rid of the paper. A good, hot fire should do the trick. Russel checked his phone. Time for World Geography. He stood up, found his sunglasses, and headed off to Phillips Hall. *Espionage is pretty serious stuff.* Russel stopped and turned around, scanning back the way he came. He checked out the people behind him. *Just a bunch of college students.* A little bit of paranoia accompanied Russel to Geography. He thought to himself, *the sooner I destroy the note, the better.*

CHAPTER 74

AGENT STONE HAD JUST FINISHED REVIEWING THE Oval Office surveillance recordings from the previous day and thought he had Hastings' problem solved. One camera caught McDonald moving from his desk, picking up a pen, and then sitting on the couch. In doing so, the recording showed the president's suitcoat knocking a paper into the wastebasket. *Bingo! Mystery solved.* Stone picked up his desk phone and asked the White House operator to get Hastings on the line.

Secretary Hastings was in a meeting with Intel executives when Stone tried to reach him. He let the phone call go to voicemail. After his meeting, Hastings retrieved the communication and immediately called the Secret Service agent.

"Did I get that right, Stone? You saw the note fall into the trash."

"You did and yes I did, Mr. Secretary. The camera angle was perfect. No mistaking what happened."

"Thanks, agent. You did good work. I need to make a few calls now so thanks once again."

"Certainly, Mr. Secretary."

Hastings put his phone down for a moment. *What an oaf. McDonald could fuck up a wet dream.* The secretary noted the time on his wall clock. He thought about calling off the M.I. guys but reconsidered. *They've probably already interviewed Nelson, and if they haven't, hell, let them do it. Scare the shit out of the kid. It would be good practice for my guys.* Hastings sat back in his chair and relaxed for a moment. He buzzed his aide, inquired about his schedule, and was informed he was free for the rest of the day. After checking his wall clock again, he decided a sauna right before dinner seemed like a good idea. He grabbed his suitcoat and headed for the building's gym.

The low sun was throwing shadows across the Foggy Bottom campus. Russel emerged from Phillips Hall and headed back to Mitchell Hall. He was hungry and hot. A quick shower and then some fast food seemed like a good idea to him. Geography had been pretty interesting. The lecture discussed border changes in the Middle East and the political motivations that instigated the drawing up of new geographic lines. It concluded by mentioning some of the regional disturbances caused by relabeling of areas.

Russel's computer case bumped against his hip and he thought about the White House note. Burning it tonight, outside near the dumpster, and throwing the ashes into the big can seemed like a good idea. His problem would be solved then. As he entered Mitchell Hall, an eerie feeling engulfed him, and spinning around, he quickly checked out who was behind him. Russel saw only fellow students lounging around, conversing, or monitoring their phones. He turned back to the stairwell, and continued slowly up the steps to his dorm floor. The oppressive, spooky feeling resurfaced as he neared the top of the stairs and his floor. Again, he whipped his head around, this time checking out the descending stairwell. There was nothing to be seen. Russel slowly stepped onto his landing and peeked around the corner at his room. It was located at the end of the hall. He jerked his head back behind the corner. *HOLY SHIT!* Two uniformed military men were talking with his roommate. *How could they know?* Russel began to sweat and his pulse raced. *Shit, shit, shit, what should I do?* He pulled out his wallet and checked for his Visa card. It was there along with about a hundred dollars cash. *Okay, no time to panic. Make a plan.* Russel panicked. He ran out Mitchell Hall's back door and sped through the alley to the street. The anxious student hailed a passing cab and jumped into the backseat. .

"Where to, young man?"

"The airport."

The driver laughed and asked, "Which one?"

Russel froze for a second. "The closest international airport."

"You've got it, boss."

The taxi entered the traffic and headed off to Ronald Reagan. It dropped Russel off about twenty minutes later. While in transit, using his phone, Russel found an Alaska Airlines flight leaving for Portland in an hour and a half. He quickly bought a ticket and went through TSA. Finding his gate, he sat down in the corner of the waiting area and surveyed the scene. *I'm totally visible.* The young student jumped up, found the closest "buy anything" airport shop, purchased a *Washington Post*, headed back to the gate, pulled his sunglasses out of his computer case, and put them on. This maneuver caused him to view his White House paper directly. *No destroying you, now. You could be my saving grace.* Russel held the newspaper in front of his face and waited for his boarding call. *What will I do when I get to Portland?* He thought about possible arrival scenarios, but couldn't make a choice. He'd have to think more about his predicament while traveling to Oregon. Hopefully, something would feel right by the time he deplaned in Portland. With his sunglasses on, Russel lowered his paper and studied the people standing and sitting around him. Nobody appeared suspicious. He re-hoisted his publication, and began reading the front page news.

CHAPTER 75

THE BIG CROWN VIC SLIPPED INTO ITS PARKING slot and came to a stop. Superintendent Philip Ross stepped out of his cruiser and adjusted his hat. Looking at the Capitol Building, he noticed a slight haze partially obscuring his vision. The hot dry summer and early fall had allowed numerous fires to get started east of the mountains, and easterly winds were blowing the smoke into the valley. The Gilded Pioneer atop the Capitol Dome shone an orangish, golden hue in the early morning light. Ross headed for the governor's office.

Oregon's Attorney General looked up as Ross entered the room. He smiled at the superintendent and greeted him. Governor O'Connell and her chief of staff sat off to the side and were conversing, and they too smiled at Ross and welcomed him. The earth tones of the office were mellowed by the filtered burnt-colored haze entering the room through translucent white drapes. As Ross sat down, he took in the governor's inner office, and as always, it elicited gratifying emotions from Oregon's top cop. Ross sat down by the politicians and removed his hat. Ross always enjoyed visiting the governor's office.

Attorney General Smith spoke first. "Out of the pan and into the fire!"

Ross smiled at Smith's statement. "Yep. If we thought we had it bad before, we've got it worse now."

The two ladies to his right nodded in agreement. O'Connell spoke to her police superintendent. "How bad is it?"

"Technically, it's the same as before, but more venomous. These old boys can strike out at us. They hold the summit and are armed with automatic rifles. Their request is the same as the students; promise not to log the forest, and they'll give it back to us."

Chief of Staff Roberts spoke next. "Should our strategy change because of these silverbacks and their rifles?"

Philip Ross thought about this question. His immediate thought was *yes and no*.

"I think 'no,' our strategy shouldn't change. We can wait them out, although I need to take more precautions now, in order to keep people safe from possible gunfire."

Robert Smith joined in again. "I think our problem will be solved any day now by the Ninth Circuit Court of Appeals. They're going to weigh in on the president's decree, and all my people tell me they'll throw out his 'order.' Also, the Sierra Club's suit focusing on the Endangered Species side of the issue will regain attention. It's a 'no brainer' the site will be shut down because of the bull trout in the Metolius."

Everyone present thought about Smith's comments, and the room was silent for a moment. Ross glanced over at the governor's desk and appreciated its craftsmanship.

The governor spoke next. "Okay, the strategy is the same. Wait them out. Laura and I, and my press secretary, will put together a 'response' for a press release."

Everyone listening nodded their agreement. Superintendent Ross spent the rest of the meeting talking about defensive measures needed to keep the area safe. Monetary issues were also discussed because of the magnitude of the plans.

As Ross walked down the Capitol steps, he called his aide, Lieutenant Peters, who'd already set all the necessary puzzle pieces into place, and was waiting for Ross's call before getting everything moving. The superintendent knew once he called Peters, one of the more unique OSP maneuvers in state history would be under way. *All over a small logging show. Amazing.* Ross got into his Crown Vic and drove out of the parking lot, heading for Highway 22. His OSP cruiser would not be the only State Police rig on Highway 22 today. Numerous other OSP vehicles planned to rendezvous at the Big Eddy Rise. The occupation site was going to get crowded.

CHAPTER 76

Ranger had heard a "squelch" come from his walkie-talkie while he stood guard duty the previous night. The other silverbacks hadn't noticed the call. They were eating dinner near the fire pit and conversing. It wasn't the agreed-upon contact time, and Ranger had wondered what the content of Bridger's communication would be. He concealed his conversation with Woody's grandson by lowering the volume and gazing away from the group. The young man's news wasn't good. Russel, a high school buddy who worked as a White House intern, had just called Bridger and told his friend about McDonald's plan to kill the silverbacks. Ranger's worst fear was becoming a reality. A military assault seemed likely. The ex-Marine concluded the conversation by assuring Bridger his dad and friends would be all right. Their citadel was bulletproof. After the communication, Ranger decided not to convey the alarming message to his friends until the next day because it would be a serious downer, and letting them have one more carefree night seemed like the right thing to do.

In his early morning communication with Woody's grandson, Ranger asked him to purchase seven New York steaks and a short case of blonde ale at the Sisters store. He was to pack these items and some ice into a dry bag and toss the whole bundle into the river at about 10:00 p.m. Before the drop, Bridger was to paint a big X on both sides of the bag with "glow in the dark" acrylic paint. The ex-Marine explained that when the bundle eddied out below the occupiers' fort, he'd snag it with a grappling hook and hoist it up into camp. Bridger and Rachael, after the conversation, went to Sisters to fulfill their instructions.

All the silverbacks woke around 7:15 the next morning. Dakota started a fire. Hang, after standing guard duty, was relieved by Woody. He joined all the others who were drinking coffee by the fire and slowly waking up. Doc warmed up some previously cooked black beans and rice, added some smoked salmon to the mix, and served the occupiers a bean, rice, and smoked salmon burrito for breakfast.

The light smoke from the campfire rose straight up from the pit and then dispersed high above the rise. It was a chilly, windless morning. All the men were thankful for the fire and the warm food and coffee.

Ranger surveyed the campsite, noting how uncluttered it appeared. The men had slept in the cavern last night. They'd packed all their small, backpacking tents up and stowed them in the big canvas tent, and this endeavor made the bowl appear relatively empty now. Like most camps, the fire pit and cook station were the main gathering points. The large, prominent hunting tent sat off to the side now and received little attention.

Woody stood guard duty and was currently peering out his rifle portal with a pair of binoculars. He was watching the lone state trooper move around at his location when Ranger walked up to his friends and stood in a manner so they all could see him.

"I have some bad news to share."

This statement got all the silverbacks' attention.

"Woody, I want you to listen to what I'm saying."

Woody gave Ranger a thumbs-up sign and Ranger continued.

"Yesterday, Bridger raised me on the walkie-talkie and told me an incredible story. Bottom line, we're probably going to be attacked by the military."

All the men began looking at each other with curious expressions. Doc voiced everyone's questions. "What did Bridger tell you, and how did he get the information?"

The rest of the men nodded their heads in agreement with the inquiry.

"It seems Bridger has a friend who works in the White House. He served food to the president in the Oval Office, and overheard conversations discussing our demise. His friend also stole a paper off the president's desk, stating the same thing in writing."

The silverbacks were silent for a moment and looks of curiosity changed to expressions of concern.

Dakota spoke to Ranger. "Okay, shit, the worst case scenario has bit us in the ass. We knew this could happen. We're in a fricking fort. How can they get to us, Ranger?"

"Well, you're right about the fort part, Dakota, but here's the rub. This is where things get bad. Our location has great defenses against a ground assault. Troops coming up this hill would be easy targets so the most likely military tactic would require some sort of artillery or airstrike preceding the ground attack. Mortar or cannon fire is not likely. They'll probably drop a bomb on us."

The silence in the bowl became tangible. Two ravens, who were sitting above the men, flew down to the basaltic rim and shuffled back and forth, closely watching the humans.

Ranger broke the quiet. "They'll use a smart bomb, which means somebody will light up our camp with a laser, and a jet will fly overhead, dropping ordnance onto our location. The bomb will be drawn to our camp by the laser. These bombs are very accurate."

Hops spoke. "Will we know when they're going to strike?"

"I'm not sure. If they use a fighter bomber, we could hear the jet. The dropping bomb creates a distinctive noise, but when you hear it, you've only got seconds to react."

Hops spoke again. "Shit, this doesn't sound good."

"One thing in our favor, men, is our little cavern. It can easily withstand the explosion of a small bomb, say a 500-lb. ordnance. They'll probably use a night maneuver, and in that case, half of us will be in our bunker."

Tunes joined in the conversation. "If the guards hear the bomb, will they have enough time to jump over the wall and get on the lee side of the explosion?"

Ranger thought for a moment about Tunes' question. "Possibly, but you'd be jumping into plain sight of the ground troops. The bad guys down below will duck their heads when the bomb goes off, but they'll spot you immediately when they return their gaze to the summit. You'd be a sitting duck, out in the open. Easy pickings for a marksman."

Dakota surveyed all his friends and saw various expressions on their faces. Mostly, he saw grim looks of anxiety and frustration. He mentioned what most were pondering. "You know, guys, we could give up and avoid this attack."

Woody had been listening to the discussion. He'd become somewhat nervous by Ranger's frankness and the scene he'd depicted, and Dakota's remark created a "knee jerk" reaction from him. "I'm not giving up. They'll have to chop these trees down over my dead body."

Woody was startled by his own outburst and his friends were, too. Each of them was surprised by its intensity. Their amiable friend rarely appeared this deadly serious or concerned. Ranger reflected about Dakota's and Woody's thoughts and spoke to his friends. "Maybe this would be a good time to take a vote on whether we stay or leave."

A murmur of agreement arose from the friends.

"All right, raise your hand if you want to continue with our occupation."

Woody's hand went up first, followed by Hang's and Tunes'. Dakota raised his next. Doc and Hops examined each other, and both slowly raised their hands.

"Okay it's unanimous, gentlemen. Let's get on with our business, then. I've got a few more tricks up my sleeve and we need to get them operational by this evening. First of all, there needs to be a change in our operating procedures. We need three people on guard duty during the night because all our firing fields need to be viewed on a regular basis. We don't need to worry about the cliff. I set up another motion detector there, and its light and auditory alarm will go off when activated."

Ranger studied his friends and noticed most had partially eaten burritos on the plates. "Let's finish our morning meal before I continue." All the men nodded in agreement and continued consuming their breakfast.

The two camp ravens bent their legs, flapped their wings, and jumped off the basaltic rim. They slowly gained altitude, and croaked loudly several times before gliding down to the OSP encampment.

Ranger left the group and went down into the cavern. Returning to the fire pit area, he held aloft an odd pair of binoculars for his friends to see. "These are night vision goggles, NVGs. They'll allow us to see the laser we'll be targeted with." He walked over to a small rock ledge and rested the NVG on it. "Anytime you want to use them, they'll be here. Be sure to replace them afterwards because these need to be accessible at all times."

Ranger got Hang and Tunes back to sculpting the C-4 and moved on to another project with Doc and Hops. Giving the men a large spool of insulated copper wire, Ranger explained he wanted the wire to enter the tent on the ground, run next to the tent's sidewalls, and emerge from the tent right next to its entrance point. They were to strip the insulation off the wire in three points, and these denuded sections of wire should reside next to the middle sections of each sidewall. The stripped wire should be about seven feet long and be bent into consecutive turns, which when finished, would resemble a grill-like configuration. Drawing a picture on the bowl's dirt floor, Ranger demonstrated what he wanted. His grill pattern seemed to be about one square foot in area. All the men got to work on their projects, leaving Ranger to monitor their results and, along with Woody, watch for the authorities' movements. Ranger eventually joined Dakota, who was on KP duty for the day, and helped prep the afternoon and evening meals.

The sun had risen to its zenith and was now descending. The temperature topped out at seventy-five, and a slight breeze had started down the river. The Rise benefited from the local air movement.

Woody called out from his sentinel location, his voice betraying some nervousness. "Hey, Ranger, you need to come and see what's happening."

Ranger and Dakota left the mess area and joined Woody at the wall. Woody handed Ranger the binoculars. The old soldier stared down the slope past the overturned van and onto the gravel road. Halfway down the passage an odd caravan was approaching them. In the lead was an OSP SWAT van. Following it was a flatbed truck, running in reverse. Bolted onto the end of the rig was a small crane. Ranger wasn't sure what was being transported.

Dakota spoke to Ranger. "Looks like they forgot about our 'No Fly Zone.'"

"Yep, it sure does. These boys mean business. I'm not sure what they've got there, but I bet it doesn't benefit us."

Dakota took the glasses from Ranger and peered through them. "I believe it's a sectioned, portable wall."

Ranger took back the glasses. "You could be right. We'll certainly know pretty soon."

The procession came close to the road's bend. The SWAT van peeled off to the side and came to a halt. The flatbed backed up a little further and stopped within fifteen feet of the road's edge. Deploying from the van and truck's cab, OSP personnel found defensive positions and pointed their M4s up at the occupiers.

Ranger barked out, "Heads down everybody."

Hops and Woody followed Ranger's orders, and the other silverbacks looked up from what they were doing. Ranger went into the canvas tent and came out holding a periscopic binocular system. He crouched down and scuttled back to the rim. All of the men had gathered together by the wall now, and watched Ranger peer down at the OSP troopers.

"What's going on, Ranger?"

"Well, Dakota, it appears you're a seer with exceptional ESP abilities. The crane is lifting wall sections off the flatbed and a couple troopers are putting them together. As I'm watching, a seven- or eight-foot-high partition is being erected at our road's bend, probably bulletproof material."

Ranger kept watching the work unfold below the summit. After the wall was constructed, the SWAT team moved behind the partition, and a few AR muzzles poked through the viewing/firing ports in the panels.

The entire wall was about thirty feet long. The structure blocked the road, ran across the side ditch, and extended into the forest for about ten feet. It was a uniform, neatly sealed wall for the most part. Two sections were skewed somewhat where the wall crossed the ditch, but other than that, the pieces sealed together nicely. A porta potty sat to the side of the road, protected by the end panels of the partition. Leaving one member at the new security point, the SWAT van and flatbed moved back to the far bend in the road. Ranger picked up the binoculars and extended his head just above the basaltic rim. He focused on the furthest bend in the road. A similar wall had been erected there, somewhat inside the forest. Canopy tops appeared behind the partition and Ranger noted an OSP trailer parked near the awnings. The portable wall left the top foot of the trailer exposed. Ranger turned and sat down facing his friends.

"Well, gentlemen, it appears that the OSP have gotten themselves settled in."

Ranger's eyes were met with glum looks and nods. "Hey, gentlemen, this changes nothing. Let's get back at it, and get our chores completed."

The silverbacks returned to their various tasks and continued where they had left off.

"Doc, Hops, holler when you've got everything ready to go," Ranger instructed.

The two men continued fashioning the wire per instructions. Doc was a meticulous worker and the wire stripping went slowly. Laying out the wire course inside the tent hadn't gone much faster, either. Hops eventually stopped helping and just let Doc finish the job.

Doc hollered out, "Okay, Ranger. The wiring is ready for inspection."

Ranger left the mess area and walked over to the tent. He peered into the musty-smelling open space and observed the two men's handiwork. "Nice job."

Locating a particularly odd looking duffel bag in the tent's back recesses, Ranger brought it out into the daylight and began removing articles. A twelve-volt battery revealed itself. A small solar panel system emerged and several pink and red colored boxes with hearts adorning their sides followed. Last to be fetched was a roll of heavy duty tinfoil.

Hops watched with disbelief. "What the hell?"

Doc added another comment. "I hauled that bag up here. No wonder it bit me numerous times and was damn heavy. What are you creating, Ranger?"

"Watch and learn, my friends."

Ranger fashioned double-thick layers of tinfoil to match the shapes of the grilled wire section. The foil's dimensions were a little larger, though. He sandwiched the wire grill with the aluminum and crunched the foil down into the recess between wire runs. Next, he attached the wire ends to the battery posts. Lastly, he hooked up the small solar panel array to the battery. Ranger stood up and inspected his electrical invention. "Voilà, gentlemen! Elementary electronics at work!"

Doc and Hops peered at the wire, tinfoil, and battery system.

Hops cautioned, "All right. You've created areas of resistance, right, and those areas will heat up?"

Ranger smiled. "Let's see." He knelt down and placed his hand on top of one portion of foil. He looked up at Doc and Hops with a twinkle in his eye. "I believe my hand perceives warmth."

Doc watched with a curious expression on his face. He entered the tent, knelt down, and placed his hand on a foil package. "Really, rather clever of you, Ranger."

Hops chuckled to himself. "Well, thanks for the basic electronics 101 class, Ranger. But what does this have to do with our present situation?"

Ranger once again mirthfully smiled at his friends and walked over to one of the valentine-decorated boxes. He broke the packing tape, took the lid off, and pulled out a folded-up wad of plastic that appeared to have a mass of red hair on its top layer. With smiles on their faces, Doc and Hops focused on each other. They began to laugh.

"You shouldn't have, Ranger. Although I was getting somewhat lonely at night," Hops admitted.

Doc clapped Hops on the back and spoke to Ranger. "Do you have any blondes packaged up? I mean, if I have a choice..."

Ranger grinned. "Well as a matter of fact..." He unboxed all the sex dolls and displayed their hair colors. "We've got a redhead, a blonde, and a brunette."

Hearing the light-hearted laughter, Dakota, Tunes, and Hang joined the group. Dakota peered at the plastic bundles and began laughing also.

"Very thoughtful of you, Ranger. The nights are becoming longer and a little chilly."

Tunes and Hang watched, not understanding what the humor was about.

Doc glanced over at the young men. "These are sex dolls, boys. Take your pick."

They smiled sheepishly.

Still smiling, Hang regarded the elder silverbacks. "Well, I guess I'm partial to brunettes, but really, gentlemen, is this the time or place?"

All the older men chorused, "Absolutely!"

Ranger stopped laughing and cleared his throat. "Okay, okay, here's the deal. Remember my 'rule of thumb'? Don't let the enemy know what you're really doing. Well, these ladies will fool our adversaries into thinking we are sleeping in the hunting tent. During the night, we'll place our beautiful friends on top of the coil systems, and they'll heat up. Any thermal imaging intel gathered during the evening or early morning will register our ladies. The bad guys will think we're sleeping above ground."

Tunes looked at Ranger. "You really thought about this before arriving here?"

"Yep. I went through numerous scenarios, and an airstrike with preliminary intel was one of them. I didn't know where we could hunker down in order to avoid the ordnance, but our cavern took care of that mystery."

Doc mused aloud, "Amazing, Ranger, really amazing!"

"Okay, enough idle chatter, gents, there's more to do. Hang, Tunes, let's get the pinecones finished. Doc and Hops, blow up our female companions and place them in a prone position on top of the tinfoil. You might insulate the foil with something thin, and check to see if the system really gets our ladies hot."

Dakota called out to his friends, "Hey, it is way past lunchtime, but I threw together some peanut butter and jelly sandwiches. They're piled up over at the mess table."

All the occupiers ate the sandwiches and then continued on with their activities. Hang, Tunes, and Ranger finished off the pinecones. They had a pile of twelve cones sitting next to them.

"We'll deploy these guys tonight, but first a little paint job."

Ranger retrieved a spray can of paint from a duffel bag filled with a dull, copper colored, fast-dry acrylic paint.

"You boys paint these explosives lightly with this can; don't completely cover the cones with paint. Your work should be slightly mottled, allowing the C-4 color to mix with the paint and create a camo type appearance."

The shadows lengthened and dusk drew near. All the men noticed the temperature quickly dropping and threw on extra layers. Dakota served up rice and a smoked salmon dish covered with canned gravy, and they sat around the fire eating. The flames flickered light onto each man. The gray-haired, gray-bearded men's faces reflected their maturity. The firelight enhanced the age lines that etched their way across their faces. In contrast, Tunes and Hang's young physiques displayed the roots of their elders' beginnings. Tunes' dark complexion and short curly hair mimicked a youthful Doc, and Hang's lithe body with light complexioned, Anglo facial features mirrored the other silverbacks' younger days.

The camp ravens had returned to roost high up in the closest Ponderosa. They stretched their wings and shuffled back and forth on their branch while they watched the fire-lit scene below. The stars were subdued this evening due to a three-quarter moon, and the birds' attention was easily diverted to the men below.

Dinner was completed and Dakota gathered plates and washed them. Before he departed the group with Hang and Tunes, Ranger announced he was the chef tomorrow and had planned a meal fit for kings. This of course sparked much speculation amongst the friends because they all knew Ranger's culinary gifts were limited at best.

The ex-Marine and his young understudies gathered for the completion of the C-4 task. They placed detonators into each package and wrapped detonator wires several times around the sculpted cones. Ranger identified several places within twenty to thirty yards of the basaltic rim where he thought advancing troops would seek cover right before they intended to charge the summit. Several hours were spent running wire and placing the cones on either side of tree trunks or nearby downed logs. Hang proved to be particularly agile in placing the cones. He wore dark clothing and Ranger had painted his face and hands in night camouflage. Sitting behind the recently erected barrier, the lone OSP trooper on duty didn't notice any of the movement above him. The few times he regarded the summit, Hang wasn't moving and was not seen.

All the occupiers retired by 9:00 p.m. except for Tunes, Dakota, and Doc, who were on guard duty. At 10:15, Ranger checked on the ladies and found their bodies to be noticeably warmer than the night air. He placed sections of sheet over each and retrieved a rope ladder and grappling system from one of his duffels. Quietly sneaking to the cliff side of the summit, Ranger crawled over the wall and alit on the slight ledge beneath the basaltic rim. He used his night glasses to check on the sheriff's deputy who had surveillance duty, and noted the sentinel peacefully sleeping in the front seat of his cruiser. Next, he peered down into the Big Eddy and watched the circular pattern of white bubbles as they drifted in the sluggish whirlpool. A grin spread across his face. There below him, slowly following the Eddy's current, was a glowing X. *Bingo!* Ranger attached his rope ladder to the rim and climbed down to the larger ledge below. He uncoiled the rope and lowered the treble hooks down to near the river's surface. The dry bag floated right beneath his hooks. Ranger dropped the tines onto the bag, but caught nothing, and the X continued on for another circuit. After four tries and misses, Ranger decided to lower the hooks into the water and pull up when the bag returned. The bag came around again, and on the first try, one hook caught the dry bag's closure system and the rope became taut. Ranger hauled up his prize, and after regaining the ledge just below the basaltic rim, he checked to see if the deputy was still asleep. Finding the guard resting, Ranger gathered together all of his essentials and clandestinely reentered the bowl. He stashed his dinner behind a large rock next to Woody's latrine, figuring nobody would be poking around the "shitter" and accidentally discover his surprise. It had been a long day filled with unnerving news, and lots of activity. Thinking about tomorrow's dinner buoyed Ranger's thoughts. The ex-Marine quietly climbed down Hops' ladder and found his sleeping mat and bag. He bedded down listening to old men's loud breathing and occasional snoring.

CHAPTER
77

THREE HUMVEES DROVE SOUTH TOWARD CENTRAL Oregon, leaving behind sagebrush and rabbit brush. Highway 97 eventually took them through orchards, wheat fields, and windfarms. The convoy crossed the Columbia River, went through Biggs Junction, and continued south on 97. For a while, the cavalcade passed through wheat fields, then, once again it found an arid environment filled with sagebrush and juniper trees.

One Hummer pulled a communications trailer with satellite capabilities. Another hauled a utility trailer loaded with the squad's bivouac and personal gear, and the front Humvee carried the squad leader, Sergeant First Class Robert Jefferson, and his close friend, Staff Sergeant Bodhi Forrest. Both men were southerners and prided themselves on their "deep south" family heritage. Forrest could trace his ancestry back to Lt. General Bedford Forrest of the Confederacy. The staff sergeant rarely missed a chance to inform a newcomer about his ancestral link to the infamous cavalry officer.

As the small convoy traveled south, Forrest and Jefferson reminisced about their numerous antics at Yakima Training Center, their present military assignment. One such situation dealt with the Confederate flag. The men had been chastised in their CO's office for driving onto the base with Rebel flags flying off the back of their pickups. The sergeants had been flaunting the flags for several weeks before Lt. Colonel Henry heard of the situation. A number of soldiers had complained about the pennants, and eventually, through the chain of command, the problem had reached Henry.

The lieutenant colonel called the two sergeants into his office and had quickly noted their haughty, superior attitudes. He flatly stated to them they needed to "cease and desist" from the irritating display of the Rebel flag, and they were reminded the Army was a desegregated force where rank, not ethnicity, determined superiority. Lt. Colonel Henry further suggested if the sergeants didn't agree with his order, they would be court-martialed and busted several ranks. Both men had left Henry's office soberly, but upon entering the hall, grinned at each other and high-fived. Even though their insulting behavior had been banned from the base, the two soldiers knew their "off duty" lifestyle for the most part was not the Army's business, and the Rebel flags displayed on their porches would remain in place.

While Jefferson and Forrest began talking about the soldiers in their command, the caravan continued south on Highway 97. Directly behind their rig was the Hummer pulling the communication trailer. The communication trailer Humvee was manned by Spec 4 James Lee and Private First Class Thomas Fitzgerald. Lee, a signal corpsman, was of American Chinese ancestry. He was responsible for setting up and maintaining communications with Lt. Colonel Henry. Private Fitzgerald was an infantryman assigned to the Yakima Training Center (YTC) Security Force. In the last Humvee, which pulled the utility trailer, rode Spec 4 Eddy Turner and Private First Class Howard Abramson. Turner, the squad's medic, was a young black man from Boston. Private Abramson, from Brooklyn, New York, was also assigned to YTC's security detail. First Sergeant Jefferson and Sergeant Forrest had privately given their troops nicknames: Spec 4 Lee was "China," Private Fitzgerald was "Irish," Spec 4 Turner was "Blackie," and Private Abramson was "Moses." This blatant use of ethnic racism would have brought the hammer down on the two sergeants, but the two men were smart enough to keep it to themselves, and for their private amusement, only.

The convoy entered Madras and turned west, heading in Lake Billy Chinook's direction. Eventually the Humvees found logging roads, and the sergeants used their satellite navigation system to reach Camp Sherman.

Upon arriving at the Camp Sherman store, three of the camo-dressed personnel, one from each Humvee, got out of their rigs. They entered the small grocery and bought snacks. When the owner, Jack Smith, rang up their purchases, he jokingly asked the soldiers if they were lost and got a vague response about local maneuvers. Only the sergeant talked with Smith. After purchasing their munchies, all three soldiers left the store, rejoined their comrades, and loaded up. The convoy rolled out of the cramped parking area, across the small Metolius Bridge, and headed out of town. At a three-way stop, they turned right and traveled on to the occupation site.

Most of the soldiers had grown up far away from old forests. Spec 4 Lee was the only member of the squad who'd seen ancient trees firsthand. He'd been raised in the Seattle area, and as a boy had camped and hiked in the North Cascades. The rest of the squad hailed from the East Coast, Midwest, or Deep South. None of them had seen big trees like the tall, stately Ponderosas.

Private Abramson gazed at Specialist Turner, "Holy cow! These are monsters! What do they feed these things?"

"You asking me, Abramson? Hell, I don't know. Biggest tree I've ever seen is my family's Christmas tree."

Abramson laughed at Turner's remark. "Shoot, we don't have a Christmas tree. I guess the one at the White House is about the same size as these."

"Probably so, Abramson."

The two soldiers drove on, annoyed by the dust from the Humvees ahead of them. Abramson continued examining the huge conifers.

Spec 4 Lee and Private Fitzgerald were right behind the sergeants' rig. They'd also been scanning the forest as they drove along.

"Hey, Lee. Let's drop back a bit, and lose some of this dust."

"Can't. The sergeant wants a tight formation."

"Well, hell yeah. He's in front and not swallowing dust like we are."

"We're almost there, Fitzgerald. Sit back and enjoy the scenery."

The private gazed out his window. "I've never seen anything like this, Lee. These trees look like skyscrapers. How tall are they?"

"Well, they seem just as big as the old Doug firs and hemlocks I used to hike and camp under. I bet some are close to three hundred feet."

"Shit, that's like a twenty-story building."

"Never really thought of it that way, Fitzgerald. Any way you cut it, they're pretty tall."

Sergeant Jefferson and Forrest were enjoying watching the two Humvees in their rearview mirrors.

"They're eating a lot of dust, first sergeant."

"Yes they are, Sergeant Forrest."

Both men laughed and knocked knuckles.

"Got to keep a tight formation and be 'Army Ready.'"

The two men laughed some more. They turned away from the mirrors and focused forward. They'd already passed through the first OSP blockade and now, the second barricade appeared ahead of them along with the Command Center.

"Looks like we're here, Forrest."

"Yep, it certainly does."

First Sergeant Jefferson halted his Humvee about twenty feet from Superintendent Ross's command trailer, and the Army sergeants stepped out of their vehicle and looked around. Sergeant Forrest noticed the desert camo pattern he'd chosen matched the surrounding forest's colors. He mentally congratulated himself. The two soldiers were wearing fatigues with soft caps, and wore only pistols for weaponry. They peered at the OSP trailer and noticed a trooper walking their way. They began moving to the officer.

Superintendent Ross was aware of the small convoy. His initial roadblock had radioed Ross and told him of the military's presence. Upon receiving this information, Ross sent Lt. Peters into Camp Sherman to phone Attorney General Smith. He'd need to know about the military's arrival. The superintendent and the two sergeants met in the roadway and shook hands. Jefferson noted the two stars on Ross's collar. *We've got a big dog, here.*

"First Sergeant Jefferson and Staff Sergeant Forrest, sir. Pleasure to meet you."

"Good morning, boys. I'm Superintendent Ross. What brings you gentlemen to my neck of the woods?"

Jefferson noted the "my" in Ross's greeting and responded. "Our orders are to offer assistance, sir, and if you need none, we'll just maintain our position, and communicate our surveillance to Command."

"What Command would that be, sergeant?"

"Lt. Colonel Henry from Yakima Training Center gave us our orders, sir. He is in direct command of this mission."

Ross thought a training center was an odd origination for a military convoy and deployment.

"Do you have any written orders I could see, sergeant?"

"Not at this moment, sir. They are forthcoming."

The three men quietly focused on each other. The sergeants offered no more conversation and Ross had gotten the information he needed.

"Well, sergeants, you can set up camp across from me."

He motioned to the other side of the road. The OSP boss wanted the soldiers nearby so he could keep an eye on them.

"No fires, gentlemen, and feel free to avail yourselves of the food under the blue canopy. There's a coffee urn, and several coolers filled with sandwiches, pop, water, and the like. The awning's shade feels pretty good around midday, too."

Ross eyed the team leader. "Sergeant, after you've seen to your camp deployment, come to my trailer, and we'll figure out some ways for your men to help our situation."

"Roger that, superintendent."

After their short, to the point, conversation, the three men returned to their responsibilities and departed. As Sergeants Jefferson and Forrest walked back to their convoy, Jefferson directed Forrest, "Get the grunts setting up camp. I want everything 'Army Ready' in two hours."

"Roger that, first sergeant."

All the soldiers were standing together next to the second Humvee. They also were in camo fatigues with soft caps and were brandishing sidearms. The two sergeants walked up and stopped next to their troops.

First Sergeant Jefferson instructed, "Lee, get our communication link set up with Colonel Henry. Give me a shout when it's operational."

"Will do, first sergeant."

Lee studied the tree canopy above, searching for a direct satellite shot, and finding one, he returned to his Humvee and began maneuvering his trailer into position. Jefferson returned to his Humvee, fetched some maps, and walked over to the OSP canopy. Sitting down at a long table provided for the troopers and sheriff's deputies, he spread his maps out and began familiarizing himself with the terrain. Several OSP personnel in tactical gear sat at another table and greeted the sergeant. The first sergeant acknowledged the troopers with a nod.

Staff Sergeant Forrest directed the unloading of the utility trailer and the establishment of the squad's bivouac. The soldiers had two yurt-styled, teepee tents, and Spec 4 Turner and Privates Fitzgerald and Abramson were raising the structures. They'd cleared an area of bunchgrass, pinecones, and manzanita bush. With the three soldiers working together, the two tents went up quickly. After the camoed structures went up, Abramson and Turner started moving cots and personal gear into their living quarters. Fitzgerald began setting up the mess area. Sergeant Forrest helped him erect the mess canopy, and then went to check on the progress of Spec 4 Lee. Lee had stabilized the trailer, and a generator was humming away, providing power for the unit.

After a couple hours' work, the soldiers had completely set up their base camp. They hadn't needed to fashion a commode because of the nearby porta potties provided by the OSP. To a man, the small squad was thankful for the portable "shitters," and they would not miss the awkwardness of a pit toilet. Turner, Fitzgerald, and Abramson sat in the shade of their mess canopy and took a break. Abramson reached into a cooler and brought out three sports drinks for his comrades.

As the soldiers sat back and enjoyed their beverages, two ravens alighted above them in the nearest Ponderosa. The birds cocked their heads from side to side and took in the scene below. Humvees, soldiers, trailers, tents, and mess area were all noticed. Satisfied with their observations, the ravens squawked loudly and returned to their previous perch, calling out to anyone who cared to listen.

Sergeant Forrest left the communications trailer and tracked down his squad leader. "Our link is operational, first sergeant."

"Excellent. Let's call home and get Lt. Colonel Henry up to speed with our progress."

The two sergeants walked over to the trailer and climbed inside. Spec 4 Lee was adjusting several knobs on the main board. He wore a headset and was talking with Lt. Colonel Henry. When the first sergeant entered, Lee handed him the headset and showed Jefferson how to adjust volume and reduce chatter. Forrest dismissed Lee and after the spec 4 left, shut the trailer's rear door. Lee joined his fellow soldiers at the mess area and grabbed a drink.

After talking with Lt. Colonel Henry, First Sergeant Jefferson left the communications trailer and walked to the OSP encampment. Henry had reminded his sergeant about offering his assistance, and he was ready to negotiate with Superintendent Ross about his squad's potential responsibilities. The first sergeant's military boots forcefully crunched the road's gravel as he approached the trailer. He knocked on the door and was ushered in. Upon entering the OSP trailer, he saw the superintendent conversing with another trooper. This officer was much younger, and wore the dark blue tactical fatigues of the OSP, but didn't have body armor or helmet on. Ross introduced Trooper Mills to Jefferson. The two men shook hands and extended introductory courtesies. After formal greetings, all three sat at the dinette and commenced talking.

"We've got our position operational, superintendent. How can my troops help your situation here?"

"Mills and I have been talking about what you and your men could do, sergeant. Extra bodies could help our containment of the occupation greatly."

"Containment, sir?"

"Yes. The governor has asked us to respond to the occupation in this manner."

Jefferson thought to himself, *that's pretty limp. Eco-terrorists, brandishing assault rifles and threatening people, are just going to be contained?*

"What can my men do to help your operation, sir?"

"I think nightly 'recon' would be extremely helpful."

The first sergeant blankly looked at Ross. *I bet it would be extremely helpful and a big pain in the ass for my men!* "What exactly did you have in mind?"

"Some foot recon in the forest and some vehicle patrols on the lower road between 2200 hours and 0600 would be very helpful. We'll have to get our transmitters on the same frequencies and some other logistical matters in line, but those security measures on your part would tighten things up."

First Sergeant Jefferson stood up. "It all sounds doable, superintendent. Let me confer with my men and work out a duty schedule. I'll get back to you with the details."

The sergeant left the trailer and headed back to his bivouac site. Mills eyed Ross and smiled. "He didn't seem too happy with your suggestions, superintendent."

"No he didn't. I really screwed up his 'simple surveillance' mission. All joking aside, trooper. I'm a little concerned that the U.S. Army is on site. This is really strange, and possibly a breach of legal protocol. I'm anxious to hear from Lt. Peters. Hopefully he can provide some information and answers from Attorney General Smith about the military presence."

"Does anything change for us because of the soldiers?"

"I'm not sure. Let's hear from Peters first before we address that question. Although one thing needs to happen: We need 24/7 surveillance of our military guests. I want to know what they're up to at all times."

" Easily accomplished, sir. There's always at least one trooper under the canopy. We'll make it a standing order for the lowest rank present to watch our friends."

"Good, Mills."

Mills stood up and took his leave. Ross glanced out his trailer's window at the Army's encampment. He noted First Sergeant Jefferson addressing his men. *What's this all about?* He arose from the dinette, went over to the refrigerator, and pulled out fixings for a sandwich. *The U.S. military should not be encamped next to me. Something is terribly wrong here.*

CHAPTER
78

THE MOON HAD RISEN AND WAS HIGH IN THE EVEning sky. It was nearly full and cast eerie, well-defined shadows throughout the forest. In several more nights, the orb would reach its zenith, which meant the contrasts would be even more vivid.

First Sergeant Jefferson left his tent, leaving Sergeant Forrest asleep, snoring in his cot. The sergeant was in full tactical gear. He'd donned his body armor, plus wore a headset for communications. He carried an M4 with a night scope in one hand and a partially filled field pack in the other. Due to the evening's brightness, he'd left his NVGs behind. Having been informed of his squad leader's recon mission, Spec 4 Lee was in the communication trailer with his headset on, monitoring his assigned channel and equipment.

Earlier in the day, Jefferson and Forrest created the duty schedule for their squad. Spec 4 Turner and Private Abramson were to patrol the lower Metolius road in two-hour intervals during the late evening and early morning hours. They'd sleep during the day. Sergeant Forrest and First Sergeant Jefferson were to do forest recon, and Spec 4 Lee and Fitzgerald were to man the communication center, keeping in contact with Lt. Colonel Henry and the recon patrols. Sergeant Jefferson had relayed all these details to Superintendent Ross.

Ross told the first sergeant his men should not engage anyone in a hostile manner. The soldiers were to communicate any possible breaches of security to Ross, and OSP troopers would be dispatched to the soldiers' location. There were a half dozen OSP troopers and county deputies on site at all times, available to handle any possible situation. Sergeant Jefferson agreed with Superintendent Ross and dismissed himself from the meeting. On the way back to his bivouac area, Jefferson visibly smiled and chuckled. The idea of calling for the police to take over a possible breach of security made him laugh. *Not likely, Superintendent Ross, not likely.*

Jefferson raised Spec 4 Lee and told him of his deployment. Lee "Rogered" the message and continued his watch. Jefferson, in his camo and painted face, headed for the unkempt portion of forest about a quarter mile from their location. On his back was his field pack. He moved from tree to tree in a clandestine manner, and eventually reached the scrubby, forested area. Yesterday, while arriving on site, Jefferson saw a particularly tall tree that now was his destination. He crossed the road and disappeared into the dense tree stand. Finding the tall Ponderosa, he noted with pleasure it was easily climbable because the big yellowbelly's limbs started about ten feet from the ground and continued upward in a fairly uniform manner. The sergeant dropped his pack and removed from it a chair system. It was very similar to a deer hunter's tree stand, except legs did not extend from the chair to the ground. One simply tied this system to the hoist tree. Finding a bushy manzanita plant, the soldier cut it off at the ground, attached the bush and his small saw to a short piece of rope pulled from his pack, and secured the rope to his belt. Next, Jefferson threw another line over the closest stout branch, and created a loop in the rope's end. He threaded the line's other end through the eye and pulled everything taut. He now had an access rope he could climb. Next, the soldier attached the tree chair to his back using the seat's shoulder straps. He pulled himself up onto the conifer's lowest branch and rested for a moment. The first sergeant caught his breath, then headed up the old giant, branch by branch, being careful not to snag the brush or saw on any limbs he passed. He occasionally checked out the Big Eddy Rise while he moved upwards, trying to find the best tactical location for his perch.

Jefferson's tree was about two hundred fifty feet tall, about one hundred feet higher than the Rise. He eventually stopped in a position where he could see into the summit's bowl. After attaching the chair to the Ponderosa, he took a break and relaxed in his perch. He smelled his hands and enjoyed the sweet aroma of pitch. His bird's eye view was unique and otherworldly. The dark shadows on the forest floor formed linear patterns tilting away from the moon's location. The soldier pulled up the manzanita bush and secured it in front of his stand for camouflage. Next, he climbed higher until he found a relatively straight, stout branch. He cut it from the tree and lopped off the branch's end; this left him a needleless length of wood about five feet long. Returning to his perch, he secured the branch to two limbs, radiating away from his position. It rested just above the newly positioned camo barrier. The leafy bush would hide the first sergeant from view and the newly hewed branch would offer a secure mount for his sniper rifle. When he completed his roost, he swung his M4 off his back and held it up in firing position. He peered into the bowl through the night scope and targeted an occupier.

"Bang, you're dead, old man."

The sergeant was pleased with his accomplishment. The tree stand stood where he could target the tent, allowing the smart bomb to do its job, and if any occupiers survived the hit, the first sergeant would neutralize them using his Remington 700 sniper rifle. He was very accurate with it at this range. Jefferson climbed back down from his stand and continued on with his recon. He raised Lee again, and told him of his return. The spec 4 "Rogered" the first sergeant's message, and Jefferson headed for the Metolius and its riverbank. He followed the stream's course. The water's black surface sparkled with moonlight in the rippled areas, and in the quiet eddies, the moon's reflection was brilliant. If you stared closely at the still waters, you could see craters reflected in the smooth surface. Leaving the river bank just south of the eddy, the soldier again moved from tree to tree. The rise occupiers were unaware of his presence, and as he passed the OSP barricade and its lone sentinel, Jefferson targeted the officer on duty with his rifle.

"Bang! You're dead."

He smiled to himself, *this is too easy,* and continued on to his encampment. He quietly slipped into the bivouac area and into his tent. Placing the barrel of his M4 onto Forrest's neck, the first sergeant said aloud, "You're dead, sergeant."

Forrest woke immediately and brushed away Jefferson's rifle barrel.

"Very funny." He rubbed the sleep out of his eyes.

"I got our stand into position. Piece of cake. Could have taken out one of the old farts too if I had my Remington 700."

Forrest yawned. "Got to wait for orders, Jefferson, got to wait for orders."

"Well anyway, Forrest, tag, you're it."

The sleepy sergeant got up and put on his gear. Jefferson took off his equipment and fatigues, climbed into the sack, and was asleep before Forrest left the camp. The staff sergeant "keyed" Lee and headed north. He wanted to scout a ravine he'd noticed earlier in the day. It ran from the road all the way to the summit's basaltic lip. Forrest felt it could provide easy, undetected access to the hill's summit, and this could greatly benefit the squad's assault of the occupation campsite. He stepped out of camp and quietly blended in with his surroundings, disappearing from view.

CHAPTER
79

It was a rather somber day in the Big Eddy Rise's bowl. All the men had spent their waking moments the previous night thinking about the imminent attack. None had really thought this would happen, and the reality of their situation weighed heavily on the silverbacks.

The men climbed out of their cavern around 7:00 a.m. and constructed a fire. Their supply of branches, cones, and pine needles was almost depleted, but nobody seemed concerned. In the back of each person's mind rested the thought that a surplus of fuel was no longer needed. Woody fixed coffee and a scramble of potatoes, onions, mushrooms, and beef jerky. The occupiers sat quietly and enjoyed his breakfast entrée.

After eating, Ranger gathered everyone together near the fire pit and discussed defense strategy for the fortress. He left Doc on guard duty. Ranger showed them how to twist the Hellbox's dial in a quick, decisive manner allowing the handheld device to send the necessary electrical charge to the plastic explosive detonator. He also discussed how to use the rifle ports in a safe, effective manner. Each person was to cover the firing field directly in front of him. These ranges overlapped so the entire hillside was covered by the four rifle positions. Nobody needed to endanger themselves, unnecessarily, by looking up and away from their position.

The ex-Marine told each man to load a daypack with his extra banana magazine and the Hellboxes for their position. Upon arriving at their post, each person was to connect the detonator wires to the Hellboxes. It was an easy one-step process requiring no tools.

Ranger continued by discussing the possible scenario: they might get overrun. For this situation, he directed Woody and Tunes to make the narrow, cavern tunnel into an egress route. During the previous night, the ex-Marine and Hang had cut a manzanita bush from the hillside and brought the plant into the bowl.

Woody and Tunes were to remove rock from the small entrance and create a hole at the top of the rock pile barrier big enough for the silverbacks to crawl through. After creating their escape route, they were to hide the new opening with the manzanita bush. After discussing the exit strategy, Ranger continued detailing the defense of their position. He stressed once the bomb exploded, they needed to quickly regain the bowl and their rifle positions because the bad guys would soon advance on the summit, and the silverbacks needed to be in position.

Being on guard duty the previous night, Ranger had watched a Humvee travel the lower road several times. His responsibility also had been the gully side of the basaltic rim. Upon observing Sergeant Forrest crawl up the ravine toward the summit, he'd targeted the soldier with his weapon. Fortunately for Forrest, he turned back down the hill before becoming a threat to the encampment. The old soldier told his friends about the military vehicles and the perimeter probe of their defenses. Hearing proof positive of the military's presence quieted the silverbacks, and Ranger chose this moment to retrieve his river package from behind the latrine. He brought the dry bag to the fire pit and began unpacking it.

Doc smiled at his old friend. "What surprise do you have for us? A seven-passenger helicopter would be great!"

The men laughed at Doc's comment.

"Nope. No whirlybirds, Doc, but maybe something even better. I'll let you be the judge of that."

Ranger pulled out of the rafting duffel several bags of ice and three six-packs of blonde ale. This received smiles and oohs and aahs from his friends. With a final, magician-like movement, he pulled out seven steaks from the bag, and his effort was rewarded with applause and laughter.

"Tonight's dinner, gentlemen, consists of a potato skillet dish and a thick-cut, rib eye steak. Oh, am I forgetting the beverages? Yes, I am. We have a locally brewed ale which I've heard is exquisite."

The silverbacks were once again smiling, animated, and conversing with each other.

Hops called out to Ranger. "My hat's off to you, Ranger. You know how to treat your friends."

Ranger accepted the warm thanks from his companions. He then sent Woody and Tunes off to prepare the escape route. Next, he directed the remaining silverbacks to "police" up their rifle positions, removing anything that might trip them up. Also, each rifleman was responsible for creating a safe, explosion-proof area for the detonation wires.

After sending everyone off to fulfill their tasks, he and Doc cleaned up the mess area and put the beer and steaks back on ice. Then they stood guard duty while the others continued with their jobs.

Ranger picked up the binoculars and was scanning the terrain. He didn't expect to see the military out and about in the daylight, but was nonetheless vigilant to his task. While he scanned the forest, both near and far, an aberration caught his attention. It was in a tall, benign tree a good distance away, one he'd viewed many times before. It now had an unusual bundle of vegetation near the top. Ranger refocused the binoculars, and again inspected the greenish vegetation cluster. *So that's how the bad guys will light us up.* Ranger had Doc come over and use the binoculars. With a little verbal instruction, Doc found the manzanita cluster in the tree. The ex-Marine explained the significance of the tree stand.

"Seems like they're getting ready to attack us, Ranger."

"Yep, it most certainly does, Doc."

Doc dropped the binoculars down and gazed at his old friend. "Can you keep us alive?"

Ranger thought for a moment before answering his good friend. "I think so. Our best defense is the bunker that nobody but us knows about. Everyone's ignorance is a huge plus for us. Repulsing the attack is dicey. It won't be easy, but I believe all we have to do is beat them back once. If we inflict some pain on them, they'll think twice about a second attempt." After a moment, Ranger added, "How complete is your medical kit?"

"I've got everything we need for bleeding, broken bones, and pain. If there's any serious injuries, we'll need a real ER."

"Well then, let's keep the injuries nonexistent or minor, Doc."

"Sounds like an excellent plan, my friend."

The old physician looked down at the overturned van with its gaping hole in the roof, facing them.

"Seems like a year since we rushed out of Woody's truck."

"Yep, it truly does."

"You know, Woody never said anything about the hole you cut into his van's top."

Ranger smiled at Doc. "He's probably got bigger, more important things on his mind."

"Yeah, you could be right. Although, I think he might just be a forgiving, 'wine glass half full' type of guy who sees the possibility of a really cool moon roof in his rig."

Ranger laughed out loud and clapped his friend on the back. "You're probably right, Doc. You're probably right."

Ranger left Doc on guard duty and began checking on everyone's progress. After reviewing his friends' endeavors, he gravitated to the mess area and started prepping for his steak dinner. He was going to make a skillet potato entrée like Woody's breakfast dish, although he was going to add some spicy summer sausage for a little "zing."

The ex-Marine glanced up at the orangish sun, noting it was past midday. The haze had cooled things down considerably, and all the men were now wearing long-sleeve shirts and pants. He thought about the temperature adjustment and wondered about the other changes he'd soon see. The possibilities were many. Some were just plain frightening.

CHAPTER
80

The night was awash with shadows, and everything was black or white. Colonel Rodgers drove his personal car from the Administration Building over to the Operations Center, parked near the front entrance, and passed through security. A number of salutes and expressions of "Good evening, sir" accompanied him as he walked to the base's small operations room. One last salute with the outside guard allowed Rodgers access to his "eye in the sky" facility. Two airmen monitoring screens quickly rose to their feet and saluted the colonel.

Rodgers saluted back. "At ease, airmen."

Both the E4s sat down in front of their computers.

After removing his hat and laying it on a nearby table, the colonel surveyed his Operations Center. There were multiple screens located on all the walls above head height and slightly tilted downwards, and in the middle of the room, a long table ran almost the entire length of the space. Computers and screens with chairs sitting in front of them lined both sides of the tables. An airman at the end of the table called out to her CO, "Sir, you'll want to sit next to me. Our drone's been in the air for about an hour, and should be over the coordinates in about ten minutes."

Rodgers sat down next to the young airman. She was a pretty, Hispanic woman who appeared to be all business. Before her sat a board with several joy sticks she was manipulating. Numerous buttons, dials, and levers were mounted on the mainboard, and occasionally she adjusted one of them.

"The screen directly in front of me, sir, will be our 'real time' monitor, and up on the wall, across from us, those screens can freeze shots, enlarge images, or go back to previous settings or pictures."

Rodgers always liked participating in intel gathering. The Operations Center was technical and powerful. It could do almost anything. As he watched the closest monitor, the colonel witnessed a sagebrush landscape acquire juniper trees, and then become divided into farmland with scrub growth between agriculture plots. Eventually, large tree tops began to cluster together and the moon's light began to reflect off numerous bodies of water. Some were ribbon like and others depicted lakes and reservoirs.

"Getting close, colonel."

The drone began following a silvery, snake-like waterway. On either side of the stream, large canopies partially covered the stream's aerial view. At one location, a small gathering of buildings sat on either side of the river, and numerous roadways converged. Occasionally, soft yellow light shone into the forest from one of the dwellings the drone's camera system was picking up.

The airman slowed the drone up as the picture showed a straight section of river with no dwellings nearby.

"We're almost on site, sir. Watch the monitor and tell me when to maintain my position."

"We're looking for a small rise. There may be a few tents at its summit and a fire pit. It should have roughly a half dozen people camped there."

"Okay, sir. I'll begin circling the area and hopefully find your summit."

Colonel Rodgers and the E4 watched the drone's feed as it tightly circled the location.

"There, sir. I think we've got it."

The moon's glow lit up the scene below.

"Let's enlarge this, airman."

The E4 adjusted a few dials and the drone's camera zoomed in, staying in focus. Still navigating with her sticks, the airman adjusted a few knobs, improving the picture's brightness.

There, below, in plain view, was the summit of Big Eddy Rise. The hunting tent could be seen clearly resting next to a smoldering fire pit, and a wisp of smoke still drifted up from the embers.

"Okay, airman. Let's get a thermal reading from the site."

The airman made some more adjustments using different knobs and levers, and eerie ghost-like figures appeared on the screen. The fire pit became exaggerated with frosty, white light. Three thermal images of sentries appeared on the inside of the summit's rock wall, while more images appeared inside the silhouette of the hunting tent. Three more occupiers were in the shelter, asleep.

"Okay, airman. Let's back out a little and check the surrounding area." The E4 did as instructed. Rodgers got a birds-eye view of the surrounding region. He noted the various roadblock locations and the OSP Command Center near the summit. After Rodgers was sure of his intel, he told the airman to bring the drone "home."

"Good work, airman. You did yourself proud tonight."

"Thank you, sir."

Rodgers went over to where he'd placed his hat and readjusted it onto his head. The two airmen came to attention and once again saluted their CO.

"At ease."

Instead of returning to his office, the airfield CO headed for his "off base" residence. He thought about his ensuing phone call to Secretary Hastings. He would be pleased to know a 500-lb. bomb could easily take out the occupiers' encampment. Rodgers thought some more about the president's contribution to his financial stability. *Two million dollars would be a great retirement nest egg.* He'd find out more about his illegal pension when conversing with Secretary Hastings.

CHAPTER 81

IN THE DARKNESS OF THE MORNING, THE PHONE'S alarm went off: "...*what a wonderful world.*" Brian groggily rubbed his hand across his eyelids, trying to massage the blurriness from his eyes. The comfortable bed invited him to stay and sleep longer. *Nope, I've got to roust Cassie, and get us going to our interview.* Brian rolled over onto his right shoulder and reached out with his left hand, gently shaking Cassie until she murmured a response.

"Up and at it, partner. We've got an important interview to do."

Cassie rolled over and gazed at the young, handsome reporter lying next to her. "This will cost you, of course!"

Brian smiled back at his co-anchor. "Name your price."

Without hesitation, Cassie responded, "Strong coffee with cream, and one of your scones."

"That's asking a lot from someone this early in the morning."

"I know you can do it, mister. I've seen my asking price delivered, several times before."

Cassie leaned over and kissed her co-anchor tenderly on the lips. Then she quickly rolled over, swinging her feet onto the floor, and stood up. Facing away from Brian, she arched her back and stretched. Her partner was mesmerized by the sight. *What a beautiful lady!* Cassie walked into the adjoining bathroom and started a shower. Brian got up quickly, dressed, and headed for the kitchen to make some drip coffee and heat up some scones in the microwave.

Brian's Subaru slowed up next to the first barricade. Numerous news rigs sat parked along both sides of the road. He noticed their parent station, WNN, had a vehicle there. They drove up to the roadblock and were met by an OSP trooper whom Brian recognized from Bend co-ed softball games.

"Good morning, officer."

"Hello, Brian."

The trooper bent over and looked to the adjacent seat. "Hello, Cassie."

She remembered the trooper's name. "Hello, Robert." Cassie pointed at all the news rigs. "Seems like we've got lots of company now."

"Yes, they all started showing up yesterday. I bet they'll be swarming you two after your interview."

"You're probably right. Can we go in now?"

"Certainly. Stop at the boss's trailer. He wants to talk with you before you interview the silverbacks."

"Will do, Robert, thanks."

The trooper swung the barricade open for them and the reporters continued down the road.

The brisk fall morning was cool and hazy. Cassie's forecast from the night before, expecting the high to be around seventy-five, seemed likely. The dryness of the road allowed dust to lift from behind the Subaru even at the slow speed Brian was maintaining. A slight breeze was blowing up in the tree canopies but it wasn't strong enough to wash away the smoky haze. The rising sun, like the haze, had an off-color tint to it.

As Brian and Cassie drew nearer to the Command Center, they noticed the military encampment off to the left. This didn't catch them by surprise since Jack Smith had called Brian and told him about the soldiers, but seeing their bivouac was startling nonetheless. Brian saw Philip Ross standing outside his Command trailer. He wore his uniform coat and his trooper hat. The superintendent waved him down, and walked over to the passenger window. Bending down, he greeted the young reporters. "Hello, Cassie, Brian."

They responded in a like manner. Brian stared back at the military encampment, "Seems like this situation is a little more serious than the last time Cassie and I visited."

Ross's gaze also scanned the tents, then returned to the young reporters. "Yes. I think we've got the feds' attention. Governor O'Connell is trying to figure out exactly whose feathers we've ruffled and why. For now, this is just an annoyance. Anyway, I'd like to ask a favor of the two of you. See if you can arrange a meeting between the occupiers and me."

Brian replied, "We'll try to arrange a parley for you, superintendent."

"Thanks. The sooner the better."

Ross' focus shifted from the reporters to the SWAT van. A full body armored, helmeted trooper carrying an M4 was approaching from that direction.

"Trooper Wilson will accompany you to our blockade near the summit. You'll need to park your rig behind my trailer."

Brian and Cassie parked their car, and were escorted by Wilson to the SWAT van. The trooper opened up the back door, and helped them step up into the van's interior. Inside, the van was dark and business like. Compartments hung on the walls and two bench seats hugged the van's sides. Numerous armaments, vests, and other military gear were hanging within arm's reach. The van moved slowly forward, coming to a stop near the bulletproof barricade. Trooper Mills, who had surveillance duty, turned and saw his friends disembark from the black armored vehicle and join him.

"Cassie, Brian. Good to see you."

Mills wore his body armor and helmet, also.

Cassie smiled at Mills. "You're looking pretty macho today."

He smiled back at Cassie. His squareish jaw and stubble beard made him appear like the perfect fighting man.

"Comes with the territory, Cassie. Our friends on the hill have AK-47s so we have to take them very seriously."

Cassie walked over and peered through a partition's view hole. She scanned the Big Eddy Rise.

Without turning back she said, "The old van made it pretty far up the hill."

Mills and Brian joined her at the wall. They both peered through other ports.

"Yeah, the whole scene was quite a show. It came flying down the road, busted through our barricade, plowed its way up the hill, and died right where you're looking. Surprised the shit out of all of us."

"I bet it did."

Trooper Mills picked up his bullhorn, keyed it, and called up to the occupiers. He announced the reporters' arrival, and their desire for an interview. A response returned from above, inviting the news anchors up to the overturned step van. Ranger heard Mills' request. He'd wondered when a meeting would be arranged, and was a little surprised it had taken so long to materialize. Mills focused on his two friends. "We'll have you both covered from down below, and if anything happens to frighten you, like you're threatened by the occupiers, or they intend to take you hostage, just drop flat to the ground. We have marksmen here who are very good."

Brian glanced around and saw four other armed OSP taking up positions.

"This sounds pretty scary, trooper."

"Well it's a whole different ballgame now. I don't think anything unusual will happen, but just in case, remember what I said."

Cassie and Brian walked around the barricade and up the hill. A small dust cloud created by their footsteps followed their progress. They studied the STRONG Alliance's orphaned articles: ropes hanging from the trees, blankets, water bottles, and even drums lay where they'd been abandoned. They stopped just above the overturned van. Cassie noted the crudely cut out hole on the van's roof. She nudged Brian, and he also observed the opening. Their gaze returned to the summit. A figure slowly and somewhat stiffly was crawling over and down the basaltic lip. The individual walked with a slight limp down the hill to them and came to a stop a couple feet from the young couple. Cassie and Brian studied the old gentleman who was extending his hand in greeting. His short, gray hair was matted down, a gray, stubble beard was getting started, and a pair of black-rimmed glasses sat atop a pointed nose.

"Good morning, young people. You've probably got a few questions for me."

Cassie spoke first. "Yes we have, sir. You've created quite a stir with your takeover of the hill."

"I imagine we have. A bunch of old farts rattling their swords and shields. I bet we've got lots of people's attention."

Brian responded, "Yes you have, sir."

Cassie held up her phone and the station's microphone. "Do you mind if we record this?"

"Yes I do, young lady. I'm sorry, but we can't have any pictures."

Cassie was disappointed, but didn't let her emotions show. Their interview with Ranger lasted about fifteen minutes. He was somewhat guarded in his responses, not wanting to compromise the occupiers' position by divulging information in unnecessary conversation. At the end of the interview, Brian told Ranger about Philip Ross's request, and Ranger acknowledged the invite, telling Brian he'd think about it.

After leaving the hill, the two reporters were driven back to the superintendent's trailer in the SWAT vehicle. They shared Ranger's response to the meeting request with Ross. After that, the two reporters quickly said their good-byes and drove off, heading for Bend. At the next roadblock, Brian's Subaru was mobbed by local and national news reporters. He focused straight ahead, slowly plowing through the crowd. After they got past the news rigs, Cassie reached over and took Brian's hand in hers. The two young reporters tenderly gazed into each other's eyes, and for a moment, Brian felt a tingling sensation again.

Cassie whispered, "Thanks for the..."

Brian grinned and interrupted, "I totally agree. Last night was fantastic. You're such a great lover."

Cassie's blissful expression turned into a mischievous one. "Well, yes it was, but I was wanting to thank you for the yummy scone and great cup of coffee you gave me this morning."

Brian's face turned a slight reddish shade and he sheepishly turned away. He began quietly laughing. "Anytime, partner. It's the least I can do for my hardworking co-anchor."

Cassie gave Brian's hand a gentle squeeze. "I agree, partner. Keep 'em coming."

The Subaru turned east onto Highway 20 and headed to Bend and the station.

CHAPTER 82

President McDonald was eating in his per-

sonal dining room on the White House second floor. He'd been joined by his new chief of staff, Ted Horner, and his press secretary, Lesley Brown. The two men wanted to brief McDonald on several media strategies they'd developed. A new TV mounted above the fireplace now held the president's attention. The screen replaced a large mirror, which was repositioned next to the hall's doorway so McDonald could view himself when he entered and exited the room.

At this particular moment, Lesley Brown was reviewing the newly minted media schemes, but McDonald was not listening to him. Allen Rodrigues was greeting his national news audience, and his opening remarks about the trade talks with Mexico and Canada falling apart captured the president's attention. Rodrigues ran an interview with the two heads of state showing them discussing going elsewhere for a close trade partner and trade agreements. Both men mentioned focusing on Japan, Europe, and China as possible new, important commerce allies. McDonald's left eye tic began to act up. Rodrigues then welcomed the station's political analysis expert onto the show. Steve and Allen further discussed the deeper ramifications of the trade talk collapse.

"Well, Steve, this doesn't bode well for U.S. businesses when Mexico and Canada leave without a new trade agreement."

"Certainly not, Allen. These two countries buy huge quantities of U.S. goods. Having them shop elsewhere for a trading partner can only hurt the U.S. worker and eventually the U.S. consumer."

"What do you think happened, Steve?"

"My sources say the U.S. wasn't prepared for serious negotiations with the two countries and the heads of state took exception to this and basically are taking their business on the road."

After more pertinent dialogue, Rodrigues thanked his political reporter, Steve, and then moved on to a related story.

"WNN has learned from a White House source that President McDonald actually didn't meet with the Mexican President and the Canadian Prime Minister today for their scheduled 'Trade Summit.' The same source tendered further information saying Vice President Robinson at the last moment was asked to preside in the president's place. Our confidant said the president chose to focus on a smaller, personal issue rather than meet with the two heads of state."

WNN went to a commercial break following Rodrigues's piece about McDonald's "summit meeting" absence. McDonald was furious at this bit of reporting. His face was red and his eye twitch became noticeable. His fists came down hard on the dining table, causing glasses and silverware to jump off the surface.

"I've got a God-damn, sneaky-ass traitor selling information to the God-damn sleazy, liberal media!"

Both Ted Horner and Lesley Brown stared at each other with frightened expressions, unnerved by McDonald's tantrum.

WNN went into its weather segment. McDonald focused on his dinner guests.

"We need to find out who our asshole snitch is. I want you two to get on it, ASAP!"

Lesley Brown responded to McDonald. "Certainly, Mr. President. Also, I think we need to create some news about Robinson's failings in the 'summit talks.' Maybe he didn't do as you instructed."

"Good idea, Brown. Also let's get out there some shit about a National Security matter of the greatest importance keeping me away from the 'Summit.'"

"Okay, how about something dealing with Iran or North Korea?"

"Yeah, you've got the idea, Horner. We need to get me off the hook."

"Certainly, Mr. President."

"All right, boys, you best get on it."

The chief of staff and press secretary studied each other. They'd barely touched their dinner, and now apparently they were being dismissed. Both staffers rose from the table and excused themselves.

McDonald once again viewed his new flatscreen. Allen Rodrigues was now focusing on the Northwest and the silverback occupation. McDonald spoke out loud to the screen. "Go ahead, Rodrigues, paint a pretty picture of our damn eco-terrorists. There won't be much left of them pretty soon to talk about, so get in what you can now."

McDonald pushed his chair away from the table and walked briskly out of the dining room. Right before the door, he stopped and adjusted his tie, sucked in his gut, and stood sideways, viewing his profile. Seemingly satisfied, the president headed for his personal living room and another channel to watch.

He missed numerous other Rodrigues stories by changing rooms and channels. The most ominous piece dealt with Congressional Republicans openly discussing their misgivings with the McDonald administration and their lack of support for his vague agenda. A few senior members were even thinking about an unofficial "vote of confidence" by Republican congressmen to see where everyone stood regarding his presidency.

McDonald had found a conservative news show to watch and he eventually relaxed and became more even tempered. He glanced over at the room's landline. It sat on a nearby end table. He decided to order a dessert from the kitchen to find out which young intern was on night shift. The president picked up his receiver and waited for a response.

CHAPTER 83

Cassie sat upright in her studio chair, squared her shoulders, and smiled at the camera. Her hands were resting on the anchor desk, one on top of the other. Her left foot was rubbing Brian's right leg. Brian sat unflinching, smiling and facing the camera, waiting for his cue. Their multi-screened backdrop showed Mt. Hood.

Brian led off. "Good evening, Bend. It's another beautiful Central Oregon day. Cassie and I are still wearing our sandals. We'll find out later in her weather segment if these shoes stay on much longer. Our lead story today is about the silverbacks and their occupation. Cassie and I had an exclusive interview with one elderly occupier this morning."

Brian discussed Ranger's demands. They pretty much mirrored the STRONG Alliance requests. He mentioned Ranger's quiet, calm, yet strong presence, and how the silverbacks were totally prepared for any kind of action presented to them by the authorities.

Brian quoted Ranger as saying everything would be resolved soon, because the logging site would be found to be illegal and the silverbacks' occupation wouldn't be needed.

He continued quoting Ranger, stating, "All the silverbacks hoped for a peaceful resolution of the site, and to a man, felt one was forthcoming."

Tarri McGrath sat in front of her TV watching the co-anchors. Wendy called out from the kitchen, "Is the show on yet?"

"Yep, just started."

"How are our young lovers doing?"

"They're being very professional."

Wendy walked into the TV room and handed Tarri a beer. "Too bad. They'd better not let me down. If they do, I'm calling the station and complaining."

Tarri focused on Wendy and smiled. "I love you."

Wendy reached over and squeezed Tarri's extended hand. "What would you do without me?"

The two women studied each other for a moment. "I don't want to know what that would be like."

Wendy's smile turned into a laugh. "Hey, save this mush for later. I've got a news show to dissect. Please, no more interruptions."

The two women returned their attention to the newscast. Brian had just finished a piece about the local fires when Cassie stood up and flip-flopped her way to the green screen.

"Well, sun worshippers, your sacrifices and prayers have been answered. The sandals stay on for at least five more days. Our extended forecast may have some rain coming in the future, but probably not for another week."

After describing the upcoming week's weather, she continued on with her forecast, noting the air quality emergency caused by the fire's smoky haze, and finished her segment statistically commenting about the record summer temperatures they'd just endured and the record low precipitation amounts, coinciding with the heat wave. Channel 19 went to break.

Wendy focused on Tarri. "Are you sure I didn't miss any flirtatious stuff while in the kitchen?"

"Yep, like I said, they were very professional."

"Something's wrong, then."

"Or, maybe something's changed."

"Um, maybe so."

When Channel 19 came back live, the camera framed Cassie. "I visited with demonstrators who took over Riverbend Park this afternoon for a rally supporting the silverbacks and their cause. No counter-demonstrators were present. About a thousand people were in attendance."

Cassie interviewed several of the protesters and the overall consensus was the logging show should not happen. The recorded feed ended and Cassie's smiling face once again greeted her Bend audience. The field of view widened, allowing Brian into the picture.

"You kind of wonder why the logging site continues, Cassie. The public certainly appears to be against the logging of our old growth Ponderosa pine."

"I agree, Brian. The general opinion in the Bend area is totally against these trees being cut down."

The camera now focused on Brian as he delivered another piece, highlighting Professor Anderson. He noted the "hot spot" beneath Mt. Hood was becoming more volatile, and a slight spewing of volcanic ash had been recorded in the early morning hours. The interview ended with numerous charts and graphs, all depicting a heightening degree of volcanic activity on the mountain, and an ominous statement from the professor predicting lava flows in the near future. The camera once again backed out, allowing both reporters to be seen.

"Whoa, Oregon skiers. Looks like warming huts won't be necessary on Hood this ski season."

Brian smiled at Cassie. "We're dealing with educated speculation here, Cassie. Don't count your chickens before they've hatched."

"Still, Brian, I might be dressing with fewer layers when skiing Meadows or Timberline this year."

Brian continued with the newscast. "We're ending tonight's show with two personal interest stories. We've got a piece which pleasantly ends one of the Big Eddy's sagas. Cassie was there when two young Alliance members left St. Charles Medical Center."

The camera changed angles, showing only Cassie. "Sasha of the STRONG Alliance was released by St. Charles Medical Center today. The young college student moved slowly as she left the hospital. She was escorted by Dread, the Alliance leader, and they both drove away in an old school bus. Sasha declined to talk with us, but I caught up with OSP Trooper Mills later on in the day, and he filled me in on her release particulars." The station went to a feed showing Cassie interviewing Trooper Mills. In the interview, he explained Sasha's freedoms were restricted. She was to inform the OSP about her whereabouts and was not to leave the state. The Attorney General's Office wanted to question her about the STRONG Alliance takeover, but when that would occur had not yet been determined.

The camera angle changed again, allowing both Cassie and Brian to be seen. The two young news anchors gazed pleasantly at the camera, and no unusual body movements portrayed any hanky-panky. Brian closed the show with his piece about the ninety-eight-year-old Sisters quilter. Numerous quilted pieces were shown, displaying the elderly woman's talents and creativity. The segment finished the show with a warm feeling.

The field of vision enlarged, showing an expansive studio scene. Cassie and Brian lifted one sandaled foot, each, onto their anchor desk and rested them on the table top. They waved their good-byes to their audience, and Channel 19 went to commercial break.

Wendy stood up and contemplated Tarri. "Something's definitely changed. There should have been some flirtation stuff right at the sign-off."

"Yeah, I'm thinking something's different, too."

Wendy walked into the kitchen and got two more beers. Tarri followed her in. Wendy suddenly turned around, holding the beers victoriously above her head. "You're damn right something's different. They've made love together."

Tarri started to laugh. "You just figured that out?"

Tarri laughed with Wendy. The two women walked to each other and hugged.

Wendy leaned back. "The obvious always escapes me."

"Your naiveté is one of the reasons I find you so attractive."

The two women hugged again. Their beers began to gather moisture on their sides, and rivulets of water descended onto the countertop.

CHAPTER 84

THE FLIP PHONE'S VIBRATOR STARTED BUZZING IN Secretary Hastings' inside breast pocket. He was conferring with McDonald in the Oval Office, and knew this call was either from Rodgers or Henry. Information from either man would be welcomed by the president, who sat across from Hastings with a scowl on his face. He'd just recapped the evening's news with the Defense Secretary, and was still agitated because of the White House leak. Just then, Janet knocked on her Oval Office door jamb.

"Mr. President. Your chief of staff and press secretary wish to meet with you."

McDonald didn't look up and responded, "Not now, Janet. Tell them I'll get to them later."

"Certainly, sir." Janet returned to her desk and told the president's men they'd have to wait.

Hastings opened up his phone. He was greeted by Colonel Rodgers. The colonel filled in the secretary on the intel he'd gathered, and suggested one 500-lb. smart bomb would neutralize the site. Hastings agreed with Colonel Rodgers' assessment. There was a slight pause in the conversation, then the colonel enquired about his retirement fund.

"I'll ask the president about it right now, colonel. He's sitting across from me as we speak."

McDonald looked over at Hastings upon hearing his name and registered the conversation. Without asking, he reached over and took Hastings' phone.

"I set up your offshore account, Rodgers. It's got two million in it for you upon the completion of your job."

Colonel Rodgers was startled by the president's sudden access to the line and by his curt remark. He took a moment to think about what he would say in return.

"Hello, Mr. President. So the two million's in place. All I need to do is drop our package on the occupiers and I can collect."

"That's how it works, Rodgers. The account is loaded, but withdrawals can't start until after our mission is finished. I'll give you the withdrawal sequence then and only then."

Rodgers thought about McDonald's stipulation and responded. "Good, Mr. President. I'll give you a call after our package is delivered."

Without saying "good-bye," McDonald handed the phone back to Hastings.

The secretary and Colonel Rodgers talked more about delivering the payload and other technical points before terminating their conversation. The last few remarks dealt with when the attack would occur. Hastings said "within the week" was the unofficial timeline and he'd contact Rodgers with more details when he knew them.

Closing up his phone, he glanced across at McDonald. The president sat chewing on his sandwich and viewing his phone.

"Well, good news, sir. This operation looks like a slam dunk."

"Damn right. When can we drop the bomb and get rid of the ape men?"

"We have to hear from Lt. Colonel Henry, sir. I expect he'll call soon and tell us about his squad's deployment."

"Well, shit, Hastings. Don't wait on him. Give him a call and stir the pot."

Hastings thought about McDonald's request. "Good idea, sir. I'll get on that soon, but right now, I need to be at another meeting. The Intel execs have a new missile guidance system they want to sell me. I'll call you later. Keep your flip phone close to you, Mr. President."

"I will, Hastings. Shit, I've got it figured out. Don't badger me."

Hastings left the Oval Office and headed for the West Wing's North Entrance.

McDonald browsed his phone and thought again about his White House leak. He glanced over at the marble fireplace. He could clearly see the patch job where he had broken the fireplace façade. *Damn shitty repair job. I'll call Peterson and get the sloppy mess redone.* His eyes drifted back to his phone.

Janet lowered the desk phone from her ear and called out to the president. "Your chief of staff and the press secretary want to know when they're meeting with you."

McDonald glanced at Janet's doorway. "Tell them now would be fine, but they need to make it brief."

"Will do, Mr. President."

Janet replaced the phone to her ear and relayed the president's message. McDonald moved back to his desk and sat down behind the polished eagle. He looked around him, noticing very little of personal importance. His thoughts drifted back to the annoying and damaging Oval Office leaks. His fingers began drumming the desk top as he mused about the possible sources of these betrayals.

CHAPTER
85

JANET WAS CHECKING HER EMAILS WHEN SHE noticed a flurry of activity in the Oval Office. She glanced in the room and saw Chief of Staff Ted Horner nervously flitting around. Press Secretary Lesley Brown was sitting on the couch, facing President McDonald, and Secretary Hastings had just entered the room through the hall doorway. McDonald was talking to his chief of staff and press secretary about preparing a really "big" press conference in a few days that needed to be sharp and attention grabbing. After Hastings had met with the Intel sales team, he had started back to the Pentagon. Partway there, Janet had contacted him, telling him to return to the Oval Office because McDonald needed to see him again. His driver drove the limo to the West Wing. The Secretary reentered the Oval Office, sat down across from McDonald, and cut into the conversation.

"What do you need, Mr. President?"

McDonald was not pleased with the interruption, but addressed Hastings' question. "I thought we'd get Horner and Brown up to speed with our mission."

"Not advisable, sir. Too many risks at this point. A 'need to know' basis is preferable."

McDonald did not like to be rebuffed. There was silence in the room and all eyes were on President McDonald. Ted Horner stopped fidgeting and sat down next to his boss.

McDonald glared coldly at Secretary Hastings. "I want a press conference, mid-morning, after our attack, Hastings. My team needs to be prepared to deliver news promptly and accurately.

Horner and Brown stared at each other and Brown ventured, "What attack, Mr. President?"

Secretary Hastings quickly interrupted Brown's inquiry. "Again, Mr. President, this is a premature meeting. Your people will have plenty of time to create a story after the attack."

McDonald and Hastings continued to focus sternly at each other. The afternoon sun shone through the Rose Garden window and bathed the presidential desk with light.

"God damn it, Hastings! We're going to get my team on board so they can begin scripting my news conference. No arguments!"

Secretary Hastings' flip phone began buzzing in his inner suitcoat pocket. "Excuse me, Mr. President."

Answering his phone, Hastings had a short conversation with the caller. He closed the flip-top and returned it to his pocket.

"That was timely, sir. Lt. Colonel Henry just checked in."

"Who?"

There was a pause and Hastings continued, "He's our ground troop commander."

"Oh."

"Henry informed me our people are on site and will be ready for a 'green light' by tomorrow."

McDonald's irritated expression changed to one of pleasure, and he switched positions, sitting erectly on the edge of the couch. "Are you saying we can bomb those hippy-dippy ape-men tomorrow night?"

"Probably not, sir, but possibly. We've got a problem with ash in the area. I've talked with my weather people about this and..."

McDonald stared at Hastings with a confused expression. He interrupted the secretary. "What the hell do you mean, an ash problem?"

"Mt. Hood had an eruption, Mr. President."

McDonald looked on blankly.

"You can't fly a plane into an area with volcanic ash suspended in the air."

Chief of Staff Horner stared at Hastings. "Are we going to bomb the silverbacks?"

McDonald snapped, "Quiet, Horner."

The thin, nervous young man put his hands on his knees and apologized for the interruption.

"Tell me more about the ash, Hastings."

"Well, sir. We need an ash-free night to drop our bomb."

"Okay, we play it by ear then."

"Correct, sir."

"So, God damn it, it's a day-by-day situation, gentlemen." McDonald clapped his hands together. "Those damn old farts won't know what hit them."

He faced Ted Horner and slapped him on the back. The young man winced but said nothing.

McDonald focused on Secretary Hastings, "Tell me again who our people are, Hastings."

"You shouldn't mention their names, sir."

"How can I have a God-damn press announcement with no names? Who are our men?"

Hastings surveyed the room for a moment, mentally freeing himself from the conversation. His eyes met President Lincoln's gaze. Then, they drifted back to McDonald.

"That would be Lt. Colonel Henry of the Army, and Colonel Rodgers of the Air Force."

McDonald showed some recognition when Rodgers' name was mentioned.

Secretary Hastings abruptly stood up. "Well, gentlemen, I'll leave you to discuss your news conference. The president can fill you in on the details."

Without waiting for McDonald to dismiss him, Hastings turned and left the Oval Office. Horner and Brown gazed at each other.

Brown spoke to the president. "We're really attacking the silverbacks?"

McDonald's face spread into one of his rare smiles. "You bet your sweet ass we are. Any day now. This will bring back my voting base. I told them I'd be tough on terrorism."

Chief of Staff Horner joined in on the conversation. "It most certainly will. Tell us more about this operation, sir."

The three men talked at length about the mission. McDonald had to wing it mostly, because even though he'd heard everything about the operation from Hastings, he'd retained very little of it.

Janet continued with her Oval Office duties. She read her emails, lined up the president's agenda, and for the most part kept herself busy. She'd even had a lengthy, cozy conversation with ex–Agriculture Secretary Billings while at her desk. The Texas oilman had invited her to his ranch in West Texas for a weekend, and Janet had gladly accepted the invitation. The dark-eyed brunette sat thinking about her visit, and was fantasizing about the hopefully romantic vacation.

She was brought back to reality by McDonald barking in her direction. She noted the president was alone in the office.

"Janet, get me some sandwiches and coffee, ASAP."

"Certainly, Mr. President."

CHAPTER 86

THE MORNING AFTER THEIR CONVERSATION WITH Ranger, Bridger and Rachael had gone to the Camp Sherman store for supplies. While shopping, they overheard the locals talking about the military's arrival, and how they were camping near the OSP Command Center. Late last night, Bridger heard loud diesel rigs routinely driving by their campsite. He hadn't checked to see what vehicle created the commotion, but upon hearing the store gossip, immediately thought, *Humvee*. The two young students replenished their foodstuffs and walked back to the campground on the river trail. A cool breeze was moving downstream. Fortunately, they both wore hoodies and jeans. The tall, streambank Ponderosas stood all around them. Their branches formed the young couple's roof, and the conifers' fallen needles created the carpet they strolled upon.

"I'll need to tell Ranger about the military presence. He might not have seen them yet."

Rachael focused on Bridger and took his hand in hers. They continued on toward their camp. "Aren't you scared for your grandpa's safety?"

Bridger gazed at Rachael thoughtfully. "Yeah, I'm really worried about Gramps. I want those guys to give up the site before anything serious happens, but it's not my decision."

"I couldn't do what they're doing," reflected Rachael.

"I'm not sure if I could either. I have faith in Ranger, though. If anyone can keep them safe, he can."

The two college students continued walking along the river, hand in hand, but now they endured a pensive silence. When they neared camp, Bridger' mood changed and he asked Rachael if she wanted to practice nymph fishing. She smiled at Bridger, noting the youthful smirk on her boyfriend's face. She responded, "I'd love to. Let's see what we can catch."

Bridger's smirk turned into a broad grin.

"Will you do your hip boot/bikini thing again?"

"If it will help us net some browns or rainbows, you bet."

"Under the circumstances, I'm thinking we won't be able to keep them off our lines."

Bridger and Rachael grew close together, and, with arms around each other's waist, walked over to their fishing gear. Rachael slipped away to change and when she returned they walked to the river and drifted some nymph patterns through the pools right in front of their camp. The smoky haze shut down the bite, so the fishermen just went through the motions and enjoyed the beautiful river flowing past them.

A small, white sedan hastily left the road, pulled into their campground, and abruptly came to a stop near where Bridger and Rachael fished. The driver's door flung open and a red-haired young man jumped out and headed their direction, hollering, "Bridger! Bridger!"

Bridger peered upstream at the advancing, shouting person. His expression went from curious to recognition.

"Russel? What the hell!!" Bridger focused on Rachael. "It's Russel, you know, the..."

Rachael smiled and interrupted his thought. "Yes I know. Your D.C. friend."

Bridger splashed his way to the bank and headed for Russel. The two friends met and hugged. They separated, and laughed and talked for several minutes. After their initial greeting, Bridger turned around and beckoned for Rachael to join them. Rachael carefully walked to the shore and over to the young men. Russel's eyes got big. He couldn't stop examining the slender, pretty, redhead standing before him in her wild, sexy fishing outfit.

"Holy shit, Bridger! I should have started fishing a long time ago. If I'd only known."

The three young people stood together and laughed. Rachael gave Russel a hug as Bridger wiped the tears from his eyes.

"Okay, Russel. What's the deal? How come you're here?"

"I guess I'm on the run. I mean seriously, on the run!"

The D.C. college student told Bridger and Rachael all about the two military men he'd seen at his dorm. He talked about his spontaneous flight back to Portland, and how, upon arrival, the only reasonable thing to do seemed to be finding Bridger. No one would think to search for him at Camp Sherman.

Russel went back to his car and retrieved his laptop. The three young people sat at the picnic table and Russel showed them his White House note. Seeing the presidential letterhead on the paper, and the messages written upon it, frightened Bridger and Rachael.

Rachael left the two friends together, and went to the store to buy a sleeping bag for Russel. When she returned to camp, Bridger had started making a rice stir fry dinner. He and Russel were still talking nonstop as she approached. While sipping cold beers, the trio consumed their rice, veggies, and chicken dinner. The sun was beginning to set and the western sky was a solid mass of dark orange. Bridger lent Russel a hoodie and pair of pants, and for a moment, all three stopped and listened to the river flowing past them. Everything was so beautiful and peaceful. The three young people embraced what surrounded them, momentarily forgetting about all their worries and fears.

CHAPTER 87

THE SURREAL, DARK COPPERY SUNSET COLORS flooded the forest. Ranger stood at the mess table cooking over the propane stove, preparing his skillet dish. He'd resurrected from the Alliance discard pile a small cooler that now rested nearby, filled with ice and beers. Hops and Doc scavenged as much burnable material as possible from their compound, and added it to their meager wood supply. All the friends agreed the evening's dinner was worthy of the last campfire. The fire was laid and the tenders awaited the ex-Marine's okay to start the blaze. Ranger put all the sautéed ingredients together, stirred them up, and added some hot sauce to the dish. After he was satisfied all the ingredients were mixed up nicely, he set the dish to the side so the flavors could blend together.

All the silverbacks gathered near the fire pit and sat on the surrounding logs, rocks, and camp chairs, talking together, and enjoying the aromas wafting off the potato dish. Woody volunteered to take guard duty during the evening's dinner party. Ranger peered over at his friends and the young college students who all sat around the communal, gathering place.

"Light 'er up, Hops."

Hops struck a match and set the pine needles ablaze. Soon a warm, bright campfire took the edge off the cool evening temperature.

"All right, gentlemen, two things: first, how do you want your steak cooked?"

Ranger got a variety of responses from the group.

Dakota faced Doc. "I'm glad Ranger's cooking. You know how these steaks would be fixed if Hops were the chef!"

Doc smiled, "This did work out nicely, didn't it? Although Hops does cook a mean medium rare steak."

It was Dakota's turn to smile, "Yeah, too bad he's the only one who likes steaks medium rare."

The two men laughed quietly together.

"And secondly, gentlemen, grab yourself a beer. Please be mindful of our supply, and allow everyone their rightful share."

This comment was greeted with cheers and claps from the occupiers, and everyone grabbed a beer and began consuming it with enthusiasm.

Hang walked over to Woody and handed him a beer. He looked seriously at his surrogate father. "You know, Mr. Thompson, when teachers asked me to talk or write about my hero, I always said you were my Superman."

Woody, clutching his beer, focused on his son's best friend. He couldn't find the words for a response.

"And, Mr. Thompson, you still are my hero, bar none. No one holds a candle to you."

Hang raised his beer to Woody, toast fashion, and the two men touched their bottles together. Then he turned away from Woody and walked back to the fire pit. Bob Thompson returned his gaze to the forest and wiped the tears off of his cheeks.

Soon the odor of cooking steaks filled the air. A wind sprang up from the northwest and the fire's smoke column now bent in a southeasterly direction, dispersing itself in the tall Ponderosa canopy. Within a few minutes, all the men had juicy steaks and Ranger's skillet dish on their plates. They found their personal knives and began carving bite-size pieces off their rib eyes. A second round of beers was procured, and the silverbacks began sharing stories of their younger years with Tunes and Hang. Doc talked about his med school stint in ER, Dakota told stories about being a gandy dancer, Ranger riveted everyone with Vietnam War tales, and Hops talked about living in Hawaii during the early seventies. The two young college students laughed and were awed by the experiences shared by their comrades in arms.

Later, after everyone finished dinner, Tunes and Hang found their instruments and began drumming. Soon, Beatles lyrics accompanied by African rhythms began drifting through the forest. The residual sunset turned to dusk with the sun's departure, and a few of the brighter stars became visible. As night descended, the summit's smoke pointed directly at the OSP Command Center. The moon rose above the horizon and was nearly full. Its face, like the sun's, was off colored by the ever-present smoky haze. When a silence from drumming and singing presented itself, Ranger called out. "We have one problem, gentlemen. Only four beers remain and there are seven of us."

Woody, Hang, and Tunes deferred to the others and after a moment of bottle top removal, they received a grateful salute from their friends. As the last beers were consumed, the drumming and singing continued.

Eerie, brownish shadows began covering the forest floor. Bats could be easily seen weaving their way through the forest's canopy, and two ravens peered into the summit's bowl at the men and their fire. They stretched their wings and continued watching their neighbors. Dakota, Hops, Tunes, and Hang continued singing and drumming while their friends finished off their KP duty and ales. Eventually, all the occupiers, minus Woody, regained the fire pit and watched the flames burn down. They'd exhausted the burnable material, and stared at the glowing coals and embers.

Ranger spoke to no one in particular. "Who's got guard duty tonight?"

Dakota, Hops, and Woody answered in the affirmative.

Earlier in the evening, Ranger heard the now familiar squelch of his walkie-talkie. He hadn't answered it immediately because just then, all of his friends were eating their steaks and enjoying the moment with their young companions. Later, Ranger quietly slipped away to the latrine area and raised Bridger. He heard about Russel's arrival and the White House note being shown to the two campers. Bridger suggested again to the old soldier that maybe surrendering was the best thing to do, and the older man reminded him that giving up was not an option. Their conversation ended with Bridger asking the ex-Marine to give his love to his gramps.

"All right, gentlemen, here's the deal. I talked with Bridger tonight; from our discussion, there is no doubt about a possible attack. It really comes down to when it will happen. You guys on guard duty must be very vigilant, and check the tent with the night optics on a regular basis." Somberness once again befell the silverbacks.

Tunes spoke up. "Hey, Ranger, this wasn't like our last meal, was it?"

Nervous laughter followed his comment. "Hell no! A good army is a well-fed army. I was just preparing you for our probable engagement. Now, sleep well tonight and dream about steaks, beers, and lovely ladies. Oh yeah, you married men, please dream about your wives. I don't want you to get in trouble." This bit of levity was well received by the group, and numerous "amens" followed Ranger's comment.

The friends watched the embers cool off and die. One by one, they made their way to the cavern entrance and descended into the sleeping quarters. Woody, Hops, and Dakota warily took up guard positions, and occasionally glanced over at the canvas tent. More than once, one of them walked over to the rock shelf and grabbed the night goggles. None of their inspections found a laser light's terminus. The moon rose higher, and the quiet evening continued without alarming circumstance.

CHAPTER 88

First Sergeant Jefferson and Sergeant

Forrest sat on their cots talking. The tent's central pole separated their beds, and a lantern hanging off the stanchion threw a soft white light into the interior of their living quarters. The gear packs and weapons were neatly arranged in the tent's recesses and were partially illuminated. It was near the time for a nightly recon and Jefferson was preparing for the task.

"Those god damn Yankee-Apers ate a steak dinner tonight. Did you smell meat cooking?"

"Couldn't miss it, first sergeant."

"Our eco-terrorists had a little party complete with drumming and singing. They had themselves a fine time tonight at our expense."

"They most certainly did."

"Here we sit, twiddling our thumbs, while they have steak dinners and parties."

"Doesn't seem right."

"No it doesn't, and on top of that crap, I'm missing my 'bow tag' season in Eastern Washington."

"No shit? Those tags are hard to get."

"Yeah, and here I sit losing my hunting days to this mission."

"Doesn't seem right, first sergeant."

"No it doesn't, so I've got a little plan to speed up the end of our deployment. I think a little aggression by the Apers targeting the local cops could get things moving."

"How so?"

Jefferson walked over to his gear sack and pulled out a rifle wrapped in cloth. Forrest focused on Jefferson. "Why you pulling out your granddaddy's old AK-47?"

Forrest knew about the Vietnam War era rifle Jefferson's granddad had given him. He took it on maneuvers as a reminder of his family's military heritage.

"Well, I was talking with a deputy sheriff today under the canopy. Guess what kind of ARs our Apers have?"

"Really?"

"Yes, really, and guess who's going to accidentally fire down into the OSP surveillance position tonight and wake everyone from their sweet slumber? This bit of deception should get us the green light from Command to finish off those old farts. If I'm lucky, maybe I can get in a few days of bow hunting as a bonus."

"It's worth a try. On one of my recons, I checked out a ravine on the north side of the Rise that ends right at the base of the rim. You could use it for cover going up and down the ridge."

"Way ahead of you, Forrest. Already got it planned out."

Jefferson unwrapped his granddaddy's AK-47 and inserted a banana magazine. He loaded a round into the chamber and looked through the sights.

"This should do the trick."

Jefferson put on his night camo and body armor, strapped on his helmet, and "keyed" Spec 4 Lee.

"I'm going out on recon, Lee. Do you copy?"

"Loud and clear, first sergeant."

"Keep your ears on."

"Roger that."

Jefferson opened the tent flap and entered the encampment. He gazed up at the moon and the surrounding, dully lit, forest floor. His camo and face paint would help hide his movements, but he still didn't like working in the moon's glow, even if it was mitigated by the haze. He headed off in a westerly direction. Jefferson moved stealthfully, observing his surroundings as he maneuvered, and eventually turned north and then east to gain the base of the ravine.

Deputy Sheriff Johnny Edwards rode down from the Command Center in the SWAT van toward the OSP surveillance position. Gravel crunched under the heavy vehicle as it slowly moved forward. He was going to visit with Trooper Mills, who had surveillance duty. The deputy wore his brown vest and helmet and carried an M4 with him. After the van stopped, Edwards stepped down onto the ground from the passenger's side and walked over to his friend.

"Howdy, partner."

Mills focused on Edwards. "What brings you out to 'no man's land,' deputy?"

"Just thought you might want some professional guidance, officer."

Mills smiled at this friend. "Are you going to tell me what to do in a hostage situation?"

It was Johnny's turn to smile. He walked over to where his friend stood and punched him on the shoulder.

"How are things going tonight, officer?"

"Pretty quiet, Johnny. Just like all the other nights, although earlier, the silverbacks had a steak dinner, and a gala event followed."

Deputy Edwards examined his friend questioningly.

"Yeah, they ate steaks, drummed, and sang till about 10:00."

Edwards laughed. "No kidding, steaks?"

"Yes, deputy. Their singing wasn't too good, but the steaks smelled great."

Edwards smiled. Both he and Mills focused at the summit through viewing portals. There was still a whiff of smoke emerging from the bowl. The campfire's smoke was the only movement showing. In the evening's murky darkness, the Ponderosa trunks were a dark brown and their needles were a dark blue–forest green color. The two officers looked away from the rise and continued talking about the occupiers' party. As they averted their eyes from the summit, a camoed figure scurried out of the black ravine and found a shadowed spot at the base of the basaltic rim.

Woody was slumped down inside the bowl thinking about his wife, Karen, and Bridger. He also was thinking about Hang and the nice words the young man shared with him. *God, I was lucky to parent Bridger and be so close to Hang for all these years.* His thoughts were interrupted by the sound of crunching rock. Woody's position was the rifle port next to the pruned Ponderosa tree. *What's out there?* As he stood up, the "pop, pop, pop" sound of AK-47 automatic fire rang out into the forest. Woody slumped back down defensively and gripped his CZ AR tightly. *Shit, shit, shit! Here it comes!*

Down below, at the barricade, Deputy Edwards had excused himself and headed for the shitter. When he reached for the porta pottie door, the AK-47 rounds fired off. The bullets raced across the bulletproof wall and ended at the barrier's terminus adjacent to the latrine. One bullet found the gap between panels and Deputy Edwards' right forearm. It smashed through his radius bone and exploded a main artery. Blood pulsed out of Edwards arm and dripped onto the ground.

"Shit, I'm hit, Mills! I'm hit!"

Mills quickly miced the Command Center. "We've got a man down. Send a medical team."

The SWAT van was already filling with troopers and deputies. The two medics stationed at the scene bolted into the rig's back, and the big black van quickly gained the surveillance barricade. After throwing on his body armor and helmet, Superintendent Ross roared down the gravel road in his Crown Vic, bringing it to a sliding stop next to the SWAT van. He jumped out and joined his troops at the barricade. In less than a minute's time, a half dozen M4s were pointed up at the Big Eddy Rise.

Dakota called over to Woody. "Where'd those shots come from, Woody?"

Woody rose and focused down onto his firing field.

"I don't know, I don't know. They didn't come from me."

Ranger, wiping sleep from his eyes, appeared from nowhere and stood next to Woody. He also peered down the hill. His trained eye was searching the ravine for movement. Ranger's CZ was in firing position but nothing presented itself as a target. He noted a shadow joining a shadow at the base of the hill near the culvert's mouth and then it was gone.

"God damn it. These guys are setting us up!"

Woody regarded Ranger. "What do you mean?"

"They've made it look like we've started the battle."

Woody responded, "Yeah, they'll think we fired the first shots."

Ranger rubbed his short beard with his right hand. "Yes it does, God damn it, yes it does."

The medics found Deputy Edwards sitting on the ground with his back against a Ponderosa. His freckled face was ashen, and the officer grimaced in pain as he held his hand over his wound. A stream of blood ran down his arm and was staining his pant leg. The pressure he was applying on his limb sent shooting pains up his arm. The EMTs quickly assessed Edwards's condition; they immediately gave him a shot of morphine and lessened the bleeding. The two experienced EMTs then stabilized his arm and got him into the SWAT van. He was driven back to the Command Center and quickly transferred to their ambulance. The big, squareish red and white Camp Sherman emergency vehicle with lights flashing headed off to St. Charles in Bend. Deputy Edwards lay on his back focusing on the van's ceiling. He watched the saline solution swing back and forth as the clumsy vehicle moved down the gravel road. He didn't feel any pain now. His fright began to diminish and he somewhat relaxed. *I'm all right, things are okay. I'm all right.* The EMT at Edwards' side looked down at his patient.

"You're going to be fine, deputy. You're stabilized, we've got the bleeding under control, and we know what we're doing. Just try and relax now. We'll be at the hospital in no time."

The medic patted Edwards' good arm in a reassuring manner.

Superintendent Ross walked along the barricade talking to his troopers and county deputies, although, there really wasn't much to say. The attack had come out of nowhere and ended quickly. The forest was strangely quiet after the volley of bullets had smashed into the protective wall. A pair of ravens left the Command area and flew back up the hill to the summit, but other than their movement, nothing else even so much as twitched. Ross walked over to the porta pottie and shined his flashlight beam around the area. Inspecting crime scenes was second nature to the experienced cop. His flashlight beam rose up onto the big Ponderosa trunk next to the commode and stopped about four feet off the ground. It illuminated a fresh, woody scar. Ross knew what he'd found. He pulled a knife from his pocket and, opening up the blade, the superintendent began probing through the shattered bark and the tree's woody, outer layer. *There you are.* He gently pried out a bullet from the tree trunk, and held the projectile up for a better look. *Hardly a scratch.* He dropped the bullet into his pocket and returned to his men.

Ross found Officer Mills. "Hold the fort down for a few hours. If nothing else happens, send the troops back to the Command Center."

"Will do, superintendent."

Ross continued. "I'm not sure what happened here, except we've got a wounded deputy on our hands."

"Edwards can't get a break, sir."

"It would seem so, wouldn't it? Anyway, have everybody stay behind the barricade and remain vigilant."

The superintendent turned, walked over to his patrol car, then pulled a U-turn and headed back to his trailer. He thought about the slug in his pocket. *I'll need to get a ballistics profile on my little friend.* Ross returned to his trailer and found a Ziploc bag to put the bullet in. Tomorrow, he'd give it to Peters, and off to the lab it would go. Ross yawned and stretched. It was hard to predict what would happen next. Hopefully, tomorrow would be incident free.

First Sergeant Jefferson quietly slid open his tent flap and side-stepped into the dimly lit interior. Forrest lay awake on his cot, listening to music through his ear buds. Jefferson tickled the sergeant's neck with his rifle's muzzle.

"Boo!"

Forrest bolted upright and knocked the gun away from his neck.

"Well, staff sergeant. Mission accomplished."

"Shit, would you stop with the gun muzzle! Crap, Jefferson, that's creepy!"

"You've got to be more aware, sergeant. I'm just helping you become a better soldier."

The two men sat across from each other on their cots.

"You must have hit somebody with your shots. An ambulance drove away earlier with lights flashing."

"All the better. Nothing like a casualty to get people moving and making decisions. We should be out of here in no time. Anyway, tag, you're it. Oh yeah, if I were you, I'd let the cops know you're out and about. People might be a little jumpy tonight."

"Yeah, thanks."

Jefferson smiled and laughed, "You're welcome, Staff Sergeant Forrest."

Forrest parted the tent's entrance flaps and disappeared into the night. First Sergeant Jefferson dressed down to his skivvies and got into his bedroll. He fell asleep immediately.

Ranger moved from sentry position to sentry position and noticed nothing unusual. He gathered together Hops, Dakota, and Woody for a quick briefing.

"I don't expect anything else to happen tonight, boys. We've been set up, for sure. Its tomorrow night or the night after I'm worried me. If you see anything weird or different out there, give me a shout."

The three men acknowledged Ranger's comments and returned to their posts. The ex-Marine climbed down the wooden ladder into the cavern. The remaining occupiers had all gotten back to sleep. Ranger quietly walked around the basaltic pillar and shined his flashlight on the ancient Indian. *Sorry, my long dead friend, but I need your help.* He bent down and rolled the skeleton up into the woven mat it lay on. Next, he tied some rope around the bundle in several places, trussing the bones up in the mat. Then, he moved the mat closer to the ladder's opening, but left it out of view, still behind the rock pillar. After he had accomplished his task, Ranger had one more job to do before bedding down. He regained the basaltic bowl and moved to the backside of the latrine. *Need to make a call.* He pulled out the walkie-talkie and keyed the mic.

CHAPTER
89

A WHITE, COMPACT RENTAL CAR TURNED OUT OF the Metolius River campground and headed for Camp Sherman. Three young college students sat nervously, focusing straight ahead, as the car entered the small hamlet. Russel anxiously secured his computer to his lap with both hands, and Rachael and Bridger were unusually quiet as their vehicle crossed the bridge and headed out of town. None of the young people knew what to expect from the meeting they were about to initiate.

Ranger had contacted Bridger late in the evening and told him to meet with Superintendent Ross. He was to tell Ross the silverbacks had not fired the shots at the barricade. The rounds were from an AK-47, and the occupiers had Czech CZ rifles. Also, Bridger was to suggest the silverbacks were being "set-up" by the shooting incident. The retired Marine also told Russel to show the OSP boss his Oval Office note. He didn't know if Ross could thwart the anticipated military action, but the shared information at least gave him some ammunition to use. Each of the young people felt Ranger's request was reasonable, but they were all scared about their possible arrest and incarceration.

The rental car slowly came to rest in front of the first barricade. Numerous reporters and camera crews were standing nearby, but after noting the car's occupants, they mostly ignored the young people. Bridger left the car and approached the roadblock's OSP trooper. He got close to the officer so he could talk softly and not be overheard by the reporters, but the officer spoke first.

"You're not allowed to block the roadway, son. You'll have to move your vehicle."

The trooper wore the traditional OSP uniform, complete with Mountie-style hat.

"I need to talk with whoever is in charge, sir."

The OSP officer cocked his head to one side and gave Bridger a questioning look. "Why's that, young man?"

"I have a message for him from the silverbacks."

Philip Ross looked down the road and saw the white sedan approaching. It stopped a few feet from the OSP superintendent, and three young people emerged from the vehicle. Ross noted two redheads and a ponytailed young man walking in his direction. The trio stopped in front of him.

"Hello, sir." Bridger extended his hand and the two men shook. "I'm Bridger Thompson; this is Rachael and my friend Russel Nelson."

Ross focused on his new acquaintances. "What can I do for you?"

Bridger gulped and took a deep breath. "My gramps, Woody Thompson, is one of the silverbacks and I have a message for you from them."

Superintendent Ross surveyed the threesome before him and shook his head slightly. "Well, son. I wish you'd come to me earlier."

Bridger, Rachael, and Russel were ushered into the Command Center trailer. They shared with Ross Ranger's message about the gunshots and Russel retrieved his White House note from his laptop case, making it available. He also related the dorm scene where M.I. seemed to be searching for him. As the foursome talked, Lt. Peters arrived and joined the group. Ross asked how Bridger communicated with the silverbacks, and Bridger pulled out his walkie-talkie, laying it on the table. The superintendent reached out, picked up the handset, and keyed it.

"Yeah, Bridger. How'd things go?"

"This is Superintendent Ross of the OSP. With whom am I speaking?"

There was a slight pause.

"You're speaking with one of the silverbacks, sir. Did you get my message?"

"Yes I did. You think it was an AK-47 last night?"

"Most definitely, sir. I've heard enough of them in my day. They don't sound like any other AR. We've got Czech CZs up here. If you can find an AK down there, you'll locate who shot at your barricade."

Ross thought about Ranger's comments. "I'm not sure if we'll be able to secure the AK-47 you allude to, sir. I agree with your assessment about being set-up. We've got a small squad of Army regulars down here who are out of place and very suspicious. Young Russel's note would suggest your days are numbered."

"We realize that, sir."

"May I suggest you gentlemen give up your position and bring this altercation to a close?"

"No can do, superintendent. We, to a man, will not give up this position until you can promise the logging operation has been scuttled."

Ross continued. "I can't oblige your request." The OSP boss thought for a moment. "You know I have no control over the regular army's presence."

"Yes, sir. I understand that."

Ross thought, again.. "My military experience tells me you'll be hit at night, and a bomb will probably be used to soften you up. Are you prepared for this type of assault?"

"Yes, sir. We are."

Ross shook his head and sighed. "Good luck." Then he impulsively asked, "What's your name, soldier?"

Ranger responded, "My friends call me Ranger, sir."

"Well, good luck, Ranger."

"Thank you, superintendent."

Ross set the walkie-talkie onto the dinette's surface. He gazed at the young people and then at Lt. Peters.

"Excuse us, please. Lt. Peters and I need to confer in private."

Ross and Peters walked to the trailer's door. The superintendent stopped and turned. "May I have your note, Russel?"

Russel looked at Bridger and Rachael and then back at Ross. "I think I need it for my safety, sir."

"I'll keep it safe, son." Ross then added, "And I'm going to keep you safe, too."

Russel gazed at Ross anxiously and then handed him the White House paper.

Leaving the trailer, the troopers stood next to each other in the hazy mid-morning sunlight.

"I think we've got an illegal, rogue operation going on here and it originated from the Oval Office."

"I agree with you, Phil."

"These guys have no orders to show me and I agree with Ranger; those shots set the silverbacks up for a retaliatory attack."

"That appears to be the case."

"We need to find our AK-47, and my money's on it being in the first sergeant's tent."

Peters nodded his head in agreement.

"Let's try and bluff this guy. Get us a search warrant for his encampment from the Attorney General. Who knows, maybe this sergeant doesn't know the rules."

The OSP Superintendent reached into his pocket and pulled the slug out of his pocket. He handed it to Peters.

"Have ballistics do their magic with this."

He also handed Russel's note to his lieutenant. "We need to keep this safe, and I want Russel put into protective custody. Also, contact his parents."

"Anything else, Phil?"

Superintendent Ross shook his head in disbelief and glanced at the ground for a moment. He raised his gaze up to the Big Eddy Rise's summit.

"Shit, is this really going to happen, Peters? Those old men are going to get killed by an illegal Army operation and I can't do a thing about it."

Peters' gaze joined the superintendent's. "Hopefully not, sir. Hell, the Ninth Court is supposed to weigh in any day now. Their determination could be stop all of this."

Ross focused on Peters. "I'm not sure they can influence this outcome. In a perfect world, probably, but this whole scene seems far from perfect."

"I'll get moving on everything we've talked about, sir. I'll get Russel into a safe house in Salem. What about the other kids?"

"We need to contact their parents and get them home."

The two troopers reentered the trailer and stood next to the young people. Superintendent Ross spoke to the trio.

"Russel, we're putting you into protective custody. I'm going to contact your parents and let them know of your situation. This is for your own good, son. Taking a presidential note from the White House has put you in serious danger. Lt. Peters will drive you into Salem today, and your parents will be able to visit you right away."

Ross then fixed his gaze onto Bridger and Rachael. "You two need to be home and with your parents. I'm going to..."

Bridger interrupted the superintendent. "I'm not going home. My gramps is here, and I don't want to leave him."

Bridger was near tears, and Rachael grabbed his hand tightly in hers. Ross took off his hat, and wiped his short salt and pepper hair with his free hand. He looked first at Peters and then back at Bridger. He knew what he should do, but the young man's devotion to his grandfather got the better of him.

"All right, son. You and your friend can stay." Ross picked up the handset and checked its frequency. "You are to contact me if anything unusual happens near you, understand?"

Bridger wiped tears away from his eyes. "Yes, sir."

"Where are you staying?"

"The first campground downriver from the store."

"All right. If you hear from your grandpa or Ranger, you are to contact me, and let me know what's up. That's our deal. If you stay, you're to help me out. You won't be betraying them, son, you'll be allowing me to help them."

Bridger studied Rachael and got a reassuring gaze from her. "Okay, sir. I can do what you ask."

Lt. Peters and Russel left together in the trooper's cruiser. Rachael and Bridger followed right behind in their rental car. The vehicles were mobbed by news personnel as they passed through the roadblock, but the reporters were soon left behind in their dust. The cars parted ways at the three-way stop. Peters and Russel headed for the main highway, and Rachael and Bridger drove back to camp.

The young people emerged from their rental and walked over to the picnic table. They sat down next to each other and Bridger put his face into his hands. Rachael slipped her arm around her boyfriend and hugged him to her side. She tilted her head over until it rested on his shoulder. The lovers sat like this, not moving for a long time. A nearby Ponderosa branch bent down as two ravens came to rest on it. They sat quietly on their perch and watched the couple's moment of uncertain trepidation.

CHAPTER 90

THE PRESIDENTIAL ENTOURAGE LEFT THE WHITE House residence and headed for the Grand Staircase. Secret Service escorts walked in front of and behind the president. He reached the second floor landing and froze. He was viewing his smartphone and just noticed a recent Allen Rodrigues piece that referred to a new ACLU lawsuit targeting the president and his administration. The ACLU was suing the federal government for its biased arrest of immigrants. They referred to the incarcerations as an unconstitutional attack upon the states by a politically motivated agenda. Because the proof of these accusations was blatantly apparent within the arrest logs of the ICE agents, the ACLU lawyers were certain of legal victory.

"God-damn liberal do-gooders!"

McDonald's outburst was ignored by his escorts. He lifted his eyes from the phone and became transfixed by the stairwell's chandelier.

The nearest agent, noticing McDonald's frozen position, inquired, "Are you all right, Mr. President?"

This query seemed to break his trance, and without acknowledging the question, he descended the stairs.

Upon reaching the White House ground floor, the procession headed for the Palm Room and the West Colonnade. McDonald refocused his attention on his phone, and partway down the wide hallway he blurted out, "Shit!"

Once again all movement stopped as the president viewed his phone's screen. Rodrigues was reporting about the numerous demonstrations occurring around the country supporting the silverbacks' occupation in the National Forest.

"God-damn liberal, Democratic tree huggers!!! Damn ACLU's probably paying all those sniveling pantywaists to demonstrate against me!"

The two escort agents focused on each other with blank stares as McDonald abruptly headed for the West Wing. He continued viewing his phone while they walked through the Palm Room and gained the West Colonnade. A brisk fall breeze greeted the entourage and McDonald pulled his suitcoat together by the lapels. The balding, gray-haired, president's pants were flattened against his thin, knobby-kneed legs as they continued forward. Just before entering the West Wing, the president abruptly stopped and raised his hands in a victorious gesture and shouted out, "Yes, you God-damn Ape-men can kiss your sweet asses good-bye!"

The two Secret Service agents viewed each other, this time with questioning, raised eyebrows. McDonald's face broke into a broad smile as he entered the West Wing. He walked down the hallway, and his escorts opened up the Oval Office, checking it out before allowing him to enter. All this activity was lost upon the president, who continued to view his smartphone. He walked by the Oval Office fireplace, and as he passed Janet's doorway, without glancing her way, he ordered some sandwiches and coffee. Sitting down at his desk, McDonald continued scanning his phone. His guardians closed the hall doors, stationed themselves adjacent to the entrance, and shared eye contact again; one agent slightly shook his head in disgust and the other responded with a nod of agreement. More damaging news met the president's critical observation.

Allen Rodrigues just noted a Capitol Hill leak had disclosed to WNN some very ominous news directed at the present administration. It appeared an unofficial Republican "vote of confidence" regarding President McDonald had failed, and Republican congressional power brokers were now determining what to do with the results.

McDonald muttered to himself. "Like I really care what those bought and paid for politicians are doing or saying."

Janet sat in her office reading her emails and listening to McDonald talking to himself. She raised her eyes to the ceiling. *Thank God I get a weekend pass from this place.* She was thinking about her mini-vacation to Texas. Staying on Ray Billings' ranch sounded like heaven to her right now. She missed the short, stocky oilman from Houston.

"Janet, what's next on my agenda?"

Janet's daydreams dissipated. "Secretary Hastings will be here in fifteen minutes, sir."

President McDonald smiled and clapped his hands together. "Perfect timing!"

His eyes took in the Oval Office. The repair work on the marble fireplace would need to be redone again. *Shit, I can't get any good work done around this place.* The president eventually locked eyes with Lincoln's cool, discerning gaze. He made a mental note to have the portrait removed soon. He remembered a painting of Napoleon in one of his Miami condos, and thought about replacing the Lincoln portrait with it. *It will be nice to have a winner on my wall for a change.*

Secretary Hastings was shown into the Oval Office. He acknowledged the president with a nod, walked over to a couch, and sat down. Following right behind him was a pretty, well-endowed intern carrying a tray filled with sandwiches and coffee. As she set everything onto the central coffee table, McDonald ogled her with raised eyebrows. The young woman straightened up, turned, and left the office. Hastings cleared his throat loudly, which seemed to regain McDonald's focus, and the president inspected the secretary.

"Perfect timing, Hastings. Did you hear the news about our Ape-men?"

"Do you mean the shooting?"

"You're damn right I mean the shooting. Seems like our old fart tree huggers have given us a perfect reason to take them out."

Hastings watched President McDonald leave his desk and sit down across from him. He had to admit things couldn't have gone better for their operation. The shooting with U.S. military personnel in the area could be their legal rationale for the upcoming attack. The shots could be construed as an assault on U.S. Armed Forces, and this could allow for a legal retaliation based on self-defense.

"Yes, Mr. President. It was a dumb move on the eco-terrorists' part, which plays right into our hands."

McDonald scooted forward onto the couch's edge. "Well then, let's get the old farts."

"I think the timing's right, sir. I'll need to get Rodgers and Henry coordinated and barring any unpredictable problems, like ash fall, we should be able to neutralize the terrorists tonight."

McDonald smiled and jumped to his feet. "Can we watch the attack from the Situation Room?"

Hastings thought to himself then said, "I think so, Mr. President. We could use our drone again for a visual."

"Great! Hastings! This is fantastic. I'll fill in Horner and Brown about the attack date. Can they watch the show with us?"

Hastings mentally reeled at the term "show" being used to describe a lethal military operation.

"Yes they can, sir. But no one else. The fewer people the better, Mr. President."

"Of course, of course. Hastings, you know what's best."

Secretary Hastings blankly studied McDonald. Standing up, he excused himself from the president's presence.

"I need to get Henry and Rodgers up to speed, sir."

"Certainly, certainly, Hastings, by all means. God damn it, Hastings! Those Ape-men are going to get theirs!"

"Yes they will, sir."

Hastings turned away from the president and visibly rolled his eyes as he left the Oval Office.

McDonald returned to his desk and sat down. He began drumming his fingers on the desk's top and fantasizing about the upcoming assault. He hoped the surveillance would be detailed enough to clearly define the personnel involved.

"Janet, clear my afternoon schedule, and get my press secretary and chief of staff here, ASAP."

McDonald continued sitting at his desk and his mind drifted back to the young intern who had delivered the coffee and sandwiches.

"Janet."

"Yes, Mr. President."

"Have Horner and Brown meet me here at two p.m. I'm going to have lunch up in my residence."

"Will do, sir."

McDonald rose from his desk and left the Oval Office. His entourage headed back to the White House and his personal quarters. He'd find out if the young, pretty intern was still serving his food.

CHAPTER 91

Secretary Hastings sat back into his limo's rear bench seat and relaxed.

"Where to, sir?"

"Back to the Pentagon, lieutenant."

"Shouldn't take long, Mr. Secretary. Traffic's moving smoothly."

His Lincoln Continental followed the curving road off of the White House grounds and turned south. Hastings thought about the recent events at the occupation site. The shots fired by the silverbacks were an egregious error on their part, and he felt if push came to shove, lawyers could show a military retaliation was within legal grounds. After all, the U.S. military was within range of the volley and it could be construed as an act of aggression against his troops. This logic would be "pushing it" of course, but that's what lawyers were for, making the whimsical appear real. *Maybe my job won't be endangered by this operation after all.* Hastings looked out his car's window at the D.C. streets and districts he passed through. He continued thinking about the attack and how pleased he was with the potential notoriety it would give him. *I'll be the only recent Secretary of Defense with the "balls" to take care of business in regards to these left wing eco-terrorists.* The secretary's predecessors had pushed situations like this onto other agencies to avoid controversy. The limo turned onto Highway 395 and headed in the Potomac River's direction. *Too bad I'm saddled with the McDonald presidency. He'll claim all the glory and downplay my efforts! Shit, what do I care what the clown says or does? Real players will know who pulled all the strings.* He continued musing about the pending military action, and after further contemplation, felt reasonably certain a disappearing act would not be necessary. Thanks to the silverbacks' mistake, the Secretary of Defense would come out of this smelling like a rose and appearing like a decisive, tough-minded champion of freedom. Hastings' Lincoln turned north off of 395 and headed to the Pentagon. He reached into his pocket and pulled out his flip phone.

"Hello, Rodgers?"

"Yes, Mr. Secretary. I thought I'd be hearing from you. Seems like our silverbacks were getting a little bored."

"Yes, it does seem that way. They certainly opened the door for us."

"I think you're right, sir."

"Let's send them a greeting card at 2400 hours Pacific time tonight."

"Okay, I've got a good pilot picked out for the mission, Mr. Secretary. I'll brief him today and we'll be operational tonight."

"Great. I'm just thinking aloud now, colonel. Will our ordnance do the job?"

"Most certainly, Mr. Secretary. Nothing in the bowl will survive."

"Okay, Rodgers, I'm calling Henry next, and getting him up to speed. After I brief him, he'll contact you and discuss the mission. I don't want any miscommunications to jeopardize our success."

"Good idea, Mr. Secretary. I'll be waiting for the lieutenant colonel's call."

"One last thing. Can your drone feed the White House Situation Room with a visual?"

"Yes it can, sir."

"Well, get it operational, too. The president wants to watch the operation in real time."

"Consider it done."

"All right then, Rodgers. Be in your Operations Room at 2300 hours Pacific time tonight and we'll get this rodeo going. Have your flip phone with you; I still want to use our personal phones for communications."

"Roger that, Mr. Secretary."

Hastings closed his phone and peered out of his car window at the Pentagon. His driver was just passing through Security. *One last phone call and our eco-terrorists' fates are sealed.* Hastings speed dialed Lt. Colonel Henry. The black Lincoln Continental pulled into the Secretary of Defense's parking slip and came to a stop. Hastings' driver noted the secretary talking on his phone, and remained seated behind the wheel. The lieutenant would wait for his boss's conversation to end before opening the limo's rear door and helping the secretary exit the vehicle.

CHAPTER 92

THE SILVERBACKS CLIMBED SLOWLY OUT OF THEIR sleeping quarters. The late September, chilly morning air had stiffened the joints of the elder men. There was no firewood, so they wore extra layers. They fired up the large, two-burner, propane cook stove, warming up a pot of water above one flame and a group of cold hands around the other.

Breakfast was simple; they heated beans and rice, adding some smoked salmon to the mix. Most of the silverbacks and their young accomplices added some hot sauce to the entrée to liven up the flavor. The group habitually sat around the fire while they consumed meals, and a fireless pit did not change their choice of dining areas. Conversation was light to nonexistent. Mostly, the men talked about the morning chill and how they'd slept.

After the group ate and warmed up, several men exchanged places with the evening guards, and the relieved sentries warmed their hands and grabbed plates filled with food. They, too, sat quietly while they ate, only occasionally offering up conversation.

Ranger walked over to the basaltic rim and peered down at the surveillance barricade. Nothing seemed to be happening. The old soldier's gaze moved to the OSP Command Center and military encampment. Those positions seemed quiet, too. The passive existence and lack of activity at the Army's bivouac belied the obvious deadly potential residing there. *Can we repulse their attack?* The unanswered question was disturbing to Ranger.

Ranger's attention was drawn to the closest Ponderosa by a chuckling sound descending from the upper branches. He focused on the two camp ravens. *Well, our two feathered friends haven't deserted the ship.* The ex-Marine smiled to himself, thinking their presence, hopefully, was a good sign. Looking past his dining friends, Ranger focused on the cavern's entrance, and was thoughtful for a moment. He left the wall, quietly walked to Hops' ladder, and descended into the cave. No one seemed to notice his movement. He entered their sleeping chamber and, stooping, rounded the basaltic pillar. After picking up the bundled ancient one, the ex-Marine left the chamber and carefully climbed the ladder. He poked his head above the lip of the cavern's entrance, and noticing nobody was gazing in his direction, stealthily stepped up and onto the bowl's floor. Ranger entered the nearby tent, and set the large, tube-like bundle on the ground between two sex toys. With his chore completed, the ex-Marine reached a hand out and felt the heat emanating from the plastic dolls. *Thanks, ladies. I hope your warm bodies fooled the bad guys.* After patting one doll on her rear, the old soldier left the tent.

Walking over to the rim again, he nervously picked up the binoculars and scanned the surrounding area. Ranger hadn't felt this anxious in many years. Turning his back to the basaltic barrier, he studied his close friends and their young companions. *How will trying to kill someone affect these men?* Ranger rubbed his stubbled chin with his free hand. His gaze went from one silverback to another. They had all aged gracefully, but due to active lives, showed their years. Gray beards and hair greeted his stare, and deep age lines were etched into their faces. Their hands were wrinkled and showed age spots. Yet these men's minds were clear and their morals strong. Ranger was proud to call each one of them his friend.

A melancholy mood transfixed the old soldier and bothered him. His anxiety was intensifying and the need to lose himself in a project became obvious so he decided to check on all the defensive positions and then make the noon meal.

The sun progressed slowly upward, and a southwest breeze began, blowing much of the haze out of the forest. Cirrus clouds were slowly drifting by at their high altitude. Hops gazed up and noticed the wispy clouds floating past. He knew from experience a weather change would follow these "mares' tails," and wondered how drastic it would be.

Hops, Dakota, and Woody spent part of the day sleeping. They arose at noon and ate several peanut butter and jelly sandwiches. Hops pulled out a bag of apples and located some processed cheese, so the occupiers finished off their meal with apple and cheese slices.

After lunch, the idle men, minus Ranger, played a marathon game of cribbage. It lasted all afternoon, and their tally marks, drawn into the ground with pointed sticks, began to surround the players. A large bag of M&Ms was within arm's reach of his friends, and Ranger assumed the men were keeping score, and whoever won a game gobbled up his winnings after determining how many points he'd beaten his opponents by. Eventually, the ex-Marine grew tired of creating things to do, and took a nap while the never-ending card game continued. The dark cavern had become noticeably colder over the last few days, and he had to add an extra blanket to his bedroll. His sleep was fitful. He arose only somewhat rested. Again, he needed something to do so Ranger lost himself in preparing the evening meal. Canned soup and grilled processed cheese sandwiches were offered up for everyone's consumption.

The encampment chilled as the sun receded, and a peachy colored sunset developed but quickly dissipated. The card players huddled together as they ate. The hot soup and grilled cheese sandwiches were great comfort foods and well received. The sentry's mouths were watering by the time they were relieved, and they too huddled together while consuming Ranger's cooking.

After dinner, Ranger and Doc cleaned the dishes while Tunes and Hang drummed together. Hang was becoming fairly talented with the djembe and could hold his own with Tunes' rhythms. The ancient forest easily accepted the African percussions and the northwest wind carried the beat down to the OSP Command Center and the military bivouac. The nearby encampments quietly listened to the rhythmic music.

With the onset of darkness, Ranger spoke to his friends. He reiterated the sequence of events, following their bombing, and specifically assigned people to particular firing positions. He and Dakota would take the ports facing the OSP locations. Hang was to man the southeast portal and Hops was to protect the northwest side. Woody and Tunes were to guard the escape route.

After Ranger's defense discussion, Tunes, Doc, and Hang retired for the evening. The others continued guarding the encampment. Before retiring, Ranger reminded his friends to be vigilant and to check the canvas tent periodically for the laser's beam. This comment sent a chill down Woody's spine, and he became nervous and worried. Ranger left his friends and climbed down into the cavern, and was greeted by Doc's snoring. Soon, his own version would reverberate through the chamber. The ex-Marine knew he needed to rest. This evening could well test everyone's mettle.

CHAPTER
93

Spec 4 James Lee left the communication trailer and approached the first sergeant's tent. The flaps were tied open and Lee could see both sergeants inside their bivouac talking. He barely heard the last comment between the men, but it seemed to reference him. Sergeant Forrest said to Jefferson, "Here comes China." The two men were now smiling and looking his way. Lee, bristling at the obvious ethnic reference, stopped at the tent's doorway.

"First Sergeant."

"Yes, Lee. What do you need?"

"The lieutenant colonel wishes to speak with you."

"Roger that, Lee."

Jefferson and Forrest walked to the trailer, entered, and closed the rear door. They were in the communication trailer for about ten minutes. When they emerged, both sergeants wore serious expressions on their faces. Forrest went into his tent, and Lee watched while the staff sergeant brought his sniper rifle over to his cot and secured a laser to the barrel's underside. Forrest studied the spec 4.

"Return to your post, soldier."

After preparing his weapon for use, Staff Sergeant Forrest rounded up the troops and gathered them together under the mess canopy. He sent Private Abramson to fetch Lee. They returned to the canopy area and sat with the other lower ranked men.

"Listen up, soldiers. The first sergeant will get you up to speed on our mission."

The men gazed at each other with questioning expressions. They all believed their objective was simple surveillance and nothing more. Jefferson entered the mess area and stood before his troops.

"All right, men, listen up. At 2400 hours tonight we will take the Aper's Hill. The Air Force will soften our target with a five-hundred-pound ordnance, and it's our job to make sure all the occupiers are neutralized or captured."

Private First Class Fitzgerald spoke, "We're really going to attack those old guys?"

"We certainly are, soldier. Did you think this was a Girl Scout picnic you were on?"

"No, first sergeant, but..."

"No 'buts,' private. You've been trained to kill people, and tonight, it may be a gray-haired eco-terrorist who's pointing an AK-47 at you. These are not your loveable grandparents, ladies. These are hard-core terrorists who have already shot at us. I want all of you here at 2300 hours in full tactical gear. Did you hear me, soldiers?"

A chorus of "Yes, sir, first sergeant" responded to his question.

"All right, soldiers. You're dismissed."

Jefferson turned to Forrest. "I want the men eating C rations for dinner. We don't need any bloated bellies out there tonight."

"Copy that, first sergeant."

Forrest returned to his tent and brought out his Remington 700. He tested the laser on a far-off tree. Satisfied, he returned to the bivouac and began gathering equipment and dressing for the assault. After he'd geared up, Forrest broke out enough C rations for the squad and then went to check on the men's progress.

OSP Trooper Jackson, sitting under the Command awning, watched the first sergeant talk to his squad and the men disperse. The body language he observed was of a serious nature. He wasn't going to alert Superintendent Ross of the soldiers' activities yet, but if any further curious actions occurred, he was going to inform his boss about his observations.

CHAPTER
94

The Metolius River danced moonlight off its surface as it flowed north. Along its banks, ancient Ponderosas reached out toward one another, and beneath the large trees, a big cat slowly walked next to the stream. When it neared the Big Eddy Rise, the cougar veered off and headed for the summit. Partway up the hill, the cat stopped and shook her coat. The tan animal began to transform its color; a dark, bluish-black pelt enveloped its host, and the animal's soft yellow eyes turned into brilliant golden orbs. As if nothing surreal or magical happened, the Black Panther continued up the slope. She eventually reached the base of the summit's basaltic wall, where she crouched down and swept the forest floor with her tail. Her leg muscles flexed and she leaped upwards, finding the top of the basaltic rim as she landed. The panther stared down into the camp. Her fore body was silhouetted by the rising moon. The big cat's head reached forward and feline lips parted, exposing ivory colored canines. She screamed into the night.

Woody was directly below the big cat and froze. The hair on his arms raised and his heart pounded. Dakota was stationed across from Woody, and was now gazing directly at the beautiful panther, backlit as she was by the moon's glow. Without looking away from her, Dakota spoke. "Don't shoot, Hops. It's all right. Woody, focus on me and slowly walk over here."

Ranger's rifle barrel emerged from the cavern, followed by his head.

"Go back down, Ranger. Everything's fine. We're having a very cool visitation. It's amazing."

Ranger peered over at Dakota and followed his directive.

Woody slowly walked across the basin. Sweat was beading up on his forehead and he gripped his CZ tightly. When he reached Dakota, his old friend gently turned him around, allowing him to view the majestic animal. All three sentinels watched the Black Panther. She sat down examining the occupiers. Now, her whole body seemed surrounded by the moon. The three men were speechless and mesmerized by the vision before them. The cat raised one paw up to her face, licked it several times, and then cleaned her whiskers and head. After grooming, the panther stood up and walked past Hops' position. She stopped, lowered herself, and checked out the OSP encampment. Once again her lips parted, her neck extended, and she screamed a terrifying cry that carried through the trees, past the military bivouac, and lost itself in the distant forest. After calling out again, the big animal rose up gracefully, and as she walked back to her initial perch, the night's orb seemed to accompany her. She paused and viewed the occupiers again. Then, turning around, the cat gathered herself and leapt from view. Only the moon remained where the Panther once had been.

Woody looked at Dakota with wide eyes. "Jesus Christ, Dakota. What we just saw was unbelievable."

Dakota smiled at his old, grade school friend and patted the ex-teacher's right upper arm. "We've witnessed a pretty good omen, my friend. It's not every man who gets a visit from his spirit helper in a time of need."

Woody's left hand unconsciously moved to his right arm and rubbed the same area Dakota had patted. He continued watching his friend.

"No, Woody. I did not have a vision."

Hops smiled to himself at this comment.

"But I feel pretty good right now. Your cat is a powerful spirit helper and I believe she's on our side."

Woody simply nodded at Dakota. In a state of awe, he slowly returned to his sentry post and stared into the forest, hoping to catch sight of the departing cat. Hops, shaking his head in disbelief, returned his view to the hillside. He peered into the woods at all the shadows and big trees. *This is just plain crazy. A Black Panther! What will happen next?* For a moment, he forgot about the imminent military assault.

CHAPTER 95

First Sergeant Jefferson mustered his squad behind the bivouacs at 2300, keeping his troops hidden from the OSP canopy area. The spec 4s and privates assembled before him.

"Check your weapons, soldiers."

All the squad dropped their night vision goggles into place and sighted through their short, ACOG scopes. They checked chambers for live rounds.

"Sergeant Forrest. Get those men's 'pack sets' on line."

Forrest went from man to man and encoded their personal radio set with the mission's "crypto."

"Are the men speaking the same language, sergeant?"

"Yes, first sergeant."

The small squad looked prepared for anything. Their bulky body armor, helmets, small miced headsets, personal armaments, and camouflaged faces depicted a fighting unit ready for action. The moon had risen, and the forest was bright with light and filled with shadows.

First Sergeant Jefferson checked his watch and then focused on his staff sergeant. Forrest carried his sniper rifle in one hand and returned his gaze.

"Check your radio, staff sergeant."

Forrest had a second radio positioned on his back. A small hand set was attached to the front shoulder of his body armor. It was a PRC 117, capable of long-distance transmissions and communications with high flying aircraft. He keyed his radio, and spoke to the first sergeant. Jefferson carried the same radio on his back.

"Loud and clear, staff sergeant."

Jefferson studied his squad. "This should be a body count, soldiers, but as we all know intel can be wrong, and we could have a firefight on our hands. Do not treat this like a walk in the park, ladies. Is that clear?"

A chorus responded to Jefferson's statement. "Yes, first sergeant!"

Jefferson again checked his watch, 2315. He examined Forrest. "Get into position. Raise me when you're operational."

Forrest quietly and stealthily left the encampment. His destination was Jefferson's tree stand.

The first sergeant studied his squad. "Who's got the M203?"

Private Fitzgerald held up his M4, so the first sergeant could clearly see his grenade launcher.

"Stay close to me, Fitzgerald. Within a few feet. Do you copy what I'm saying, soldier?"

"Yes, first sergeant."

"All right, ladies, are you ready?"

A chorus again responded to Jefferson's question. "Army ready, first sergeant."

The sergeant again checked his watch. It was 2330.

"Move out."

The squad left in various directions. Like Staff Sergeant Forrest, they moved quietly and carefully through the forest, continually noting their surroundings.

During the team's earlier briefing, each squad member's assault path had been delineated. Abramson was to utilize the ravine for his ascent. Spec 4 Lee was to come up the southeast flank and Spec Turner, Sergeant Jefferson, and Private Fitzgerald were to approach the summit from the southwest. The squad was to maneuver to within fifty yards of the summit and wait for the ordnance delivery. After the explosion, they would slowly climb the hill, soldier by soldier, with the others covering each man's movement.

Their call sign was introduced during the squad's tactical meeting. Ghost was chosen to denote the squad members. First Sergeant Jefferson was Ghost one, Forrest was Top Ghost, and the privates and specialists were given their separate numbers. Jefferson checked his watch; it was 2340.

"All Ghosts. This is Ghost one. Secure your positions and await further orders. Over and out."

Jefferson and Fitzgerald knelt behind a huge Ponderosa trunk and peered around either side. Turner was to their right, prone, using a log for cover. He peered around its decaying end, taking in the Rise's summit. The first sergeant couldn't see Lee or Abramson. He waited for Sergeant Forrest's communication.

Now we wait. I love this shit. Maybe one of these old Apers will survive the blast and put up some resistance. That would be fun. Jefferson stared up the hill. Nothing moved on the summit. It was perfectly still.

Sergeant Forrest slowly made his way to the sniper Ponderosa. After locating it, he climbed up the access rope, and carefully, branch by branch, stepped and pulled himself upwards. Upon gaining his perch, he unslung his Remington 700 and waited for his breathing to return to normal. The seat was positioned so his feet rested comfortably on a lower branch. He rested his rifle onto the cross branch, dropped down his night vision goggles, and gazed through his scope. The rifle sat in a perfect firing cradle. He noted his roost provided only a small view of the Rise's bowl, but he could see part of the elk tent and a little ground before it. *Damn lucky this position worked.* Forrest checked his watch. It was 2345. In ten minutes, he would raise the F-16 and communicate with its pilot. He looked through his scope again, and tested his IR laser on the distant elk tent. Satisfied with his weapon, Forrest used his optics to survey the slope's western flank. He could see a small portion of the hill clearly, but most of it was a surreal jumble of lines created by tree trunks and shadows. The staff sergeant keyed Jefferson and communicated his status. Checking his watch again, Forrest noted the time. He hadn't been in a real tactical operation for years. *God damn! Bring it on!* The minutes couldn't go by quickly enough for the seasoned sergeant.

CHAPTER 96

AS TED HORNER AND LESLEY BROWN ENTERED the Oval Office, the president sat at his desk drumming his fingers on its top. He glared up menacingly at his chief of staff and press secretary. Ted Horner visibly shrank backwards from the stare. The darkness outside filled the Oval Office windows with a blackish void. Simultaneously, as the president's staff entered his office space, Janet's lights came on, drawing McDonald's attention.

The president barked, "Who's there?"

Janet came to the doorway. She was surprised to see the president in his office at this hour. Ray Billings had flown into D.C. in the afternoon because he wanted to accompany Janet on her flight to Texas. They had dined at Murphy's and conversed with other D.C. regulars until midnight. At that time, Janet departed for the White House, giving Ray her apartment key. She kissed him on the cheek, told him to make himself cozy, and to not wait up for her because she would be awhile. The president's secretary had copious instructional notes to create for her temporary replacement.

"Mr. President, I'm sorry to disturb you. I was going to write up some directions for my replacement."

"Damn late to do so, isn't it?"

"You're right, sir. I could come back later this morning."

The president had already dismissed Janet's presence by refocusing on his minions. Janet turned from his office and returned to hers. As the men walked to the couches, McDonald revealed why he was in an angry, foul mood.

"God damn it, we've still got a sneaky ass snitch running around these halls."

WNN, earlier in the day, had reported on the president's planned attack on the silverbacks. Allen Rodrigues cited an anonymous White House staffer close to the president as his source. This news had already prompted quick responses against the attack by the ACLU and other humanitarian organizations. Numerous important governmental officials had also voiced negative opinions about the military action. The Joint Chiefs of Staff hadn't weighed in yet, but everyone knew their reaction would be against such a move. McDonald was furious about this latest leak and wanted someone's head to roll.

"You two need to find this rat. Shit, what are you doing all day? Sitting on your thumbs?"

Horner and Brown focused on each other in bewilderment as they sat down. Brown stared at the president and swallowed hard. He had some news he felt could potentially derail the upcoming mission. McDonald left his desk and sat across from the men.

He hollered at Janet. "Get us some sandwiches and coffee, Janet."

Janet looked up from her keyboarding and sighed. "Certainly, Mr. President."

Brown swallowed hard again. "Mr. President, the late news discussed your logging operation decree, and noted an unofficial spokesperson, privy to the Ninth Court's decisions, stated your logging proclamation will be struck down by the court tomorrow. The same source said a conservationist suit against your Metolius River logging show will be upheld. I think, sir, under the circumstances maybe we should reconsider..."

McDonald could tell where this line of thought was going. "Hell NO! We aren't going to stop this mission. Those candy-ass Ape-men need to get their butts kicked! We're going to show every activist in this country who's in charge here and who they shouldn't mess with."

McDonald slammed his hand down on the cushion next to him as he spoke. Brown and Horner watched as McDonald brought his hand up and clenched it into a fist, shaking it at the two men.

"Those Ape-men are Dead Meat! Hear me?"

McDonald's chief of staff and press secretary dutifully nodded their heads in agreement.

There was a knock on the door and Secretary Hastings entered the Oval Office. He glanced at Janet's lit-up doorway.

"Is your secretary here?"

"Yes, she's writing out some dumb instructions for a temp."

Hastings thoughtfully examined the empty doorway for a moment, and then sat down next to the president. He checked his watch.

"I just left the Situation Room, Mr. President. Everything is in place." Hastings eyed his companions and rubbed his hands together. "Are you men ready to see history being made?"

Everyone present focused a quizzical expression at Hastings.

Horner spoke. "What do you mean?"

Hastings looked from person to person. He waved the question off with his hand.

"Nothing, nothing, gentlemen." He checked his watch again. "Mr. President. It's about 2:00 a.m. We should go to the Situation Room and begin following our operation."

"Damn right we should."

McDonald jumped up and almost ran out of the Oval Office. Just before his hall doorway, he turned toward Janet's office and hollered in her direction, "Send those sandwiches to the Situation Room."

The president turned and left his work space, followed by Hastings, Brown, and Horner. They picked up two Secret Service personnel as they left. It wasn't far to the Situation Room, although the entourage had to access the recesses below the West Wing's ground floor. Two Marine guards marked the Situation Room's entrance. As McDonald drew close, they opened the door for the Commander in Chief and his team. Inside, two more Marines ushered everyone into chairs that sat next to a large flatscreen. McDonald surveyed the room. There were about six of these big monitors sitting on the walls, and a long rectangular table took up most of the floor space. A few staffers were looking at live screens. The walls were dark mahogany paneling, and the lighting system was recessed fluorescent tubes. On top of the central table sat numerous laptop computers. Some had attendants monitoring them. McDonald returned his gaze to the nearest screen and was greeted by a bluish field of vision.

A fortyish, neatly groomed man approached the group. He wore a dress shirt, tie, and slacks.

"Mr. President, we have your live feed ready." He faced Hastings. "Mr. Secretary, do you have an auditory track for us to acquire?"

Secretary Hastings responded, "No, sound won't be necessary. The visual is all we need." As he spoke, he reached into his inside suit pocket, retrieved his flip phone, and laid it onto the table next to him.

The dress shirt spoke again. "Its 2330, Pacific time, Mr. Secretary, would you like to see your visual?"

Hastings nodded an affirmative. As he responded, he picked up his phone and triggered one of his speed dial numbers.

Colonel Rodgers stood inside his Operations Room behind a young airman who was flying the observation drone. The spec 4 displayed total concentration while performing his task, as one hand flew the drone and the other deftly directed the robotic plane's camera angle. Rodgers opened his phone.

"Yes, Mr. Secretary."

"Is everything operational?"

"Yes, sir. Our F-16 is in flight as we speak and my drone is relaying a nice picture back to us and, I assume, to you."

Hastings gazed up at the screen, which now showed a ghostly picture of the Big Eddy Rise. "We've got our visual up now, Rodgers. Detail looks good."

"Excellent, sir."

"I'll get back to you later."

"I'll have my ears on, Mr. Secretary."

Both men closed their phones.

McDonald and his contingent watched the screen. The drone's camera captured the top of the Rise and the surrounding area. Inside the bowl, three sentinels were clearly shown and several sleeping individuals were noted in the tent. As they watched, more ghostly bodies appeared, surrounding the summit near its base.

"Those are our men, Mr. President."

"You're damn right! Those are my boys!" The president clapped his hands together in excitement and sat on the edge of his chair, physically leaning toward the assault's monitor. The perimeter forces became stationary and for a while all the humans depicted were motionless.

McDonald became antsy and squirmed around in his chair. He blurted out, "What the hell are they waiting for?"

Hastings stared at his Commander in Chief. "The ordnance to be dropped."

McDonald nodded his head and returned his view to the flatscreen. Except for the Marine guards, who stood "at ease" gazing blankly into the room, all the Situation Room personnel sat or stood silently watching the panel.

CHAPTER 97

Staff Sergeant Forrest checked his watch.

It was 2355. He keyed his PRC 117 radio.

"Falcon One, Falcon One. This is Top Ghost. Over."

Forrest waited a few seconds.

"Top Ghost, this is Falcon One. Over."

The F-16 had descended and its targeting systems were activated. The pilot nervously looked to the northwest at a huge plume of ash rising above Mt. Hood. It extended upwards for thousands of feet. *Shit, an ash eruption is not good. Let's get this over with.* The pilot checked his watch. It was 2356.

"Falcon One. This is Top Ghost. The target is lit up. Over."

"Top Ghost, this is Falcon One. Copy that. Over."

The F-16 navigation system had brought the plane into perfect position. The aviator watched his targeting instruments. *Yes. Target acquired.* It was 2357 when the pilot released his five-hundred-pound bomb. It quickly changed inclination and pointed down to the Big Eddy Rise.

"Top Ghost, Top Ghost. This is Falcon One. Package delivered a little early, boys. Duck your heads. There's a storm a-coming. Over and out."

The F-16 pilot banked sharply to the south and brought his plane around and onto a northeasterly flight path. He turned his head back, viewing Mt. Hood, and watched the ash column grow taller. A slight southerly wind was bending the gray, billowing pillar's top directly at the Big Eddy Rise.

Sergeant Forrest remained motionless. He could see his IR laser targeting the canvas tent. He waited patiently for the bomb's impact.

Colonel Rodgers stood behind his airman and watched the screen in front of him. An E4, monitoring communications with the F-16, turned and spoke to his CO. "Falcon One is transmitting, sir."

Colonel Rodgers faced the airman.

"You can speak at will, sir. We've got 'open' communications," he told the colonel.

"Falcon One, this is Team Leader, over," Colonel Rodgers initiated.

"Team Leader, this is Falcon One. Sir, our package has been delivered. I snuck in under the wire, colonel. A cloud of ash is descending upon the drop site as we speak, over."

Rodgers had seen the whitish flash illuminate his screen as the ordnance hit the rise. He now watched in amazement as the silverbacks appeared from nowhere and took up defensive positions near the summit's rim. *What the hell?*

"We may need to do a 'turn around,' captain. Our targets survived the attack."

"That would be a negative, sir. The ash will drop this bird faster than a Sidewinder."

Rodgers contemplated his pilot's words. The airman was right. There would be no more flights tonight. "Copy that, Falcon One. Return to base."

Colonel Rodgers watched the Big Eddy Rise engagement commence as he spoke with his pilot. It was obvious the Army regulars were now at an extreme disadvantage. He pulled a chair up close to his monitor and continued watching the firefight. His mood became somber. The CO had seen military operations go bad before, but those experiences could not lessen the feelings of failure and frustration he felt now. He nervously ran his hand across his short-cropped hair and, while staring at the floor, sadly shook his head from side to side. Regaining his composure, the Air Force colonel returned his attention to his screen and watched the compromised assault stumble ahead.

CHAPTER 98

WOODY, DAKOTA, AND HOPS NERVOUSLY WATCHED the hillside below. The silverbacks knew their time was up and anxiously awaited the assault. A number of times during the evening, each sentinel had left his post, donned the night goggles, and checked out the tent. Each time, nothing was noted.

The two camp ravens peered down at their hosts and nervously began to sidestep back and forth on their branch. The birds' movements became exaggerated and quickened. They began calling out loudly in their harsh voices. At first, the surrounding forest echoed their calls, and then more ravens and crows called back and forth. The crescendo became louder and louder, and birds began flying to the Big Eddy Rise, sounding an alarm. From down below, near the river, came the scream of a big cat. The hairs on Woody's arm raised and he nervously surveyed his friends. "What the shit?"

Dakota glanced over at Hops. He called out to his two friends, "Someone put on the goggles, check the tent."

The birds were now circling the Rise and calling out to the occupiers. Hops ran for the goggles, but before he could reach them, Ranger's hand grabbed the NVGs from their perch. He quickly entered the tent and peered around, looking through the goggles. *Shit! Here we go!* Ranger jumped out of the tent and urgently called out to his friends. "Heads down! Get into the cavern, NOW! Move it! Move it!"

Ranger grabbed Woody by the arm and pushed him down the ladder. Dakota and Hops were right behind and almost dove into the dark entranceway. Another screeching cry from the big cat rang through the forest. The circling birds flew outward and away in all directions from the hill. Ranger bolted down into the cavern.

"Grab your packs and rifles."

The nervous men did as they were told.

"Now get over next to the pillar and cover your ears."

Everyone responded immediately. They all waited in defensive positions for the inevitable. An eerie, whistling sound was heard momentarily, and then a huge concussion rocked the ceiling above them and the cavern's floor jumped. The basaltic roof held. The sound of the explosion was deafening. Dust from the floor was thrown upwards into the cavern and small rocks were falling from the roof. Ranger waved dust particles away from his vision.

He shouted to his friends, "All right, packs and rifles! Move it, move it, move it!"

He pushed Hops and Dakota to the ladder, and they scrambled out of the cavern. Ranger stopped Woody from following.

"Woody, you and Tunes are guarding our escape route." He focused on Tunes. "All right, young man, get yourself and Woody going."

Holding his medical bag in his left hand, Doc went up the ladder next. Hang and Ranger were the last to exit their bomb shelter.

The bowl smelled of acrid explosives, and the dust from the explosion was obscuring everyone's vision. Ranger searched through the dust and observed the southwest rim. It had been completely blown open by the ordnance, and a gaping hole greeted his view. *Shit!* In his right hand, he held his Italian 501 sniper rifle. Ranger knew the first thing he needed to do; the Army sniper needed to be neutralized.

"Dakota, get down next to the blown-out rim. Don't look out until I tell you to."

Ranger lay prone on the ground, rested his rifle on a chunk of basaltic rock, and peered through his scope. The blown-out portion of rim rock was perfectly in line with the tall Ponderosa that held the sniper stand.

In the huge old giant, Sergeant Forrest was waiting for the bowl's dust to clear. He was hoping to scope the summit and report "no movement" to the first sergeant. What Forrest saw next was a sniper's worst nightmare.

As Ranger gazed through his scope, the dust continued settling and the visibility slowly improved. The tall Ponderosa's upper canopy became clear to Ranger. As he lowered his barrel minutely, a clump of manzanita presented itself. The old soldier made out a scope peering his way and a helmeted head bent over, peering through it. He took a breath, held it, slowly exhaled, and squeezed his 501's trigger.

Sergeant Forrest saw Ranger's scope and rifle targeting him. He instinctively took a breath and breathed out. *Don't jerk this shot.* He began squeezing his trigger, but the Remington didn't discharge. His head jerked backwards and his body twitched. Then, Forrest's head slowly rocked forward and his chin came to rest on his upper chest. A smear of blood remained on the yellowbelly's orangish outer bark where Forrest's head had struck it. The sniper rifle quietly slipped from his lifeless hands and dropped straight down. Ever so slowly, Forrest's body leaned forward until it too, fell from its perch. The dead soldier bounced off several branches before landing with a solid thud next to his rifle.

"Top Ghost. This is Ghost one. Over. Top Ghost. This is Ghost one. Over."

Forrest's PRC 117 spoke to no one.

First Sergeant Jefferson was surprised by his comrade's silence. *Shit! These damn radios!* Moments before, he had begun telling his squad to hold their positions. Coinciding with his orders was a barrage of nervous jabber coming from Fitzgerald. The annoying banter had distracted Jefferson somewhat, just as a slight "thud" emanated from the bowl.

"Shut up, Fitzgerald!"

Jefferson listened intently for a second more. No other sound came from the summit.

Secondary explosion?

"Ghost two and Ghost three. This is Ghost one. Move out."

A choral "Roger that Ghost one" came back to the sergeant.

Abramson and Lee began climbing up the slope from their flanking positions. The three soldiers in front of the rise scoped the rim with their optics. Their lasers danced about on the basalt surface above them as they keenly checked for any movement. Lee moved from shadow to tree trunk and then back to shadow. He gained about twenty yards, then stopped.

"Ghost one. This is Ghost two. I'm in position."

"Copy that, Ghost two."

Abramson was slowly moving up the ravine. He too found a secure location after ascending about thirty yards.

"Ghost one. This is Ghost three. I'm in position."

"Copy that, Ghost three."

Now it was the flankers' turn to cover the other team members' movements.

Ranger scanned the shooting positions. Only Hang's firing port had an active plastic explosive set-up, and he already had connected his Hellbox. All the other wires were destroyed in the bomb blast. He and Dakota moved into position on either side of the blown-out wall. The ex-Marine told Dakota to keep his head back and cover the center left side of the hill and Ranger would protect the center right. Next, the old soldier reached into his bag and brought out his extra banana magazine, plus three fragmentation grenades. Dakota watched and brought out his extra magazine, too. It was a waiting game now. All the occupiers, in one state of mind or another, viewed their firing fields intently.

Ranger called quietly over to Dakota. "I've got two bad guys below me."

Dakota gazed over at Ranger and raised up his right index finger, then motioned down the slope with it. Ranger nodded. The two men quietly waited for the attacking force to get closer.

Spec 4 Lee was twenty yards below the south rim. He felt for his grenades. He was scoping the rim, but saw no activity. First Sergeant Jefferson and Fitzgerald moved upwards and found a log to lie behind. Spec 4 Turner knelt down behind a tree. All the soldiers scoped the rim rock.

"Ghost two and Ghost three. Advance to the rim, over."

Again, a choral response. "Roger that, Ghost one."

Lee, holding his M4 in firing position, stepped out from behind his tree, and in a half crouch, scuttling gait, approached the summit. Hang stared at the advancing soldier, picked up the Hellbox, and turned the handle sharply. A double explosion rocked the hillside. Turner glanced over and saw Lee's body lifted up off the ground and thrown sideways. It landed heavily about ten feet from his original position. The crumpled body lay motionless.

The first sergeant yelled into his headset microphone, "Light 'em up!"

Automatic fire raked the basaltic wall above the Army regulars.

Ranger and Dakota, using their CZ burst option, shot down at the soldiers' position. The first sergeant's log was taking direct hits from Ranger. Turner's location was getting bullets spraying all around it. Sergeant Jefferson sent a volley of shots into the ragged basaltic hole above him. As his laser danced over and through the opening, bullets began ricocheting off the basaltic rock. *God-damn body count, my ass. Whose fucking bodies?* He looked over and saw Turner exchange fire with the hillside's summit. The first sergeant shouted to Fitzgerald, "Frag 'em!"

The private cocked his M203 and loaded a grenade. He'd have to lob it into the encampment. Fitzgerald knelt upwards while Jefferson gave him cover fire, and pulled the grenade launcher's trigger. There was a thump, and the grenade arced toward the summit. Ranger hollered, "Grenade!" Doc and Hang jumped behind the mess area's large boulders. Hops dove next to the latrine's chunk of basalt. His upper torso was protected by the large rock, but his legs sprawled out past the boulder's side.

Ranger and Dakota simply curled up by their firing positions. The fragmentation grenade landed by the shitter and exploded, sending hot shrapnel spraying through the compound. Hops screamed out. His legs had been lacerated by metal and began bleeding profusely. Doc ran over to his friend and began administering first aid.

Ranger focused back on Doc and hollered to Hang, as he had left his position to help Doc. "Get back to your position, Hang. Move it, move it."

Dakota kept Specialist Turner pinned down behind the big Ponderosa. Ranger grabbed a grenade, armed it, and tossed it down the hill. It bounced and rolled to a stop next to the first sergeant's log and exploded. Dead wood, shrapnel, and bark hurled away from the log as Jefferson was littered with debris. He hollered at Fitzgerald, "Give 'em another frag!"

Ranger was ready for this move. Fitzgerald took his firing position too quickly, and didn't have cover fire from the first sergeant. Ranger's burst echoed down the hillside. Fitzgerald yelled in pain and dropped down, grabbing his arm. Blood streamed out from between his fingers. One of Ranger's bullets had shattered his elbow.

Abramson, upon hearing the firefight erupt, had stealthily moved upwards. He had gained the backside of a large Ponderosa that stood ten yards from the summit's wall. He released a grenade from his belt, and jumped in front of the tree. The private armed his grenade, and instantly his position was flooded in light.

Woody stared through the manzanita bush, down his rifle's barrel. Tunes knelt behind him. The motion detector's brightness made Woody wince and blink his eyes. When he refocused, he saw Fitzgerald draw back his arm.

"Shoot, Woody! Shoot!"

Woody froze. The scene before him was terrifying. Tunes reached down and inserted his finger in front of Woody's index finger, and pulled backwards. The AR was set on fully automatic. The rifle jumped up as it spewed out bullets. Private Abramson was hit several times, twice in his leg, and three bullets embedded themselves into his chest armor. His rifle and grenade both fell off to his side and tumbled down past the tree's trunk. There was a loud explosion. Rocks, metal fragments, dirt, and debris scattered away from the tree's backside. The CZ burst had knocked Abramson down, and he now sat with his back up against the tree's trunk, his legs splayed out before him. His right leg's femur was broken and his main artery ruptured. Abramson fought back hysteria. *Shit, I'm going to die. I'm going to fucking die.* A dark patch of blood showed through his camo pant leg and increased in size rapidly.

He reached for his med kit and blurted out, "Don't shoot. Don't shoot. I'm getting a tourniquet."

Woody watched in horror through the manzanita bush at the young soldier dying before him. Abramson screamed as he positioned the tourniquet and cinched it up. *Shit, don't panic.* He tried to roll over and gain his feet, and screamed out in pain, again, when he twisted his broken leg. His tourniquet slipped down and the private clumsily readjusted it.

Woody looked back at Tunes and handed him the AR. "Hold this."

He then crawled out of the tunnel, pushing the manzanita bush ahead of him as he left the small opening. Tunes watched in bewilderment. *What the hell?* Woody knelt by the grimacing soldier.

"What can I do?"

Abramson turned and looked up at the older man who knelt beside him. He couldn't believe his eyes.

His voice was strained. "I need to get to the road."

The young soldier keyed his pack set and talked into his mic. "Ghost one, this is Ghost three. Over." His voice was weak and wavering.

"Ghost three, what is your position? Over."

"I'm fucking hit bad. Need medical assistance immediately. Retreating to the road."

"Copy that, Ghost three. We'll come and get you."

Sergeant Jefferson surveyed the scene around him. He'd placed a tourniquet on Fitzgerald's arm and tightened it into place above his elbow. The private lay next to him grimacing in pain. Turner was pinned down to his right. He could see Lee's motionless body and now Abramson was out of the fight. *Fucking body count.*

"Ghost four. This is Ghost one." Turner focused on the first sergeant.

"Get Lee and move back to our base. I'll cover you. Over."

"Copy that."

Up in the ravine, Abramson tossed off his helmet and unhitched his body armor on his left side. He pulled the double-sided vest off with his right hand and grunted in pain. Abramson spoke to Woody between gasps and grunts.

"All right, I need to get down to the road. Help me up."

Woody put his hands under the soldier's arm and hauled him upright. Abramson felt a shot of pain wrack his body. He felt for the tourniquet. It was still in place, but blood continued running down his leg. The private fought off waves of nausea. The ex-teacher and young soldier stumbled down the ravine together. Abramson used the elder man for a crutch. When they reached the road, Woody dragged the young soldier up onto its surface. After gaining flat ground, he crumpled down, next to the soldier, and both men gasped for air. Abramson grimaced and called out in pain between mouthfuls of air.

The young soldier was feeling lightheaded, and knew his loss of blood was critical. Reaching into a velcroed pocket, he pulled out a small saline pouch, IV needle, and drip hose. Next, the private procured a small flashlight from another pocket and gave it to Woody. The dizzy soldier told him to shine the beam onto his hand. Woody watched as the soldier inserted an IV needle into a large vessel, and then, connecting his sodium solution to his drip hose, started the saline transfusion. Woody held the bag above the soldier as he lay down.

Abramson closed his eyes. His body seemed to spin round and round as he lay on the gravel road, still nauseated. The lunar orb was high in the night sky now, and flooded the forest with brilliant light. Woody peered up at the Big Eddy summit and could see it clearly from where he knelt. Gunfire still occasionally burst through the night air. Abramson inspected the man who had shot him, then saved his life.

"I don't get it, Gramps. I just don't get it."

Woody looked down at the private. "I don't want to kill anybody, soldier. I just want to save some trees from being cut down."

Woody wiped a tear off of his cheek. The two men sat quietly together for a while, listening to the nearby shots. Abramson became less woozy and started to regain his faculties. Reaching up, he took the saline bag out of Woody's hand.

"You better get out of here sir, before my gun-toting friends arrive. I'm going to make it. Keep your head down and go back up the ravine."

Woody patted the soldier's arm, then turned and left. Partway up the ravine, he stopped and looked back at Abramson. The moonlight lit up the road. The soldier's dark, camouflaged body was deathly still as it rested on the gravel road. One hand was still raised aloft holding up his saline drip. The moon's light shone through the solution, giving it a crystalline, ethereal glow. Woody turned away and climbed upwards, hoping upon hope the young man below him would survive.

CHAPTER
99

FIRST SERGEANT JEFFERSON AND RANGER WERE exchanging volleys with each other. Fitzgerald had moved down the slope, aided by cover fire, as had Spec 4 Turner, who carried Lee over his shoulder. As Turner moved down the hill, he stumbled occasionally from the weight of his fellow soldier.

Doc had called out for help. Ranger motioned for Hang to aid Doc. Hang wasn't sure what the ex-Marine wanted so he stooped over and ran to him.

"Go help Doc, Hang."

Hang nodded and without thinking, stood erect and turned around. Just then, Sergeant Jefferson raised up and targeted the gap. To his surprise, his laser beam lit up an upper torso. He fired off a volley. The body crumpled out of sight.

"Take that, Aper!"

Ranger stared at Hang, who was rocking on the ground in agony holding his right shoulder. He quickly turned back and fired a burst at the first sergeant's position. He focused on Dakota.

"Get Hang back to Doc. Keep your damn head down."

Dakota crawled back to Hang and rolled him over onto his side. Blood was running down his chest. He'd also been hit in his right buttocks, and blood was now soaking through his rear pants pocket. Doc ran over and the two men pulled the young man away from the basaltic rim. Ranger fired another burst at Jefferson's log, although the first sergeant had already left his position and was crawling down the hillside. At about fifty yards from the summit, he stood up behind a Ponderosa trunk. He keyed his pack set.

"Ghost four. This is Ghost one. Over."

"Copy you, Ghost one."

"What is your position? Over."

"I'm at camp. We've got serious injuries. We need medical assistance. Over."

First Sergeant Jefferson shook his head in disgust. *What a shit show!*

"Ghost four. I'm coming in. Over and out."

The first sergeant headed for his bivouac at a run. He skirted the OSP Command Center and arrived at their encampment to find Spec 4 Turner loading Lee, who rested on a stretcher, into the back of a Humvee. Private Fitzgerald was helping as best he could. His arm was in a sling. Blood had soaked through the fabric where his elbow bulged outward.

Turner stared at the first sergeant. "We need to find Abramson. I believe he's on the road past the OSP barricade. I've talked with Lt. Colonel Henry. We're to abort this mission and get our wounded medical help."

Jefferson stared at Turner. "The hell I am!"

He turned, ran to his tent, and entered it. The flap flung back open, and Jefferson burst out into the moonlight carrying his sniper rifle.

"I'm going to find Sergeant Forrest. I'll be damned if these Yankee Apers are going to chase me the fuck off. They'll be God-damn sorry they messed with me."

Jefferson jumped into a Humvee and drove off toward the tree stand. Turner watched the Humvee leave. Then he focused on Fitzgerald.

"God-damn cowboy! Can you drive, private?"

"I think so."

"Well, give it a try."

Turner ran over to the gear trailer and pulled out another stretcher. He put it in the Humvee's bed, next to Lee, and closed the rear lid.

"Let's move, private. I'm going to sit next to Lee and help keep his head stationary."

Fitzgerald grimaced in pain as he sat in the cramped Humvee's driver's seat. He got the diesel rolling and drove past the OSP Command Center with his head lamps off. Partway to the barricade, he left the road and, using the moon's light to navigate by, circumvented the barricade. He regained the road and continued on.

"Holy shit, Turner! You've got to see this!"

Turner leaned forward and peered through the Humvee's windshield.

"What the hell?"

There, lying on the road's edge, was Abramson. He still held his sodium solution above him. Turner jumped out of the Humvee and grabbed the stretcher from the back. He and Fitzgerald ran to and knelt by Abramson. The young private looked up at his fellow noncoms.

"Glad you guys could make it."

Pain still registered on his face. Turner checked out his injuries. As Fitzgerald and Turner carefully got the private onto the stretcher, Turner asked, "How the hell did you get down here messed up like this?"

Abramson studied Turner and managed a smile. "You wouldn't believe me if I told you straight up."

"Okay, okay, Abramson. Be mysterious. It's okay with me."

They put Abramson into the Humvee next to Lee, and the four soldiers left the Metolius River behind them.

"Where to, specialist?" Fitzgerald asked.

Turner looked out the Humvee's windows at the big trees they were passing by. He held Abramson's saline bag with one hand and kept Lee's head secure with the other.

"We need an ER, pronto. Head to Bend."

The clumsy, camouflaged Humvee turned east onto Highway 20 and slowly picked up speed. Turner focused down at Abramson.

"You ready to tell me how you got off that hill?"

"Nope."

"Okay, I can wait you out. Don't think I can't."

Turner peered out the Humvee's window again as more Ponderosas passed by. No other vehicles were on the road. It was 0130 and all of a sudden, Spec 4 Turner felt very tired.

CHAPTER 100

The Situation Room erupted into applause when the ordnance detonated. A blurred, whitish mass exploded on the screen and slowly dissipated before the onlookers' eyes. Hastings had leaned forward in his chair when human bodies appeared from nowhere and, like ants, scurried to the rim's wall. They evenly spaced themselves in a defensive position. Hastings counted five live bodies ready to repel his team's assault.

"Shit!"

He reached for his cellphone. McDonald glared at Hastings.

"What are you doing?"

"Hell, I'm giving Lt. Colonel Henry a call to have him abort this mission. Our guys are walking into a damn ambush!"

McDonald grabbed Hastings' phone. He stared at the Marine guards and blurted out, "Arrest the secretary if he tries to call anyone again!"

The Marine guards nervously glanced at one another and then responded in the affirmative to the president. Hastings glared at the president. *What an asshole. These men are going to die because of your ego!* All eyes were back on the screen watching the soldiers slowly ascend the hill. One of the soldiers separated from two others, who seemed to be moving in unison.

The Situation Room gradually became more and more quiet and somber as the short firefight played out. Hastings looked around the room at the paneled walls with their inset screens, and shook his head in disbelief. He watched some "dress shirts" return to their computers and begin typing on keyboards. He focused back on his screen. No military personnel were visible. The Situation Room had watched the regulars get shredded by the occupiers. The assault was intense. At one point, a dress shirt upon seeing Woody's image appear from nowhere uttered the obvious, "There must be a tunnel network up there."

No one responded. Everyone present had watched as the soldiers retreated and eventually left their field of vision. Now the Situation Room focused on the Big Eddy Rise's summit. Images of seven people appeared on their screens. Two were immobile and assumed to be wounded since their bodies' eerie glow maintained its normal intensity. The president stared at Hastings with an angry expression.

"What the hell just happened?"

Secretary Hastings took a deep breath. "We just got our asses handed to us by the silverbacks, Mr. President."

As Hastings spoke, his phone, which rested by McDonald, began to buzz and slightly move across the table's polished surface. McDonald picked it up with a quick, annoyed swipe and opened it.

"Who's this?"

There was a pause. Lt. Colonel Henry was startled by this abrupt challenge, and this only irritated his angry, agitated state more.

"It's Lt. Colonel Henry. Who's this?"

"It's your God-damn Commander in Chief who just watched your men get their asses kicked! Were those the best soldiers you could find?"

Henry's anger boiled to the surface. He shouted into his phone, "My fucking men got ambushed. God-damn 'body count.' What kind of intel did you people gather? Your sloppy work got my team destroyed!" Henry paused for breath and thought for a moment. "And where are my God-damn orders?"

Hastings grabbed the phone from McDonald. The Marine guards stiffened, quickly glancing at each other. They held their positions.

"Henry, this is Hastings." The secretary took a deep breath. "You won't be getting any orders."

"What the hell are you saying, Hastings?"

"I'm saying there won't be any orders. I'm sorry, Henry. You need to get your 'affairs' in order. There's no telling what will come down the chain of command because of this mission."

There was a pause from Henry's side and then the connection went dead.

Secretary Hastings closed the phone, set it on the table, and looked between his legs at the floor. The phone began buzzing again. McDonald once more swiped it from the table's top and flipped it open. Again he threw out the challenging, menacing question. "Who the hell is this?"

Colonel Rodgers recognized the president's voice.

"It's Colonel Rodgers, Mr. President."

McDonald continued on with his rantings. "Your God-damn pilot missed, Rodgers."

Colonel Rodgers was a proud, experienced military commander. Nobody was going to bullshit him like this, not even the President of the United States.

"I watched the whole mission, sir. My pilot nailed the drop. He didn't miss a God-damn thing."

"Well how the hell did the Ape men survive the blast, Rodgers?"

"Apparently, there was a bunker system in place, Mr. President, which our intel didn't detect."

"Your shitty intel screwed this mission up, Rodgers."

McDonald had worked himself up into a frenzied state, and was shouting into the phone. Rodgers was through with his presidential conversation.

"I need the access code to my bank account, sir."

McDonald screamed, "What?"

There was a pause and Rodgers spoke coldly and deliberately. "I need the access code to my bank account."

The president stiffened and held the phone away from his face. He yelled even louder. "I don't give money to losers."

McDonald threw the phone across the room and it smashed against the opposite wall, dropping to the floor in several pieces.

"Worthless meathead!"

The president looked around the room at his audience. He sat back down abruptly and drummed his fingers loudly on the conference table's top.

Colonel Rodgers placed his flip phone quietly onto his desk top. He'd left the Operations Center, and now sat in his drab office. One small desk lamp provided the only light for the room. The space's perimeter was only partially illuminated. *Okay, so that's how it's going to be.* Rodgers contemplated a moment longer and then unplugged a small recording device from his landline. He held it in his hand for a while before putting it into his pocket. He then reached for his landline's receiver and punched in a long distance number. The colonel waited patiently for the ringing to end. After hearing the recorded message, he left a lengthy response and returned the phone to its base. Rodgers stood and walked across the dimly lit room. In a solemn manner, he collected all the Douglas A-1 Skyraiders pictures from the wall, leaving "A Higher Calling" surrounded by faded, rectangular, ghostly images. The CO's door quietly closed, and Rodgers headed for his parking space. A military career spanning four decades was nearing an abrupt and unceremonious ending. Rodgers came to a stop at the base entrance, saluted the guard, and drove home. His next move was already planned, and it would be the last time the colonel wore a military uniform.

CHAPTER 101

McDonald abruptly stood up and announced,
"Well, this God-damn shit show is over! I'm going to bed!"

He quickly left the Situation Room without acknowledging anyone else's presence. His two Secret Service escorts got in step with the president and accompanied him as he walked back to his White House residence. Secretary Hastings inspected the remaining personnel in the Situation Room.

"That will do it, everyone. Thanks for your good work."

Grim looks followed the secretary as he left the room. He called his chauffeur while heading to the North Entrance. Hastings focused straight ahead, lost in thought.

Brown and Horner nervously left their seats. They rose to the first floor, walked down the hall to the chief of staff's office, and found comfortable chairs to sit in. The two men began talking about possible ways to separate the president from this debacle.

The Situation Room staff returned to their business. Cups of coffee were poured; flatscreens displayed newscasts from around the world. The dress shirts sat attentively watching their TVs and keying their computers. No one talked about the tactical mission they'd just seen. The night shift continued on with their jobs. The two Marine guards stood at rest and watched the team at work. They simply waited for their "relief" to arrive.

CHAPTER 102

THE CAMP RAVENS HAD RETURNED TO THEIR perch and peered down at the occupiers. The moon had moved farther across the sky, but the old forest was still brightly lit up. All the men circled around Doc, who was finishing bandaging up Hops and Hang.

Doc addressed Ranger. "I've got the bleeding controlled. Both men have received codeine for the pain, but infection is the real problem. Hops and Hang need to get to an ER, soon."

Ranger checked his watch; it was now 1:30 in the morning.

"Can they wait until 8:00? That's six and a half hours from now."

"I'm not sure, Ranger. We'd be pushing it. I've got antiseptics in their wounds, but I couldn't clean all the damaged tissue, and I couldn't get all the shrapnel out of Hops."

Ranger peered around the bowl. It was unrecognizable. All their equipment was blown apart or now simply nonexistent. He focused back on Doc, but spoke to everybody. "I want you men to surrender at 8:00 a.m. tomorrow. I can protect you in the daylight."

Woody stared at Ranger. "What do you mean, protect us?"

"The bad guys may still try something, Woody. I'm going to be out in the woods making sure they're not successful."

Doc studied his good friend. "You're not going down the hill with us?"

"No, I'm not. I'm actually leaving all of you very soon."

His friends all studied Ranger, wondering what he was saying.

"I'm going to disappear, gentlemen. At some point, someone's going to ask where all our illegal armaments came from. And the penalty for their possession may be too harsh for my liking. So here's the deal."

Ranger glanced over to where the canvas shelter used to be.

"Tell the authorities I was in the tent when the bomb exploded. My friends, I need you to do this for me." All the silverbacks nodded their heads in agreement.

"When things have settled back to normal, we'll all get together again. Trust me. I wouldn't have it any other way."

Ranger tossed the walkie-talkie to Woody. "Call your son, Woody, and tell him everything's okay. He'll want to hear from you. The sooner you call, the better. Also, tell him to raise Superintendent Ross and explain your surrender schedule." Ranger smiled at Woody. "Copy that, soldier?"

"Roger that, Ranger, sir."

Tired, smiling faces watched as the two men hugged. Ranger quietly walked over and picked up his pack and sniper rifle. Then, with a running jump, he gained the basaltic rim above the Metolius River's Big Eddy and flung himself outward. Tunes, Doc, and Woody ran to the rim and climbed on top. They peered down through the darkness to the swirling eddy. Ranger was swimming to the near shore. He emerged from the river, dripping wet. The old soldier looked up in the moonlight, waved to his friends, and then disappeared from sight as he moved upstream.

Tunes peered over at Doc and Woody. "Damn, can an old guy really pull off a stunt like that?"

Doc laughed softly. "Seeing is believing, young man. It appears at least one old guy can do it."

Woody rejoined Dakota and the others. He keyed the walkie-talkie.

A metallic voice answered back. "Ranger, is that you? Is Gramps all right? Shit, the explosions and shots have really freaked us out. We're…"

"Bridger, Bridger. It's Dad."

There was a long pause, then Bridger's voice came through, but was garbled by sobs. "Shit, Dad, we thought you were dead!"

"I'm not, son. I'm fine. A few of us are hurt but everyone will make it."

There was another long silence. Bridger had somewhat regained his composure. "Dad, get the hell off the hill!"

"We will, Bridger. I promise. Contact Superintendent Ross and tell him we're surrendering at eight o'clock tomorrow morning. Also, tell him we've got two wounded people. Did you hear me, Bridger?"

"Yes, Gramps, I did. I'll do it right now."

"Good. Bridger, I love you, don't worry. I'll see you in the morning."

Woody put the walkie-talkie into his pocket, and sat on a nearby rock. He wiped tears from his eyes.

Two young people stood next to the Metolius River with a beautiful moon shining on the water. Rachael and Bridger hugged as Bridger cried. Rachael just held her boyfriend tightly. "Everything is going to be fine, Bridger. It's over. They're all right."

She rubbed Bridger's back with her hands. The blond, ponytailed, young college student slowly stopped crying.

"Shit, I'm such a baby."

"Well, yeah, that's fairly obvious."

Bridger smiled and focused on Rachael through blurry eyes. He wiped tears from his cheek. "God damn it, Rachael. You're not playing fair. Kicking a guy when he's down."

"It may not be fair, but it sure is fun."

She handed Bridger the car keys. "We need to find the OSP superintendent, and tell him what your gramps said. Let's get this occupation over with."

Bridger and Rachael started their rental up and drove out of the campground. They passed through Camp Sherman, and after crossing the river, Bridger glanced over at Rachael. Her red, frizzy hair bounced with the car's movements and he could see her freckles. "This sure wasn't a simple camping trip, was it?" he remarked.

Rachael focused on Bridger but didn't say anything. She grasped his hand and held it. The car continued to the OSP Command Center.

CHAPTER 103

GRAY ASH DRIFTED FROM THE SKY LIKE DIRTY snow. The summit's bowl had a dusting of the gritty stuff covering every surface. Footprints could be seen trailing between the cavern's opening and a lone tarpaulin structure erected near the bowl's center. Inside the protective covering, Hops and Hang rested on Insulite pads covered with blankets. Doc, with Tunes' help, had given them more codeine and checked their temperatures on a regular basis. He had changed bandages once, and finding no sign of infection, thought of himself and his friends as being very lucky.

Woody and Dakota fashioned two stretchers by pushing several delimbed juniper poles from the cave's stash through numerous zipped-up sweatshirts and jackets. The portable cots weren't pretty, but they were functional.

All the men wore kerchiefs over their noses to help keep the ash from their respiratory systems. Looking like the Hole in the Wall Gang before a stage coach robbery, the silverbacks prepared themselves for departure.

Woody checked his watch. "It's time."

His friends gazed at him. He got thumbs up and understanding nods from all of them. Woody picked up the bullhorn, walked over to the blown-out portion of wall, and taking a few steps through the gap, looked down at the OSP barricade. He keyed the mic once, and a familiar metallic screech greeted the forested slope. "We're coming down."

The retired school teacher returned to the tarpaulin structure and dropped the bullhorn on the ground inside the shelter. "Okay, everyone. Let's do this."

He and Dakota grabbed Hang's cot and dragged it out from underneath the tarp. Doc and Tunes also maneuvered Hops out into the falling ash. Hoisting their wounded comrades to waist height, the occupiers began moving though the basaltic rim's gap. Ranger's remarks, suggesting that exposing themselves on the hillside might be dangerous, weighed heavily on everyone's mind.

After peering through his scope, Sergeant Jefferson leaned back against the tree trunk. His view of the bowl was extremely limited because tree trunks and branches blocked most of his vision. Making matters worse was the falling volcanic ash. His optics magnified the grit, and the linear range he viewed registered hundreds of fallen particles, severely compromising visibility. Earlier, Jefferson had noticed movement in the bowl, and the men seemed to be readying for their departure. He'd also noted what appeared to be stretchers. The sergeant leaned forward and checked out the slope again. He found an uninterrupted, exposed section of incline about midway down the hill. This would be his "killing field." *God-damn ash.* The first sergeant continued looking through his optics, trying to adjust physically and mentally to the continuous motion. *Damn, a head shot's not possible under these conditions. I'll have to go for the upper torso. Come on, Apers. First Sergeant Jefferson is waiting for you.* Jefferson continued watching through his scope. It wouldn't be long before his field of vision filled up with targets. *Hurry up, old men. I'm getting stiff, sore, and bored up here.*

The two stretchers moved, one behind the other, through the rim's opening. Down at the road, Superintendent Ross and ten OSP troopers in tactical gear awaited the silverbacks. Two panels had been dislodged and removed from the barricade, allowing for a passage point. Ambulances, cruisers, and the SWAT van sat behind the police on both sides of the gravel road. A few troopers looked through the rifle ports using their M4 scopes, but mostly the men, with weapons at their sides, watched and waited for the silverbacks to start down the hill. One trooper called out, "There they are!"

All eyes focused on the summit. Woody had just appeared. He and Dakota, with their stretcher, moved slowly down the incline, and Doc and Tunes, carrying Hops, followed right behind. The small contingent slowly picked their way downward to the barricade. The ash was somewhat slippery because the exposed slope had accumulated some early morning dew.

Tunes pulled abreast of Woody, and the two stretchers continued forward, side by side. All the men scanned the woods nervously, but they saw only ash-flocked Ponderosa pines surrounding them. Suddenly, Woody's lead foot rolled on a piece of wood. His back foot couldn't control his step because it slipped in the damp ash, and Woody fell backwards, landing awkwardly. He winced in pain and Hang groaned. Off in the distance a muffled rifle report sounded and a projectile zipped above and past Woody's head. Tunes yelled out and fell sideways onto the ground. He clutched his stomach with both hands, as blood wicked through his T-shirt and seeped between his fingers. Dakota and Doc instinctively knelt down, still holding onto the stretchers. Woody stared in the direction of the rifle report.

Shit! Where's Ranger?

Superintendent Ross watched from behind the barricade as Woody fell down and Tunes was hit by the sniper attack. He immediately called out to his troopers, "Cover fire! Move it! Move it!"

The troopers rushed through the barricade. The first two instantly sent rifle bursts in the shot's general direction. Two more troopers ran up the hill, lodged behind trees, and returned fire in a southerly direction. While four officers raked the forest with cover fire, more officers ran to the occupiers and knelt beside them, scoping the forest and searching for targets. A couple more officers had gained the hill, and were producing cover fire from higher ground. Within a blink of an eye, eight OSP troopers created a firing wall between the silverbacks and their attackers. Ross focused on Trooper Mills.

"Grab the stretcher, Mills. Let's get these men off the hill."

Mills sprinted up the slope. He shouted to the occupiers, "Get up! Get behind the barricade."

He grabbed Hops' stretcher and pulled it upward. He and Doc quickly slipped and trotted their way down the slope. Rifle volleys continued echoing through the woods. Woody couldn't get his footing in the ashy muck, and was having trouble getting up. Two hands grabbed onto him and pulled him to his feet. Superintendent Ross assessed the anxious retired school teacher.

"Get down the hill pronto, sir. Don't hesitate."

Dakota and Woody stumbled their way down the hill and, bursting through the barricade, came to a halt. Their shoulders ached and both men's legs trembled. First responders exchanged places with the older men, and quickly transported Hang to an awaiting ambulance. Its emergency lights were activated, throwing rhythmic flashes of light onto the scene. Hops had already been loaded into the other ambulance, which was now leaving with its lights blinking. Superintendent Ross, holding onto and partially supporting Tunes, rushed into safety behind the bulletproof wall. An EMT relieved Ross of his charge, and laid the injured occupier onto a gurney. Lifting up the young man's T-shirt, the medic inspected his wound. Tunes was nervous and worried about his injury, and the first responder noted this; he gently patted the anxious occupier on his shoulder.

"It's just a flesh wound, young man. You're going to be just fine."

Rising to his feet, the medic addressed Mills. "You'll need to administer first aid, trooper. I've got to get moving. Do you have large butterfly bandages?"

Mills answered with an affirmative. Satisfied, the first responder went to his ambulance, hastily shut its rear doors, and disappeared around the rig's back corner. Within seconds, the emergency vehicle pulled away, racing off to Bend with Hang inside.

OSP troopers were slowly maneuvering their way down the hill. No shots were being fired, and each officer carefully moved from tree to tree. They all returned to the barricade safely. Walking over to the bulletproof wall, Woody nervously sat down with his legs drawn up to his chest and buried his face into his hands. Bob Thompson sat on the gravel road and softly cried.

After Dakota watched the last ambulance depart, he began searching for the remaining silverbacks. He located Woody sitting next to the barricade and observed him for a moment. A smile spread across the old shaman's face, and as he walked to his friend, he slightly shook his head in amused bewilderment. Dakota sat down next to the retired teacher. "You're embarrassing me. For just once in your life, could you not cry?"

Woody nodded his head, and sniffled. "I know. I'm trying not to cry."

Dakota gave his friend a side hug. "Well try harder, Woody."

Doc found his friends and sat next to them. He patted his grieving compadre's forearm.

"Its okay, Woody. We're all safe now. Everyone's going to make it."

He got a nodding head as his response. The tired physician looked over at Dakota and then back to his distraught friend.

"I'm proud of you, Bob Thompson. You made us all do the right thing."

Dakota mirthfully regarded Doc. "Don't pander to him. He'll never stop crying."

The two friends looked over Woody's head at each other and smiled. Their heads rolled back, rested against the barricade, and they laughed heartily. They began laughing away their anxiety and fears. Dakota gave his old friend a stronger side hug. Woody raised his head and wiping the tears from his eyes, joined his friends in their emotional release.

A third ambulance arrived on scene, and Tunes was loaded up and driven off. After putting away his first aid kit, Trooper Mills sought out Ross. They stood off to the side of the silverbacks, discussing what recourse should be taken against the sniper. As they spoke, three officers approached the occupiers with intent to handcuff them. Ross focused on his men. "No handcuffs, officers."

The troopers were surprised by their boss's statement.

"And they ride together in the same cruiser."

One officer responded, somewhat hesitantly, "Yes, sir."

"They're not criminals, gentlemen. Let's not act like they are."

Ross thought for a second and then commented again. "Make sure the deputies lodge these men away from the general jail population. They're to be isolated from the others, and treated with the utmost respect."

"Certainly, sir."

The officers helped the occupiers to their feet, walked them to a squad car, and situated them into its backseat. Blue and red lights flashed as the small motorcade pulled away from the barricade with the silverbacks sitting in the middle car. The state cruisers receded down the road, and at the distant corner, the procession was lost from sight.

Ross turned to Mills. "Get some people out into the woods and find our sniper. Careful, I think it might be one of those Army sergeants. Jefferson took off in a Humvee last night in the general direction today's shot came from."

"All right, superintendent."

Mills rounded up six officers and they departed in their cruisers.

The superintendent left one trooper at the barricade. He had one more job to do before contacting Salem. He was going over to the Metolius River campground, rustle up young Thompson and Rachael, and then escort them to the Deschutes County Jail, where he would arrange for an impromptu meeting between grandson and grandfather. Ross's Crown Vic pulled away from the Big Eddy Rise with blue and red lights flashing. *This reunion is long overdue.*

CHAPTER 104

IN THE OPEN, FORESTED AREAS, AN ACCUMULAtion of the gray volcanic spew slowly dusted the ground. Ranger looked out of the old garage and watched the ash fall lightly onto the ground. He'd overslept, and his stiff, cold body spoke to him. Quickly, he put on a camo coat and pants. Next, the old soldier strapped a chest holster to his upper torso and inserted a 40-caliber Beretta into place. Its long silencer protruded past the holster's terminus through a hole Ranger had cut out of the sheath. He grabbed his Beretta 501 rifle, slowly opened the garage door, and peered into the near forest for anything of concern. The ex-Marine wanted to find the sniper's tree quickly. Hopefully, from its perch, he could see the forest clearly and protect his friends from further attacks. As he moved through the woods, tracks in the gray volcanic ash followed his every movement. The daylight troubled Ranger, making him hurry faster than he liked. There could be military or civilian officials lurking in the woods, and he was fair game.

He moved silently through the dense, unkempt forest on a path he intuitively felt more than saw. Ranger's feet stepped over and around dead branches and pinecones. After traveling about two hundred yards, he stopped and crouched near a large tree. He'd just passed through an unruly patch of seedlings and young Ponderosas, and at its edge, the woods opened up somewhat. Dusted with a mantle of ash, the scene before Ranger took on an unearthly appearance. He scanned area in front of him, feeling certain the sniper Ponderosa was close by, and as he surveyed the forest, his gaze stopped at one big conifer. The tree had a rope hanging down to the ground from a low branch. *There she blows.* Ranger pulled his binoculars out of an oversized pocket in his camo jacket, and although falling ash somewhat obscured his view, he looked at the site. He surveyed the rope and the ground around it, again. *Yep.* Ranger's glasses stopped moving. Protruding from behind the tree was a human, lower torso. Booted, camoed legs, slightly covered with a film of ash, lay lifeless on the forest floor.

A muffled shot rang out as the old soldier peered through his glasses. *Oh shit! I'm late to the fucking dance!* Ranger ran for the tree, jumping over and around fallen branches and manzanita bushes. His heart was pounding as he fronted the tree and stared up into its top. Focusing, he saw a soldier leaning forward, peering through his scope. A bullet casing fell to the ground and landed next to him. The sniper's neck and chin were exposed to the ex-Marine and he quickly lifted his Beretta upwards, held his breath, exhaled slowly, and squeezed the trigger. The soldier's head jerked upwards and fell back down. Drops of blood reddened the ash near the spent casing. The camo-clad body slowly leaned forward and fell head first onto the ground, creating a shower of ash as it descended. The sniper's rifle also cascaded downwards. Ranger jumped to the side as the soldier's body and rifle hit the ground with multiple thuds. Sergeant Jefferson's body lay crumpled on the ground next to Forest's stiff and cold corpse. The ex-marine slowly reached down and felt for a pulse on the first sergeants neck. There was none.

When Ranger stood up, the quiet of the forest erupted with automatic rifle fire. He quickly stooped and ran to the backside of the Ponderosa. He knelt behind the tree, listening to bullets whiz by or strike nearby tree trunks. *Damn, are these shots meant for me or the bad guy?* The volleys continued for a couple minutes, then stopped. The old soldier peered around his tree and surveyed the forest. He couldn't see any movement nearby. *If those shots were meant for me, I'll be a dead man if I try to advance.* Ranger looked around the other side of his tree. Again, nothing was moving. *Think, man, think.* He saw the recent scene in his mind. The shots were random and seemingly picking no particular mark. *Okay, okay. I probably wasn't the target.* The ex-Marine rose up and dodged from tree to tree as he ran back to the dilapidated garage and his truck. *That was cover fire protecting my friends. The good guys fired those shots.*

Returning to the outbuilding, he pulled open the single-hung door and moved it aside. Next, he tossed his rifle into the back of the truck and shut the canopy's flap. He brushed the ash off his coat and jumped into the driver's seat, grabbing the keys, which rested in a cup holder. Ranger held his breath and turned the ignition switch. The old truck engine turned over immediately. Throwing the transmission into reverse, he backed out and turned his rig around. The rusty old pickup's tracks joined the other tread patterns on the gravel road's surface as the vehicle moved discreetly in Highway 20's direction.

The lone OSP trooper who stood sentinel at the first roadblock stared past all the news vehicles and reporters at the departing truck. He wondered where it had come from, but at the moment, other, more pressing uncertainties gained his attention. A long barrage of gunfire had just moments before ended. In the distance, coming from the Camp Sherman direction, another ambulance with lights flashing was heading to him. The trooper hastily opened up his barricade in preparation for the emergency vehicle's arrival. The first responders passed by his station and headed for the occupation site. The trooper closed his barricade and focused down the road at the receding ambulance. *What the hell just happened?*

CHAPTER
105

THE BIG, COBALT BLUE CROWN VIC WITH ITS golden, stylized stripes was driving through Mill City on its way to the state Capitol. Superintendent Philip Ross steered the old cruiser and thought about the last few days. They had been harrowing. At this moment, Ross felt certain the fight for the Big Eddy Rise logging show was over.

As the car moved west, the windshield wipers slapped a slow, deliberate rhythm. A light, fall rain was wetting down most of Oregon. While the superintendent thought about his postponed golf games, he inwardly laughed about how Murphy's Law had controlled most of his time in Central Oregon. *Well, I'll get a round of golf in soon enough, hopefully without any distractions.*

Ross was to meet with the governor and her staff upon arriving in Salem. He had much to tell them. When the bomb had exploded on the Rise, in order to keep his troopers safe, Ross had immediately called back all the OSP sentinels from the barricades, and all the officers watched from the Command Center as the firefight developed. They couldn't see much, but knew the attack was brutal due to the various ordnances being used. After the attack on the silverbacks, Ross and his team watched the small squad of Army Regulars leave in disarray, and noted their vehicles departed in opposite directions. The significance of this was not ascertained until the next day.

Earlier in the day, Peters had given the superintendent a search warrant Attorney General Smith had managed to get signed. The OSP boss vividly remembered what transpired next. With the warrant and a flashlight in hand, Ross, after the soldiers' hasty departure, walked into the first sergeant's tent. Shining the beam around the small, cramped quarters, he noticed a battery-powered lamp hanging from a central post. Stepping over sundries, Ross turned the lamp on and used its illumination to inspect the tent's interior. He observed, resting on top of a field pack, a banana clip protruding from a towel, wrapped around a rifle.

The OSP superintendent walked over to the bundle and shined his flashlight onto it. *Just as I thought.* He picked up the rifle and unwrapped its covering, finding an AK-47. The sturdy, square-jawed OSP boss rewrapped his find, left the tent, and returned to his command trailer where Trooper Mills and Lt. Peters sat at the dinette. They focused on their boss's parcel. Ross unwrapped his find for the second time. After he showed the AK-47 to his troopers, a conversation ensued.

"Where'd you find our missing weapon, sir?"

"In the first sergeant's tent."

The OSP boss sat down across from his troopers on the trailer's couch.

"This is a game changer, gentlemen. It appears, not only do we have an illegal, rogue military operation on our hands, but the shots fired at us came from one of the sergeants."

Lt. Peters nodded his head in agreement. "Hard to argue with the evidence, Phil. What should we do?"

Ross quietly viewed his men. He laid the AK-47 on the couch, and ran his hand over his crew cut.

"Mills, I want you to find the hospital those regulars went to. You're to take several troopers with you and arrest the soldiers who aren't being medically treated. Jail them at the nearest facility. I suspect they went to St. Charles. Some of those boys looked to be in bad shape, and I believe a long road trip would have killed them, so the Bend hospital seems like their likely choice."

"I'll get right on it, sir."

Mills left the trailer quickly and began rounding up his men.

"All right, lieutenant." Ross handed Peters the AK-47. "Get this back to Salem and run ballistics on it. The outcome is a no-brainer, but let's get the data."

"Okay, anything else, Phil?"

"I can't think of anything."

"I'm off then." Lt. Peters picked up the AK-47 and left the trailer.

As Superintendent Ross reflected on the evening attack, his AK-47 discovery, and his conversation with his troopers, he neared Salem's city limits. He continued musing about the firefight and the next day's events. The following day's attack on the surrendering silverbacks had been a mystery for a while. After the occupiers were dispatched to the Deschutes County jail, Ross sent Mills and several troopers out to find where the sniper fire came from. It didn't take them long to locate one of the missing Humvees. They scouted outward from the Humvee's position in the ash-laden forest until they came upon the two sergeants' bodies. Finding the soldiers' corpses answered a few questions, although the bullet's path running up and through the first sergeant's head was puzzling. The projectile's angle probably didn't occur because of OSP cover fire. Ross still wasn't sure how to address this enigma. *Had Jefferson taken his own life?* What the troopers found next suggested another possible solution. They located footprints in the ash coming to the sniper's tree and then returning to an abandoned summer home's garage. Confusing things even more were the vehicle tracks leading from the garage to the nearby gravel road. Ross formulated an explanation for these circumstances, but decided to let the whole matter remain innocuous. Sleuthing out a possible unknown silverback or one who'd escaped the summit, and rejoined the fray from the forest floor, only hindered the termination of the "Logging Site Occupation" saga. Philip Ross was ready to move on and let this chapter of Oregon history come to a close.

After the bodies were discovered, a forensic unit from Salem arrived on site. They combed the summit's bowl searching for evidence and the missing body of one of the silverbacks. The surviving occupiers said their friend Ranger had been in the tent when the bomb exploded. Ross's team had, to the best of their ability, searched the site for clues that would clarify Ranger's disappearance. The wet ash and a slight drizzle severely hampered their efforts. At the end of the day, however, the forensic personnel felt certain they'd found pieces of hair and bone fragments, and these were bagged up and returned to Salem with them.

Ross motored past the detention center on the outskirts of Salem. He thought about the irony that became apparent right after the silverbacks were ambushed during their surrender. News reached Superintendent Ross via Lt. Peters who stated the Ninth Circuit Court of Appeals had finally weighed in on McDonald's logging regulation decree. They had struck it down, citing an obvious abuse of the Executive Branch's Governmental Powers. In the same breath, the Ninth Circuit Court had upheld the Sierra Club's suit asking for a termination of logging at the Big Eddy Rise. The litigation cited the Endangered Species Act for its legal grounds, noting the native bull trout population would be harmed by the logging effort.

Ross pulled into the parking lot and found his reserved space. He placed the protective plastic cover over his trooper's hat and stepped out of his cruiser. Once again, Ross climbed the Capitol steps, and paused for a moment looking upwards. Small rain drops caused his eyes to blink as he viewed the Gilded Pioneer. He shook his head in disbelief. One last thought reentered his mind. Lieutenant Peters had been present when the silverbacks were booked into the Deschutes County jail. As the elderly men were escorted to an isolated holding cell, the jail had slowly erupted into foot stomping and chanting. The inmates beat the floor with their shoes, and sang out, "Stop the Greed, Save the Trees!" Those prisoners who could reached out and shook the hands of the men as they walked by. Peters relayed that he'd never seen anything like it.

Superintendent Ross quickly ascended to the second floor of the Capitol Building. He entered the governor's greeting room and stopped at the closed double doors. As he opened the doors, Ross removed his hat.

Governor O'Connell focused on Ross as he entered the room. Her expression was serious. She welcomed the superintendent by pulling outwards an empty chair next to her. On one side of the long, oval table sat the governor, Chief of Staff Roberts, and Attorney General Smith. On the other side sat Lt. Peters, Russel Nelson, Air Force Colonel Rodgers, and Spec 4 Turner. Lying on the table's surface was an AK-47 in a large plastic bag and a smaller Ziploc Ross assumed held the rifle's spent slug. Russel's White House note was also present, sealed into another Ziploc. Ross nodded his greetings to everyone present and sat down next to the governor. The office was dimly lit. The gray, rainy, mid-valley day offered little illumination. The overhead lights were off and the few table and standing lamps throughout the room lit only their close, surrounding proximity. The subdued lighting created a somber stage for the meeting.

Governor O'Connell spoke. "Superintendent, I believe you know everyone here except for Colonel Rodgers." The governor facilitated the two men's introduction. "What news do you have for us, superintendent?"

Ross reviewed all the thoughts he had revisited while driving over to Salem. A few questions were asked of him for clarification and then the governor pressed on.

"We have signed affidavits by Colonel Rodgers and Russel depicting an illegal military act against Oregonians carried out by the U.S. Government and the United States Army. This action seems to have been ordered by President McDonald and facilitated by Secretary Hastings. Lt. Peters relayed to us that OSP has proof the U.S. Army attacked our containment operation and in so doing wounded a Jefferson County deputy."

O'Connell stared at Mills and Colonel Rodgers. "Why would the Army shoot at us?"

She then focused on Spec 4 Turner. He nervously stared down at the table.

"Why did the Army shoot our deputy, young man?"

Turner glanced up at the governor and then back down at the table. He didn't know what to do.

The young Army specialist cleared his throat. "Honestly, ma'am, I don't know why or who fired those shots. All of us privates and specialists were not privy to our mission's real objective until the day of the attack."

"All right...all right."

Superintendent Ross addressed the governor's question. "I believe the Army created the false attack to villainize the silverbacks. By making them appear to be the aggressors, any retaliation by the regulars could be considered justified."

Governor O'Connell thought for a moment. "Seems like logical, sound reasoning, Philip. It appears the military was deceitful and treacherous at the same time."

Colonel Rodgers chose this moment to reach into his inner suit pocket to retrieve the recordings of his first conversations with Hastings. "I'd like to add this to the evidence pile, governor."

Rodgers laid his device onto the polished table top. He explained to everyone what the recordings chronicled. Attorney General Smith picked up the small plastic device and examined it.

O'Connell turned to her attorney general. "What can we do about this, Robert?"

"Normally, governor, with this much evidence and these material witnesses, I'd say a suit seeking criminal sanctions and damages would be a slam dunk, an open and shut case. But, whenever you sue the government, anything can happen, and legally, we can't sue a 'sitting' president. For the most part, they're immune from litigation while they're in office. That said, I think we should sue the government and McDonald's and Hastings' asses and see where the chips fall."

Chief of Staff Roberts joined in. "Sarah, if we make a lot of noise, get our case presented openly, and use our press conferences wisely, a lot of pressure will be put on the McDonald administration. The American people are looking for just one more unconstitutional, immoral act from this guy so they can hang him out to dry. We could be providing just what is needed."

O'Connell focused on her OSP superintendent. "What do you think, Philip?"

Ross gazed around the room and back to his peers. "I agree with Laura, governor. Let's go after McDonald and Hastings. Oregonians, and Americans for that matter, deserve to be rid of this president. Maybe we'll be the straw breaking the camel's back."

O'Connell looked around the table. She noted serious, hopeful expressions returning her gaze.

"I hear what you're all saying, but what will the State of Oregon get from this lawsuit?"

Attorney General Smith addressed this question. "That's a big unknown, Sarah. We're navigating rarely frequented waters here. Again, suing a sitting president cannot be done. I believe, when the dust settles from this litigation, we may be awarded some damages, but only if we find friendly judges at the various court levels this case will travel through."

"All right, then so be it. Robert, I want a legal brief before me by this time tomorrow. We'll give a press conference the next day, explicitly detailing our evidence and suit against the federal government, naming McDonald and Hastings as principal defendants in the case."

The governor adjourned the meeting. Two OSP troopers entered the room; one handcuffed Spec 4 Turner and led him out of the governor's office while the other officer escorted Colonel Rodgers and Russel out of the room. They would both be taken to a safe house in Salem. Superintendent Ross and Lt. Peters excused themselves. They descended to the first floor and stood surrounded by the murals depicting Oregon's earliest days.

"We need to go back to Central Oregon, lieutenant. I want you to supervise the breakdown of our Command Center. Also, I want troopers standing vigil at the military encampment, the jail, the morgue, and the hospital where the soldiers are recovering. I want to know when and who comes to retrieve these people and gear. If the military personnel arriving on scene don't present written orders to our troopers, they are to be turned away."

"I'll get everything operational, Phil. Maybe we can flush out some more bad guys."

"Maybe so, lieutenant."

Ross and Lt. Peters headed down the Capitol steps and went their separate ways.

The OSP boss sat down behind the steering wheel of his Crown Vic. He was going to go home and spend the evening with his spouse. *What a thought. A real, quality moment with my wife.* Tomorrow, he'd talk with Attorney General Smith and arrange for the silverbacks' release. Ross wanted to drive to Bend and personally facilitate the occupiers' discharge. He was going to offer the silverbacks and their families a stay at Black Butte Ranch paid for by the State of Oregon. Ross doubted they'd take him up on his gesture, but he held out hope for their acceptance of his gift. He wanted to talk with these men and get to know them a little bit. Heroes were hard to define and sometimes were unrecognizable. These older men and their college student companions would be villainized by some and applauded by others. Ross knew how he felt. He hoped to simply talk and share a moment with these noble men who were willing to die for their beliefs.

CHAPTER
106

STRAIGHT DOWN THE FAIRWAY, FRONTED BY HILLS covered by Ponderosa pines, was North Sister. A light dusting of snow softened the jagged, craggy summit's appearance. Superintendent Ross smiled as he pulled an oversized driver from his golf bag.

"I've been waiting for this, John."

"I know you have, superintendent. It's been a long time coming."

Ross practiced a few swings, and addressed his ball. The metallic "ping" as the club face met the ball was music to the OSP boss's ears.

"Sounded good, sir."

The ball arced skyward and landed, bouncing a few times before rolling to a stop about two hundred fifty yards away. Ross picked up his broken tee. He couldn't stop smiling.

"You played your fade nicely, sir."

Ross focused on his good friend, Lt. Peters. "I don't want to hear any sirs, or superintendent, today, John."

John Peters laughed and slapped Ross on the back as he passed him, club in hand. "Sorry, Philip. It's hard to switch hats."

John nailed his drive and drove straight down the fairway. His ball landed just past Ross's. The two men picked up their bags, slung them over their shoulders, and headed down the 10th fairway.

As they walked, Peters caught Ross up on the latest national and local news. Peters was a news junkie, and DVR'd a couple news shows each day. Recently, he'd locked onto local Channel 19 and recorded it along with his favorite national broadcast, WNN. A few days ago, Allen Rodrigues reported the station's White House confidant leaked information affirming that McDonald's team had knowledge of the Ninth Court's judgment prior to attacking the silverbacks, and McDonald chose to ignore this information. Peters continued by saying this knowledge added more fuel to marches against McDonald. Washington D.C. had been receiving several hundred thousand protesters a day since the WNN disclosure, and the demonstrators, ignoring required permits, mostly congregated around the White House, demanding the removal of President McDonald from office. Peters furthered this White House discussion by adding McDonald was holed up in his second floor residence and hadn't been seen since the silverback attack. In addition, Secretary Hastings was AWOL. Nobody had seen him since the military assault.

The two friends dropped their bags near their lies. Ross swung a three wood by his ball and loosened up his shoulders. With a nice stroke, he pushed his ball up onto the apron of the 10th green.

"You should stay away from golf more often, Phil. That's a beautiful shot. I'm smelling a possible birdie here."

Ross laughed at John's comment. Peters used the same club, but faded his shot off the right of the green. After their shots, the OSP officers picked up their bags and continued down the fairway.

It was Ross's turn to add information to the conversation. Peters had been in Central Oregon and missed the governor's news conference and some recent information pertaining to the state's case. The attorney general informed Superintendent Ross and all the pertinent state officials that Lt. Colonel Henry, who'd orchestrated the Army's involvement at the Big Eddy Rise, had been killed by an accidental shot fired from his service revolver. This was tragic news, but the loss of Henry would not influence the state's case. After noting Henry's death, the superintendent switched gears, and with a smile and some laughter told Peters about the forensic team's report on the hair and bone fragments found in the Big Eddy Rise's bowl. They informed Ross the remains belonged to a two- to five-hundred-year-old Native American female. Peters stopped in his tracks, bent over, and laughed heartily at this information. After regaining his composure, he asked the superintendent what he intended to do with the knowledge. Ross's response was simple; he was going to round file it. He didn't want any more distractions derailing the closure of this case. The two men brought out nine irons and pitched onto the green, leaving themselves doable puts. Ross rimmed the hole and two-putted. Peters one-putted for a one under par.

"Nice putt, John. A birdie on your first hole. No betting today, lieutenant. I'm sensing an ambush in the making here."

"Let's talk after a few more fairways. You know how it is when you haven't golfed for a while. My ugly habits will soon raise their heads and bite me in the butt."

The two men picked up their bags and moved toward the 11th tee. They noted the expensive homes off to their right and a pond system fringed with cattails to their left. Past the water was a commons area with grass and nature trails that dissected the space. They dropped their bags and pulled out drivers. The tee-off area was surrounded by aspen and pines. Down at the end of the hole sat North Sister. Their drives landed squarely in the middle of the fairway, and once again, Ross played his fade nicely. As they walked to the green, Peters mirthfully told Ross about some local news. He was enamored with the Cassie Williamson/Brian Larson newscast. The two young reporters had finally tossed their sandals at the camera. The slight rain, which recently wetted down the Central Oregon dust, triggered the promised response. The next evening, Brian and Cassie showed up wearing long-sleeved Aloha shirts, and Cassie adorned her neck with a lei. These apparel items weren't coming off until the first snows hit Bend. Their audience loved this gimmick, and the few Hawaiian shirts left on local store racks quickly disappeared. Also, Peters mentioned Professor Anderson had announced to Bend the tremors under Mt. Hood had ceased, along with the erupting ash clouds. It appeared the big volcano was through with its displays and was settling in for the winter. Of course, Cassie bemoaned this fact by saying she'd already picked out a nice bikini to wear while skiing, and couldn't return it because of a lost sales slip. Both men laughed at the young anchor's humor. As the two men prepared for their approach shot, the lieutenant told Philip in a serious tone about the wounded Jefferson County deputy. Channel 19 had broadcast an interview done by Brian with Deputy Edwards. He'd been released from the hospital and now, while mending from his wound, held down a desk job at the Sheriff's office in Madras.

Ross's approach shot found one of the infamous bunkers on the Big Meadow course. It took him two strokes to chip out of the sand. Peters played the hole nicely. Ross wrote a bogey into his score card, and Peters recorded a par.

As the two friends walked onto the 12th tee, they continued sharing information. Ross highlighted the governor's address for Peters. O'Connell had named as plaintiffs in the state's suit the State of Oregon, all the silverbacks, Hang and Tunes, and Deputy Edwards. The state sought monetary damages for all the plaintiffs and charged the two defendants in the suit, President McDonald and Secretary Hastings, with aggravated assault and attempted murder. The governor realized she was "breaking ground" in a legal attack of this nature on the Commander in Chief and his secretary of defense, but felt due to the atrocious and deliberate acts perpetrated against the plaintiffs, the State of Oregon was within its moral if not legal rights to sue McDonald and Hastings. Ross and Peters mused the Supreme Court would eventually be drawn into this fight, and the outcome would probably go against the state. Although, both men felt the facts and evidence supporting the law suit, which the governor presented in her news conference, would spell the end of the McDonald administration.

The 12th hole proved to be a challenge for Peters. He'd found two sand traps and headed for the 13th tee registering a double bogey on his score card.

The 13th hole was a pretty par three, and both men teed off with five irons. The OSP officers found the green with their drives. As they walked down the fairway Ross told Peters about the silverbacks' release from jail. The superintendent had arranged to be there when the occupiers departed. He conveyed seeing a white rental minivan enter the jail's parking lot. Bridger and Rachael emerged from the van, followed by two women wearing jeans and sweatshirts. One was a brunette and the other a redhead. Both ladies wore their hair pulled back in ponytails, and wisps of gray highlighted their temples. As the foursome neared the jail's entrance, Doc, Dakota, and Woody walked out of the double doors. Doc slowed up and allowed his friends to meet and embrace their loved ones without his distraction. The two couples hugged for a long time. Woody wiped tears from his eyes, and both couples talked for a moment as they continued holding onto each other. Rachael walked over to Doc and gave him a big hug. Bridger joined his grandparents and all three embraced. After some more discourse, the small group moved to the van. At this moment, Superintendent Ross walked over to the gathering and introduced himself to the women. He offered everyone a few nights' stay at Black Butte Ranch on the state's tab. The group politely refused his gesture, and conveyed their need to return home and relax with loved ones in a comfortable, familiar environment. Before Ross took his leave, he offered his apologies to the silverbacks for their ordeal and wished them all the best.

Peters had listened thoughtfully to Ross's summation. He interjected how lucky the silverbacks were; one or several of them could have easily been killed during the assault. The superintendent mentioned how he wished Ranger was around to talk with. He'd like to meet the old soldier who'd kept his friends alive while facing a well-planned military attack.

The two friends both two-putted the 13th green and parred the hole. Ross dropped the pin back into the cup and the men walked to the 14th tee. As Peters pulled out his driver, he gazed down the fairway. Three Fingered Jack greeted his view; the jagged summit, covered with the season's first snowfall, looked beautiful. The fairway was straight, with homes sitting on either side. Peters let her rip, and the ball burst off his club's head, coming to a stop about three hundred yards from the tee.

"Nice shot, John. You opened it up on that one."

Ross also swung away. His fade got the best of him, and the ball landed past the out of bounds marker.

"Going to have to add a stroke because of my miscue."

As the two friends reached their first shot, Peters peeked ahead at his lie.

"I'm going to try an 8 iron. What do you think?"

"Go ahead. Swing conservatively. You'll make it easily."

As they walked to the 14th green, John told Ross about Colonel Rodgers' Salem arrival. It had awed the experienced OSP trooper. Rodgers called Oregon's attorney general the night of the attack and left a message explaining his part in the assault, and his wish to become a material witness for the state. Attorney General Smith gladly welcomed his offer. Rodgers requested a state official meet him at the Air National Guard's headquarters next to Salem's municipal airport. Peters had gotten the nod, driven over to the Guard's offices, and parked near the tarmac. He was standing next to his cruiser when the whining sound of a jet turbine caught his attention. An F-16 taxied to a stop near his position. An Air Force ground crew immediately ran to the plane, and chocks were thrust beneath the wheels. While a crew member visually inspected the plane, another helped the pilot disembark. The aviator was unbuckled, and, leaving his helmet in the plane, replaced it with a soft cap.

As the airman walked to Peters, his cap's insignia caught the sunlight. An eagle with outstretched wings glinted in the afternoon brightness. Colonel Rodgers and Lieutenant Peters exchanged greetings and shook hands. Both men walked to Peters' cruiser, where the lieutenant opened the passenger door for the colonel and closed it behind him. He drove Rodgers to meet with Attorney General Smith, and eventually, later in the day, the lieutenant escorted the colonel to a safe house.

After Rodgers' arrival was described, Ross and Peters separated and headed for their respective lies. Peters' 8 iron dropped the ball onto the 14th's green and Ross found the apron to the right side. The OSP superintendent hit a nice chip shot and one-putted, saving his par. Peters two-putted and walked to the 15th tee, scoring another par.

"Hell, you're not going to cool off today, are you?"

Peters smiled. "Maybe this will be one for the books, Phil. I don't know what I like best about this course, my score or the scenery?"

The two friends continued playing the Big Meadow course. After several hours of pleasurable golf, they availed themselves of the clubhouse bar. Later on in the evening, they dined at the Ranch's restaurant, which overlooked the commons, and sat in the lower level's corner table, which provided a perfect view of a small casting pond and the undeveloped meadow area. Ross had offered a toast to the silverbacks and the end of the Big Eddy Rise standoff. As the two uniformed OSP troopers dined, the sun slowly receded, and dusk engulfed their view. Both men knew it was back to work tomorrow. This required their return to Salem, but for a while longer, they enjoyed their freedom and continued talking about the oddities of the Big Eddy Rise occupation. The friends skipped dessert and after enjoying a couple of Irish coffees, they left the restaurant. Outside, cool, dry evening air greeted the troopers. Central Oregon's atmosphere was always more refreshing than the valleys. The men separated and walked back to their rooms.

Superintendent Ross reflected somberly to himself as he walked. *This is one for the books.* He'd never forget the young college students and the elder silverbacks. They inspired Oregon's top cop with their bravery and resolve. The occupiers reminded Ross about his own responsibilities in regard to being vigilant, and defending Oregon's citizenry from wrong no matter where it came from. Oregon's top cop neared his room, surrounded by big Ponderosas. Ross hoped the Big Eddy Rise occupiers would inspire others as well.

CHAPTER 107

A SMALL MOTORCADE, ESCORTED BY D.C. POLICE, slowly moved in the White House's direction. It carefully pushed through protesters who encircled the Capitol grounds, demanding the removal of McDonald from office. Six black Lincoln Continentals, carrying important Republican Party members and prominent business leaders, resolutely forged on to the West Wing and the Oval Office. The mobile entourage was about to have an impromptu meeting with President McDonald wherein his future political path would be discussed. Cavalcades moving down Pennsylvania Avenue were not uncommon in the Capital, but this one was extremely relevant and embarrassingly overdue. When it neared the Library of Congress, the number of protesters had greatly increased and the motorcade began to inch forward. Eventually, the limos reached the White House gate and turned onto the grounds. They drove slowly on the circular path, leading to the North Entrance of the West Wing, and one by one, the limos stopped at the main entrance.

High-ranking Republican officials were ushered into the building and waited in the foyer for all of the participants to assemble. Three of the limos held major corporation bigwigs: Boeing and U.S. Steel had their leaders present, all the major U.S. car manufacturers and high tech industry CEOs were in attendance, Wall Street was well represented, and the apparel industry giants had lent their managers to the gathering as well. The formidable assembly numbered about twenty big stakes players, and they all had one destination in mind, the Oval Office. As the gathering proceeded from the West Wing's entrance, the Republican leaders walked in front of their industrial counterparts. The president pro tempore of the senate walked with the speaker of the house; the Republican Party chairman and the majority leader strode side by side; accompanying them was the Chief Justice of the Supreme Court. It was a powerful gathering that intended to address the President of the United States.

White House Secret Service personnel facilitated the group's entrance into the president's office. Some of the contingent sat on couches conversing while others stood near the presidential desk discussing the immediate situation and its agenda.

The president's temporary secretary didn't know how to contact McDonald in his residence, and she nervously asked the Secret Service personnel to retrieve the president from the second floor. They dutifully left the West Wing and headed for the president's residence. Gaining the second floor, one agent knocked on McDonald's living room door. An irritated voice greeted his second rap.

"What do you want?"

The agent opened the door and entered McDonald's living room. All the big screen TVs were on, showing newscasts. The president peered through bloodshot eyes at his Secret Service staffer.

"I don't want to be disturbed."

The agent somberly examined McDonald. "Your presence is required in the Oval Office, Mr. President."

McDonald, sitting on his couch, ran his hand across his head. "I'm not interested in meeting with anybody right now."

The agent broke protocol and responded with a personal judgment. "You need to meet with these people, sir. They're all big players who normally don't wait for anyone."

"Shit, they can wait for me."

"Not advisable, sir."

McDonald stared sharply at the agent, contemplated for a moment, then stood up. He walked over to a chair that had his suitcoat draped over its back and slipped it on. His clothes were wrinkled to an excess, but he didn't seem to notice or care. The agent stepped aside as McDonald entered the second floor hallway. His Secret Service staffer noticed with raised eyebrows that the president passed by a floor-length mirror without admiring himself. McDonald walked down the Grand Staircase. He forgot his phone, but didn't seem to notice that, either. Partway down the steps, he stopped and looked at the stairwell's walls, noticing portraits of Washington, Lincoln, and Teddy Roosevelt. McDonald gazed at them for the first time, then blankly looked away and continued down to the ground floor. In the Palm Room, McDonald stopped once again. Directly before him hung the painting of "Liberty," a visual masterpiece completed in 1869 by the Italian artist Brumini. The remarkable oil canvas evoked no momentary hint of recognition or emotional response from the president. He simply registered the painting for a moment and moved on. His procession walked down the Colonnade, entered the West Wing, made their way down the hall, and stood facing the Oval Office doors, waiting for them to open. Once they swung inward, McDonald stood still, gazing into his work space, but did not proceed. Those in attendance turned, facing the president. They said nothing. His Secret Service personnel guided McDonald forward, and moved him to his desk. The motorcade members parted, allowing his passage. One agent pulled the president's chair out and McDonald slowly sat down, warily eyeing those in attendance.

"What the hell do you all want?"

The senate majority leader spoke to McDonald. "The Democrats have begun formal impeachment proceedings, Mr. President. The Republicans in Congress will not stop their efforts, sir. A 'vote of confidence' was taken, Mr. President, and very few Republicans will stand by your side. Your national approval ratings have dropped to below twenty-five percent and most of our constituents want you out of office."

The Republican Party chairman took the ball. "Mr. President, your administration is destroying our party's backing, and at this point, you've set us back twenty years. We'll have a hard time regaining the Oval Office for quite some time."

"I'm the best president you ignorant D.C. lifers have ever had!"

Silence engulfed the room as the occupants, in disbelief, looked back and forth at each other.

The president pro tempore of the senate spoke next. "General consensus would disagree with you, Mr. President. The bottom line, sir, is you'll be forced out of office in probably two months. These impeachment hearings will advance quickly because none of your party members will support you."

McDonald started to drum his fingers on his desktop. "And what do you bright public servants suggest I do?"

The speaker of the house removed a sheet of paper and a pen from his attaché case, and placed both in front of McDonald.

"We suggest you sign your resignation, Mr. President, and help us stop our party's bleeding."

The president continued drumming his fingers. He stared at the paper before him, and reached for the pen.

"Hell, you dipwads don't deserve me. I'm tired of this third-rate carnival, anyway."

McDonald signed the statement with a flourish and dropped the pen on top of it. He thrust both dramatically away from him. Next, ex-President McDonald stood, pushed his way through the gathering, and left the Oval Office behind him. The Secret Service escort ran to catch up with McDonald and strode behind him as he hurried away from the West Wing. He rose quickly to the residence floor of the White house and slammed his hallway door behind him. Taking up stations on either side of the closed doors, the Secret Service escorts briefly faced each and smiled before returning their gaze back to the empty hallway.

In the West Wing, the Oval Office assemblage had moved to the vice president's office. Robinson was awaiting them. The president pro tempore of the senate had called Robinson earlier and asked him to meet with the Capitol Hill entourage after they left McDonald's office. As Robinson's office filled up with politicians and business executives, he smiled and stood up from behind his desk, noting the power players standing before him.

"What can I do for you, gentlemen?"

The speaker of the house removed McDonald's signed resignation from his briefcase and placed it before Robinson. He cleared his throat. "You can become the next president of the United States."

Robinson sat back down slowly and picked up the official document. He read the resignation. From his sitting position, the VP viewed everyone standing before him.

"I'd be glad to, gentlemen." In a somber manner, he continued, "Where do I sign?"

The Supreme Court's Chief Justice administered the Presidential Oath in Robinson's office. After the swearing into office, everyone attending applauded for the new President of the United States, and feeling hopeful about a possible GOP recovery, they all shook the young African American politician's hand.

As most of the men departed Robinson's office, the big Republican dogs stayed behind. The house speaker explained how McDonald had two days to vacate the White House. During this time, the speaker asked Robinson to continue on with his vice presidential duties while subtly taking over the president's role as well. President Robinson agreed to the little charade. He realized a smooth transition in this case would require a little deception. The house speaker, president pro tempore of the senate, and the Republican Party chairman left Robinson to himself and headed for their limo.

Leaving his work space, the new president walked down the long hallway to the Oval Office. He politely greeted his escorts as they joined him. The agents let Robinson into his office. He walked to the Presidential Seal, knelt by it, and brushed the insignia's nap in one direction until the seal's colors shone brightly. He then gently patted the rug. Robinson rose and turned to the portrait of Lincoln. He focused on the long dead, assassinated leader.

"I'll make you proud, Mr. President."

President Robinson turned and left the Oval Office, and returned to his old work space. He checked his emails noting tomorrow's agenda and read his messages. It appeared there was much to be done.

CHAPTER 108

PRESIDENT MCDONALD'S CHIEF OF STAFF SCURried up the Grand Staircase and alighted onto the second floor landing. He quickly checked his watch. The slight, weasel-faced young man noted it was quarter to twelve. Lesley Brown, McDonald's press secretary, followed Horner and came to stand next to him. Both men peered down the hallway and acknowledged two Secret Service men guarding the entrance to the president's living room. They walked down the corridor and were let into his apartment. The ex-president sat on the couch facing his four flatscreens with his hard-soled leather shoes sitting atop the coffee table's polished surface, once again creating irreparable scratches. The president sat stone-like, holding his smartphone in one hand and a remote in the other. All four screens showed the many demonstrations erupting throughout the country. McDonald was in a foul mood.

"God-damn liberal bastards. Can't tell their asses from a hole in the ground! They deserve Robinson! He's a nice, polite "blackie" from the South. Make 'em all feel warm and cozy about themselves."

Horner and Brown heard the racial slurs directed at the new president and stared at each other in disbelief.

"Mr. President, it's quarter till. Time to make your departure via Marine One."

President McDonald glanced over at his two flunkies with a slight snarl on his face. "God-damn right it is. I've had enough of this shit show!"

He rose, put on his suitcoat, walked over to the floor-length mirror near the hallway entrance, and primped. His press secretary handed the ex-president a copy of his speech, and with the two men following, McDonald left his living quarters. Four flatscreens still showed marchers thrusting protest signs into the air and chanting. The procession was joined by two Secret Service agents, and the enlarged group moved to the ground floor level via the Grand Staircase.

Several days earlier, the White House chief usher had met with Ted Horner. The chief of staff had discussed with Peterson McDonald's requests regarding his departure. Since their meeting, large tiered bleachers had been erected, allowing seating for hundreds of attendees. A raised platform was built for the president's Marine Band. Positioned directly in front of everything and facing all of the South Lawn seats was a podium, complete with the Presidential Seal.

McDonald had planned a regal and stately departure for himself. All the well-known Washington dignitaries had been invited, and a large group of corporate executives would be in attendance, too. Massive flower arrangements sat in huge vases, creating an aisle from the Diplomatic Reception Room's stairs outwards all the way to McDonald's dais. Floral arrangements also sat on tripods surrounding the lectern. The band was to strike up "Hail to the Chief" as McDonald entered the South Lawn. They were to softly play Sinatra's classic "My Way" as he spoke and then finish with a flurry by playing "America the Beautiful" as McDonald boarded Marine One. The White House chief usher had dutifully arranged every detail of the Departure Gala as instructed.

The presidential procession gained the ground floor. They turned right and McDonald motioned for the lead Secret Service agent to follow him. They turned left and walked through the Diplomatic Room. Horner realized the hallway and Diplomatic Room were vacant of well-wishers and completely empty. His boss didn't seem to register the obvious slight by the White House staff, and the group stopped at the South Lawn entrance to the Diplomatic Room. McDonald stared down the floral aisle past his podium, noting the Sikorsky SH-3 Sea King helicopter awaiting his boarding.

"Brown, check things out and cue the Marine Band. They should start playing when I begin my descent."

"Certainly, Mr. President."

He left and quickly returned with a worried expression on his face. "There seems to be a problem, sir. Nobody..."

McDonald interrupted his press secretary in mid-sentence. "There's always a problem around this shithole place. Let's go!"

McDonald sucked in his stomach, squared his shoulders, and strutted out into the Washington D.C. sunshine. His entourage had to slightly trot to keep up with him. He raised his hand in a thumbs-up salute and smiled broadly for the attending audience. The ex-president's rapid movement had carried him to the bottom of the South Entrance stairs before he realized no music greeted him. His risers were empty and the presidential band was absent. Two Marine guards stood at attention on either side of Marine One's open, exterior door. That was it. Nobody else appeared to be present. A look of disbelief followed by a red-faced expression of near tantrum spread across the president's face. "God damn it, where is everyone?"

McDonald glared at Horner in an accusatory manner. "Did you screw…?"

He never finished the sentence directed at his chief of staff.

A small group of reporters, who had been off to the side, rushed the president. Questions were called out as microphones were shoved into his face.

"Is it true you ordered the attack on the silverbacks?"

"How does it feel to be the second sitting president to be forced out of office in the last half century?"

"Do you have any advice for President Robinson?"

McDonald's face became a deeper shade of red, and he glared at the media. He twirled around, seeing a distant, unfriendly White House surrounded by a beautiful cloudless sky. He turned back, facing the helicopter. McDonald noted all the emptiness surrounding him except for the maddening crowd of news people. He was about to strike an aggressive woman reporter when two strong hands grasped his upper arms and partially lifted him off his feet. Another hand stopped his punch from ever connecting. The Secret Service detachment lifted the president and carried him through the throng of reporters, who trailed behind, shouting out more questions. McDonald was thrust into the hands of the two Marines, who walked him firmly into the helicopter and forcefully sat him into a chair. They buckled him in and cinched the seatbelt tightly around his waist. The two soldiers quickly exited, closed the door, and latched it shut. They ran a safe distance from Marine One, turned, and gave the pilot the thumbs-up signal. Rotor blades began turning as the Sikorsky's engine revved up. McDonald's vacant gaze registered the small crowd of reporters now holding recorders and microphones at their sides. They unemotionally stared back at him. A few photographers took pictures of McDonald's small face peering through the helicopter's window. The large Sikorsky Sea King slowly lifted off into the cloudless afternoon sky, cleared the trees, and headed for Andrews, and as the copter's sound and size diminished, it became lost in the Washington skyline.

A long white curtain slowly closed in the Green Room. White House Chief Usher Don Peterson and staffer Preston Lincoln eyed each other and smiled.

"Seems like you're losing your touch, Mr. Peterson."

"Yes it does, Preston, yes it does."

The middle-aged chief usher and the young black man walked out of the Green Room and headed for Peterson's office.

"I'll have to check my emails and see where my timing went wrong with McDonald's departure." Peterson focused on Preston and with a slight smile on his face said, "It's hard to imagine only the media received the correct exodus schedule. You know I haven't been myself these last few months, Preston. This job really got under my skin."

"We all got a little frazzled, sir. The man was hard to work with. 'Bat shit crazy,' really."

Peterson continued smiling at Preston and rested his hand on the young man's shoulder. "Yes, I think 'bat shit crazy' describes the man perfectly."

They stopped at the chief usher's door. "Well, Mr. Peterson, I got tasks to do. We've got a brother moving in upstairs, and I need to rid his new residence of some bad juju."

The chief usher responded to the young staffer. "You do that, Preston. Seems like we should clean things up."

Preston turned away from his boss, slipped his hand into his pocket, and felt the sage bundle and his disposable lighter. Preston Lincoln walked across the Entrance Hall and started up the Grand Staircase. It was time to set things right in the White House.

CHAPTER
109

BRIDGER, RACHAEL, TUNES, AND HANG ENTERED the McNary/Wilson food service area from its east entrance. They walked toward a large crowd of several hundred students who were all watching a huge flatscreen mounted on a wall in the Commons. As they neared the throng, a loud round of applause greeted them. Several African drums delivered a cadence and the gathering erupted into a rhythmic chant, "Stop the Greed, Save the Trees." The crowd parted, allowing the Camp Dogs to sit close to the screen. They found the STRONG Alliance members already seated, and the two groups greeted each other with hugs and smiles.

The Alliance and the 11th Streeters were campus celebrities. The *Daily Barometer*, a student-run campus paper, had done an extensive piece on the student occupiers. The campus openly embraced their peers and the part they played in stopping McDonald's attack on Oregon's old growth. The young militants graciously accepted the fuss. Dread and the STRONG Alliance took advantage of their popularity by producing several campus forums focusing on natural ecosystems and their importance to the planet. The ecological meetings were well received.

Because of the day's national and international political importance, Oregon State University announced classes would be suspended for the day. The campus was eerily quiet. Very few students could be seen walking on the sidewalks, and the buildings were mostly empty. Even the library was vacant of activity. Most everybody had gravitated to a TV. All the national news networks were running coverage of President McDonald's departure from the White House.

Hang and Tunes slowly sat down in chairs next to Sasha and faced the big screen. All three were still mending, but had not completely healed, and their injuries still caused them pain. Dread, Bridger, and Rachael sat together on the floor in front of their injured friends.

Allen Rodrigues was summarizing the Big Eddy Rise standoff. WNN saved this discussion for the show's ending segment. He had previously depicted the many missteps taken by the McDonald presidency that brought the administration perilously close to collapsing. McDonald's response to the occupation of his chosen logging site was shown to be the "last straw," and this action brought his regime tumbling down. When Rodrigues mentioned the STRONG Alliance, the Wilson/McNary crowd applauded, whooped, and hollered their approval, and the same response greeted the silverbacks' acknowledgment by WNN. Tunes stood up for a moment and surveyed the cavernous eatery's commons. He couldn't sit for too long because his stitches were still in place and the pressure on them while sitting eventually became too much. He scanned the back of the gathering where the food service staff and latecomers congregated. The café workers wore their aprons and hats, and some still had serving utensils and towels in hand. His gaze turned to those around him. The faces he saw were from all ethnicities and from every corner of the world. Tunes visibly smiled. *This is how it should be.* He raised both hands into the air in a triumphant salute, and those close by mimicked his gesture and shouted their approval. Tunes, feeling emotionally buoyed and connected with everyone, turned back to the TV and sat down. The camera showed Allen Rodrigues's face. His gaze was serious and somber.

"The following tape was shot by a WNN photographer as President McDonald departed the White House and his presidency."

The photographer had set up on the bleachers to the right of the South Lawn's steps. His angle and height provided a perfect view of the setting and the president's humiliating departure from the Capital.

A hush enveloped the student audience as they watched McDonald get mobbed by the reporters. The silence continued as they saw his Secret Service escorts physically pick him up and carry him to the waiting Marine guards. Nothing stirred in the Commons area as McDonald was pushed inside the Sikorsky helicopter. As the copter lifted off and turned away from the White House, a crescendo of applause, shouts, and drumming erupted from inside the eatery. Students jumped up and down and hugged each other. Soon the throng began to bob up and down in rhythm with the Alliance's drumming, and a spontaneous chant of "Stop the Greed, Save the Trees!" once again engulfed the interior space.

Sasha, Tunes, Hang, Bridger, Rachael, and Dread sat motionless and smiling. They still held each other's hands as they had throughout WNN's portrayal of McDonald's last steps upon the White House grounds. Tears glistened in the young friends' eyes as they slowly stood up and hugged each other.

Sasha was tired from the exertion and needed to return to Callahan Hall to rest. Dread took the hand of the pretty, dark-complexioned, dark-haired activist, and escorted her from the complex.

The 11th Streeters slowly moved through the crowd. Rachael and Bridger were somewhat protective of their friends and made sure no reveler bounced into them. Outside, the air was crisp and the sky clear. As the foursome walked slowly to their apartments, more shouts of happiness and drumming could be heard coming from the green space adjacent to McNary Hall. Partway home, Rachael skipped out in front of the group, turned, and walked backwards while facing them. She got a mischievous expression on her face and teasingly addressed her friends. "Hey, we've got some time on our hands. Anybody want to go on a simple, quiet camping trip with me?"

Tunes and Hang laughed and gave Rachael a resounding, choral booing as their response. Bridger swooped her up in his arms and cradled her into his body. He twirled, holding her tightly.

"No, thank you, sweetheart. I think I'd like to try being a college student. Maybe even attend a class, someday."

All the friends laughed together and physically grew closer as they neared their 11th Street house. Bridger still held Rachael in his arms as the foursome trooped up the porch steps.

Two ravens sat in a huge old tree across the street from the yellow apartment house. Most of the leaves had fallen off the giant maple and the birds had a perfect view of the Adams Street porch. They stood staring down at the now empty space. Becoming anxious, the birds shuffled back and forth on their perch, and cleaned their beaks on the branches' bark. One bird raised its head and called out in a harsh voice. The other chuckled a raspy response. They both preened for a moment and then stretched their wings. Folding their feathered arms back against their bodies, the guardians gazed a little longer at the yellow building below them. Without any more fuss, they jumped from their roost and took several strong wing beats. They glided for a moment, and then flapped their wings again. The sun illuminated the birds' iridescent feathers, and a bluish-black sheen flashed in the afternoon light. The ravens headed east. They had a long journey ahead of them.

Epilogue

IN THE DAYS, MONTHS, AND YEARS FOLLOWING the Big Eddy Rise conflict, much has happened to those involved with its resolution.

Sasha and Dread graduated from OSU, married, and set about raising a family together. They both took full advantage of their degrees. Dread works for the U.S. Park Service in south central Oregon and Sasha teaches elementary school.

Hang received a handsome settlement from the U.S. government. After several years of college, he hooked up with Shelley, his Corvallis neighbor, and the two of them moved to Maui and bought property there. They built a beautiful three-story tree house and a world-class zip line course that drops through the jungle on the windward side of Haleakala. Presently, the two are the reigning champs in "Up Country's" mixed-doubles corn hole league. They've held the title for two years running, and odds are, they'll capture it again next year.

Tunes continued on with his OSU education and graduated with an English degree. He currently lives in Sisters, Oregon, and teaches writing classes. The young teacher is an extremely wealthy individual. Not only did he receive compensation from the U.S. government for his injury, but he also receives royalties from the novel he wrote detailing the STRONG Alliance's role in stopping the Big Eddy Rise's logging show. Further, Tunes received a lump sum of money for the movie rights to his book.

Rachael and Bridger fell further in love, graduated from OSU with education degrees, and right after college began raising a family. They moved to Camp Sherman, Oregon, and teach alongside their good friend, Tunes, in the Sisters School District. Both Rachael and Bridger love living and recreating in Central Oregon, being parents, and spending time with their children's godparent, Tunes.

Russel Nelson enrolled in Willamette University and within three years had his Political Science degree. Shortly thereafter, he became the youngest person to ever serve in the State of Oregon's legislature. Russel has aspirations of holding higher offices, and the Oregon Democratic Party is delighted to have Russel on their side of the fence.

After the occupation, the silverbacks continued their lives with varying degrees of alteration. Hops received a settlement from the feds. He and his wife moved to Papeete, Tahiti, where they opened a brew house featuring Hops' creations. His "Tahiti Blue Pale Ale" became a South Pacific favorite, and eventually found a worldwide market. His Island Villa and Brew House developed into a favorite vacation destination for the silverbacks and their families.

For several years, Ranger's whereabouts remained a mystery, which caused his friends much grief. Eventually, the master of deception cryptically created a Big Eddy Rise reunion on the southern Oregon coast. It was partway through the first evening's dinner when all the attendees realized that none of them had arranged the gathering. Coinciding with this epiphany, the dining room lights had gone dark and when they came back on, Ranger was standing on the dais with his glass held high, toasting his close friends. Jubilation followed as everyone, with tears in their eyes, hugged their long-lost friend.

Ranger eventually settled near his children who, after leaving the military, resettled in the Cave Junction area. The monies they received in compensation for their father's demise facilitated the continued production of his tools. Ranger's two sons established a small factory near Cave Junction that employs about a hundred locals who build the best firefighting tools on the planet. Upon his return to the Cave Junction area, Ranger joined his sons in the management of their business.

After the occupation, Dakota dove back into his artwork, creating a series of surreal oil pieces depicting scenes from the Big Eddy Rise standoff. This artistic production was well received by art critics and patrons. Many of his canvases sold for hundreds of thousands of dollars, and one large triplex mural sold for nearly a million dollars.

Dakota's newfound wealth hasn't altered his essential core principles or disrupted his worldly journey. He continues loving, helping, and enjoying his family and tends to his First People's values and shamanic responsibilities.

Doc returned to the coast and his clinic. He finished his novel and then self-published it through a local Portland publishing house. His book received positive recognition, both locally and nationally. Because of the themes portrayed in his writing, Doc became a speaker for the "Equality Now" movement in Oregon and the West Coast. His personal and poignant message has helped solidify the connection of the past to the present, allowing everyone to move forward. Between speaking engagements and clinical work, Doc has made time to continue recreating with his old, coastal friends. Trout fishing and upland game bird hunting in Eastern Oregon remained high on the priority list. Now that Ranger has rejoined the excursions, the play, once again, includes all of its actors.

Woody and Karen bought property in Central Oregon and dropped a modular home on it. Now they divide their time between the coast and their new abode. Bridger, Rachael, the grandkids, and Tunes often meet over at their house and they all spend the afternoon together. The kiddie pool is filled with water, the barbecue is fired up, and classroom tales both old and new are kicked around.

Woody retrieved his van from the occupation site, and after a couple more years of restoration, the old P10 step van looked brand new again. The satellite dishes were removed, but the striping and the station logo remained. Many of Woody's friends believe the addition of the moon roof adds the touch of "class" the old rig deserves.

Cassie and Brian's flirtatious, young, budding romance turned into a full-blown love affair, and the two eventually wed. They continued on with Channel 19 newscasts and branched out by creating and hosting a hugely popular *Central Oregon Destination* show. The newlyweds continue enjoying their Central Oregon lifestyle and friends, and have begun planning for their parental roles. Hold onto your hats, Bend, there's going to be more from these two!

Deputy Edwards quit the Jefferson County Sheriff's Department. He also received a large settlement from the federal government and with it, opened up numerous coffee shops and coffee wagons throughout Central and Eastern Oregon. He named his espresso business "Peace Officer Grounds" and frequently works shifts in his Bend, Madras, and Redmond locales.

Trooper Alec Mills continues on with his OSP career. He had a slight sojourn into acting when he played himself in the Hollywood movie adapted from Tunes' book. His strong acting persona opened up numerous doors for him in Southern Cal, but Mills chose to return to Central Oregon and continue on with his police work. At this moment, he's the CO of the Bend outpost and has risen to the rank of Captain.

Wendy and Tarri continue with their relationship. They officially married and with the help of modern IVF, the couple began raising their own family. Tarri continues with her Forest Service career while Wendy relishes her role as a stay-at-home mom. Tarri still enjoys working outside in her Central Oregon office, and occasionally she, Wendy, and the kids will catch John Hanson's "Summer Campfire" lectures. John has added another layer to his Central Oregon history, which Tarri and Wendy love. He now ends his discourse with an abridged discussion of the Big Eddy Rise standoff.

Dennis Stafford stopped logging and took over his father's log cabin construction business. He and his family moved into the Ochoco Mountains close to his mother's property, and pretty much pester her on a daily basis. The entire Stafford family feels blessed to be in the Ochocos, surrounded by beautiful Ponderosa pines.

All the surviving, regular Army troops who attacked the Big Eddy Rise received dishonorable discharges from the military. Several of them suffered disabling injuries from the mission and the State of Oregon gave each man a free ride to an Oregon state college of their choice. The state continued to aid in their rehabilitation by facilitating their acquisition of jobs and their eventual, successful immersion back into private, civilian life.

Superintendent Philip Ross retired from his OSP job. He, like Mills, played himself in the *Big Eddy Rise Standoff* movie, and also, like Mills, returned to Oregon after filming. Now he lives in Black Butte and plays golf often. He and his wife enjoy riding bikes to the Camp Sherman store, getting an espresso drink, and sharing a scone together while they sit next to the Metolius River. Occasionally, Ross returns to the Big Eddy Rise, climbs to its summit, and pays homage to those people who risked everything to protect the hill's forested slopes.

Janet's romantic weekend with ex-Secretary Billings blossomed into a romantic lifelong journey. She stayed in Texas, never returned to Washington D.C., and became Billings' personal secretary. On every anniversary of McDonald's exodus, they sit on their West Texas ranch house porch at sunset and toast the STRONG Alliance and the silverbacks for their help in ridding America of McDonald. After their toast, Billings toasts Janet for her small role in purging the White House of her former boss. She graciously accepts his praise with a laugh and slight curtsy.

Secretary Hastings mysteriously evaporated and dropped off the radar after the occupation assault debacle. Coincidentally, after his disappearance, a small rental house in San Pedro, Belize, welcomed a long-term renter. The unit came with its own private dock and fishing boat. The new tenant, a dark-haired, slender, older man with a military style haircut, occasionally takes clients out on fishing trips, but mostly he stays to himself and rarely entertains guests.

Colonel Rodgers received a dishonorable discharge from the military. Due to some insightful financial planning, Rodgers cultivated a personal nest egg that now augments his new part-time job's income. He was given a position at OSU that allows him to instruct ROTC students. Previously, Rodgers had spent a short time within the military intelligence service and had friends who retired from or still worked within the intelligence community. He made it a life goal to find the whereabouts of Secretary Hastings, and he and his friends feel it is only a matter of time before they sleuth him out. What happens at that point is anyone's guess.

McDonald eventually made his way to his privately owned resort on one of the Maldives' islands. The Republic of Maldives currently has no extradition treaty with the United States, and of course, this prompted McDonald to choose the Maldives property for his new home. Occasionally, he receives visits from loyal cronies, but these social events are few and far between. Most of his old business associates and peers choose to distance themselves from the disgraced former president. Numerous outstanding warrants for his arrest remain active in the United States, which pretty much means our soil will never again be tainted by McDonald's presence.

About the Author

Don Mackie is a retired educator who lives on the north Oregon coast. He is surrounded by family and beautiful coastal vistas.

Don has lived in Oregon most of his life and is an outdoor enthusiast. He enjoys hiking, scuba diving, camping, whitewater rafting, hunting, skiing, and fishing in his state's many stunning environments.

He received a degree from Oregon State University in Physical Geography, which furthered his love and appreciation for the terrain surrounding him while he recreates or travels.

During his life, he has been dismayed and saddened by the overuse and over-harvest of Oregon's natural resources. He watched while the lack of planning and foresight repeatedly caused a "boom and bust" business model in his state, particularly in rural Oregon.

His future plans include enjoying his family, continuing with his recreational passions, and writing more novels that explore the uses of Oregon's natural resources.

Acknowledgments

In the completion of this novel, I had loads of help. First of all, I'd like to thank my wife, Becky, for her patience and assistance. Simply reading my chicken scratch requires decoding skills any cryptologist would be proud of, and dealing with my dysfunctional, electronic ineptitudes requires superhuman powers rivaling any of those found in contemporary comic book characters.

Secondly, I wish to openly profess my thanks to my close friends. Each of you have inspired and humbled me. Your ethics and morals have constantly held the bar high and challenged me to do better.

Thirdly, I'd like to thank those individuals who shared their knowledge and collaborated with me, allowing this fictional piece to be realistic and logical. "Jack, Joe, Troop, Jay, Michael, Ryan, and Linda," your expertise and experiences gave me the confidence to write about situations that were alien to me. I can never thank you enough.

Lastly, my gratitude goes out to all those people who have spoken out in favor of protecting Mother Earth: Thoreau, Mardy Murie, Edward Abbey, Dayton O. Hyde, and Al Gore are a few individuals who come to mind, and dear reader, I hope your name can be added to this list, too.